PENGUIN BOOKS

THE RED ROOM

'Brilliantly plotted, crisply written and very, very frightening, French's latest is definitely one to read with the lights on' *Cosmopolitan*

'An intelligent and gripping thriller' *Punch*

'An absorbing, highly addictive read' *Evening Standard*

'Haunting, harrowing . . . sends you on a knuckle-biting roller-coaster ride of fear' *Good Housekeeping*

'Gripping, chilling but also moving' *Observer*

'French confects some of the best cliff-hangers in the business and her handling of frightened female sensibilities is acute and exemplary' *Literary Review*

'The characterization is first-rate, and the solution to the mystery comes as a real surprise' *Sunday Telegraph*

Nicci French is the pseudonym for the writing partnership of journalists Nicci Gerrard and Sean French. The couple are married and live in Suffolk.

There are now eight bestselling novels by Nicci French: *The Memory Game, The Safe House, Killing Me Softly, Beneath the Skin, The Red Room, Land of the Living, Secret Smile* and *Catch Me When I Fall*, all published by Penguin.

The Red Room

NICCI FRENCH

PENGUIN BOOKS

PENGUIN BOOKS

Published by the Penguin Group
Penguin Books Ltd, 80 Strand, London WC2R ORL, England
Penguin Group (USA) Inc., 375 Hudson Street, New York, New York 10014, USA
Penguin Group (Canada), 90 Eglinton Avenue East, Suite 700, Toronto, Ontario, Canada M4P 2Y3
(a division of Pearson Penguin Canada Inc.)
Penguin Ireland, 25 St Stephen's Green, Dublin 2, Ireland (a division of Penguin Books Ltd)
Penguin Group (Australia), 250 Camberwell Road, Camberwell, Victoria 3124, Australia
(a division of Pearson Australia Group Pty Ltd)
Penguin Books India Pvt Ltd, 11 Community Centre, Panchsheel Park, New Delhi – 110 017, India
Penguin Group (NZ), 67 Apollo Drive, Rosedale, North Shore 0632, New Zealand
(a division of Pearson New Zealand Ltd)
Penguin Books (South Africa) (Pty) Ltd, 24 Sturdee Avenue, Rosebank, Johannesburg 2196, South Africa

Penguin Books Ltd, Registered Offices: 80 Strand, London WC2R ORL, England

www.penguin.com

First published by Michael Joseph 2001
Published in Penguin Books 2002
This edition published 2008 for Index Books Ltd
1

Copyright © Joined-Up Writing, 2001
All rights reserved

The moral right of the author has been asserted

Typeset by Rowland Phototypesetting Ltd, Bury St Edmunds, Suffolk
Printed in England by Clays Ltd, St Ives plc

www.greenpenguin.co.uk

Penguin Books is committed to a sustainable future
for our business, our readers and our planet.
The book in your hands is made from paper
certified by the Forest Stewardship Council.

To Karl, Fiona and Martha

Beware of beautiful days. Bad things happen on beautiful days. It may be that when you get happy, you get careless. Beware of having a plan. Your gaze is focused on the plan and that's the moment when things start happening just outside your range of vision.

I once helped out my professor with some research on accidents. A team of us talked to people who had been run over, pulled into machinery, dragged out from under cars. They had been in fires and tumbled down stairs and fallen off ladders. Ropes had frayed, cables had snapped, people had dropped through floors, walls had tipped, ceilings had collapsed on to their heads. There is no object in the world that can't turn against you. If it can't fall on your head, it can become slippery, or it can cut you, or you can swallow it, or try to grab hold of it. And when the objects get into the hands of human beings, well, that's a whole other thing.

Obviously there were certain problems with the research. There was a core of accident victims who were inaccessible to our inquiries because they were dead. Would they have had a different tale to tell? That moment when the basket slipped and the window-cleaners fell from twenty floors up, their sponges still in their hands, did they think anything apart from, Oh, fuck? As for the others, there were people who, at the time of their mishap, had been tired, happy, clinically depressed, drunk, stoned, incompetent, untrained, distracted or just the victims of faulty equipment or what we could only and reluctantly characterize as bad luck, but all of them had one thing in common. Their minds had been on something else at the time. But, then, that's the definition of an accident. It's something that breaks its way into what your mind is on, like a mugger on a quiet street.

When it came to summing up the findings, it was both easy and hard. Easy because most of the conclusions were obvious. Like it says on the bottle, don't operate heavy machinery when intoxicated. Don't remove the safety guard from the machine press, even if it seems to be getting in the way, and don't ask the fifteen-year-old doing a week's work experience to use it. Look both ways before crossing the road.

But there were problems, even with that last one. We were trying to take things that had been on the edge of people's minds and move them to the front. The obvious problem with that is that no one can move everything to the front of their mind. If we turn to face a source of danger, something else has an opportunity to sneak up behind us. When you look left, something on your right has the chance to get you.

Maybe that's what the dead people would have told us. And maybe we don't want to lose all of those accidents. Whenever I've fallen in love, it's never been with the person I was meant to like, the nice guy with whom my friends set me up. It hasn't necessarily been the wrong man, but it's generally been the person who wasn't meant to be in my life. I spent a lovely summer once with someone I met because he was a friend of a friend who came along to help my best friend move into her new flat; the other friend who was meant to come and help had to play in a football match because someone else had broken his leg.

I know all that. But knowing it isn't any help. It only helps you understand it after it's happened. Sometimes not even then. But it's happened. There's no doubt about that. And I suppose it started with me looking the other way.

It was towards the end of a May afternoon and it was a beautiful day. There was a knock at the door of my room and before I could say anything it opened and Francis's smiling face appeared. 'Your session has been cancelled,' he said.

'I know,' I said.

'So you're free . . .'

'Well . . .' I began. At the Welbeck Clinic, it was dangerous ever to admit you were free. Things were found for you to do, which were generally the things that people more senior than you didn't want to bother with.

'Can you do an assessment for me?' Francis asked quickly.

'Well . . .'

His smile widened. 'Of course, what I'm actually saying is, "Do an assessment for me", but I'm putting it in a conventionally oblique way as a form of politeness.'

One of the disadvantages of working in a therapeutic environment was having to answer to people like Francis Hersh who, first, couldn't say good morning without putting it in quotation marks and providing an instant analysis of it, and, second . . . Don't get me started. With Francis, I could work my way through second, third and all the way up to tenth, with plenty to spare.

'What is it?'

'Police thing. They found someone shouting in the street, or something like that. Were you about to go home?'

'Yes.'

'Then that's fine. You can just pop into the Stretton Green station on your way home, give him the once-over and they can send him on his merry way.'

'All right.'

'Ask for DI Furth. He's expecting you.'

'When?'

'About five minutes ago.'

I rang Poppy, caught her just in time and told her I'd be a few minutes late meeting her for a drink. Just a work thing.

When someone is doing the sorts of things that are likely to cause a breach of the peace, it can be surprisingly difficult to assess whether they are bloody-minded, drunk, mentally ill, physically ill, confused, misunderstood, generally obnoxious but harmless, or, just occasionally, a real threat. Normally the police handle it in a fairly random fashion, only calling us in when there are extreme and obvious reasons. But a year earlier, a man who had been picked up and let go turned up a couple of hours later in the nearby high street with an axe. Ten people were injured and one of them, a woman in her eighties, died a couple of weeks later. There had been a public inquiry, which had delivered its report the previous month, so for the time being the police were calling us in on a regular basis.

I'd been to the station several times, with Francis or on my own. What was funny about it, in a very unfunny way, was that in providing our best guesses about these mostly sad, confused, smelly people sitting in a room in Stretton Green, we were mainly providing the police with an alibi. The next time something went wrong, they could blame us.

Detective Inspector Furth was a good-looking man,

not much older than I was. As he greeted me, he had an amused, almost impudent, expression that made me glance nervously at my clothes to make sure nothing was out of place. After a few moments I saw that this was just his permanent expression, his visor against the world. His hair was blond, combed back over his head, and he had a jaw that looked as if it had been designed all in straight lines with a ruler. His skin was slightly pitted. He might have had acne as a child.

'Dr Quinn,' he said with a smile, holding out his hand. 'Call me Guy. I'm new here.'

'Pleased to meet you,' I said, and winced in the vice of his handshake.

'I didn't know you'd be so . . . er . . . young.'

'Sorry,' I began, then stopped myself. 'How old do I need to be?'

'Got me,' he said, with the same smile. 'And you're Katherine – Kit for short. Dr Hersh told me.'

Kit used to be the special name my friends called me. I'd lost control of that years ago, but it still made me flinch a bit when a stranger used it, as if they'd come into the room while my clothes were off.

'So where is he?'

'This way. You want some tea or coffee?'

'Thanks, but I'm in a bit of a hurry.'

He led me across the open-plan office, stopping at a desk to pick up a mug in the shape of a rugby ball, with the top lopped off like a breakfast egg.

'My lucky mug,' he said, as I followed him through a door on the far side. He stopped outside the interview room.

'So who am I meeting?' I asked.

'Creep called Michael Doll.'

'And?'

'He was hanging around a primary school.'

'He was approaching children?'

'Not directly.'

'Then what's he doing here?'

'The local parents have started an action group. They give out leaflets. They spotted him and things got a bit nasty.'

'To put it another way, what am *I* doing here?'

Furth looked evasive. 'You know about these things, don't you? They said you work at Market Hill.'

'Some of the time I do, yes.' In fact, I divide my time between Market Hill, which is a hospital for the criminally insane, and the Welbeck Clinic, which provides assistance for the middle classes in distress.

'Well, he's weird. He's been talking funny, muttering to himself. We were wondering if he was a schizophrenic, something like that.'

'What do you know about him?'

Furth gave a sniff, as if he could detect the man's stench on the other side of the door. 'Twenty-nine years old. Doesn't do much of anything. Bit of minicabbing.'

'Has he got a record of sexual offences?'

'Bit of this, bit of that. Bit of exposure.'

I shook my head. 'Do you ever think this is all a bit pointless?'

'What if he's really dangerous?'

'Do you mean, what if he's the sort of person who might do something violent in the future? That's the sort of thing I asked my supervisor when I started at the clinic. She answered that we probably won't spot it now and we'll all feel terrible afterwards.'

Furth's expression furrowed. 'I've met bastards like Doll, *after* they've done their crime. Then the defence can always find someone who'll come in and talk about their difficult childhood.'

Michael Doll had a full head of shoulder-length hair, brown and curly, and his face was gaunt with prominent cheekbones. He had strangely delicate features. His lips in particular looked like a young woman's, with a pronounced Cupid's bow. But he had a wall-eye and it was difficult to tell if he was staring at me or just slightly past me. He had the tan of a man who spent much of his life outside. He looked as if the walls were pressing in on him. His large callused hands were tightly clutched as if each was trying to prevent the other trembling.

He wore jeans and a grey windcheater that wouldn't have looked especially strange if it weren't for the bulky orange sweater underneath, which it failed to cover. I could see how, in an another life, another world, he might have been attractive, but weirdness hung about him like a bad odour.

As we came in he had been talking quickly and almost unintelligibly to a bored-looking female police officer. She moved aside with obvious relief as I sat down at the table opposite Michael Doll and introduced myself. I didn't get out a notebook. There probably wouldn't be any need.

'I'm going to ask you some simple questions,' I said.

'They're after me,' Doll muttered. 'They're trying to get me to say things.'

'I'm not here to talk about what you've done. I just want to find out how you are. Is that all right?'

He looked around suspiciously. 'I don't know. You a policewoman?'

'No. I'm a doctor.'

His eyes widened. 'You think I'm ill? Or mad?'

'What do *you* think?'

'I'm all right.'

'Good,' I said, hating the patronizing reassurance in my voice. 'Are you on any medication?' He looked puzzled. 'Pills? Medicines?'

'I take stuff for my indigestion. I get these pains. After I've eaten.' He rapped his chest.

'Where do you live?'

'I've got a room. Over in Hackney.'

'You live alone?'

'Yeah. Anything wrong with that?'

'Nothing. I live on my own.'

Doll grinned a small grin. It didn't look nice. 'You got a boyfriend?'

'What about you?'

'I'm not a poof, you know.'

'I meant have you got a girlfriend.'

'You first,' he said sharply.

He was quick-witted enough. Manipulative, even. But not all that much more crazy than anybody else in the room.

'I'm here to find out about *you*,' I said.

'You're just like them,' he said, a tremble of rage in his voice. 'You want to trap me into saying something.'

'What could I trap you into saying?'

'I dunno, I . . . I . . .' He started to stammer and the words wouldn't come. He gripped the table hard. A vein on the side of his forehead was throbbing.

'I don't want to trap you, Michael,' I said, standing up. I looked over at Furth.

'I'm done.'

'And?'

'He seems all right to me.'

To my side I could hear Doll, like a radio that had been left on.

'Aren't you going to ask him what he was doing outside the school?'

'What for?'

'Because he's a pervert, that's why,' said Furth, finally not smiling. 'He's a danger to others, and he shouldn't be allowed to hang round kids.' That was for me. Now he started talking past me at Doll. 'Don't think this is doing you any good, Mickey. We know you.'

I glanced round. Doll's mouth was frozen open, like a frog or a fish. I turned to go and from that point on I had only flashes of awareness. A smashing sound. A scream. A push from one side. A tearing sensation down the side of my face. I could almost hear it. Quickly followed by a warm splashing over my face and neck. The floor rising to meet me. Lino hitting me hard. A weight on me. Shouting. Other people around. Trying to push myself but slipping. My hand was wet. I looked at it. Blood. Blood everywhere. Everything was red. Unbelievable amounts everywhere. I was being dragged, lifted.

It was an accident. I was the accident.

I

'And I said, "Yes, yes, I do believe in God," but God can be the wind in the tree and the lightning in the sky.' He leant forward and pointed at me with his fork, this man who I wasn't going to be going home with at the end of the evening, and whose phone number I would lose. 'God can be your conscience. God can be a name for love. God can be the Big Bang. "Yes," I said, "I believe that even the Big Bang may be the name for your faith." Can I top you up?'

That was the stage of the evening that we'd arrived at. Six bottles of wine between eight of us, and we were only on the main course. Sloppy fish pie with peas. Poppy is one of the worst cooks I know. She makes industrial quantities of unsuccessful nursery food. I looked across at her. Her face was flushed. She was arguing about something with Cathy, waving her arms around over-emphatically, leaning forward. One of her sleeves trailed in the plate. She was bossy, anxious, unconfident, perhaps unhappy, always generous – she was throwing this small dinner party in honour of my recovery and my imminent return to work. She felt my eyes on her and looked my way. She smiled and looked suddenly young, like the student she'd been when I met her ten years ago.

Candlelight makes everybody look beautiful. Faces around the table were luminous, mysterious. I looked at Seb, Poppy's husband, a doctor, a psychiatrist. Our territories bordered. That's what he had once said. I'd never thought of myself as having a territory, but he sometimes seemed like a dog patrolling his yard, barking at anyone who came too close. His sharp, inquisitive features were smoothed by the kind, guttering light. Cathy was no longer brown and heavy but golden and soft. Her husband at the other end was cast into secret shadows. The man on my left was all planes of light and darkness.

'I said to her, "We all need to believe in something. God can be our dreams. We all need to have our dreams."'

'That's true.' I slid a forkful of cod into my mouth.

'Love. "What is life without love?" I said, I said' – he raised his voice and addressed the table at large – '"What's life without love?"'

'To love,' said Olive, opposite me, lifting her empty glass and laughing like the peal of a cracked bell. A tall, dark, aquiline woman with her blue-black hair piled dramatically on top of her head. I've always thought she looks like a model rather than a geriatric nurse. She leaned across and planted a smacking kiss on the mouth of her new boyfriend, who sat back in his chair looking dazed.

'More fish pie, anyone?'

'Is there someone in your life?' murmured my neighbour. He really was quite tipsy. 'Someone to love?'

I blinked and tried not to remember. Another party, another life away, before I'd nearly died and come back to life as a woman with a scar bisecting her face: Albie in a spare bedroom in a stranger's house, with someone else. His hands on her strawberry-pink dress, pushing its straps off her shoulders; her creamy breasts swelling under his hands. Her eyes closed, her head tipped back, the bright lipstick smudged. He said, 'No, no, we mustn't,' in a drunken slur, but let her anyway, slack and passive while her fingers unpeeled him. I had stood there on the landing, gazing in, not able to move or speak. There are only so many things one can do in sex, I thought then, watching this tableau; all the gestures we think are our own belong to other people too. The way she rubbed her thumb across his lower lip. I do that. Then Albie saw me and I thought, There are only so many ways you can catch your lover with somebody else. It seemed unoriginal. His lovely shirt hung loose. We had stared at each other, the woman lolling between us. We stared and I could hear my heart beat. What's life without love?

'No,' I said. 'Nobody now.'

Poppy rapped her knife against her glass. Upstairs I heard a child shriek. There was a loud thump on the ceiling above us. Seb frowned.

'I want to make a toast,' she said. She cleared her throat.

'Hang on, let me fill the glasses.'

'Three months ago, Kit had her terrible . . . thing . . .'

My neighbour turned and looked at my face. I put up my hand to cover the scar, as if his gaze was burning it.

'She was attacked by a madman.'

'Well . . .' I began to protest.

'Anybody who saw her in that hospital bed, like I did, what he'd done to her . . . We were desperate.' Drink and emotion made Poppy's voice wobble. I looked down at my plate, hot with embarrassment. 'But nobody should judge her by appearances.' She blushed with alarm and looked at me. 'I don't mean the . . . you know.' I raised my hand to my face again. I was always doing that now, the gesture of self-protection I hadn't managed at the time. 'She may look gentle, but she's a tough, brave woman, she's always been a fighter, and here she is, and on Monday she returns to work, and this evening is for her, and I wanted everyone to raise their glasses to celebrate her recovery and . . . well, that's it, really. I never was good at making speeches at the best of times. But anyway, here's to darling Kit.'

'To Kit,' everyone chorused. Glasses, raised high, chinked across the debris of the meal. Faces glowing, smiling at me, breaking up and re-forming in the candle-light. 'Kit.'

I managed a smile. I didn't really want all this, and I felt bad about that.

'Come on, Kit, give us a speech.' This from Seb, grinning at me. You probably know his face or his voice. You've heard him giving opinions on everything from serial killers' motivations to toddlers' nightmares to the madness of crowds. He compliments and smiles and does his very best to make me feel good about myself, but really, I suppose, sees me as a hopeless beginner in his own profession. 'You can't just sit there looking sweet and shy, Kit. Say something.'

'All right, then.' I thought about Michael Doll, lunging across the room, hand upraised. I saw his face, the glint of his eyes. 'I'm not really a fighter. In fact I'm the opposite, I –' There was a loud howl from upstairs, then another.

'Oh, for God's sake,' said Poppy, rising in her chair. 'Other children are in bed asleep at ten thirty, not beating each other up. Hang on, everybody.'

'No, I'll go,' I said, pushing back my chair.

'Don't be daft.'

'Really, I want to. I haven't seen the children all evening. I want to say good-night to them.'

I practically ran from the room. As I climbed the stairs,

I heard footsteps pounding along the corridor, and little whimpers. By the time I reached their bedroom, Amy and Megan were in bed with the covers pulled up. Megan, who is seven, was pretending to be asleep, though her eyelids quivered with the effort of keeping them shut. Amy, aged five, lay on her pillow with her eyes wide open. A velvet rabbit with shabby ears and beady eyes lay beside her.

'Hello, you two,' I said, sitting on the end of Amy's bed. In the glow from the night-light, I could see that there was a red mark on her cheek.

'Kitty,' she said. Apart from Albie, they were the only people I knew who called me Kitty. 'Megan hit me.'

Megan sat up indignantly. 'Liar! Anyway, she scratched me, look. Look at the mark.' She held out her hand.

'She said I was a bird-brain.'

'I did not!'

'I've come to say good-night.'

I looked at them as they sat up in their beds with their tousled heads, bright eyes and flushed cheeks. I put a hand on Amy's forehead. It was hot and damp. A clean smell of soap and child's sweat rose off her. She had freckles across the bridge of her nose and a pointed chin.

'It's late,' I said.

'Amy woke me,' said Megan.

'Oh!' Amy's mouth opened in a perfect circle of outrage.

Downstairs I could hear the hum of voices, the scrape of cutlery on china, someone laughing.

'How shall I get you to go to sleep?'

'Does it hurt?' Amy put out one finger and poked my cheek, making me flinch.

'Not now.'

'Mummy says it's a shame,' said Megan.

'Does she?'

'And she said Albie's gone.' Albie had tickled them, given them lollipops, blown through his cupped hands to make owl noises.

'That's right.'

'Won't you have babies, then?'

'Ssh, Amy, that's rude.'

'Maybe one day,' I said. I felt a little throb of longing in my belly. 'Not yet, though. Shall I tell you a story?'

'Yeah,' they said together, in triumph. They'd got me.

'A short one.' I searched around in my mind for something usable. 'Once upon a time there was a girl who lived with her two ugly sisters and . . .'

A joint groan came from the beds. 'Not that one.'

'Sleeping Beauty, then? Three Little Pigs? Goldilocks?'

'Bo-o-ring. Tell us one you made up yourself,' said Megan. 'Out of your own head.'

'About two girls . . .' prompted Amy.

'. . . called Amy and Megan . . .'

'. . . and they have an adventure in a castle.'

'OK, OK. Let's see.' I began to talk without any idea of how I was going to continue. 'Once there were two little girls called Megan and Amy. Megan was seven and Amy was five. One day they got lost.'

'How?'

'They were going for a walk with their parents, and it was early evening, and a great storm blew up, with thunder and lightning and winds howling round them. They hid in a hollow tree, but when the rain stopped they realized they were all alone in a dark forest, with no idea of where they were.'

'Good,' said Megan.

'So Megan said they should walk until they came to a house.'

'And what did I say?'

'Amy said they should eat the blackberries on the bushes around them to stop themselves from starving. They walked and walked. They fell over and scraped their knees. It got darker and darker and lightning flashed and big black birds kept flapping past them, making horrible screeching sounds. They could see eyes peering at them from the bushes . . . animal eyes.'

'Panthers.'

'I don't think there were panthers in that –'

'Panthers,' said Megan firmly.

'All right, panthers. Suddenly, Megan saw a light shining through the trees.'

'What about –'

'Amy saw it at the same time. They walked towards it. When they reached it, they found it came from an oil lamp hanging above an arched wooden door. It was the door to a great ruined house. It looked scary, a spooky place, but by now they were so tired and cold and frightened that they decided to take a chance. They rapped on the door, and they could hear the sound echoing inside, like the beat of a drum.' I paused. They were silent now, their mouths open. 'But nobody came, and more and more big black birds screeched around them, until there was a dark cloud of birds in the sky. Black birds and flashes of lightning, and rumbles of thunder, and the branches of trees swaying in the wind. So Megan pushed hard on the door and it swung open, with a squeaky creak. Amy took the oil lamp from the entrance, and together the two little girls went into the ruined house. They held hands and stared around.

'There was a passageway, with water running down

the walls. They followed it until they came to a room. It was painted all blue, with a cold blue fountain bubbling in the middle and a high blue ceiling, and they could hear the sound of waves crashing on the shore. It was a room of water, of oceans and faraway places, and it made them feel that they were further from home than they had ever been before. So they walked a bit further and came to another room. It was a green room, with ferns and trees in pots, and it reminded them of the parks they liked playing in and made them feel more homesick than they had ever felt before. So they walked a bit further and came to a third room. The door was shut. It was painted red. For some reason they felt very scared of this room, before they even opened the door.'

'Why?' asked Megan. She reached out a hand and I clasped it in my own.

'Behind the red door lay the red room. They knew that inside this room was everything they were most afraid of. Different things for Megan than for Amy. What are you most scared of, Megan?'

'Dunno.'

'What about being high up?'

'Yeah. And falling off a boat and dying. And being dark. And tigers. And crocodiles.'

'That's what was inside the red room for Megan. And Amy?'

'Amy hates spiders,' said Megan gleefully. 'She screams.'

'Yeah, and poison snakes. Fireworks exploding in my hair.'

'OK. So what did Megan and Amy do now?'

'Run away.'

'No, they didn't. They wanted to see inside. They wanted to see those tigers and boats and crocodiles –'

'And poison snakes –'

'And poison snakes. So they pushed open the door and they went into the red room, and they looked around and it was red everywhere. It was red on the ceiling and red on the walls and red on the floor.'

'But what was in it?' asked Megan. 'Where was the crocodiles?'

I paused, nonplussed. What actually was in the room? I hadn't thought of this bit of the story. I toyed with the idea of a real live tiger that would eat them both.

'There was a little stuffed tiger,' I said. 'And a stuffed crocodile.'

'And a stuffed snake.'

'Yes, and a little toy boat and there was lovely food to eat and a big lovely soft bed. And Megan and Amy's parents. And they tucked them up in the bed and gave them a big kiss and they fell asleep.'

'With a night-light.'

'With a night-light.'

'I want another story,' Megan said.

I leaned down and kissed two grumpy foreheads. 'Next time,' I said, backing out of the room.

'Tailed off a bit at the end, I thought.' I started and looked round. Seb was smiling at me. 'Where did you get it from? The Bruno Bettelheim collection of bedtime stories?'

He said it with a grin, but I answered him seriously. 'It was a dream I had in hospital.'

'But I don't suppose there were toys and a warm bed in your red room.'

'No.'

'What was there?'

'I don't know,' I said. I was lying. I felt my stomach lurch at the memory of it.

★

Later, I refused the offer of a lift home from my drunken friend who believed God was the Big Bang, and walked the mile from Poppy and Seb's to my flat in Clerkenwell. The cool, damp wind blew in my face, and my scar tingled faintly. The half-moon floated between thin clouds, above the orange street-lamps. I felt happy and sad and a little bit drunk. I'd made my speech – about friendship helping me through, all of the trite, true phrases about valuing life more now – and eaten apple crumble. Made my excuses and left. Now I was alone. My footsteps echoed in the empty streets, where puddles glinted and cans rattled in gateways. A cat wrapped itself around my legs then disappeared into the shadows of an alleyway.

At home, there was a message on the answering-machine from my father. 'Hello,' he said, in a plaintive voice. He paused and waited, then: 'Hello? Kit? It's your father.' That was it.

It was two in the morning and I was wide awake, my brain buzzing. I made myself a cup of tea – so easy when it's just for one. A bag and boiling water over it; then a dribble of milk. Sometimes I eat standing at the fridge, or prowling around the kitchen. A slice of cheese, an apple, a bread roll past its sell-by date, a biscuit munched absent-mindedly. Orange juice drunk out of its carton. Albie used to cook huge and elaborate meals – lots of meat and herbs and spices; pans boiling over; strange misshapen cheeses on the window-sill; bottles of wine uncorked at the ready; laughter rolling and swilling through the rooms. I sat on my sofa and sipped the tea. And because I was alone, and in a maudlin kind of mood, I took out her photograph.

She was my age then, I knew that, but she looked ludicrously young and long ago. Like a faraway child;

someone glimpsed through a gate at the end of the garden. She was sitting on a patch of grass with a tree behind her, wearing frayed denim shorts and a red T-shirt. The gleam of sunshine was on her, dappling her bare, rounded knees. Her pale brown hair was long and tucked behind her ears, except for a strand that fell forward over one eye. A moment later, and she would have pushed it back again. She had a soft, round face, sprinkled with tiny summer freckles, and grey eyes. She looked like me, everybody who had ever known her always said that: 'Don't you look like the image of your mother? Poor dear,' they would add, meaning me, her, both of us, I suppose.

She died before I was old enough to keep her as a memory, though I used to try to edge myself back through the foggy early years of life, to see if I could find her there, on the bleached-out edge of recollection. All I had were photographs like this, and stories told to me about her. Everyone had their own versions. I had only other people's word for her. So it wasn't really my mother I was missing now, but the impossibly tender idea of her.

I knew, because of the date my father had written punctiliously on the back, that she was already pregnant, though you couldn't tell. Her stomach was flat, but I was there, invisible, rippling inside her like a secret. That's why I loved the photograph: because although nobody else knew it, it was of both of us together. Me and her, and love ahead. I touched her with my finger. Her face shone up at me. I still cry when I see her.

2

I have always been nervous of New Year's Eve. I can't make myself wholly believe in a fresh start. A friend once told me this meant I was really a Protestant rather than a Catholic. I think she meant that I trail my life behind me: my dirty linen and my unwanted baggage. Nevertheless, I wanted my return to work to be a new beginning. The flat was cluttered with all the things that Albie had left behind. It had been six months, yet I still had a couple of his shirts in the cupboard, an old pair of shoes under my bed. I hadn't properly thrown him out. Bits of him kept turning up, like pieces of wreckage washed up on a beach after a storm.

That Sunday evening, I put on a pair of white cotton trousers and an orange top with three-quarter-length sleeves and lace around the neck, like a vest. I put mascara on my lashes, gloss on my lips, the smallest dab of perfume behind my ears. I brushed my hair and piled it, still damp, on top of my head. It didn't matter. He would come, and then a bit later he would go away again, and I would be in my flat on my own once more, with the windows open and the curtains closed and a glass of cold wine and music playing. Something calm. I stood in front of the long mirror in my bedroom. I looked quite steady. I smiled and the woman smiled back, raising her eyebrows, ironical.

He was late, of course. He is always just a bit late. Usually he arrives panting and out of breath and smiling and talking before the door is even half open, sweeping in on a gust of conversation, on the crest of some idea or other, on a boom of laughter. I heard him laugh before I ever saw him. I turned round, and there he was, delighted with himself, enviable in that, I thought at the time.

He was quieter today; his smile was wary.

'Hello, Albie.'

'You're looking very fine,' he said, contemplating me as if I were an artwork on a wall that he hadn't quite made up his mind about. He leaned forward and kissed me on both cheeks. His stubble scratched my skin, my scar, his arms held my shoulders firmly. There was black ink on his fingers.

I allowed myself to look at him, then stepped back, out of his embrace. 'Come on in, then.'

He seemed to fill my spacious living room.

'How have you been, Kitty?'

'Fine,' I said firmly.

'I came and saw you in hospital, you know. When I heard. You probably don't remember. Of course you don't. You were quite a sight.' He smiled, and put up a finger to trace my injury. People seemed to like doing that. 'It's healing well. I think scars can be beautiful.'

I turned away. 'Shall we get going?'

We started in the kitchen. He took his special mushroom knife, with a brush on the end to flake away dirt, his fondue set with its six long forks, his ludicrous striped apron and chef's hat that he insisted on wearing when he was cooking, three cookbooks. Eel stew, I remembered. Passion-fruit soufflé that had risen too much and blistered on the roof of the oven. Mexican tacos filled with mince and sour cream and onions. He ate with gusto too, waving his fork around and stuffing food into his mouth and arguing and leaning across the candles on the table to kiss me. Last Christmas he'd eaten so much goose and swigged it back with so much hearty red wine that he'd gone to the casualty ward thinking he was having a heart-attack.

'What about this?' I held up a copper pan we'd bought together.

'Keep it.'

'Sure?'

'Sure.'

'And all those Spanish plates that we –'

'They're yours.'

But he took his dressing-gown, his South American guitar music, his poetry and physics books, his aubergine-coloured tie. 'I think that's everything.'

'Do you want a glass of wine?'

He hesitated, then shook his head. 'I'd better be getting back.' He picked up his bag. 'Funny old world, isn't it?'

'That's it, then?'

'What?'

'Your epitaph on our relationship. Funny old world.'

He frowned at me. There were two vertical creases above his nose. I smiled to reassure him that it didn't really matter. Smiled when he got up to leave with his boxes, smiled when he kissed me goodbye, smiled as he walked down the steps to his car, smiled as he drove away. Now I was going to look ahead, not behind.

The Welbeck Clinic stands in a quiet residential street in King's Cross. When it was built in the late fifties, the whole point was that it shouldn't look like an oppressive institution. After all, it was going to be a building in which psychiatrists solved people's problems and made them happy and sent them back into the world. What was meant by not looking institutional was that it didn't look Victorian, with Gothic towers and small angled windows.

Unfortunately the design was so successful and highly praised and prize-winning that it influenced the construction of urban primary schools, medical centres and old people's homes, and the Welbeck Clinic now looked very institutional indeed. Normally I didn't really see the building, just as I wasn't conscious of my own breathing. I went to it every day, worked and talked and studied and drank coffee there. But now, walking up the steps after weeks away, I saw that the building was middle-aged, the concrete stained and cracked. The door dragged on the stone step, scraping like fingernails as I pulled it open.

I arrived at Rosa's office and she immediately came out and gave me a long hug. Then she held me back to contemplate me with a semi-humorous expression of inquiry. She was dressed simply in charcoal slacks and a navy blue sweater. Her hair was quite grey now and when she smiled her face almost shimmered in all its fine wrinkles. What was she thinking? When I had first met her, almost seven years earlier, I had already known her extraordinary work on child development. I'd occasionally been puzzled by this great expert on children who had never had children herself, and I sometimes wondered if the rest of us at the clinic were competing to be her cleverest son or daughter. There may have been something maternal about the way she presided over the Welbeck, but it wasn't necessarily wise to rely on a mother's softness and forgiveness. She had a steely objectivity as well.

'We've missed you, Kit,' she said. 'Welcome back.' I didn't speak. I just pulled a face that was meant to look affectionate. There were butterflies in my stomach; it felt like my first day at secondary school. 'Let's go outside and talk,' she added briskly. 'I think it's cleared up. Isn't the weather funny at the moment?'

We walked towards the garden at the back and Francis met us on the way. He was also dressed casually, in jeans and a dark blue shirt. As usual he was unshaven, his hair rumpled. He was a man who wanted to look like an artist rather than a scientist. When he saw me, he held out his arms and we had rather an awkward few seconds of walking towards each other, before I could step into his embrace.

'So good to have you here again, Kit. You're sure you're ready?'

I nodded. 'I need to work. It's just . . . this bit is rather like getting back on a horse again after a fall.'

Francis pulled a face. 'I'm glad to say I've never been anywhere near a horse. Best idea is not to get on one in the first place.'

It had rained earlier but now the sun was out and the wet flagstones glittered and steamed. The benches were sodden so we stood in a group self-consciously, like people who had just been introduced at a drinks party.

'Remind me of today's schedule,' said Rosa, for something to say.

'This morning I'm going to see Sue.' Sue was an anorexic twenty-three-year-old, so thin she looked as if the light could shine through her. Her beautiful eyes were like brimming pools in her shrivelled little face. She looked like a child, or an old woman.

'Good,' she said crisply. 'Take it at your own pace. Let us know if there's any help you need.'

'Thanks.'

'There's one more thing.'

'Yes?'

'Compensation.'

'Oh.'

'Yes. Francis is certainly of the view that you should consider legal action.'

'Open and shut case,' said Francis. 'It was even done with the policeman's own bloody mug, wasn't it? What on earth did he think he was up to?'

I looked over at Rosa. 'What do you think?'

'I would rather hear what you think.'

'I don't know what I think. It was all so confused. You know that the Crown Prosecution Service has . . .' I tried to recall the wording of the letter I'd received '. . . declined to proceed against Mr Doll. Maybe it was their mistake. Maybe it was my mistake. Maybe it was just an accident. I'm not sure what I'd be after.'

'About a couple of hundred grand, some of us reckon,' said Francis, with a smile.

'I'm not sure that Doll really meant to hurt anybody. He was just flailing around, panicking. He picked up the mug and smashed it against the wall, and cut himself, and then he cut me. He was a mess even before the police had finished with him. You know what happens to people in police cells. They go crazy. They kill themselves or fly at other people. I should have been prepared for that.' I looked at Rosa and Francis. 'Are you shocked? Do you want me to be angrier? Out for Doll's blood?' I shuddered. 'The police beat him up pretty badly before throwing him into a cell. By the sound of it, they thought they were doing me a favour. They must be furious that he got off.'

'They are,' said Rosa drily.

'And it was Furth's mistake, though he will never admit to that, of course. And mine, too. Perhaps I wasn't concentrating hard enough. Anyway, I just don't see the point of suing them. Who would it help?'

'People should be held responsible for their mistakes,' Francis said. 'You could have died.'

'But I didn't. I'm fine.'

'Think about it, at least.'

'I think about it all the time,' I said. 'I dream about it at night. Somehow the idea of getting someone to compensate me by giving me money doesn't really seem relevant just now.'

'I hear what you're saying,' said Francis, in a tone that made me want to tweak his nose.

It was raining steadily as I drove back; warm summer rain that splashed on my windscreen, and sprayed up in iridescent arcs from the wheels of the lorries that thundered past. The rush-hour traffic was building, and my eyes felt gritty, my throat a bit sore.

As I pulled up outside my flat, I saw that a man was standing at the front door. He had on a raincoat, his hands in the pockets, and he was looking up at the house. He heard my car door slam, and turned to me. His blond helmet of hair gleamed in the rain. His thin lips stretched into a smile. I looked at him for a long time and he just looked back at me.

'Detective Inspector Guy Furth,' I said.

I felt myself surveyed and evaluated under his gaze and I tried not to flinch.

'You look good, Kit,' he said, and smiled, as if we were old mates.

'What's this about?'

'Can I come in for a moment?'

I gave a shrug. It seemed easier just to agree.

3

'I've never been here before,' he said, looking around.

I couldn't help laughing at that. 'Why on earth should you have been? We've only met the once. Remember?'

'Feels like more,' he said, walking around as if he were thinking of buying it. He went across to the back window, which looked out over the expanse of grass. 'Nice view,' he said. 'You don't see that from the front. Nice bit of green.'

I didn't reply, and he turned round with a smile that was betrayed by his eyes. They flickered warily around the room as if he were an animal that feared being caught from behind. I always felt that my flat changed with each person who entered it. I would see it through their eyes. Or, rather, I would see it the way I imagined the person would see it. This flat would look too bare to Furth, lacking in comfort and decoration. There was a sofa and a rug on a varnished wooden floor. There was an old stereo in the corner and a pile of CDs stacked next to it. There were bookshelves full of books, and books on the floor. The walls were whitewashed and almost bare. Most pictures irritated me or, worse still, they stopped irritating me. I found it painful the way, after weeks or months, a picture that had unsettled me would become unnoticed, just another part of the decoration. When I stopped noticing a picture, I put it away or got rid of it until I had only two. There was a painting of two bottles on a table that my father had given me when I was twenty-one. It was by a hopeless old friend of his, a distant cousin. I could never walk past it without it stopping me. And there was a photograph of my father's father and his brother and sister in front of a studio backcloth somewhere in what must have been the mid-1920s. My grandfather was wearing a sailor suit. All three of them had a strange suppressed smile on their faces, as if they were holding back a giggle at a joke out of our view, out of our hearing. It was a lovely photograph. One day, maybe in a hundred years' time, someone would have that picture on the wall and they would be amused by it and they would wonder: Who were those children?

I looked at Furth and saw that for him, of course, it meant nothing. Maybe there was just a touch of bafflement and scorn. Is this *all*? This is what Kit Quinn comes back to every night?

He stood too close to me and looked into my eyes with an expression of concern that turned my stomach. 'How are you now?' he said. 'Everything all right with the face?'

I stepped back before he could stroke my scar. 'I didn't think we'd ever meet again,' I said.

'We felt bad about you, Kit,' Furth said, before adding hurriedly: 'Not that it was anybody's fault. He was like a mad animal. It took four of us to lay him out. You should have paid more attention when I told you he was a pervert.'

'Is that what you've come round to say?'
'No.'
'Then why are you here?'
'Chat.'
'What about?'
He looked shifty. 'We wanted some advice.'
'What?' I was so startled by the wild unexpectedness

of this that I had to make some effort not to giggle. 'You're here about a case?'

'That's right. We wanted a chat. Have you got anything to drink?' he asked.

'Like what?'

'A beer or something.'

I went and found a bottle of something Bavarian-looking in the back of the fridge and brought it to him.

'Do you mind if I smoke?'

I fetched him a saucer from the kitchen. He pushed the glass I had given him to one side and took a swig from the bottle. Then he lit the cigarette and drew on it several times. 'I'm working on the Regent's Canal murder,' he said finally. 'You've heard about it?'

I thought for a moment. 'I saw something in the paper a few days ago. Body found by the canal?'

'That's the one. What did you think?'

'Sounded sad.' I grimaced at him. 'A little story at the bottom of a page. A young drifter. The only reason there was any story at all was that there were some nasty injuries. They didn't even know her name, did they?'

'Still don't. But we've got a suspect.'

I shook my head. 'Well done. Now –'

He held up his hand. 'Ask me the name of the suspect.'

'What?'

'Go on.' He grinned widely and settled back in the chair with his arms folded, waiting.

'OK,' I said obediently. 'What is the name of the suspect?'

'His name is Anthony Michael Doll.'

I stared at him, taking it in. He looked back, cheerily triumphant. 'There now, see why you were just the person for the job? Perfect, eh?'

'Chance to get my own back,' I said. 'I missed out on

my chance to give him a kicking in the cell, so perhaps I can help to send him down for murder. Is that the idea?'

'No, no,' he said, in a soothing tone. 'My boss was interested in you doing some work for us. Don't worry, you get your fee. And it might be fun. Ask your friend Seb Weller.'

'Fun,' I said. 'How could I resist? And we had such a good time before.'

I went over to the fridge and pulled out an open bottle of white wine. I poured myself a full glass and held it up to the fading light. Then I took a mouthful and felt the icy cold liquid trickle down my throat. I stared out of the window, at the red sun low in the turquoise sky. The rain had stopped and it was going to be a beautiful evening. I turned back to Furth.

'Why do you think it's Doll?'

He looked surprised, and then pleased. 'You see? You're interested. He spends his days fishing on the canal. He's there every bloody day. He came forward when we had our appeal for anybody who'd been in the area.' Furth looked sharply round at me. 'Does it surprise you?'

'How?'

'A man like that, coming forward.'

'Not necessarily,' I said. 'If he's innocent, he's better off identifying himself. And if he's guilty . . .' I stopped. I didn't want to be sucked into a consultation based on Furth's thumbnail sketch of a suspect.

He winked at me anyway, as if he'd caught me. 'If he's guilty,' he said, 'he might like to get involved in the inquiry, even in a small way. What do you think?'

'It's been known,' I said.

'Of course it's been known. People like that love it.

They want to be close to it, to feel how clever they are. A little extra kick. The sick bastards.'

'So what did he say?'

'We haven't interviewed him.'

'Why not?'

'We'll let him stew a bit. But we haven't been lying down. We've got this young officer called Colette Dawes. Nice lady. Clever. She's got to know him. In plain clothes, of course. Got him talking. You know the sort of thing. Bit of a drink, bit of flattery, bit of crossed legs when he's looking, steer the conversation. In the meantime, she's wearing a wire and we've got the tapes. Hours of them.'

'That's your investigation?' I said, baffled. 'Getting a female officer to flirt with him?'

Furth leaned forward with an urgent expression on his face. 'I'm not going to say anything,' he said in a conspiratorial whisper. 'We just want your professional opinion of him. Off the record. It wouldn't take long. Just look at his file and then have a brief talk with him. You know the kind of thing – a preliminary assessment of him.'

'Talk to him?'

'Sure. Have you got a problem with that?'

Of course I had a problem with that and now I knew that I couldn't say no. 'No problem,' I said. 'This woman, Colette Dawes, does she know what she's doing?'

Furth pulled a face. 'She can look after herself. We're always around, anyway. Look, Kit, I can understand you feeling nervous. We thought it might be a way of making you feel better.' He took a sip from his beer. And you wanted to make sure I wouldn't sue for compensation, I thought to myself.

'Thank you, Doctor,' I said. 'Maybe it would.'

'So, what do you say?'

I stood up and walked to the window, looking out over that hidden lawn trapped between the backs of office buildings. It was early evening now but it wasn't dark or even twilight. The light was softening from harsh yellow into gold.

'It's a plague pit, you know,' I said.

'What?'

'Bodies were tossed in a pit there during the plague. Covered with quicklime. Buried. Forgotten about.'

'Bit creepy.'

'No, it isn't,' I said, turning back to him. 'I'll just say one thing now. I don't know anything about your case. I think this woman playing Mata Hari is a crackpot idea. I don't know what authority you're doing this on and I don't want to know. To me it seems irresponsible, it may even be illegal, but then I'm a doctor, not a lawyer.'

'Will you let me know, though?'

'Yes.'

'When?'

'How about a couple of days? There's someone I need to talk to first.'

'You'll ring?'

'Yes.'

He went and I stayed for many minutes looking out of the window. Not at Furth, not out of that window. I looked out at the grass, watching the green change and fade in the glorious evening. Dead people. Dead people everywhere.

4

I phoned Rosa at once, at home. I couldn't wait.

'Furth came to see me,' I said.

'Who?'

'The detective. The one who was there when it happened, when I was attacked.'

I told her the whole story and as I told it the more bizarre and unprofessional it sounded.

'And what did you say?' she said finally.

'I was taken aback.'

'But curious.'

'Curious? I felt pulled.'

'What does that mean, Kit?'

'I wake in the night. Or sometimes I don't wake in the night. It hardly seems to make a difference. And I go over and over it, as if it is still happening to me. Or as if it is about to happen and I can do something to stop it, wind back the clock. It's like I am back in that room again, and there's red blood everywhere. Mine. His.'

'So you want to meet Doll again and reduce him to his human size?'

'You're a clever woman, aren't you?'

'You know, I've never thought being clever was very important. Look, Kit, I'm just going to say two things to you and they're the two things you must have had in mind when you decided to ring me. The first is whether you'll do yourself any good by seeing this man. The second is that it doesn't really matter what good it does you. You're being brought in to do a job. Can you do that?'

'Yes. I think so.'

There was a pause.

'It's dangerous to ask for advice, Kit. You might not get the advice you wanted.' She gave a sigh. 'I'm sorry. In my opinion you shouldn't do this. Now why do I think you're not going to pay any attention to what I say?'

'It must be a bad line.'

'Yes, it must be that.'

I put down the phone. It was twilight outside. Once more the rain splashed down the window-panes and rattled and slapped in the wet trees outside. Wild July, bashed and drenched by warm gales. I went and stood by the window and looked out at the garden below, the waterlogged lawn.

A couple, holding hands, sloshed together across the grass, through the piles of sodden blossom and the shallow puddles. She turned her face towards his, laughing in the half-darkness. I moved away from the window. Love and work, that's what gets you through the days.

The phone rang, startling me out of my reverie. 'Is that Kit?'

The voice sounded very far away. Crackly. Was it abroad? Maybe not. New York can sound closer than South London. It is, in a way.

'Yes?'

'It's Julie.' Dull silence. Julie. Julie. Julie. Couldn't think of anybody. 'Julie Wiseman.'

'Oh, *Julie*. But I thought you were . . .' She'd gone away. Dropped off the face of my earth.

'I'm back in London.'

Back from *where*? Should I know? I tried to picture her

as I'd last seen her. Dark curly hair – pinned up, wasn't it? There was a rush of memory, like a breath of warm air, that made me smile. Cigarettes late at night in cheap restaurants. One night we were all there so late that the cooks came out of the kitchen with a bottle of wine and sat with us. Above all, Julie had done the thing we all said we wanted to do and secretly knew we would never dare to. She had been a maths teacher in a secondary school and she handed in her notice and set off around the world or around South America or wherever it was. I felt myself soften. I said that we'd missed her and that it would be great to see her. And she said it would be great to come and see me, and then it quickly emerged that it would be great if she could do even more than that. I remembered now. She'd given up her flat when she left. What had she done with her stuff? Given it all away, knowing her. That was Julie, generous with her own possessions, generous with your possessions. Could she stay for a day or two? I paused for a moment. I couldn't think of a single reason why it wouldn't be better to have somebody else here with me for a bit.

She came through the door with a waft of elsewhere about her. A vast rucksack and a brown canvas bag hit the floor so that dust rose off them. She wore brown leather shoes, rough khaki trousers, a blue padded jacket that had a sort of Tibetan look to it. Her face didn't just look tanned. It was beyond tanned. It looked sanded, seasoned, weather-blown, polished. Her hands and wrists were brown as well, and her eyes, bright as semi-precious stones, were grinning at a joke you hadn't seen yet.

'Blimey, Kit, what on earth happened to your face?'
'Oh, well, as a matter of fact . . .'
But she was head down, rummaging in a plastic bag.

'I've got something for you,' she said. I expected her to produce some hand-carved antique Buddha but it was a bottle of duty-free gin. 'I thought you might have some tonic to go with this,' she said. 'I could pop out and get some.'

Clearly there was no doubt that this was to be opened and poured straight away.

'It's all right,' I said. 'I've got some.'

'And could I make myself something? I slept for about thirteen hours on the plane.'

'Where have you come from?'

'I stopped over for a couple of weeks in Hong Kong,' she said. 'Amazing. Some fried eggs maybe.'

'And bacon?'

'That would be great. And fried bread if you've got some. For the last couple of months I've been having a dream about coming back to England and having a real old fry-up – eggs and bacon and tomatoes and bread all fried up together.'

'I'll get some tomatoes while I'm at it. There's a twenty-four-hour shop on the corner.'

'I've got something else for you too.' She got out a huge duty-free carton of Marlboro cigarettes.

'Actually I don't smoke.'

'I sort of knew that,' Julie said with a smile. 'Do you mind if I light up?'

'Not at all.'

Fifteen minutes later, I was sitting opposite Julie at the kitchen table. I was sipping at my gin and tonic. She was alternating sips from her gin with gulps of treetrunk-brown tea and assaults on the great platter of her very, very late breakfast. As she ate she told me bits of stories: treks at altitude, canoes, hitchhikers, campfires, strange foods, a flood, war zones, brief sexual encounters, a full-blown affair in a harbour-front apartment in Sydney, crewing on a yacht between Pacific Islands, waitressing jobs in San Francisco and Hawaii and Singapore, or was it São Paulo and Santo Domingo? And all this – it was understood – was like a film trailer advertising coming attractions. The full stories, in all their texture, would be told to me in due course.

'I love this flat,' she said. 'I always did.'

I was puzzled for a moment.

'Was I living here before you left?'

'Of course,' she said, mopping up a thick pool of yolk with a corner of greasy bread. 'I've been here several times. I've been to dinner here.'

That was right. I remembered now. It felt like a rebuke. She had done so much, seen so many strange sunsets, had so many 'experiences', all those sights, and all the time I'd been here in Clerkenwell, going out to work, having a room painted. My work had seemed so important, I hadn't even taken a holiday in the time Julie had been broadening her mind. I caught a glimpse of myself in the mirror. I looked so pale. As if Julie had come back from being in the sun and lifted a stone and found me stuck to the underside, damp and sickly.

'But in a way I really envy you,' she said, not meaning it at all. 'I stepped off the ladder. I mean the career ladder. Now I'm back and I've got to find a way back on. Here I am. Back and totally unemployable.' She gave a laugh. She was clearly, and rightly I had to admit, very proud of herself. 'And you,' she said, in the moment I'd been dreading. 'What have you been up to? How did you get that amazingly sexy scar?'

'Someone attacked me in a police cell.'

'God!' She looked suitably impressed. 'Why?'

'I don't know. Because he was panicking, I suppose.'

'How awful.' She chomped loudly for a few seconds. 'Was it really bad?'

'Pretty bad. It happened three months ago and I only went back to work today.'

'Today? You don't mind me coming, do you?' Her face creased in an anxious frown. 'Landing on you like this.'

'No, it's fine. As long as it isn't for too –'

'What else is happening? Apart from being attacked by a madman and nearly dying, I mean.'

I searched for a significant event. 'Albie and I split up,' I said. 'Finally.'

'Yes,' Julie said sympathetically. 'I remember you talking about having problems.' Oh, fuck, I thought to myself. Really? Three years ago? I seemed to be living a life like one of those old-fashioned deep-sea divers, walking along the bottom very, very slowly in heavy lead boots. 'So is there anybody new?'

'No,' I said. 'It only happened recently.'

'Oh,' she said. 'What about work?'

'I'm still at the clinic.'

'Oh,' she said.

I had to think of something. I just had to. Or else I might as well leave the room and phone the Samaritans.

'I've been asked to do some work for the police. Maybe it might even turn into a kind of consultancy.' Saying it out loud to an outsider made it seem real.

She took a giant slug of gin, swallowed it, then yawned. I could see her white teeth, pink tongue, a glistening tunnel of throat.

'Amazing,' she said. 'Did I tell you about this man who picked me and a friend up when we were going up to the Drakensburg mountains?'

She hadn't but we moved over to the sofa and she did

now. The full version, this time. It felt soothing, Julie stretched out like a cat talking with fond pleasure about these faraway dangers while I took a sip of my drink every few minutes, and outside the night came on very slowly, like a game of Grandmother's Footsteps that I could never win. And finally I looked up and Julie was asleep, her drink still in her hand, her brain having told her strong brown body that it was in Thailand or Hong Kong, and that it was actually three in the morning. I slid the glass from her fingers and she murmured something unintelligible. Then I fetched a duvet from the cupboard in my bedroom and covered her with it, right up to her chin. She gave a sigh and wrapped herself up in it like a hamster in its nest. I couldn't help smiling at the sight. This wanderer was already more comfortable in my flat than I was.

I went into my bedroom and took off my clothes. It had been the strangest day – frantic with activity after so many weeks of convalescence. My head buzzed with thoughts. My skin felt cold and exposed, like a twig peeled of its bark. I climbed into bed and pulled my own duvet around me. I couldn't seem to get it comfortably over me. I knew that it was square but it felt as if it were lozenge-shaped and there always seemed to be a bit of my body exposed. At last I allowed myself to think of the girl found dead by the canal. Lianne, that was her name, or the name she called herself. Just Lianne. A lost girl with no real name. I would find out more about her soon; tomorrow, perhaps. I had to sleep, so that my brain would be clear for tomorrow. Tomorrow I had to see Doll. I touched my scar. Closed my eyes.

She wasn't by the canal any more, obviously. Lianne with no last name. She would be in a cold metal cabinet, filed away. I felt, almost physically, the size of London stretching around me in all directions. There were bad things going on in some of those houses. But I tried to convince myself that it didn't matter statistically. Think of all the millions and millions of houses in which good things were happening, or nothing much at all beyond loneliness or neglect. That was the really amazing statistic. All those houses in which no serious harm was being done. It didn't cheer me up but I fell asleep anyway.

5

Michael Doll's bedsit was above a dog-grooming parlour in Homerton, in a road full of strange and dingy shops that always made me wonder how they could possibly make any money. There was a taxidermist, with a stuffed and faded kingfisher staring with dull eyes out of the window. Who had wanted to stuff a kingfisher? There was a clothes shop selling flowery aprons and Crimplene slacks with heel straps; an everything-under-£1 shop; a twenty-four-hour grocer, where dented tins were stacked in pyramids on the shelves and a fat man sat at the till picking his nose. Number 24A. One of the windows was covered with a billowing stretch of plastic. A light was on.

I turned to Furth. 'You know, it's not meant to be this way round. You should be looking at the case, and theorizing a suspect, not looking at a suspect and seeing if he can be fitted into your case. I'm only doing this because you've already fucked up, sending your pretty Colette in with her wires and flashing her slim legs.'

'Of course, Kit,' he replied blandly, looking ahead down the grim street. 'Are you all right, though?'

'Fine.' I wasn't going to tell him that I'd been awake since three in the morning, rehearsing for this moment.

As we got out of the car, I felt a spasm of apprehension and clenched my fists. I had put on a pair of black jeans, a long-sleeved white T-shirt under an old suede jacket, which hid my alarm. My hair was loosely tied back. I wanted to look relaxed and approachable, but business-like as well. I was the doctor, friendly but not a friend.

I pressed the doorbell, but couldn't hear if it was ringing upstairs. There was no reply. I rang again and waited. Still no one came. I pushed against the door and it swung open. I stepped inside, and called: 'Hello? Michael?' My voice hung in the musty air.

The stairs were narrow and bare. Balls of fluff lay on the boards. The stairwell was painted hospital green. I put my hand on the varnished banister, which was tacky to the touch, as if lots of sticky fingers had held it before mine. There was hardly room for the two of us. I went first and Furth followed, as if we were climbing a winding staircase in the turret of a castle. As I went up the flight of steps towards the door at the top, I became aware of a thick, meaty smell. Suddenly I knew this was all wrong. 'We can't do this,' I said to Furth, in a low voice.

'What do you mean?' Furth hissed. 'Have you lost your nerve?'

I shook my head. 'No, no. I need to see him on my own.'

'What are you talking about? I can't let you do that, for Chrissake.'

'Don't you see? You and me and him all over again. What would he think?'

Furth looked around desperately, as if there was some-one else on the stairs who could take charge. 'You're not going in there on your own.'

'You told me he was a petty little pervert. What's the problem?'

'I've told you, I think he's a killer.'

I thought. 'You stay on the stairs. I'll tell him you're there. It'll work.'

Furth was silent for a moment. 'I'll be right outside.

Just shout and I'll be in. Do you hear me? One second's doubt and you scream, Kit.'

'Perfect,' I said, taking a deep breath. 'Stay a few steps down until I'm inside. Michael?' I called again, and rapped firmly against the door, painted in the same depressing green.

Someone slid a chain lock into place, then pulled the door open a couple of inches. 'What do you want?'

A tiny segment of Doll's face peered out at me. His eyes looked slightly bloodshot; his pasty forehead was covered in dozens of tiny under-the-skin pimples. The smell was stronger now.

'It's Kit Quinn, Michael. Dr Quinn. The police phoned about me dropping by.'

'But I wasn't expecting, I haven't . . . It's a mess in here. You're too early. Everything's a mess.'

'That doesn't matter at all.'

'Wait. Wait.' The door shut on me and I could hear sounds of him clearing up; things were being dragged across the floor, drawers slamming shut, a tap running.

A few minutes later the door opened, this time fully. Doll was there. I made myself smile and I saw him smile back. I made myself step forward.

He had brushed his lank hair back behind his ears, and dabbed some kind of lotion over himself. The sweet smell of it, combined with the meaty odour, caught in my nostrils.

I made myself hold out my hand. I saw it was quite steady. He shook it delicately, as if it was a bomb that might go off. His palm was soft and sweaty against mine. He couldn't meet my eye.

'Hello, Michael,' I said, and he stood back to let me into the room. As I stepped over the threshold, I heard a low growl, then a dark shape hurtled towards me. I saw yellow teeth, a red tongue, shining eyes, and smelt the fierce reek of its breath against me before Doll pulled it off.

'Down, Kenny!' Kenny was big and blackish-brown, with a large amount of Alsatian in him. 'Sorry. Sorry.'

'That's fine. He didn't even touch me.' The chemical rush of fear still sluiced through my veins. The growl was still rumbling at the back of Kenny's throat.

'No. I'm so sorry. So sorry.'

'Oh. You mean about this.' I touched my face and he stared at the scar.

'Sorry,' he said again. 'Sorry sorry sorry. I didn't mean . . . It was just the way they treat you . . . It wasn't really my fault, you were just there and they said things.'

'I'm not here to talk about that, Michael.'

'You're with them.'

'I'm not with them. I want to be straight with you. I'm a doctor, I talk to people who have troubles, or who need to talk, or want to talk. And I give the police advice. They brought me here but I told them to wait outside. I wanted us to talk, just you and me.'

'Yes. They beat me up too, you know. It wasn't only you. Both of us.'

I looked at him and considered why it might be that a man like Michael Doll would never be given a normal job, why he would scare most women away. There was no single explanation. It was simply that everything was a bit askew. I thought of the way that drunk people pretend to be sober, the way they might get all the details right but fool nobody. Doll was imitating a normal, socialized member of the public. He had even made a special effort for my visit. He had fastened the buttons of his shirt all the way to the top and he was wearing a tie. There was nothing strange about the tie, but the knot had been pulled incredibly tight and small. It looked as if it would be impossible to undo. His worn corduroy jacket was slightly too big and he had rolled one sleeve inwards and the other outwards, so that the lining showed on one side but not on the other. His belt had apparently split because it was wound about with masking tape. He had shaved but he had missed an improbably large section, an archipelago of stubble, under the line of his jaw.

I didn't know if he was an evil person or a psychopath. I knew that he was poor and always had been. I knew that he lived alone. I've sometimes thought that the most important words anybody says to us are not 'I love you' but 'You can't go out looking like that.' People say it to us over and over again as children, and as we grow up, we internalize it and say it to ourselves. So we grow up learning to do the sort of things other people do, to say the sort of things other people say, so that we can pass unnoticed in the world. There are men like Michael Doll who never had it said to them, or not in the right way. For them, doing the things people do is a foreign language that they always speak with a strange accent.

'Tea? Coffee?' Sweat was gathering on his forehead.

'Tea would be lovely.'

He got two mugs out of an otherwise empty cupboard. One was a Princess Diana mug; the other had a chipped rim. 'Which would you like?'

'How about the Diana one?'

He nodded as if I had passed some test. 'She was special, Diana.' He met my eyes for a second then his gaze flickered off again. He put his hand up under his shirt and scratched vigorously. 'I loved her. Do you want to, um . . .' gesturing at the sofa.

I sat on it gingerly, and said, 'Yes, lots of people loved her.'

He frowned, as if searching for the right words, then repeated hopelessly, 'She was special.'

In the corner of the cramped room, which doubled as sitting room and kitchen, were two large bones. A cloud of flies buzzed noisily around them, and around a bowl on the floor, half full of jellied dog meat. On the wall, over the small, greasy cooker, was one of those calendars featuring naked women with vast breasts and a dewy smile. A pan with hardening baked beans sat on the hob. A small television was on in the corner, with the sound on mute. A horizontal white line flickered down the screen. The sofa was covered in dog hairs and stains that I didn't want to think about. Beer cans and crisp packets and overflowing ashtrays lay on the floor. Through the door I could see a section of Doll's bedroom. There were pictures, torn from newspapers and magazines, all over the wall. As far as I could tell, they ranged from the semi-naked pouting page-three girls to graphic pornography.

There were shelves on the wall, but not for books – for apparently random clutter: a plastic ballerina with one leg broken off at the knee, six or seven old and cracked radios, a bicycle bell, several muddy sticks, a dog collar, a notebook with a picture of a tiger on the front, a yo-yo without any string, a cracked pitcher, a girl's pink hairband, with a rose on the front, one pale blue sandal, a hairbrush, a length of chain, a pewter basin, a ball of twine, a heap of coloured paper-clips, several old glass bottles. I could imagine that a good fifty per cent of the British public would believe Michael Doll deserved a life sentence just for what he had done to this flat.

He saw me looking and said, half proudly and half

defensively, 'That's just stuff I collect. From the canal. You'd never believe the things people throw away.'

I watched as he put a tea-bag in each mug, then four spoonfuls of sugar into his. His hand was trembling so much that sugar scattered over the work surface.

'I like it sweet,' he said. 'Want a biscuit?'

I felt I couldn't eat anything he'd even looked at. 'No,' I said. 'Help yourself.'

He took two biscuits from a packet and dipped both of them together into the tea until they touched the tips of his fingers. The biscuits were so soggy he had to hold them in his other hand. He lifted them to his mouth and ate them, licking them off his own skin with relish. His tongue was thick and greyish. 'Sorry,' he said, with a grin.

I brought my lips very close to the tea in imitation of a sip. 'So, Michael,' I said. 'You know why I'm here?'

'They said I should tell you about the girl.'

'I'm a doctor who's done some work with people who commit crimes like this.'

'Like what?'

'Violent, against women, that sort of thing. Anyway, the police have asked me for my advice on the canal case.' I saw a flicker of interest in his good eye. He looked at me intently for the first time. 'Obviously,' I continued, 'I'm interested in chatting with anybody who might have seen anything. You were one of the people who came forward. You were in the area.'

'I fish,' he said.

'I know.'

'I sit there every day,' he said. 'When I'm not working. It's peaceful down there, away from all the noise. It's like the countryside in a way.'

'Do you eat the fish?'

Doll looked appalled and disgusted. 'Can't stand fish,' he said. 'Slimy smelly things. And you wouldn't want to eat anything from that water. I took one back for my dog once. Wouldn't touch it. Now I just keep them in my net and chuck them back at the end of the day.'

'You were quite near the spot where the victim was found.'

'That's right.'

'Do you know what happened?'

'I looked for it in the papers. There wasn't very much about it. She was called Lianne. I saw an old picture of her when she was alive. She was just a girl. About seventeen, they said. That's just a girl. It was terrible.'

'Is that why you came forward?'

'The police asked. They wanted to talk to anybody who was in the area.'

'How near were you?'

'I was a few hundred feet away. Towards the river. I was there all day. Fishing, like I said.'

'If Lianne had walked along that way you'd have seen her.'

'I didn't see her. But she might have walked past. When I'm fishing I get lost in my thoughts. Did you see her?'

'What?'

'Did you see the body?'

'No.'

'The throat was cut.'

'That's right.'

'Is that a quick way of dying?'

'If you cut the main arteries then it would be quick.'

'There'd be a lot of blood, wouldn't there? The killer, he'd be covered in it.'

'I suppose so. I'm not really that sort of doctor. Have you been thinking about it?'

'Yeah, of course. I can't get it out of my mind. That's why I wanted to hear about what the police were doing.'

I pretended to take another sip from my tea. 'Are you interested in the investigation?' I asked.

'I've never been near anything like this before. I thought I could be part of it. I wanted to help.'

'You said you can't get it out of your mind.'

He shifted in his chair. He took another biscuit but he didn't eat it. He broke it into pieces and then into smaller pieces until there were just crumbs on the table. 'I go over it.'

'Go over what?'

'That girl, walking along the canal and then suddenly having her throat cut and dying.'

I took a packet of cigarettes from my pocket, lifted from Julie's stash specially for the occasion. He looked up. I offered him one and he took it. I tossed my box of matches across the table, as if I was among friends. 'The police must have asked you if there was anything at all you remembered.'

'That's right.'

'I want to approach it from a different angle that might jog a memory. I want to know a bit about what you felt.'

'What do you mean?'

'About Lianne being killed?'

He shrugged. 'I think about it.'

'Because you were nearby?'

'I suppose.'

'What do you think about?'

'I go over it in my mind.'

'Over what?'

'It. It,' he insisted. 'I think what it must have been like.'

'What do you think it was like, Michael?'

He laughed. 'Isn't that your job? Don't you try to imagine what it must be like to kill women?'

'You said you couldn't get it out of your mind.'

'I didn't see anything. So I imagine it.'

'That's what interested me,' I said. 'If you didn't see anything, why did you come forward?'

'Because I was in the area. The police asked.'

'Are you all right, Michael? Have you been talking to anybody?'

'You mean a doctor?'

'Yes.'

'What for?'

'Sometimes it helps to talk about it.'

'I have talked about it.'

'Who to?'

'To a friend.'

'And?'

He shrugged. 'We talked.'

There was another pause. 'You're interested in the case. Is there anything you'd like to know about it?'

His look shifted now. Evasively? 'I'm interested in what the police are doing. I want to know how it's going. I feel strange, being there and not knowing anything.'

'When you can't get it out of your mind, what do you see in your mind?'

He thought for a moment. 'It's like when you flash a light on and off very quickly. I see the woman.'

'Which woman?'

'Just any woman. I see her out there on the towpath. Someone coming up behind her, grabbing her, cutting her throat. I see it all in a moment. I see it over and over.'

'What does it make you feel?'

He shook himself, almost shivered. 'I dunno. Nothing. I just can't get rid of it. It's there. I only wanted to help.' His voice was plaintive and high. He sounded like a little boy.

I remembered the details I had read about his life yesterday in the files, when I'd gone into the station to talk with Furth: taken into care at eight, having been neglected by his alcoholic mother and beaten by his stepfather. Twenty residential homes and ten sets of foster-parents by the time he was sixteen. A history of bed-wetting; running away; of being bullied at school, then of being a bully. He'd tortured a cat in one of his foster-homes, and set fire to his bedclothes in another. He'd been moved to a special unit for disturbed children at thirteen, where his violent behaviour had escalated. By the time he was independent, living in a squalid bed-and-breakfast, wandering around streets with his wandering eyes, and spying on girls in the park, he was a crisis waiting to happen.

'Nobody listens,' he went on fretfully. 'That's what the trouble is. Nobody ever listens. You say something and they don't hear you because they think you're scum, or something. That's what they call you. They don't hear what you say. That's why I go fishing, where I don't have to meet no one. I can be there all day. Even when it's raining. I don't mind the rain.'

'Has nobody ever listened to you?'

'Nobody,' he answered. 'Not ever. Not her.' I guessed he meant his mother. 'She never cared. Didn't even see me after I was taken away. Never seen me. I don't even know if she's alive. If I ever have a little baby boy or girlie' – here his tone became cloyingly sentimental – 'I'll cuddle them and pet them and never let them go.' A column of ash crumbled on to his trousers.

'What about in the homes?' I asked. 'Did they listen to you there?'

'Them? That's a joke, that is. Sometimes I did bad things, I couldn't help it, like, I was all full up of stuff inside me and I had to let it out, and they hit me and locked me in my room and wouldn't let me out even when I cried and cried.' His eyes filled again. 'Nobody hears you.'

'What about your friends?' I asked cautiously.

He shrugged, ground his cigarette out.

'Girlfriends?'

Doll became agitated. He picked at the cloth of his trousers and his eyes darted off. 'There's a lady,' he said. 'She likes me, that's what she said. I told her stuff.'

'Stuff like what?'

'Like, things I felt. You know.'

'About feelings?'

'Feelings, yeah. And other things. You know.'

'Feelings you have about women?'

He mumbled incoherently.

'The feelings you have about women, Michael, do they make you anxious?'

'Dunno.'

'Do you like women?'

He tittered nervously and said, 'Course. There's nothing wrong with me in that area.'

'I mean, like them as people. Do you have friends who are women?'

He shook his head, lit another cigarette.

'When you think about the girl who was murdered, what does that make you feel?'

'That Lianne, she was a girl who'd run away. Don't blame her either. I ran away, you know. I always thought my mum would end up getting me back. I'd smash her face in if she showed up now, though. Smash it in with one of her bottles, like, till there was nothing left. That'd teach her.'

'So you wanted to help the police, because you knew you'd been in the area?'

'Right. I keep going over it in my mind. I can't stop. I make up stories about it.' He glanced at me, then away. 'I go back to the canal and sit there and I think to myself, It may happen again. It could, couldn't it? It could happen again, right where I'm sitting.'

'Does that frighten you?'

'Kind of. It . . .' He licked his lips. 'Kind of nervous and kind of, you know . . .'

'Excited?'

He stood up and started to prowl round the small room. 'Do you believe me?'

'Believe what, Michael?'

'Believe me,' he repeated hopelessly

I hesitated before replying. 'I'm here to listen to you, Michael. To hear your side of the story. That's what I do: I listen to people's stories.'

'Will you come back again? I thought you'd be all angry with me, after, you know . . . what happened. But you don't treat me like I'm no good.'

'Of course not.'

'And you're pretty. Don't get me wrong, I'm not – you know, coming on. You're a lady. I like your eyes. Grey. Like the sky. I like the way they watch me.'

Furth was sitting gloomily on the stairs. I almost tripped over him.

'So, what did you think?' he asked, as if I had just emerged from the insect house at the zoo. We walked out and got into the car. Doll would probably be looking at us out of the window. He would see me with Furth. What would he think? I wound down the window and let the warm wind gust over my face. A few heavy drops of rain splattered against the windscreen and the sky darkened.

'Poor.'

'That's it? That's your profile of him? Poor? This is the man who's wrecked your face. Remember?'

I sighed. 'OK. Poor, sad, uneducated, unloved, disturbed, self-pitying, self-righteous, vicious, lonely, damaged, scared.'

Furth grinned. 'And you've only had the starter. Now it's time for the main course.'

6

Back at the police station, I splashed cold water over my face and wiped it dry on a thin paper towel from the dispenser, scrubbing off the last traces of lipstick. I brushed my hair and tied it back more tightly, no loose strands. I took off my earrings and dropped them into the side pocket of my shoulder-bag. I felt as if something soft and almost indefinable was drifting over my face, like cobwebs or a few thin strands of hair. The air was warm and thick and stagnant. Second-hand. I was sucking in air that other people had just expelled from their lungs. I caught a glimpse of myself in the spotted mirror. I looked stern and pale. And plain – but plain was good right now.

Furth was waiting for me, standing among all the packing cases. He had a tiny mobile pressed against his ear, half hidden under his shiny hair, but he slid it into his breast pocket as soon as he saw me. 'Bloody phones don't work here any more,' he said. 'Half the computers have already gone. Nothing to sit on in half the rooms. No fucking toilet rolls in half the cubicles.' Then he jerked his chiselled jaw. 'Upstairs,' he said.

I followed him into a small square room, with a dead rubber plant drooping in one corner and a window that was painted shut. In the corner, a broken chair lay on its side. On the table in the centre of the room there was a large tape-recorder, and a box of tapes with small neat writing on the labels. Furth sat down, and I sat opposite him. Our knees were almost touching under the table and I drew back a little, put my hands on the wooden armrest of my chair.

'Ready?' he asked, lifting a hand. 'We've wound it forward to the spot you'll be most interested in.'

I nodded and he jabbed the 'play' button with his forefinger.

I didn't recognize the voice at first. It was higher, for a start. And the pace was completely different – sometimes very fast, so that I could barely make out what was being said, and then, abruptly, it would slow down and each syllable would be slurred. For a few seconds I almost thought there was something wrong with the machine, the batteries running down – except it was plugged into a wall socket and when I leaned over, I could see the spools running evenly.

'I go down there. At nights I go down there when I can't sleep and I often can't sleep, Dolly, thinking about . . .'

I pushed the 'stop' button. 'Dolly?'

Furth gave a modest cough. 'That's the name Colette – WPC Dawes – chose for herself. Delores – Dolly for short. See? He's Doll, and she's Dolly. That's how she struck up a conversation at first. You know – "What a coincidence," she said, all surprised, blinking her long lashes, "my name's Doll too!" Clever, eh?'

'I'm awestruck.'

He laughed. 'You're a hard woman to please, Kit Quinn. Do you want to continue?'

'Go on, then.'

'. . . the women. You know.'

'Go on, Michael,' said the woman. 'Go on.'

'I go to where it happened. When no one else is there and it's all dark and I stand where she was standing.'

'Yes?'

58

'Yes, Dolly. Is this right?'

'You know it is.'

'I go there and I imagine – I imagine it all happening again, just like then. This girl walking up the path and she's quite pretty, right? She's young, seventeen maybe, and she's got long hair. I like hair that's long. Like your hair, Dolly, when you let it down. And I imagine for a bit I just follow her, a few steps behind. She knows I'm there, right, but she doesn't look round. I can see she knows. Her neck's gone all stiff, right, and she walks a bit faster. She's scared. She's all scared of me. I feel tall and strong. You know. Manly. Can't mess with me. She walks a bit faster and I walk a bit faster. I get closer.'

There was a pause, just silence and breathing and an ambient hiss. WPC Colette Dawes said again: 'Go on.' Quite sharply this time, as if she was his teacher.

'I get closer,' he repeated. His voice had slowed right down. 'She turns round and as she turns round I see her mouth wide open and her eyes wide open and she looks just like a fish, like one of my fish before I throw it back in the dirty water. Like a fish under my thumb.'

I listened to the sound of Michael Doll laughing. A nervous, liquid laugh. At least the woman didn't join in.

Silence. Furth and I sat and listened to the sound of the tape turning. I looked at the other tapes in the box. There were three more, labelled and dated. Doll spoke again: 'Does that make me a bad man? What I've just said, does that mean I'm bad, Dolly?'

'Did you hate her, Michael?'

'Do I hate her?' he asked, fretfully. I made a mental note of the jumbled tenses. I wished I had a pad of paper in front of me, that I was making pedantic little notes and concentrating on that. 'No, not hate. I love her, of course. I love her. Love. Love.'

Furth leaned over and turned off the tape, then he sat back and crossed his arms.

'Well?'

I pushed my chair back and stood up. The room felt too small. I crossed over and looked out of the window at the wall opposite, the thin trickle of water coming from the leaking gutter. If I craned my head, I could almost see a line of heaving grey sky.

'I'd like to talk to WPC Dawes.'

'Come on, Kit, for Chrissakes. This isn't a big deal. We just want your professional opinion, based on his background, the impression he made on you, his taped confession. What kind of man Doll is in your considered opinion, blah blah, you know the kind of thing. You've heard him. He did it. He as good as confessed he killed the girl and now he's getting off on it, wanking in his squalid bedsit night after night, looking at his dirty pictures and thinking about it. He's a pervert, a murderer. Not someone you want to be anywhere near. You of all people know that. You know what he's capable of. Just write a few paragraphs on what you thought of him.'

'Just a word with Colette Dawes. Then I'll write up your report. All right?'

He frowned. He sighed heavily. He jammed his hands in his pockets. 'I'll see what I can do,' he said.

A woman carrying a clipboard and a bundle of envelopes came through the door. I could see immediately how Doll would have trusted her. She had yellow hair and a smooth, softly contoured face that seemed to have no edges to it, no bones. She had pale skin with a permanent blush about it. And she looked very young. We shook hands.

'Did Furth tell you about me?'

'Not really,' she said. 'You're a doctor or something.'

'Yes. Furth wanted some advice about Michael Doll. I've seen the file. I've listened to a bit of the tape.'

She lifted her bundle, holding it with both arms against her chest, like a shield. 'Yes?'

'I wanted a quick word.'

'Yes. DI Furth said. I haven't got much time. I'm emptying filing cabinets.'

'Fifteen minutes. No more. Shall we go for a walk?'

She looked wary but pushed her bundle across the desk and murmured something I couldn't make out to the duty officer. We went in silent single file down the stairs, and walked outside. Stretton Green police station is on a quiet back-street but a minute's walk brought us to Stretton Green Road. There is a health-food shop with a few tables that serves coffee during the day and we sat in the corner. I walked across and ordered two black coffees from a young woman who was sitting reading the paper by the till.

'Ten,' I said, as the woman left us with our mugs.

'What?' said WPC Dawes.

'Piercings,' I said. 'Three in one ear, four in the other, two in the nose and one through her bottom lip. And who knows what else?'

She took a sip from her coffee but didn't reply.

'Colette. Is it all right if I call you Colette?'

'Sure.'

'Well, Colette, it was remarkable what you got out of Doll,' I said. She gave a shrug. 'Was it difficult?' Another shrug. 'Where did the conversations take place?'

'Different places.'

'I mean the one in which he describes the murder in detail.'

'We were in his flat.'

'Did you like him?'

She looked up sharply and then looked away. Crimson patches had appeared through her pale skin. 'Course not.'

'Or did you feel some sympathy?'

She shook her head. 'No, no, Doctor . . .'

'Kit.'

'Kit. Look.' She was angry, or making herself get angry. 'Didn't you see the pathologist's report?' she continued.

'No, that's not my remit. I'm just concerned with Michael Doll.'

'He's a dangerous man, you don't know.'

'Oh, yes, I do.'

'What do you want, then? Do you want to wait until there's another murder and maybe we can catch him then? Or maybe the next victim will fight back and catch him for us – is that what you're waiting for?'

I sat back in my chair. I didn't reply and she continued.

'This is a piece of good old-fashioned police work. Furth and the others spent days and nights going through everybody who was in the area. It was Furth who came up with the material on Doll. Didn't he tell you that?'

'No.'

'I got friendly with him, got him to talk. That wasn't a nice thing to do. So I don't know what you're saying.'

I took a slow sip from my coffee, carefully not finishing it off. I didn't want her to go yet. 'I just want to get any information about Michael Doll that I can. All right?'

She gave the smallest hint of a nod in reply.

'So, Colette, what was your plan once you got to know him?'

'I just wanted to get him to talk.'

'About the murder?'

'That's right.'

'But that's hard, isn't it? So could you tell me about your conversations?'

A strand of hair had slipped down her forehead and she pushed it up. It slipped again and she made an effort to fasten it. 'Doll hasn't exactly got a lot of friends. I think he was desperate for somebody to talk to.'

'Or desperate for a friend.'

'Same thing.'

'Yes,' I said. 'How long have you known him?'

'Not long. Not more than a couple of weeks.'

'I understand that there were three or four taped conversations and that the one I heard came from the last of them. Is that right?'

'That's right.'

'What were the first ones like?'

'What do you mean?'

'Did he talk about the murder?'

'No.'

'Did you raise the subject?'

'A bit.'

'Did he talk about it straight away?'

'I had to get his trust.'

'You mean he had to trust you before he told you that he'd murdered someone?'

'He didn't exactly confess, did he? That's why they brought you in.'

I put both my elbows on the table, which brought my face close to Colette's. 'You know, I've talked to lots of people with terrible problems, who've done terrible things, and the barrier at the beginning is to get them to feel that their interests will be served by being honest with you, by telling you everything. How did you do it?'

'Have you got a cigarette?' she asked.

'As it happens,' I said, and took out of my bag the packet I'd brought along for Doll.

'I encouraged him to talk freely,' she said. 'I said I wanted to know his secrets.'

'You said you wanted to know his secrets and he told you he had committed murder.'

'It wasn't like that. I was talking to him about his fantasies.'

'This wasn't in the pub, I take it. These conversations were back at his flat.'

'Yes.'

'You steered the conversation towards areas of sex and violence.'

She took a drag of the cigarette. 'I encouraged him to talk. The way people do. The way *you* do.'

'Was it a sort of quid pro quo? Did you provide him with fantasies and invite him to respond with his own?'

'I tried to get him to talk. I needed to show him that I wouldn't be shocked by anything he would tell me.'

'But the first couple of big conversations you had with Doll didn't produce anything?'

'Not really.'

'Obviously Furth and the rest listened to the tapes.'

'Obviously.'

'And they said they weren't producing anything.'

'They *weren't* producing anything.'

'And they said, "Go back and get something better." '

'Not exactly.'

'And they said try harder.'

'How do you mean?'

'I imagine they said something like: "Why should Doll tell you anything? You've got to encourage him a bit more." '

'I don't know what you mean. I just got him to talk.'

'Absolutely. What I heard was great stuff. Really disgusting. There's no question, Colette, you went back in there and came away with the goods.'

'I did my job.'

'You met this strange, disturbed, highly unsocialized man and by the third or fourth meeting he's giving you a lurid fantasy about murdering a woman. You see where I'm heading, don't you?'

'I did my job.'

I leaned over so that our noses almost touched. 'Did you have sex with Michael Doll?'

She flinched. 'No,' she said, almost in a whisper. Then, more loudly, 'No.'

I kept my eyes tightly on hers. 'You were wearing a wire. Maybe sex would be a problem. Maybe it wasn't exactly sex.'

'No,' she said, shaking her head. She rubbed the corner of her right eye.

'Good,' I said softly. 'Let's go.'

We walked back in silence until we were walking up the steps to the station. I stopped and held her back. 'Colette,' I said.

She looked away.

'Who prepared you for the assignment? Who gave advice?'

'Just Furth.'

'Right,' I said. 'And how do you feel about it now?'

'How should I feel about it?'

'Troubled, maybe.'

'Why? That's the problem with people like you. You try and get everybody to feel traumatized.'

'I was trying to be sympathetic.'

'I don't need sympathy.'

We parted coolly and I called Furth immediately. He appeared looking breezily confident. 'So?' he said.

'I need to hear all the tapes,' I said.

7

I woke and slept in snatches and then finally I woke up late. I gulped some coffee as I ran around getting myself ready. Julie came out of her room wearing nothing except an old jacket of mine she must have found in the cupboard of the spare room that I had made a partial attempt at turning into a study. Now her room. We were going to have to have a talk about things. She looked like a rodent that had been dragged out of hibernation. Her hair was a mass of fluff, her eyes narrow as if she needed to keep out the light. 'I didn't know you were getting up so early,' she said. 'I'd have made you some breakfast.'

'It's twenty to nine,' I said, 'and I'm in a rush.'

'I'll do some shopping,' she said.

'Don't bother.'

'It's no bother.'

I drove back to the police station with a feeling of ominous inevitability, like when I was fifteen years old and taking my first real exams. I sat very straight in the driver's seat, and clenched my hands on the wheel. Every bit of my body felt tight. My spine was like a metal rod. My neck muscles strained. My jaw clenched involuntarily. My head throbbed as if someone was thrumming against my temples with their knuckles. 'Idiot, idiot, idiot,' I muttered to myself under my breath, stuck at a traffic light that went red, green, red without any cars moving because an articulated lorry was blocking the road. It was raining steadily. Outside, a few people scuttled by under umbrellas, side-stepping the puddles and dog shit on the pavements. Grey, clogged, mucky London. My report lay beside me on the passenger seat. It was about six hundred words long. Brief and to the point. The tapes were in a plastic shopping-bag beside it.

At the police station, I reversed into a parking space and heard the ominous scrape of metal on metal. The funny thing is that when it happens to you, you almost feel it, as if the car's bodywork was your own skin.

'Shit.'

The back of my car was jammed up against the gleaming blue paintwork of a horribly expensive-looking BMW. I climbed out into the downpour, and examined the long thin scratch I'd made on the other car. My own had suffered even more, with a light broken and one panel like screwed-up newspaper. I fished a notebook out of my bag and wrote a note of apology, together with my car's registration number and my own phone number, folded it several times to protect it against the wet, and tucked it under the BMW's wipers. I'd failed to bring an umbrella and I was already soaking. Water trickled down the back of my neck. I picked up the report and dropped it into my bag.

Furth was sitting at a table in the conference room with a clipboard in front of him, but he got up when I came in, giving a friendly nod. With him was a woman with prematurely grey hair and a smooth, placid face whom I had met once before, a young beanpole of a PC, and a bulky man with straggly hair around a bald pate and small, shrewd blue eyes.

'Just the person,' he said. 'Were your ears burning? Let me take your coat. Here, you know Jasmine, don't you? Jasmine Drake. And this is DCI Oban. He's my governor. Coffee? Tea? Nothing?'

I looked at Oban with some alarm. 'Don't mind me,' he said. 'I was just looking in.'

'No tea for me,' I said, easing myself into an orange plastic chair and putting my report, in its blank white envelope, in front of me. 'You asked me to deliver this in person. Here it is.'

'Nice one,' Furth said, with a look across at Oban, then he winked at me. 'She looks gentle, but you've got to watch yourself.'

I slid my finger under the sealed flap and tore it open. 'Do you want this?'

'Before you start, you might like to know that we've brought Doll in.'

'What?'

'Apart from your report, things are moving ahead. There are divers in the canal as we speak. His own testimony places him in the area, there's his suspicious behaviour before and after, and his own taped confession, of course. It's all bubbling away nicely. Everything done to the letter, don't worry. Legal aid, of course. John Coates. He's on his way now. You must know him.'

I'd met him once in here with Francis. Nice, smiled a lot. You'd want him for your bank manager rather than your lawyer. I looked at Jasmine Drake, but she was doodling on her notebook and wouldn't look up. I glanced across at Oban and was disconcerted to find his pale, unblinking eyes on me. I pulled out the single sheet of paper and placed it on the table in front of me.

'Is that it?' said Furth.

'Summarize it for us, please, Dr Quinn.' The voice was Oban's.

'Let him go.'

The room filled up with silence. I could hear my heartbeat. It was quite steady. I felt better with it out, now that I had crossed the line.

'What?'

'Unless there's other evidence you haven't told me about, I don't see a case. As yet.'

Furth's face flushed. That was the worst moment. I was meant to be on his side but now it seemed that I wasn't. 'You don't know what you're talking about,' he said, not looking me in the eye.

I took a deep breath. 'Then you shouldn't have asked me for my report.'

'It's your report I'm bloody talking about,' said Furth, with a sudden angry hilarity, as if this were something that could be laughed away. 'You were just asked to assess Doll. That's all. A simple brief. He's a pervert. Isn't he? That's all you have to say. Anthony Michael Doll's a pervert.'

'He's a disturbed young man with violent and lurid fantasies.'

'So what's –'

'*Fantasies*. There's a difference between the fantasy and the act.'

'He's confessed and he will confess again. You'll see.'

'No. He fantasized during sexual acts with WPC Dawes.' I looked around. That had done it. There was silence. 'Did you know? Did you know that when she *encouraged* – her word for it – him to talk, she was jerking him off, allowing him to fondle her. Did you encourage it, without actually spelling it out? Interests would be best served, that sort of thing. Wasn't she getting good enough material at first? Anyway, it doesn't matter. It's not a confession, it's a piece of pornography.'

'Listen, Kit.' His face was flushed. 'I should never have brought you in. That was my mistake. I should have realized that after your accident your judgement might be impaired. You're actually identifying with Mickey Doll, protecting him in some strange way. It's like people falling in love with their kidnappers.' He stole a glance at Oban, then turned his concerned face back to me. 'We thought we were helping you, but now I see we were wrong. It was all too early. So maybe we should just say thank you for your time, and we'll reimburse you.'

I said, as mildly as I could manage, 'You told Colette Dawes to solicit a confession from Michael Doll. Did she know what she was dealing with? Did she get carried away?'

'He's a murderer,' Furth said, openly scornful. 'We know he is and you bloody well ought to know he is. We just need to prove it before a jury. WPC Dawes did a fine job in difficult conditions.'

I looked him in the eyes. 'Was this your idea?'

Furth made an obvious attempt to speak calmly. 'We've got a murderer in there,' he said. 'In my opinion. We've built a case. We've got a confession. If we've stretched the rules a little, I'd have thought you would approve of that, Kit, of all people. We're on the side of the women – the one who has been killed and the others who will be.'

'I think you've misunderstood me,' I said, hearing my voice tremble. Was it nervousness or anger? 'I'm not saying that Michael Doll cannot have killed this woman, but you've got no case. I'm here as someone who works with the emotionally troubled and the criminally insane, not a lawyer, but I would guess that that tape would be entirely inadmissible in any trial. More than that, I reckon that if any judge heard it, he would throw the whole case out for the most blatant entrapment.' I looked at him, his handsome face. 'If I were you, I would bury that tape in a very deep hole and pray that Doll's lawyer never ever hears about it. In any case, I want no more to do with the case.'

'That's the first sensible thing you've said.'

That did it.

'This whole thing,' I said, almost gasping for breath, 'is a fucking grotesque obscenity. And you' – this was to Jasmine Drake – 'you should know better. And I don't just mean as a policewoman. As a bloody woman. And that goes for you too.' I turned to DCI Oban, who was sitting apart, with a blank expression on his large, soft, slightly florid face. I looked furiously at the report lying on the table, the report that was expressed in such calm and scientific language.

Oban didn't reply to me. He stood up and as he opened the door he looked at Furth with a gloomy expression that reminded me of a very old, wrinkled bloodhound. 'Let him go,' he said, in a voice that was soft and almost casual.

'Who?'

'Mickey Doll. Anything else?' Nobody spoke. Now he looked at me. 'Send us your invoice, Doctor, or whatever it is you normally do. Thank you.' But he didn't sound very grateful. I had spoiled his day. Then he left. Jasmine Drake followed, with a narrow-eyed glance at me before she disappeared into the corridor outside.

I was alone with Furth, who was sitting in silence, staring at the wall. I got up to go. The sound of my chair scraping on the floor woke him from his reverie. He seemed surprised that I was still there. He spoke as if he were in a dream. 'It'll be your fault,' he said, 'when he does it again. He did it to you, he did it to that girl, and outside, walking around, is someone – probably, shall we say probably? – that he'll do it to next.'

'Goodbye, Furth,' I said, leaving. 'I'm, um, you know . . .'

'Keep an eye on the newspapers,' he called after me, having to shout to be heard. 'This week, next week – it'll be there.'

8

As I reached the street I was trembling with suppressed emotion. I wanted to do something extreme and violent, like throwing a large object through a shop window or leaving the country, assuming a new identity and never coming back to Britain as long as I lived. I would settle for going home, locking the door and not emerging for a week.

When I got back to my car, the BMW was gone. Doubtless I would soon be hearing from an insurance company. 'We have been notified by our client . . .' A scrape along two panels. How much would that cost?

My flat had a wonderful clattery emptiness about it. Julie wasn't home. This was a precious opportunity. I ran a bath, poured some exotically and absurdly named salts into the water, grabbed a newspaper and a magazine and slid into it like a walrus. I quickly tossed aside the newspaper and read the magazine: I read about the five best country-house weekend getaways for under a hundred pounds, I learned seven ways to shock your man in bed, and I answered a questionnaire entitled 'Are You a Homebody or a Party Animal?' It turned out that I was a party animal. Why did I so rarely go to parties?

Finally I tossed aside the magazine as well and slowly slid down the bath until only my nose and mouth pro-truded above the surface of the water. Unconcerned I heard the phone ring, once, and the intervening beep of the answering-machine. I imagined lying in a flotation tank. A saline solution adjusted to give you perfect buoyancy, maintained at the same temperature as that of your body. Darkness. What was the point? Were you totally detached or totally absorbed? I knew that either a very short time felt extremely long or else it was the other way round.

I felt a succession of thumps and the slamming of the door. Julie. It sounded as if she had kicked the door shut. Time to get back into the world. I dried myself slowly as if to delay the inevitable, then wrapped the towel around my body and stepped out.

'Fantastic,' said Julie. 'Bath in the daytime. That's the way to live.'

'It feels a bit illicit,' I admitted, though at the same time I felt irritated at being teased for self-indulgence by somebody who had spent years drifting around the world.

'Don't worry about supper,' she said brightly. 'I was looking at a couple of your cookbooks and I went out and did some shopping. Are you in this evening?'

'Yes, but I hadn't really planned –'

'Great. Let me take care of you. It's a secret but don't worry about it. It's all very light. Very healthy. By the way there's a message for you on the answering-machine from someone called Rosa. Sorry, I didn't know you were here and I was expecting a call. I'm not sure if I pressed the right button. I might have erased it by mistake.'

She had. I went and got dressed very quickly and simply. I wasn't going out. I pulled on some white jeans and a pale blue sweater. I was tempted to ignore Rosa's message. I couldn't think of any good news it could possibly be. But I counted to ten and dialled.

'We need to meet,' Rosa said immediately.

'What for?'

'It's to do with the police. I understand you didn't follow my advice. It's not exactly a surprise, but it would have been nice to have been told.'

'Oh,' I said, with my heart sinking. 'Right. Shall I come in sometime tomorrow?'

'I'd like to see you today. Is it all right if I see you at home?'

'Why? I mean fine,' I said.

'I'll be about an hour,' Rosa said, and hung up.

I began a farcically ineffectual attempt at tidying the living room to the slightly alarming sounds of Julie doing things in the kitchen. In fact, it was barely forty-five minutes before there was a knock at the door.

I ran down the stairs and opened the door with a rehearsed cheery greeting that froze as I looked out on the step. 'Oh,' was all I could manage, which I think was what I had said to Rosa on the phone.

'I'm not alone,' she said.

She wasn't alone. Standing beside her was Detective Chief Inspector Oban. Behind him was a car. A BMW.

'I'm sorry about the car,' I said. It was all I could think of, but as I said it I realized that if you can only think of one thing it doesn't mean you have to say it. It may be that the one thing you can think of is the very worst thing to say. 'It was completely my fault. I'll pay for it at once. I know that the first rule of crashing is never to admit responsibility but it was completely my responsibility.'

Rosa looked puzzled and Oban gave a faint smile. 'A parking problem,' he said to her in explanation. Then he looked back at me. 'That was you, was it? There was a note, but it had been rained on. Don't worry, I think the damage will be treated as having happened in the course of duty.'

'Which it did,' I said. 'In a way.'

I had run out even of foolish things to say, so I held open the door and stood aside as they made their way past me. At first I'd thought, in some paranoid way, that it was because of the damage to the car, leaving the scene of a crime, or something like that. But it clearly wasn't that, so what was going on? Had some sort of official complaint been made? I followed them up the stairs. As we reached the living room, Julie came out of the kitchen looking rather striking in a striped butcher's apron, *my* apron. She looked surprised. I introduced everybody.

Oban shook hands with Julie slightly awkwardly. 'You're, erm –' he said.

'Julie's staying here for a few days,' I interrupted.

What was he talking about? Then I looked at Julie, tall, tanned, Amazonian. Oh, God, he probably thought this was some sort of gay thing. I considered trying to explain our relationship then couldn't really see the point.

'I'm just making our supper,' Julie said, sounding horribly domestic. 'Do you want to stay?'

'It's just a work meeting,' I said hurriedly. The thought of Julie and me starting to entertain as a couple made me shudder.

'You're really a detective?' Julie said to Oban.

'I really am,' he said.

'That must be amazing.'

'Not most of the time.' Oban looked towards Rosa who had picked out a book from a shelf and was flicking through it with a frown of concentration. 'Could you excuse us?' he said, with careful politeness to Julie.

'What? Me?' said Julie in surprise. 'I'll get back to the kitchen.'

She scuttled away. When she was gone, Rosa pushed the book back into the shelf and turned to me.

'Please sit down,' I said.

We all sat, slightly awkwardly, with Rosa and me side by side on the sofa, while Oban pulled over the chair so that he faced me.

'Dan Oban phoned me this morning –'

'Rosa,' I interrupted, 'I know I should have . . .'

She held up a hand to silence me. 'Wait,' she said. She turned to Oban. 'Dan?' They obviously knew each other well.

'I'm sorry about all this,' I charged in again, before he could speak. 'I was in a bit of a state anyway, and I was so cross about the entrapment, the whole idea of it, that I couldn't stop myself. But it was unprofessional and . . .'

'You were right,' Oban said.

I couldn't see his expression because as he spoke he was leaning forward, rubbing his eyes. He was tired.

'What?'

'The whole idea was disastrous. You were right. I've been talking to some people in Legal and, as you said, it's likely that the tape would be totally inadmissible as evidence. That poor girl was leading Doll by the nose. As it were.' He gave a sheepish grin towards Rosa, which he suppressed immediately when she frowned back.

'So,' I said, with a shrug. 'Good.'

'That's not what I was coming to say. I rang Dr Deitch because I want you back.'

'Back?'

'That was good, clear-headed work. I want you on the investigation.'

'I don't think that's a good idea.'

'Why?'

'Lots of reasons. For a start, can you imagine me working with Furth again? He was steaming.'

'Furth's my problem. He is no longer in charge of the investigation, anyway. I am.'

'Oh,' I said. 'But, still, I don't think I've got anything to offer. I haven't done much of this sort of thing before. Any, really. I just work with men like Doll. I've got no ideas.'

Oban stood up and paced towards the window, then turned. 'This is a simple case,' he said. 'This is the most basic, horrible murder. Find a woman in a lonely place, kill her, run away. He's still out there. We just need to get a bit lucky. Just a little bit and we'll get him.'

'Why did you ring Rosa?' I said suspiciously. 'Why not me?'

'Because he wanted to know what I thought,' Rosa said.

'You mean whether I'm crazy?' I said.

Rosa couldn't keep a straight face. 'I wouldn't presume to comment on that,' she said. 'He wanted to know if it was fair to ask you.'

'And you said?'

'That he should ask you.'

'You mean ask me whether it was fair to ask me?'

She shrugged.

'What do you think?' said Oban.

'I'll think about it,' I said tamely.

'That's good,' said Oban. 'I just want you aboard. You name the terms. You've got a free hand. I'll give you whatever you need.'

The door burst open and Julie appeared. She was carrying a tray. Where the hell had she found that? On it were three dishes.

'Before you say anything,' she said, 'this isn't supper.

It's just a snack. You'd like some, wouldn't you, Mr Detective?'

'Very much,' said Oban, looking at the tray eagerly. 'What is it?'

'They're the simplest things. This is some ham and figs, this is an artichoke salad, and this is just a little omelette made with courgettes. I'll get some plates.'

She returned, not just with plates and forks but with glasses and an opened bottle of red wine. A very expensive bottle of wine belonging to Albie that he had forgotten to collect but would remember sometime in the future. So Julie was good for something after all. She generously topped up our glasses. Both Oban and Rosa helped themselves to all three dishes.

'This is very good, Julie,' Rosa said.

'Delicious,' said Oban. 'I must say, this seems a very good arrangement. How long have you and Kit, you know, er . . .'

'Oh, just a couple of weeks,' said Julie brightly.

I drained my glass in one gulp.

9

The next day, when I went into Stretton Green for a meeting, Oban gave me a hug, which made me feel more like a favourite niece than a professional consultant. Then he led me through the office to meet the largely new team that was investigating the canal murder. 'Thanks for last night,' he said. 'Delicious food. Tell me.' He looked round with a quizzical expression. 'When did you and, er, Julie meet?'

'I don't know. Years ago. She was a friend of friends of mine. I'm not really –'

'Nice,' he said. 'You two make a good, erm –'

'Look,' I said urgently. 'I think I'd better –' I broke off because Oban was now leading me through the open-plan office, which looked a bit as if a burglar had got in recently – filing cabinets with all their drawers open, files lying scattered on a table, cardboard boxes half filled with stained mugs.

'Moving,' said Oban, kicking a roll of Sellotape out of his path.

'I kind of gathered.'

'A bloody disaster is what it is. Have you ever moved house?'

'Yes. Awful.'

I looked around for Furth but, to my relief, I couldn't see him. And then I got irritated with myself. What did I have to feel bad about? I hadn't asked for this. We stopped at the far side of the office, in a corner. Oban signalled to various people hunched over desks, and phones were replaced, files closed and a small group of detectives, male and female, gathered round. Oban gave an introductory cough.

'This is Dr Kit Quinn. She's attached to the Welbeck Clinic and to Market Hill Hospital for the Criminally Insane.' He turned to me. 'I won't introduce you to everybody now. You'll probably run up against most of them.'

'Hello,' I said, trying to aim a smile at the whole room. At that moment, Furth came in. He stood by the door and folded his arms across his chest.

'It was because of Dr Quinn,' Oban continued, 'that we let Michael Doll go.' This statement wasn't exactly greeted with a round of applause. Instead there were some murmurs at the back and a shuffling of feet. 'And if anybody has a problem with that, I'd like them to come and see me. If this case had gone in front of a judge, it would have been tossed straight back in our faces. I won't repeat here what I said in private to Guy, but let's do some old-fashioned legwork, all right? And in the meantime, give Dr Quinn what she needs.' More murmurs. I sensed that not everybody was delighted to have me foisted on them. 'Kit, is there anything you want to say?'

I started. I hadn't been prepared for this. I looked at the slightly sullen faces that were pointed at me. 'Well,' I said. I hated beginning sentences when I had no idea what was going to come next. 'I just want to say that I'm not here to tell you how to do your job. The best I can do – perhaps – is to help by pointing you in one direction rather than another, making suggestions.'

'It was Doll,' someone said. I couldn't see who.

'Was it?' I said, for want of a more effective riposte.

'Yeah.'

I could identify the speaker now, a man at the back in shirtsleeves, tall, the build of a rugby player.

Oban stepped forward. 'Then find some real evidence, Gil,' he said.

'What if you were wrong? What if Doll did it?'

'Look, I never said Doll was innocent. I said there was no evidence. What I want to do is look at what you've got and pretend that I never heard his name.' Somebody muttered something I couldn't hear and someone else guffawed.

'That's enough,' said Oban sharply. 'Meeting's over. Sorry, Kit,' he said, looking over his detectives with an expression of disdain. 'I'd say they aren't a bad lot, really, except it's not true. But I know you can stand up for yourself. I'll leave you with Guy. All right?'

'Fine.' It wasn't.

Oban left and the others drifted away, not looking very busy. I looked at Furth. 'Can I get you some tea?' he asked, with careful courtesy.

'In a minute, thanks.'

'Got any ideas, then?'

'No,' I said, honestly. 'I haven't. Anyway, at this stage, ideas would be an obstacle. I want to look through the material with an empty mind.'

Furth gave a thin smile. 'I don't see why we need to hire empty minds as long as we've got Gil. But I told you already, this is just a simple case.'

'Really?'

'A runaway found dead by a canal.'

'Is that simple?'

Furth shrugged and looked around, almost as if he was embarrassed that anybody should be eavesdropping while he stated the obvious to a stuck-up shrink. 'Perverts pick on prostitutes and runaways because they're easy targets. They pick on them by canals because they're deserted. No passing traffic.'

'Yes, I've read all that.'

'You disagree?'

'Can I make a suggestion?'

Furth tightened his lips. I think he wanted to tell me to fuck off out of the station and not come back, but this wasn't allowed. 'That's what we're paying you for,' he said.

'Sometimes it's too easy just to put a label on someone. It might help not just to think of Lianne as a runaway. It stops you seeing her as an individual.'

'She *was* a runaway.'

'I know,' I said. 'She may have been other things as well.'

'Like a prostitute, you mean?' He half laughed, then stopped when he saw the look on my face. I had had a sudden flash of him when he was a boy, pushed around by other boys until he developed his hard-man act.

'No. I don't mean that. She was a young woman. She had a history, a past, a family, a name.'

'Which we don't know.'

'How old was she, about?'

'Sixteen, seventeen – maybe a bit less, maybe a bit more.'

'How do we even know she was called Lianne?'

'We don't. We just know that's what she called herself. Character named Pavic, who runs a local hostel, identified her.'

'But presumably it's just a matter of time before you find out who Lianne actually was, where she came from.'

'What makes you think that?' He had a slight smile on his lips.

'Everyone's on some list, some computer, some register, aren't they?'

'Do you know how many runaways there are?'

'A lot, I know.'

'Tens of thousands.'

'I know,' I said.

'Those are the ones we know are missing, but can't find. The ones someone, somewhere, wants us to find. What about all of the others, like Lianne, who nobody really gives a fuck about, who just drifted off one day and never came back? How do we find them, if no one's reported them as lost? It's like a fucking missing-luggage department in an airport. Have you ever been in one of those? I have, in Cairo – a great warehouse of suitcases, most of them completely hidden from sight, gathering dust, being eaten by rats. Hard enough to find your bag even if it's got a label on, but if it hasn't, you might as well forget it.'

'Lianne's not a piece of luggage.'

He stared at me. 'I didn't say she was a piece of luggage,' he said. 'I said she was *like* a piece of luggage.'

'My point is that we have to think of her as a girl, not a stray item. Not just "the runaway".'

'What about the canal? Are we allowed to call it that or do you think it might be a river in disguise?'

'I was trying to say that it helps to come to things fresh. But maybe that's really a reminder for myself rather than you.'

'Good,' he said, very quietly. 'We're eagerly awaiting your contribution. What can I get you?'

'Didn't Oban tell you?' I tried hard to sound authoritative and as if I knew exactly what I was doing. 'I want a quiet room and then I'd like to look through everything you've got.'

'Anything else?' This last was said with grim politeness.

'Tea would be nice, please. Just a drop of milk. No sugar.'

Furth took me to a small windowless room that smelt as if it had been previously used for storing something corrosive and illegal. There was nothing but a desk and a plastic chair. Within a couple of minutes two female officers arrived carrying a bundle of files. It seemed disappointingly flimsy. Almost nothing was known about Lianne's life, and they hadn't even accumulated much data on her death. I started to read. I sat in the room for an hour and three-quarters. I read about puncture wounds, I read some statements, I looked at photographs of her pale body at the scene, face down in the scrubby grass behind some bushes by the canal and at the end I thought: Is that it?

IO

On the radio they said it was the wettest summer since 1736. I parked in a puddle and sat for a minute, while water cascaded down the windscreen and bounced off the bonnet. I closed my eyes and heard the rain inside my head like a roaring. I have not become used to seeing dead bodies.

The pathologist was waiting for me. Alexandra Harris. I'd met her before. She didn't look like a pathologist, whatever a pathologist is supposed to look like, more like an ageing B-movie actress from the thirties, voluptuous in her white coat, with dark hair falling in ringlets around her creamy oval face and a dreamy, passive air about her. Or maybe she was just tired. There were dark rings under her eyes.

'Alexandra,' I said, as we shook hands. 'Thanks for giving me your time.'

'That's OK. It's my job. Guy said you'd already looked through the files.'

'Yes. It wasn't you who did the autopsy, though?'

'No, that was his lordship. I mean Brian Barrow. *Sir* Brian. He's teaching today. What are you looking for exactly?'

'I just want to get an impression,' I said.

'An impression?' She gazed at me doubtfully, as if suddenly this wasn't such a good idea.

'A feel for her,' I added inadequately. 'Lianne.'

'Have you seen a cadaver before? There's not much to see.'

'Seen one?' I asked. 'I trained as a doctor. I had one of my own for six months.'

'Sorry. Do you want me to take you straight through?'

'Might as well.'

My fingers slipped on the handle of my briefcase. I wanted to see Lianne; really see her, not just flick through the ghastly colour photographs looking for clues. She'd had a short, lonely life, with no one to miss her much now that she'd died. I wanted to touch her; stand by her body for a while. I didn't think Alexandra would understand that, and I'm not sure I understood it either.

'Do I need to change?' I asked.

'You mean into a ball-gown?' Alexandra said, with a grin. 'No, we dress pretty informally around here.'

'I'm sorry,' I said. 'I'm fairly new to this. I haven't learned to treat it all as a joke yet.'

'You want me to talk like an undertaker?'

'I want to see Lianne,' I said gently.

Alexandra's smile faded. She wasn't quite as friendly any more. I followed her through two sets of swing doors, hearing the click of my heels across the linoleum. Here we were in another world, cold and silent and sterile. An underworld, I thought. Beneath my thin summer clothes, my skin was covered in goose-bumps. I could hear my heart thumping – how strange, all these bodies in here, but only our two hearts beating.

I could see what Alexandra had meant. Lianne looked as if every trace of evidence that she had lived in the messy crowded world outside had been scoured off her body. She was very very clean. Not clean like when you wash your hands. Clean like when you've been scrubbing a sink and your hands are wrinkled and raw. With her head exposed, the one scrap of her life I could see was the tiny fold of a hole in an ear-lobe. Sir Brian Barrow had had a tricky job. He had cut round her neck slightly above the laceration. His own incision had now been sewn back up. The knife wound remained but, cleaned up with no blood, it had a look of padded plastic. I had attended surgical operations before and the strong cat-food smell of meat and blood had never left me. But this was different. Just a sharp medicinal odour that burned my nostrils.

Lianne's face was round. There was a scattering of freckles across the bridge of her nose. Her mouth was small and colourless. I laid one finger against her cheek, felt the stony flesh. Death at my fingertips, so chill and hard it made me gasp. She had coppery hair, long, shaggy, and parted crookedly in the middle. When I leaned forward, I could see the split ends. Hair appears to go on growing after death, everyone knows that. Hair and nails – but when I cautiously lifted up one side of the sheet to expose an arm, I saw that Lianne's fingernails were chewed to the quick. She had tiny plump hands. Somehow, it was the hands that moved me most. They still looked soft, as if they could curl and hold. I touched her palm, and it was stony too.

I took a deep breath and pulled off the covering, so that only her feet were still hidden. I took in her body whole; it was as if the sight of her was pouring into my skull and fixing there. Once more there was Sir Brian's long incision down from her neck to her reddish pubic hair. Not quite straight. There was a little cut around her belly-button, like a road forking at an ancient monument. The wound had been neatly sewn up, like a demonstration in a home-economics lesson. I needed to concentrate on the relevant wounds. Her throat was neatly and efficiently cut, side to side, but there were also these small stab marks on her stomach, her shoulders, her thighs. There were seventeen of them – I lost count the first time and had to start again. Her high, shallow breasts were untouched; so too was her genital area. I knew from the autopsy report that there had been no injuries inside either the vagina or the perineum.

I stepped closer to Lianne. I tried to keep calling her that in my mind. Her legs were unshaved. Her arms were downy. There were a couple of violent scratches on her left wrist – those would be from where she'd lain among brambles by the canal. A scar on her left knee. Maybe she'd fallen over when she was little. I imagined her when she was still in pigtails, with gaps in her teeth, running around some garden one summer when it didn't rain, thinking life would be happy. That's what is so touching about children: they are sure that life will be grand for them. Ask a six-year-old what they want to be when they grow up, and they say, a pilot, a prime minister, a ballet dancer, a pop star, a footballer, a millionaire. What had Lianne wanted to be, I wondered. Well, whatever her dreams had been, there were no dreams now. Here she was – except, of course, Lianne wasn't here at all, only her wrong-coloured, chilled corpse. There was nobody here except me. No breath of life in the room except my breath. I had never before had such a sense of absence.

I lifted the sheet off her feet, and saw that the nails were painted red, the varnish chipped. I touched the scar on her knee. I touched her hand again, with its pathetic bitten nails. I lifted up a strand of copper hair. Even her hair felt dead. Each cell and particle of her had stopped in its track. I could feel the blood hammering round my body, the air rushing through it, the images flooding through my eyes, the hair prickling on my clammy skin.

Enough. I pulled up the sheet, made sure it entirely covered Lianne, not even a strand of hair showing. I wanted to say something, anything, to break the silence, but I couldn't think of anything to say so I cleared my throat loudly instead. Immediately Alexandra clipped back into the room. She must have been waiting just outside.

'Finished?'

'Yes.'

Lianne was lying in a drawer and with an effort, Alexandra pushed it back as if into a giant filing cabinet. 'Nothing you couldn't have found in the report, was there?' she asked, with a touch of sharpness.

'I wanted to look at the wounds,' I said.

I collected my case, my mac, stumbled through the door into the drenching downpour. I lifted my face up to the sky and let rain stream over it like tears.

I went back to my boxy room at the station and rifled through Lianne's file again, though I knew it pretty well by now. I looked first at the sparse sheet of biography: young woman known as Lianne, estimated age around seventeen, thought to have turned up in the Kersey Town area seven to eight months ago, stayed briefly in a hostel run by a man called William Pavic, otherwise – according to the couple of fellow drifters the police had managed to track down – slept in parks and on benches and in the doorways of shops or, every so often, on the floor of a luckier friend who lived in a B and B. That was all – nothing about her character, her friendships, her sexual history. It didn't say whether she had been a virgin or not.

I picked up the map of where her body had been found, X marks the spot. Then I dialled through to Furth.

'I'd like to see where she was found,' I said. 'Maybe this afternoon, after my clinic work? Say five o'clock, is that possible?'

'I'll get Gil to take you there,' he answered. I could almost hear him smile.

'Here's where Doll did her,' he said, glancing sideways at me. He stood back to let me see.

Lianne's body had been found on a steepish bank behind the stump of a dead tree, where ragwort, cow parsley and nettles grew. You could still see from the crushed and broken stems where she had sprawled face down. Her head had been pushed right into the green forest of weeds. Her feet, in their white pumps and perky red-striped socks, had been resting against a broken bottle. Tatters of plastic hung from the brambles and floated in the oily brown water. There were cigarette packets and old stubs ground into the mud of the canal towpath. A tiny plastic horse lay just in front of Lianne's hiding place; probably some toddler had let it drop there. Just behind it I could see a bike wheel, rusting and bent.

'And a young man found her?'

'That's right. Darryl something or other.'

'Pearce.'

'Yeah, a jogger. Serves him right. Did you read his statement? He found her as she was dying. More or less. He was staggering along here and heard her crying out.'

'But she had died by the time he found her.'

'Wanker – that's Darryl, not you. He pissed around here for ten minutes, he said, deciding what to do. Scared out of his wits, more like. Then, by the time he got his bottle back and looked and then called us and we got there, she was dead. If he'd walked straight round, she could have told him who'd done it. Saved us an inquiry.'

'Wasn't he a suspect?'

'Course. But he didn't touch the body. Old Lianne looked as if she'd been sprayed with blood. The killer must have been covered. We did swabs on Darryl, fibre tests, everything. Not a sausage.'

'And there was the woman, Mary Gould,' I said, half to myself.

'Yeah, the old dear with bread for the ducks. She came from the other side of the bushes, from the flats. She saw the body and just legged it back home. She didn't phone until the next day. We've put her medal on hold.'

I turned back to the spot and stared at it.

'And then Doll came forward a couple of days later to say he'd been lurking in the area,' said Gil. 'He didn't exactly use those words.'

I frowned and he gave me his cocky grin again and whistled through his teeth.

I tried to picture the scene to myself. When she was found, she had been wearing a very short red Lycra skirt, pulled up over her buttocks. Her underpants had not been removed. She had been wearing a purple cotton shirt with no bra underneath. She had been wearing the clothes when she died and they hadn't been removed subsequently. The stabbings had been through the shirt. On her left wrist she wore one of those digital watches they give away free at garages, and round her neck was a tacky gilt locket in the shape of a broken heart. It had curly pink writing on it: 'Best . . .'. Was someone, somewhere, wearing the other half of the heart, bearing the legend, '. . . Friend'?

I rang up Poppy, my best friend. I needed to hear a warm voice again.

'Kit! How's it gone, your first week back?' In the

background I could hear children shrieking and yelling. Poppy was stirring something, the chink of a spoon.

Only a week, I thought. Four days. 'Odd,' I answered. 'Very odd.'

'I tried to ring you before. Some woman I didn't know answered.'

'Julie. Did you ever meet her years ago? Maybe she was before your time. She's been away.'

'Didn't she give you my message?' She hadn't. 'Who is she? Hang on – Megan! Amy! Come and get your hot milk and honey! Sorry. This Julie . . .'

'She's been away, travelling round the world. She's staying here. For a bit.'

'Oh. Do you mind?'

'Not yet, not really.'

'But are you all right? Oh, Christ, clear that up now. Now! Get a cloth or something, it's running everywhere.'

'Do you have to go?'

'I think so. Call you back.'

I'd bought food the previous day, including a bag of fresh pasta, a jar of red pepper and chilli sauce and a couple of those bags of salad that you don't have to wash. But they had disappeared. So had the slice of lemon and ginger cheesecake. There was almost nothing in the fridge except for a couple of cartons of milk, some cream cheese, and – I lifted them up to make absolutely sure – a pair of new black knickers, with their price tag still attached.

I knocked on Julie's door. No answer. I pushed it open. Clothes were flung everywhere, including some of my own. There were jars of cream and tubes of lipstick on the filing cabinet, where she'd propped a mirror from the bathroom. My slippers lay by her unmade bed.

I didn't feel like going out to the shops again – I was too tired – so I made myself some toast and marmalade and a mug of cocoa. I retrieved my slippers and put on my dressing-gown. Then I got out my sketch-pad. I sat at the table, taking small sips of frothy hot chocolate, and I tried to draw Lianne – not her face, though; her small childish hands, with the nails chewed to the quick. Hands are difficult, worse than feet or faces, even. It's almost impossible to get the proportions right. Fingers bulge out like bananas; the thumb twists at an improbable angle.

I couldn't get it right, and after several attempts I gave up. I was mildly bothered by the black knickers in my fridge and the rain slapping at my window and the itchy notion that I was missing something.

11

Being busy brings its own adrenaline rush. That morning, instead of lying in a hot bath until I heard Julie leave, I took a quick shower and washed my hair. I didn't bother to dry it, just towelled it briskly then twisted it up. I drank my coffee while I pulled on a dress and sandals. Then, putting my car keys and an apple in my bag, I managed to whisk out past Julie, who sat at the kitchen table with a mug of tea, looking as sleepy as a cat in a puddle of sunlight. I drove straight to the Welbeck and parked my car in its old place, under the acacia tree. The morning was misty and damp. No one else was there yet except a cleaner, moving backwards over the lobby with a vacuum cleaner.

In my office I pulled the door shut and opened the windows, which looked out over the small patch of gardens at the back. There were no papers in my out-tray, but a small mountain in the in-tray. Patients I should see, referrals I had to deal with, correspondence I needed to reply to, forms to fill in, journals to read, invitations I was going to turn down. According to my answering-machine, I had twenty-nine messages. I switched on my computer and found a dozen or so e-mails there, too. I'd read somewhere that a busy executive can get up to two hundred e-mails a day. It was so unfair. Couldn't they be shared out among all the people sitting alone in rooms to whom nobody wanted to send messages?

By nine, the heap of paperwork had sunk and I'd refused invitations to conferences in three different countries; I'd separated requests for me to see patients into the yes, no and don't-know piles; I'd filled up my diary with satisfying little blocks of allotted time. There were crumpled balls of paper all round my chair. I could hear the sounds of the clinic coming to life: phones ringing in other offices, doors slamming, the murmur of conversations in the corridor. I went down to the coffee machine, which was on the ground floor, then bolted back to my office with my cup of coffee slopping against my fingers.

There I pulled out the notes I'd made on Lianne. I stared at the sentences I'd jotted down until they blurred, became hieroglyphics. The only name I had that could provide any kind of illumination was of the man who ran the drop-in centre where she sometimes slept or went for a hot bath, a warm meal and clean clothes. Will Pavic, that was it. On an impulse, I picked up the phone and dialled his number.

'Yes.' The voice was abrupt and impatient.

'Could I speak to Will Pavic, please?'

'Yes.'

There was a pause.

'Is that Will Pavic speaking?'

'Yes.' Crosser this time.

'Good morning. My name's Dr Quinn and I'm helping the police –'

'Sorry, I don't deal with the police. I'm sure you'll understand that, in the circumstances.' And the line went dead.

'Bastard,' I muttered.

I took the apple out of my bag and ate it slowly, everything except the stalk. Then I dialled my own number.

'Hello!' Julie sounded much livelier than she had when I'd last seen her.

'It's me, Kit. Something's been bugging me all morning. Why is there a pair of knickers in my fridge?'

'Ooops!' There was a splutter of laughter. 'I read in some magazine that if it's hot weather, it feels glorious to put on a chilled pair of knickers. That's all.'

'But it's not that hot.'

'That's why they're still there. I'm waiting.'

So that was sorted. I phoned Will Pavic once again.

'Yes.' Same voice, same tone.

'Mr Pavic, this is Kit Quinn, and please would you hear what I have to say to you before putting the phone down again.'

'Ms Quinn –'

'Doctor.'

'*Dr* Quinn.' He managed to turn the title into an insult. 'I am a very busy man.'

'As I said – or was trying to say – I am helping the police with their inquiries into the death of Lianne.' There was a pause. 'Lianne who was found by the canal?'

'I know who you mean. I don't know how you expect me to help you.'

'I wanted to talk to people who knew her. Who knew what her life was like, what company she kept, what was worrying her, whether she was the kind of person who –'

'Certainly not. I won't have the young people here badgered by you lot. They've got enough problems as it is.'

I took a deep breath. 'What about you, then, Mr Pavic?'

'What about me?'

'Can I talk to you about her?'

'I've nothing to say. I scarcely knew Lianne.'

'You knew her well enough to identify the body.'

'I knew what she looked like, of course.' His voice

was harsh. I imagined a stern grey man with a face like a hatchet and gimlet eyes. 'I hardly think that's the kind of discussion you want, is it? You want to know about her *mind*, right?' His voice dripped sarcasm.

I wasn't going to lose my temper. The more cross he became, the calmer I felt. 'I won't take long.'

I heard a pencil tapping rapidly against a surface. 'Very well, what do you want to know?'

'Can I come and see you in person?' No way was he going to tell me anything like this.

'I have a meeting in less than an hour and after that –'

'I'll be with you in fifteen minutes,' I said. 'It's very kind of you, Mr Pavic, I appreciate it.' Now it was my turn to put down the phone. I grabbed my bag and jacket and ran out of my office before he had the chance to ring me back.

The Tyndale Centre for Young People was a large and unprepossessing pre-war building with metal windows, squeezed between a slatternly pub and what must have been one of the ugliest low-rise apartment blocks in London – dirty grey breeze-blocks and mean little windows, some of which were smashed. A brightly coloured mural made its way up one edge, flowers, tendrils curling up to the roof. It might have been *Jack and the Beanstalk*. In another hand 'Fuck Off' was scrawled across the design about six feet off the ground. On the other side of the street, there were several derelict houses with boarded windows and doors, and weeds taking over the front yards. Two teenage boys with shaved heads were kicking a ratty tennis ball between them in the street, but they stopped and stared suspiciously at me as I approached the door.

'Hello?'

I couldn't work out if the person who opened it was one of the young people or a helper. She had purple hair, several studs in her eyebrows and her nose, a sweet smile. She was wearing massive shaggy slippers. Behind her, I could see a large hallway, with corridors leading off it, and I could hear, coming from upstairs, the insistent throb of rap music and someone shouting.

'I'm Dr Quinn. I've got an appointment with Will Pavic.'

'Appointment?' shouted a voice, out of sight. 'Let her in.'

The woman stepped aside. The hall was painted pale yellow. There was a spindly tree in a pot in the corner, a table stacked with leaflets against one wall, and an old sofa near the stairs where a ginger cat lay asleep. I saw at once that it had been carefully designed to be unintimidating for anyone who made it through the doors.

Will Pavic was in a small room opposite, with the door open. He was sitting at a desk staring directly at me over the top of his computer. He must have been in his forties, with hair cropped to about the same length as his dark stubble, and thick dark eyebrows. In the brightness of his office, he looked monochrome, all black and grey and chipped, as if he had been hacked out of granite. He was scowling. He stood up as I crossed the hall towards him, but stayed behind the cluttered fortress of his desk.

'Hello,' I said.

He shook my hand firmly but cursorily. 'Take a seat,' he said, nodding at a hard-backed chair in the corner. 'Just put the papers on the floor.'

I cleared my throat. I gave a nervous smile, which Will didn't return. There were yellow Post-it stickers on every spare inch of the wall behind him. Suddenly it occurred to me that I hadn't really thought about what

I was going to ask. 'I'm sorry,' I said. 'I don't really understand. Is this a children's home?'

'No,' he said.

'What then? A council half-way house?'

'The local authority have nothing to do with it. The government have nothing to do with it. Ditto the social services.'

'Then who runs it?'

'I do.'

'Yes, but who do you answer to?'

He gave a shrug.

'But what actually happens?' I asked.

'Simple,' he said. 'This is a place where homeless young people can stay for a short period. We give them some help, make some calls, whatever, and send them on their way.'

'Did you send Lianne on her way?' At that his face froze. 'Look, I'm starting from zero here,' I said, smiling at him. No response at all, like a computer that's been turned off. 'I want to find out whatever I can about Lianne – I don't mean about her movements round the time of her death, last-known sightings, that kind of thing. That's for the police. More, the kind of girl she was, you know.'

His phone rang but was picked up by the answering-machine.

'I didn't know her like that,' said Will.

'How long was she here?'

'She wasn't here. Not the way you mean. She came occasionally. She knew people.'

'This doesn't make sense. If you've got so little connection with her, why was it you who identified the body? How did the police make the connection?'

'The police made the connection because they put her

face on a poster and a concerned citizen phoned up anonymously and said that she had spent time at the Tyndale. And the reason I identified her was because I was the only supposedly respectable person they could find who admitted to ever having met her. But, then, this is Kersey Town, which isn't the sort of place you come from.'

'You don't know where I come from.'

'I can guess,' he said, with a slight smile at last.

'I just want to know what she was like, Mr Pavic. Do you know anything about her background, for instance? Or her friends?'

Now he looked uncomfortable and irritated, as if I were being obtuse.

'You don't get it,' he said. 'I don't want to know about these people's lives. I'm not going to pretend to be their friend. I try to give a small amount of practical help and most of the time I fail. That's all. Runaways have their reasons for running away, Dr Quinn. Do you think they do it for fun? Lianne probably had very good reasons for running away.'

'Do you think she might have been abused?' I asked. He didn't reply and I felt crass for asking the question.

'She was lonely,' he said abruptly. 'A lonely, eager, frightened, angry young woman. Someone like you might say she was looking for love. Enough now?'

'And you don't want to help?' I said.

He leaned over the desk, his face harsh. 'But I already failed to help,' he said. 'Again.'

'I –'

'I've got to go now. I've got a meeting.'

'Can I walk with you to the underground?'

'I'm driving.'

'You could drop me off at a station on your way, then.

I've just a few questions. Which way are you going?'

'Blackfriars Bridge.'

'Right past my front door,' I said, conveniently forgetting that my car was parked at the Welbeck Clinic.

He sighed ostentatiously. 'All right.'

We walked out into the hall together. A startlingly pretty girl, with long fair hair, ran in. *'I'm fucking trying!'* she screamed into our faces, then bolted up the stairs, sobbing.

'Was she on any drugs?' I asked, as I sat in the passenger seat of Will Pavic's rusting Fiat and we eased through the traffic.

'More questions, eh?'

'I was curious.'

'Tell me where to turn off.'

'Not yet. Why are you so angry?'

'Seems a reasonable response to me.'

'To what?'

'Everything. All this crap.' And the gesture he made, with his hands off the steering-wheel, took in everything: the traffic, the conversation, me beside him when he wanted to be alone, Lianne's death, life in general.

We drove the rest of the way in silence, apart from the instructions I gave him. He pulled up right outside the front door, and I climbed out.

'Kit! Hey, Kit – Kit!'

My heart sank.

'Hi, Julie.'

'Brilliant timing. I've forgotten my key.' She bent down and smiled in at Pavic through the open door.

'This is Will Pavic,' I said, in a muttered grunt. 'Julie Wiseman.'

She leaned right into the car, so that her skirt rode up

her thighs and her breasts swelled under the flimsy shirt. 'Hi, Will Pavic. Are you coming in?'

'He just gave me a lift. He's on his way to a meeting.'

Julie ignored me. 'Tea? Coffee?'

'No, thank you.' His voice was remarkably courteous. So it was just me, then.

'Thanks for the lift,' I called, and turned my back on them. I left the door open so that Julie could let herself in, and went upstairs, although in a few minutes I'd have to turn round and head back to the clinic and my car. Time for a cold drink, at least. I let the tap run, dabbling my fingers under the flow. I heard Julie's feet clattering up the stairs.

'Wow! He's *gorgeous*.'

'You reckon?'

'Oh, definitely my type. Grim, weathered, strong, silent. I asked him for dinner.'

I spun round. 'You *what*?'

'Invited him for dinner.' She smiled triumphantly. I spluttered something incoherent and she grinned and kicked off her sandals. 'No good hanging around waiting. I'm not like you, Kit. Did you know you can divide people into herbivores and carnivores?'

'I –'

'You're a herbivore. I'm a carnivore. And *he*'s a carnivore.'

'Is he coming?' I managed to say.

'Tomorrow. Eight o'clock. He couldn't think of an excuse in time.'

'I'm going out.'

'You never go out,' she said dismissively. 'Anyway, you can't. I said we were having a few friends round for a meal, and why didn't he join us if he was free. So who are you going to invite?'

'Julie . . .'

'And what shall I cook?'

'Listen . . .'

'And, most importantly, what shall I wear? Can I borrow your red dress?'

12

After I'd returned with my car, I went into the living room and sat down with some papers while Julie, well pleased with herself, took a shower. She took so many showers, singing unseasonal Christmas carols loudly and tunelessly. Perhaps she'd picked up all these clean habits from travelling abroad. I remembered the jokes that American and Australian colleagues had made about the English: untidy, dusty houses, bad teeth, unclean. If you want to hide something in an Englishman's bathroom, what's the best place? Under the soap. I'd been told that late at night at a conference in Sydney.

I reread the scene-of-crime report. I looked at the photographs. I closed my eyes and tried to picture what it had been like down there by the canal. Something was irritating me. It almost drove me mad, this feeling of something beyond my grasp that I was reaching for. Yet there was excitement as well. Something was coming. I had a photocopied map that showed the sites. I stared at it helplessly. What was there to worry about?

Julie came into the room, glowing, almost steaming from her shower. She was wearing her cut-off jeans, a very small T-shirt that didn't reach her belly-button, and no bra. There would have been no room for a bra. She was carrying a bottle of white wine and two glasses. Without a word, she poured it and handed me a glass. She went to the kitchen again and returned with a small Chinese bowl full of olives. She put it on the coffee table and sat on the sofa with her knees up against her chest and took a sip. I tasted mine. It was wonderfully cold. I looked at Julie. She was very attractive, tanned, so relaxed in her own body. I thought of Oban and smiled. There was something of the couple about us now, and I suppose he thought Julie was rather a catch for me. I could easily see the attraction of being gay. There was so much bother with men. Their basic foreignness, the different stuff in the bathroom, everything. I took another sip. Unfortunately there was nothing I could do about it. It was probably to do with my upbringing or the pressures of society, but I was stuck with hetero-sexuality.

'Try an olive,' Julie said. 'I was walking through Soho this afternoon. It's great, and I bought these olives stuffed with anchovies and chillies. It's like being kicked in the face by a horse. In a good way, I mean.'

I chewed one and indeed it did suddenly feel as if a match had been struck on my tongue but I took another gulp of wine and the cool dousing the hot felt wonderful. 'Nice,' I said.

'I was walking around and doing some thinking. I've got to find three things. A job, a place to live and a man. That's why I grabbed that guy outside. Is he married?'

'I don't know.'

'Or gay?'

'I've never met him before.'

'If he's not gay and he looks good and he can string a couple of words together and he's available, then you've got to act instantly.'

'It's my experience that when people are available it's often for a good reason.'

'You mean he might have a disease?'

I only laughed.

'But look, Kit, I meant what I said. I feel bad about

squatting like this. I want to say that I'm actively looking for a place.'

'That's all right.'

'I'm cramping your style, I know.'

'Do I have a style at the moment?' I asked. 'No, I know I get a bit ratty, but if I was on my own, I'd probably be crawling up the walls.'

'I thought you'd be out more. Looking for clues.'

I leaned over, took the bottle and topped up my glass and Julie's. 'I'm mainly looking at files, I'm afraid.'

Julie put two olives into her mouth then started coughing and gulped at her wine. She went very red in the face. 'Have you got a suspect?' she managed to gasp.

'That's not what I'm doing. I'm going through everything I can with a different eye, to see if anything occurs to me about the sort of person they should be looking for. I'm just supposed to look at it lucidly, with no pre-judgements – a bit like those lateral-thinking riddles. You know, Antony and Cleopatra are lying side by side, dead. Beside them is a puddle of water and some broken glass. How did they die?'

'Goldfish,' said Julie instantly. 'But what about the man who gets into a lift on the ground floor and always presses the tenth floor, then walks the last five floors, whereas on his way down he gets into the lift at fifteen and goes all the way to the ground, no stopping?'

'Dwarf.'

'So, do you think they'll find the murderer?'

'That depends. If he stops now, then no, I don't think they will.'

'That's a bit negative.'

'Do you know how many murders are committed in a year?'

'What? In the whole world?'

I laughed. 'No. In England and Wales.'

'I haven't a clue. Five thousand?'

'A hundred and fifty, two hundred, something like that. And more than half of those, maybe two-thirds, are solved straight away. Most people are killed by people they know, husbands, family members. There'll be a fight outside a club, some football fans, a burglar killing an old lady, caught by her as he's leaving. For the rest, there's the golden first forty-eight hours in which most people who are going to be caught are caught. That's when the killer is still going to be covered in blood, behaving strangely, disposing of weapons and clothes, covering his tracks. It's only days and days later when they've run out of ideas that they even think of asking someone like me to get involved. The murder weapon has been got rid of and not found. The blood has been washed away. If a witness had seen anything, they would almost certainly have come forward by now. You know when you've lost your keys and you get to that terrible stage where you're looking in the places you've already looked in? That's the stage they've reached now.'

'Sounds hopeless.'

I bit another olive. Lovely. 'The police aren't too bothered. No relatives creating a fuss. No press calling for a result. But there's a bright side. If the situation is hopeless, then at least it's difficult to make things worse.'

'Is that why you were talking to that guy, Will?'

'Yes. Lianne – well, there are a lot of people like her in this area.'

'You mean prostitutes and runaways.'

'I mean young women drifting around, not in stable relationships, earning casual money. And I think Will Pavic knows as much about that world as anybody.'

'What is he? A pimp?'

'He runs a hostel that helps some of these runaways.'
I smiled at Julie's disappointed expression. 'Sorry. He's
not a lawyer or a doctor or a television producer. I've
already gathered from the expressions on the police's
faces every time his name comes up that they don't think
much of him. Anyway, as you may have heard, he wasn't
very keen on communicating with me, so maybe your
plot to get him into your clutches could be useful. While
he's falling in love with you, he might start talking to
me. Or do you mind me being here?'

'For Chrissake, you've got to be here. You've got to
help.'

Julie was going out for the evening but I finished the
bottle of wine and read through files I'd already read. I
looked at the map again and then I gave a sort of grunt.

'That's it,' I said to nobody. It wasn't a great eureka
moment. I didn't run around the room shouting. But I
felt puzzled and that was something.

When I appeared in Detective Inspector Furth's office
the following morning, he looked as if I had arrived to
repossess his stereo. 'Yes?' he said.

'I've had a thought.'

'Good,' he said briskly. 'You didn't have to come in,
though. You could always just give a ring. It saves us all
trouble.'

'We don't have to be enemies, you know,' I said.

'What do you mean?' he asked, in a tone of innocence.

'Doesn't matter. Do you want my idea?'

'I'm agog.'

'You may want to look at the map,' I said.

'I've got my own map.'

'Do you want to hear what I've got to say?'

'Please tell me your thought, I'm on tenterhooks.'

I sat down opposite Furth's desk. The chair was irritatingly low, which made me feel as if I was looking up at the chairman of the board. 'Why the canal?' I asked.

'Because it's secluded.'

'Yes, but look at the map.' I laid out my photocopy on his desk. 'There are very secluded parts of the canal, but not where the body was found. Look. Where Lianne was found is right by the Cobbett Estate.'

'That's secluded enough,' Furth said breezily. 'I know the site backwards. There are plenty of bushes. It's poorly lit, deserted at night. Also, the murderer could escape along the canal in either direction or cut off into the streets.'

'That's what occurred to me when I looked at the map. It's a place that can be driven up to. Look, it's almost next to the estate car park.'

'So?'

'Another thing puzzled me. Lianne had her throat cut and her carotid artery severed. Her clothes were soaked in blood. I looked at the scene-of-crime report for the amount of blood found on the scene. Nothing.'

Furth gave a shrug.

'Well?'

'Isn't that strange?'

'Off the top of my head, not really. If she was pulled backwards, the blood might just go on her and the murderer. The other spots wouldn't be noticed. Anyway, the scene-of-crime guys probably didn't mention it. What would have been the point?'

'This is the point. What if Lianne wasn't killed on the canal? What if she was brought there, already dead, and dumped? The site was chosen because it could be driven up to, and it was dark and quiet, as you say.'

'Is that it?' said Furth briskly.

'Yes.'

He got up, went to a filing cabinet and opened a drawer. He flipped through it, pulled out a grey file, walked across and tossed it on to the desk. I picked it up and looked at it.

'Recognize it?'

'Yes.'

'Darryl Pearce. He found Lianne's body, remember? Remember how he found it? He heard a drawn-out groan or cry. He hung around a bit. Cowardly bastard. Finally made up his mind, rummaged in the undergrowth and found her. What's your argument? Did your murderer bring a half-dead person in his car? Do you know how long it takes someone to die after a wound like that?'

'I thought of that as well,' I said.

'Then what the fuck are you doing here?'

'One of the things I've tried to remember is not to give too much importance to any single piece of evidence. Because it might be wrong. Remember the Yorkshire Ripper hunt? They looked in the wrong place for about a year because they believed a fake tape.'

'You think that runt Darryl Pearce has the brains to fake anything?'

'I was wondering about that. I tried to work out if he might have made a mistake or fabricated the story to cover up for something, but I couldn't think of anything.'

'So?'

'Mary Gould.'

'Remind me.'

'The woman who found the body.'

Furth looked dismissive. 'She was the one who was too scared to report it and phoned up the next day. It was no big deal. She didn't have anything important to contribute.'

'She saw the body, but in her statement she didn't say anything about Lianne still being alive. What do you make of that?'

'She might have forgotten. Or not noticed.'

'You don't not notice someone bleeding to death from an artery.'

'She could have arrived on the scene just after Lianne had died.'

I looked at Furth. His expression was a little less contemptuous. He looked as if he was starting to become interested, despite himself. 'So,' I said, 'in that scenario, you imagine Darryl Pearce hearing a groan. According to his account he was on the towpath, just by the canal. Then while he is deciding what to do, Lianne dies and Mary Gould arrives from the other side, from the direction of the housing estate, she said. She is horrified and runs off before Darryl comes round and finds the now-dead body. That's quite a lot to happen in ninety seconds.'

'You got a better suggestion?'

'I've got an alternative. Mary Gould finds the body, cries out, runs off. Darryl Gould hears that cry and assumes it came from Lianne. That's all I'm saying. Darryl Pearce's statement is the only suggestion we have that Lianne was ever alive when she was lying by the canal.'

Furth leaned back. 'Fuck,' he said reflectively.

'Do you see what I mean?'

'I'm going to have to think about this one.'

'There's one more thing.'

'What?' asked Furth, looking past me into space.

'If we're agreed that the actual killing isn't tied to the canal –'

'Which we're not,' Furth interrupted.

'– then the significance is not the place but the means of killing. Which may mean that if this is a random killer on the look-out for a vulnerable victim, then there may be other killings that have been overlooked. So it would be worth checking with other cases. What do you think?'

'I'll consider it,' said Furth.

'Do you want me to talk to Oban about this?'

'I'll do it.'

'Good,' I said brightly. And, having spoiled Furth's morning, I left, feeling oddly cheerful.

13

When you've got somebody awkward coming to dinner, all the agony aunts agree on what you should do. You need to find your very best friends. You talk to them and explain the situation. You invite them round but on the firm promise that you'll repay them by inviting them for a really enjoyable evening in the near future. I considered this and then I had a moment of inspiration. I thought: Fuck it. Why should I put anybody I care about through an evening like that? I had a much better idea. I had a small group of people in the corner of my brain like a migraine that was always waiting to happen. They were like something stuck to my coat that I couldn't get rid of. They were the people to whom I owed hospitality but whom I never got round to inviting.

There was Francis at the Welbeck, for example. He had invited me to dinner at his flat in Maida Vale. There had been a terrible argument – I couldn't remember what about – and somebody had left early, and Francis had got very embarrassed and very drunk. I had described the event to Poppy and she thought it sounded funny and even enjoyable, in a Blitz spirit sort of way, but it really wasn't. In fact, Francis had actually avoided catching my eye for days afterwards, and had never referred to the evening again. Still, I suspected I ought to reciprocate in some form, some day, and this seemed like a good opportunity, not least because it was such short notice that he almost certainly wouldn't be able to come. I rang him at work and said that I was having a few people round the next day, could he come? Great, he said. See you then.

Then there was Catey. I had met Catey because at university her boyfriend was the best friend of someone I had gone out with for a while. It was a distant enough connection, God knows, and it wasn't as if we had hit it off especially. There were dozens of closer friends with whom I'd lost touch gradually or suddenly but my tepid relationship with Catey had been kept going over the years by a stubborn, persistent drip of invitations, a dinner party that year, a drinks party the next, and I would respond with an invitation ratio of about one to every four of hers. Once more I hoped that she wouldn't be able to come, and that that would be my obligations discharged for another year or two. Indeed, when I got through to her it turned out she was engaged for the evening, but then she said, 'No, no, I'm sure I can put them off,' and that she wanted me to meet Alastair, her new boyfriend, in fact, almost her fiancé. She rang back three minutes later. That was fine, she said. See you tomorrow. Lovely, I said.

Julie insisted on cooking and I agreed to that without any protest since the entire imminent disaster had been her idea. When I arrived home just before seven the flat was full of rich smells. The table was laid. The main room was tidy. I went into the kitchen. On one side there was a large dish I had forgotten I had. She must have been rooting around in the back of my cupboards. It was full of vegetables. I could see tomatoes, aubergines, courgettes, sliced onions.

'You said to keep it simple,' Julie said. 'That's the first course. Marinated vegetables. Then there's a risotto. I've got the liquid all ready. And I got some fruit and ricotta round the corner.'

'I bought some wine,' I said, faintly.

'Then we're all done.'

'How do you do all this?'

'What do you mean?'

'All this. This stuff, the laid table, the dish with veg-etables that could be put in a magazine. There are no cookbooks lying around wedged open with stains where you spilled oil on them.'

Julie laughed. 'I don't know how to cook. This isn't cooking. I just fried or boiled a few vegetables and poured some olive oil and a splash of vinegar over them, sprinkled a few herbs. This is just fast food.'

'Yes, but where did you learn how to do it without planning and worrying and complaining and making a mess?'

She looked puzzled. 'Compared with what?' she said. 'Are you comparing boiling up some rice with going and looking at dead bodies and thinking about how they died?'

I pulled a face. 'That wasn't exactly what I had in mind,' I said lamely.

'But your dress,' Julie said. 'You haven't changed your mind about that?'

Julie looked almost too sensational in the dress. With her tousled hair and still-tanned face and arms and legs, lipstick and just a touch of mascara, she looked as if she should be performing a torch song in an exotic bar rather than having dinner with a selection of my more drab friends.

'You look amazing,' I said, and she gave a half-grin as if it was all a joke, as if we were both going to dress up in grown-ups' clothes to play a game. 'I'm not going to be able to compete. I think I'll dress down this evening.'

'Is this all right?' Julie said, looking slightly alarmed. 'You want this back for this evening? I'm sure I can dig out something else.'

I shook my head. 'That's your dress,' I said. 'That dress does not want to be worn by me ever again.'

I tried on five different dresses. I was after a complicated and subtle effect. I didn't want it to seem as if I'd made an elaborate, rather pathetic attempt to impress at what was, after all, a casual dinner. On the other hand, it wouldn't do to appear insultingly casual. I settled on something simple and black, which didn't look as if it had been sprayed on but neither did it look as if I was going to a barn dance. When I emerged from the bedroom, Julie gave a whistle, which made me laugh. 'That's amazing,' she said. 'You look incredible. Is that what you call dressing down?'

I went over to her and turned her towards the large antique mirror on the wall. I leaned on her shoulder and we scrutinized each other and ourselves with a critical eye. 'We're wasted on this crowd,' I said. 'We should be going out somewhere so trendy that I haven't even heard of it.'

'I thought these were your best friends,' Julie said.

'More like obligations. You remember that detective, Oban?'

'Course.'

'He thinks we're gay.'

'What?'

'I think so.'

Julie giggled and then her face wrinkled with concentration. 'Was it something we did?'

'I think it was just that we were two women living together, you doing the cooking, all that. You know, a cosy set-up.'

'And a turn-on for him as well, I suppose.'

'Maybe.'

She turned back to the mirror. 'I can see the attraction,' she said thoughtfully. 'It's just that it's always been men with me. Don't know why.'

There was a ring at the door. I looked at my watch. It was one minute to eight. 'Don't they know that eight means nine?' I said, going across to the door that led down to the street. It was Catey, with Alastair hovering shyly behind. Catey was prettily dressed in pale green, and Alastair wore a suit and a tie. He looked as if he had come straight from work. They kissed me on both cheeks then gave me a bottle of sparkling wine and a large bunch of flowers.

'I've heard so much about you,' said Alastair.

What, I wanted to say in reply, could you possibly have heard about me? But I just smiled.

'We've got so much to catch up on,' said Catey, and ran up the stairs.

With a bit of desperate improvisation, there was just enough to catch up on to last us until eight minutes past eight when Francis arrived. He was wearing a white shirt with no tie and a suit that looked so terrible – as if it had been made out of some Terylene substitute, left out in the garden for a week and then not ironed – that I realized it must have cost more than my car. He had brought some champagne. He looked around the living room. 'This is an exciting moment for me,' he said. 'This is the flat that Kit never lets anybody come to.'

Catey and Alastair looked around it with new interest. It was like one of those moments in the National Gallery when you give a painting a casual five seconds, then you look in your guidebook and discover it's the most important German painting of the fifteenth century and you retrace your steps and say to yourself, 'Come to think of it . . .' I flashed a look at Julie, which was the closest I got to explaining that, to be more precise, this was the flat that I didn't let Catey or Francis come to.

'None of you know each other,' I said. 'This is Julie, who's staying with me and has done the cooking tonight and, well, everything, really. And this is Francis, who works with me at the clinic. And this is Catey who, er, who's an old friend. And this is Alastair.'

'Alastair works in the City,' Catey interjected. 'At something totally incomprehensible, of course. Do you know? I heard on the radio the other day that sixty per cent of people have no idea what their partner does at work. By the way, Kit, what happened to that person you were, you know . . . ?'

I was tempted to say, no, I don't know, but I said in a meek voice that we weren't seeing each other any more and there was a silence. Francis opened his champagne and filled a glass for himself, then wandered around the room looking at the furniture, pictures, books as if he was compiling a psychological analysis of me, which of course was what he was doing. He made me think of the days in summer when a big fat bumble bee would get in through a window and chunter around the flat until I could flap it back out of the window with a magazine. Meanwhile Catey began to talk about what an interesting area this was and how clever of me it had been to get in early.

His unofficial tour concluded, Francis sat down on the sofa between me and Julie. 'How's the return to work?' he said, terminating the London property conversation.

'That's a big question,' I said.

'Are you still doing the same thing?' Catey asked brightly.

'Well . . .'

'I was telling Alastair about what you do in the taxi. The reason it came into my mind was that I was wondering whether you know anything about this terrible murder the other day.'

I was puzzled. How could Catey – who, as far as I knew, still worked in a gallery – possibly have heard about my connection with the Lianne murder?

'Which one?'

'The one on Hampstead Heath. That mother who was killed with her daughter there. Philippa Burton.'

'No, I'm not involved with that.'

'It's like Lady Di. People have been laying flowers on the road nearby. They go on for more than a hundred yards. Someone's left a book of remembrance. Ali and I walked over there just to have a look and it's extraordinary. There's a traffic jam, lots of police, queues of people. Women were crying, men were carrying children on their shoulders so that they could get a glimpse. Why do people do it?'

'What do you think, Francis? What's your professional opinion?'

He looked alarmed. 'It's not really my field, of course. Maybe people believe that at the spot something happened, a good thing or a bad thing, there's a special energy. Like heat. People go there to get close to it.'

'It's exciting,' I added. 'People want to be near to feel involved in all the drama.'

'And they care,' added Julie. 'They were upset when they heard about it and they wanted to show it. There's nothing bad about that, is there?'

'No,' I said, and I looked over at Catey. 'I'm working on a murder in a place where people aren't leaving flowers.'

'Why?'

I shrugged. 'The victim was homeless. Her body was found by a canal. I don't think anybody cared much at all.'

'That's sad,' said Catey. But she didn't pursue the subject.

At ten past nine when Will Pavic still hadn't appeared, I decided that we would start eating. We sat down, leaving, on Julie's insistence, a space next to her for him, should he arrive. The vegetables, olive oil and exotic bread that Julie had conjured up from somewhere or other were all extraordinary. It was like being in a restaurant but with the added benefit of having my own furniture. The risotto was wonderfully chewy and flavoured with sorrel, which I had thought was a weed, but hugely impressed Catey. I seemed to get some reflected credit for Julie's food, as if I had been the impresario for the occasion.

The main course was almost finished when there was a ring at the door. Will was standing there in jeans and a blue shirt, rough trainers, carrying a jacket under his arm. Suddenly I felt overdressed, which was ridiculous. He was the one who ought to be apologetic. 'It's been a bad day,' he said. 'I should have rung to say I couldn't come, but I haven't got your number.'

'It's in the phone book,' I said shortly. 'Well, I don't know if it is in the phone book any more. You could probably have got it somewhere. Come and eat. We started, I'm afraid.'

He followed me upstairs. Indoors, in the brighter light, he looked tired and drawn. I introduced him to the people around the table, who looked sheepish suddenly, as if they had been caught eating when they weren't allowed to. Julie came forward, with a charming smile, shook his hand and didn't let go, leading him to his place beside her. He tossed his jacket on to the sofa as he passed it.

'You'll have to catch up,' said Julie. 'Do you mind if I pile everything on to your plate?' He smiled and shook his head. 'Red or white?'

'Whatever.'

For the next few minutes, he ate steadily, glancing around the table, but mainly concentrating on his food.

'Maybe we should try and bring Will up to date,' Julie said. 'Like in a soap opera. We talked about this area. I did my normal spiel about travelling around the world. You've never heard that, Will. I'll tell it to you later. And Catey and Alastair went to look at where a murder was committed on Hampstead Heath and they signed the book of remembrance . . .'

'We didn't actually –'

'. . . and Alastair was just talking about working in the City.'

Pavic looked round at Alastair. 'Where do you work?'

'Just off Cheapside.'

'What firm?'

Alastair looked puzzled.

'Hamble's.'

'Pierre Dyson.'

'Well, yes,' said Alastair. 'I mean, I've never actually met him, but, yes, he's the chief. Do you know him?'

'Yes.'

There was a pause. 'Sorry,' said Alastair. 'What was your name again?'

'He's called Will Pavic,' I said.

'Hang on, hang on. I remember. Wahl Baker, right?'

Will looked uncomfortable now. 'That's right.'

123

'It's great to meet you, Will. I've heard so much about you.'

'You mean about the hostel?' I asked.

'No, no,' said Alastair contemptuously. 'I don't want to embarrass your guest, but he managed the Wahl Baker fund for ten years. Legendary years. Fantastic.'

'It wasn't so fantastic,' Will said quietly.

'I'll be the judge of that,' said Alastair.

'I didn't know you worked in the City,' I said.

'I don't,' said Will. 'Not now.' And then he fell silent as the conversation drifted off in another direction.

For the rest of the meal I sneaked glances across the table at Julie and Pavic. I heard fragments of her conversation about something in Mexico and something else about Thailand. His replies were brief and I couldn't make them out.

After the meal we sat on the sofa with coffee, tea or, for Catey, a concoction that smelt medicinal. Will was clearing the table and we found ourselves in the kitchen at the same time.

'Not exactly your sort of people, I suppose,' I said.

He didn't smile. 'What do you know about my kind of people? They seem all right.'

'I meant me as well.'

He gave a smile that might have been sarcastic.

'Julie's nice, though,' I volunteered dutifully.

'She seems nice,' he said.

There was a pause. 'I can't believe you swapped being in the City for that hostel in Kersey Town.'

'You know the City?' he said.

'I know Kersey Town.'

'It seemed like a good idea at the time.'

'What about now?'

He opened his mouth, then closed it again, and seemed

to think before talking. 'Sorry,' he said. 'I think it's too big a subject for this kitchen in this dinner party.'

'Then I suppose I should be sorry,' I said. 'By the way, I talked to someone who knows you.'

A flicker of interest. 'Oh yes?'

'A detective called Furth. He's working on the Lianne case. Know him?'

'Yes, I know him.'

'He warned me against you.'

'That sounds like Furth.'

'I don't like him either.'

Will piled the plates carefully by the sink and turned to face me. 'I don't know what you want, Kit, but I don't care what you think about the police or anybody else.'

That was it. I tossed the towel on to the kitchen table and took a combative step towards him. 'What the fuck did you come here for? You come late, and then slouch in the corner like some adolescent with your sarcastic comments and grumpy expressions. You think you're better than me, do you?'

Will shoved his hands into his pockets and frowned. 'I came because I was taken by surprise by your friend's invitation and couldn't think of anything to say. And I'm sorry I was late. As I said, it was a bad day.'

'I had a bad day.'

'I'm not going to have a bad-day competition.'

'I'm not the enemy,' I said.

'Aren't you?' he said, and he walked out of the kitchen. I went after him so we arrived almost together. I was flushed and furious. I don't know what he looked like.

'We were just saying,' said Catey, 'how amazing it was to do what you did, to give up everything, a fantastic job, and work in this hostel.'

I thought he was going to be as horrible to Catey as

he had been to me, back in the kitchen, but his expression was almost benign. 'It wasn't so amazing,' he said. He turned to Alastair. 'I mean, why don't you give up your nice job?'

Alastair looked startled. 'Well, that is, I don't know, really. Because I don't want to, I suppose.'

Will spread his hands. 'I *did* want to. That's all.'

Julie came over – no, slunk over, if that's the word – with a mug of coffee and handed it to Will. 'Why are you bad-tempered with Kit?' she asked.

He gave a start and looked across at me, almost shiftily. 'Bad-tempered?' he said. 'Maybe I'm over-sensitive. When I first started the hostel, I expected help from people, from the police, from social workers. It didn't work out like that. Now I just want them to leave us alone. So sometimes I snap at people.'

'I just want to help,' I said, realizing as I spoke how pathetic that sounded.

'You're too late,' he said. 'She's dead. I was too late as well.' He gave a sad smile. 'There. That's something we've got in common.' He sipped at his coffee, then gulped it down. 'I'm sorry,' he said. 'I think I'd better go.'

'Don't,' I said. 'Not because of me.'

'It's not because of you. I'm not fit to be seen in public just now.'

He said goodbye quite graciously to everybody and was nice to Julie about the meal. Julie saw him out and when she came back murmured to me, 'The search goes on.' I managed a splutter of a laugh but I felt shaken and on the pretext of making more coffee I retreated to the kitchen and did all the washing-up. When I returned with the jug, I saw that my plan to revenge myself on these people hadn't entirely worked. Francis was talking about himself, Julie was talking about the Taj Mahal at dusk, Catey was talking about Alastair, Alastair was looking modest. I was able to pour out coffee, drink coffee and say almost nothing.

After too long, they left with ominous cries of how we must get together soon, and I even saw Francis and Alastair exchanging phone numbers on the stairs, a nightmare vision of my burdens joining together and becoming even bigger ones.

Julie and I were left alone. I pulled a face. 'Sorry to inflict all that on you,' I said.

'Don't,' she said. 'I liked them. And they like you. They all care about you – you're lucky to have so many friends, you know.' For a brief moment, she sounded almost wistful. 'I should be apologizing to you. My Pavic plan didn't really work.'

'Doesn't matter. There was nothing wrong with the plan. It was Pavic who was the problem.'

She smiled and drained her glass. She put down her glass then stepped across to me. She put one hand on my cheek and kissed me on the lips, quite lightly. 'If I become a lesbian,' she said, 'you'll be the first person I make a pass at. Night-night.'

14

I'd been right about one thing – the moan *had* come from the witness, or *a* moan had, at least. A police officer called on Miss Mary Gould and she said she wasn't sure, well, yes, maybe she might have cried out when she saw the poor girl, in fact, come to mention it, yes, she was sure she had. She wasn't in trouble, was she?

So it had been wrong to assume that Lianne had been killed by the canal.

'Which means,' I said to Furth, 'that there's no reason to think it was Doll rather than anyone else. Right?'

'Lady,' he said, thrusting his face towards mine so that I could see the yellow stains on his teeth, the shaving rash on his neck, the lines of exhaustion round his mouth, 'this is all wanking around, you know. She was murdered beside the canal, by Doll.'

'It would be worth looking into other murders, though, wouldn't it?'

'We've already done it. Gil and Sandra spent four hours this morning trawling through the unsolved murder cases in London from the last six months and no match turned up. So there goes your theory. Sorry. Just the one body for you, not a glamorous clutch of them.'

'What were you looking for?' I asked.

'We are trained police officers, you know. Similarities in methods of killing, victim, geography. That kind of thing. There was nothing. No drifter, no mutilated bodies, no common location. Zero. Nothing.'

'Can I look through the cases too?'

He rubbed his eyes and sighed. 'You're meant to be helping, not getting in the way. What's the point?'

'I'm looking for different things,' I answered mildly.

He shrugged wearily. 'If you want to waste a day off, it's your business.'

'Are there a lot, then?'

'Thirty odd, unless you want to extend your search parameters to include the Bronx.'

'How do I look at them?'

'We'll take someone away from catching criminals and you can find a spare terminal.'

'So when can I see them?'

He looked at his watch and muttered something under his breath. Then: 'Half an hour or so.'

'Thanks.'

'Can I ask you something?' he asked, in a more earnest tone.

'What?'

'Are you always sure that you're right?'

I blinked at him, feeling the little knot of panic in my stomach. 'You've got me wrong,' I said. 'I'm never sure. That's the point.'

Thirteen of the unsolved murders were of young men, who had been killed late at night or in the early hours of morning, outside night-clubs, pubs, football matches, parties. I scrolled through their cases: bludgeoned to death, stabbed, smashed in the face with a broken bottle. In twelve of the thirteen cases, they had drunk a large amount of alcohol; the thirteenth was a nineteen-year-old black man who'd been found lying underneath his bicycle, the lights still on. His skull was fractured. Hit by a car. Possible accident. Possible race attack.

Two prostitutes, one found dead in her little room

above a kebab joint, whose owners wondered what the smell was; another who'd been battered to death on some wasteland in Summertown. Not far away from Lianne. I hesitated briefly over her: Jade Brett, aged twenty-two, HIV positive, no next of kin. Probably not, but I made a note. There were several homeless people, winos with wrecked livers found dead by park benches, or in the shop doors where they usually slept. There were seven children, and although their murders were unsolved, in all except one case the police were directing their inquiries towards family members, acquaintances. They weren't relevant anyway.

And of course, there was Philippa Burton, thirty-two years old, middle class, respectable, famous now for dying. Hers was the only name I recognized. Clearly none of the others had merited more than a couple of paragraphs on page five of some newspaper. I looked at the details of her case. As I already knew, she'd been snatched from Hampstead Heath, by the playground where her little daughter had been playing, and dis-covered several hours later at the far, wild end of the Heath, face down among trees and bushes. She had been hit over the head, several times, with a stone that had been found a few feet away from her. There was a cut down her left cheek, and faint bruises around her wrists. She had not been molested. There was no sign that it had been a sexual murder.

I rubbed my eyes and stared at the screen. Then I picked up the phone and dialled Furth's extension.

'I'd like to see Philippa Burton's body. And her case file.'

'What?'

It wasn't a 'What did you say?' It was a 'What the fuck are you talking about?'

'Can I?'

'Why?' he repeated heavily. I could hear him breathing.

'Because I want to,' I said.

'Are you messing us around, Doctor? Is this something to do with your own work?'

'I realize that I –'

'You want to know what I think?'

'What?'

'You've got a problem. After Doll's attack. Other people have been saying it.'

'Then why was I asked in?'

'I've been wondering about that.'

'The fact is that I'm here. Can I see the body?'

'Just because it would be interesting? No way.'

He put the phone down on me. I stared at the computer screen for a few seconds longer, then I picked up the internal phone again and asked to be put through to Oban.

'Can I come and see you?'

'Sure. Now?'

'Please.'

'All right.'

Oban looked at me steadily over the steeple of his fingers. His eyes seemed paler than ever. It was several seconds before he responded. 'I don't quite understand, Kit, what it is you're looking for.'

I didn't reply – there wasn't much to say, since I didn't know either, and the consciousness that I was probably making an idiot of myself, to the delight of the whole police station, was growing stronger.

'You've talked about not making assumptions. Now you're assuming that Lianne's killer murdered someone else as well. Why? You think there might be a connection with the Pippa Burton case. Why? Help me out here, Kit.' His gentle and courteous tones were much harder to respond to than Furth's bluster.

'I don't think I'm assuming that at all,' I said. 'I am just saying that if Lianne wasn't murdered by the canal – and there's no reason now to suppose that she was – then there are things we should consider, that we might have missed.'

Oban was being painfully patient with me. 'For the sake of argument, let's say that you're right. Let's ignore the fact that Furth's team have already looked through the files. Why Pippa Burton? All I can see here is the lack of connections.' He started counting them off on his fingers: 'The victims are different, the wounds are different, the areas are different, the *kinds* of area are different. And it's not just that, it's office politics. You've got a fund of goodwill, guilt even. We felt bad about, you know, the accident. You don't want to use all that up.'

Again, I didn't reply. I managed to hold his gaze, and not drop my eyes.

'OK,' he said with a sigh. 'Take a look.'

'Thank you.'

'It's not in our remit, of course, but it shouldn't be a problem. I'll make sure Furth sets it up – he won't be happy, though. I know he's an idiot, but he's got instincts as well. They're not all wrong.' He looked at me assessingly and didn't smile.

'Oh, well . . .' I managed a laugh that sounded more like a sob.

'Why is this case so important to you, Kit?'

I gave a shrug. 'I'm trying to be thorough.'

'I hear you've been seeing Will Pavic.'

'How would you know that?'

'Dodgy character. You know he used to be something big in the City?'

'I heard something about that.'

'I don't know all the details, but he had a breakdown, gave it all up. He's tried to become the Mother Teresa of north London.'

'That sounds like a good thing.'

'It's more complicated than that. He's out of his depth.' Again, he looked at me searchingly. 'He's not very friendly to the police either.'

'Apparently the feeling is mutual,' I said drily.

'We've just been trying to persuade him to obey the same laws as the rest of us. Don't be fooled by his charm.'

Finally, something that made me smile. I thought of Pavic the other night, with his bristling head and scornful eyes. 'There's no chance of that.'

Oban was right. Furth was right. So why did I not agree with them? I stared again at Philippa Burton's body on the tray. A slim, smooth body, with round hips, high breasts and faint stretchmarks on the stomach, from the birth of her daughter probably. The hands were long and graceful, the manicured fingernails painted with pearly-pink polish, matching her toenails. Her body was untouched, except for the marks around her delicate wrists. She lay there like a beautiful statue, draped in the folds of a sheet. But above her smooth torso, the left side of her head was bashed in. Her cap of yellow hair stuck to the dark blood.

I felt no impulse to touch her, or linger over her body. She had a husband and a daughter to mourn her, dozens of shocked friends, a whole crowd of strangers who had fallen in love with the thought of her. There had been articles in the newspapers; politicians had queued up to pay tribute to this model mother, so brutally mown down by an evil monster, and we must not rest till he's caught, etc. Thousands of people had piled flowers and soft toys at the site where her body had been discovered. Hundreds of people would go to her funeral. Strangers would send flowers. But I stayed, staring at her, because of a feeling, like an itch I couldn't scratch. She'd been found face downwards, like Lianne had been found face downwards. Even I knew that wasn't enough to connect them. Nevertheless, I had this sense of a connection waiting to be made, if only I could think about it in a different way.

I left the morgue and went for a walk on the Heath. It wasn't raining, but it was a dull and heavy day. The grass was wet and the trees dripped steadily. There weren't many people around, just a couple of joggers, and dog-owners, throwing sticks into the soggy under-growth. I walked fast, past the playground, past the ponds, up the hill where on sunny days people fly kites. I wasn't really going anywhere, just round in circles, my brain churning uselessly.

15

I was already distrusted by one group of detectives. Now I had to deal with another. At least they were attached to the same station – or maybe, given the way I was regarded, that wasn't such a good thing after all. Oban was kind, despite all his misgivings, and spoke to the head of the Philippa Burton murder inquiry and said nice things about me. So within a day I found myself sitting opposite Detective Chief Inspector Vic Renborn. He was a large bald man, with a very small amount of ginger hair above his ears and at the back of his head. With his fiery red complexion, he was a scary sight. I could imagine doctors taking bets on whether the heart-attack or the stroke would come first. He panted slightly as he spoke, as if the effort of opening the door for me had been too much.

'Oban says you're interested in Philippa,' he said, as if he were referring casually to a friend in the next room.

'Yes.'

'Everybody's interested in Philippa.'

'I know.'

'I've got uniformed officers out directing the traffic and controlling the crowds around the area where she was found. We've had to install traffic lights and create a temporary car park. People are coming from all over the country and leaving notes and flowers. I've just had a Canadian forensic psychologist on the phone. He's in London promoting a book and he was offering his services. I've got an astronomer. Is that right?' He looked inquiringly at a female officer who was sitting in a corner with a notebook.

'Astrologer, sir.'

'Astrologer. And a couple of psychics. One woman dreamed last month that the murder was going to happen. Someone else has said that they'll be able to identify the murderer if we give them a piece of bloodstained clothing. The press are sniffing round. It's like a circus down there. I'm a lucky man. Everybody wants to help me. And I've got nothing. And we're fucking moving office so I haven't even got a place to hide. Are you here to help me?'

'I'm not specifically concerned with this case.'

'I suppose I should be relieved. Oban says you're involved in the case of a dead drifter found by the canal.'

'That's right,' I said. 'No psychics have come forward about that one. Nobody cares.'

'What do you want with Philippa Button?'

'I'm not sure.'

'It's not just that it's a higher profile case?'

'What do you mean?'

'I just want to inform you that I've already got a psychological adviser. Seb Weller – do you know him?'

'Yes.'

'Good man?'

I paused for a moment. 'I'm not here to compete,' I said tactfully.

'Our problem is that we've only got one witness and she's three years old.'

'Has she said anything?'

'Plenty. She likes strawberry ice-cream and *The Lion King* and small stuffed animals. She doesn't like avocados or loud noises. We've got a child psychologist who spends her time making mud pies with her, or something. Woman called Westwood. Know her?'

'Yes, I know Dr Westwood.' My heart banged uncomfortably. I didn't want to tell Renborn that actually Bella Westwood had taught me. We'd all revered her – a young, striking, intelligent and sardonic woman who sat on her desk swinging her slim legs when she taught – and it would always be hard for me to think of her as an equal. Once a teacher, always a teacher. When I was seventy and she was eighty she would still be the person who'd written in the margin of my project: 'Beware of confusing instinct and hypothesis, Katherine'. Now, I was muscling in on her world, questioning her judgement, even.

'So what do you want?' asked Renborn.

'I'd like to talk to the husband. Maybe see the child, if possible.'

He frowned. 'I don't see why not myself. But you'd better talk to Dr Westwood about the child. I don't know whether she'll let you anywhere near her. There are complicated rules about what people are allowed to say to her. I don't understand them, anyway.'

'That's fine,' I said. 'Ask Dr Westwood, and see what she says.'

'All right,' said Renborn. 'We'll get back to you.'

'I'll wait.'

Renborn gave a grunt. 'Well, then,' he said, 'if you'd step outside, I'll call her. Now.'

I had barely had enough time to take a drink of water from the cooler outside when Renborn came out of his office looking puzzled, and not especially pleased. 'Do you know Dr Westwood?' he said.

'I've met her,' I hedged.

'Hmm,' he said. 'I thought she was going to tell you

to sod off. That's what she's said to everybody else. Got something on her, have you?' This last was said with a wry expression close to a smile, which was better than nothing.

'So that's all right, is it?'

'She'll take you this afternoon.'

'Thanks very much,' I said, mentally rearranging my day.

'Look,' he said, 'I haven't got a clue what you're up to, but if you turn up anything, please tell me first. I'd be disappointed if I learn about it on the front page of the *Daily Mail*.'

'I only want to help,' I said, which, come to think of it, was what I'd said to Pavic as well. My new catchphrase. It had a melancholy ring.

'There you go,' Renborn said sadly. 'You're sounding like an astronomer again.'

'Astrologer,' said the female officer.

'I was testing you.'

'How are you, Kit?' said Bella, looking at me with an expression of sympathy. She had sent me flowers in hospital, I remembered, and a card of a charcoal-and-ink woman bending over and brushing her long hair; her writing was dashing and bold. I had kept the flowers long after they had started to turn brown. I had always wanted Bella to think well of me. You don't have to be a genius to know that she and Rosa were my mother-figures, my figures of authority and of comfort.

'Better, I think.'

We were sitting in Bella's battered old car, stuck in traffic, so she was able to turn and look at me without putting our lives at risk. She had a thin face, crow's-feet round her eyes now, tiny wrinkles forming above her lip, strands of grey in her curly brown hair that flowed everywhere. She was dressed in a deceptively nuanced way. In her dark trousers and light brown sweater she was smart enough to assert some sort of professional status, to show that she hadn't just walked off the street and was making it up as she went along, but she was casual enough to be reassuring.

'Thank you for letting me see Emily.'

'I wouldn't if I thought you'd be clumsy in your approach – but I must say I don't know what it is you're after here.' She put up a hand to stop me when I began to answer. 'I don't particularly mind, either, as long as you don't confuse the child, or distress her, which I'm sure you won't.' A warning was implicit in the sentence. She didn't need to spell anything out. 'My job is simply to talk to Emily and, if necessary, to offer her help. The police investigation is outside my area of expertise.' And yours, she didn't need to add.

'So what have you been doing with her?'

'I asked her what she remembered.'

'Just like that?'

'Why not? I know what you're thinking, that it sounds too simple and open-ended. Last year I had to talk to a four-year-old boy who had been in the flat when his mother was raped and murdered. He had spent eight hours alone with her body. He was severely traumatized, almost unable to speak. Remember the case?' I nodded. 'There we had the problem of healing Damien as well as finding out what he had seen. That was a complex case involving a whole lot of oblique strategies. Games, drawing, telling stories, you know the kind of thing. But Emily was just left by her mother at the playground. There's no trauma, no evident distress. She wasn't disturbed by being asked and it seems there was nothing to remember. She was playing with other girls and then her mother wasn't there. That was the distressing part but she doesn't seem to have witnessed anything of her mother's disappearance, or abduction, or whatever it was.'

'Three-year-olds aren't very good at responding to direct questions.'

Bella laughed.

'Don't worry,' she said. 'I've played with her. I've watched her interacting with friends, playing with her Beanie Babies. Sometimes, painful as it is, we've got to admit that all the sensitivity and clever tricks don't mean anything if there's nothing there to find.'

We drove up through Hampstead to the very top of the hill and then down the other side through opulent residential streets that were new to me. Bella turned into a quiet road and pulled up. 'They're staying with Philippa's mother who lives nearby. For what it's worth, it's meant to be a secret.'

'Do the police believe they're under threat?'

'From the press, I think.'

Bella sat still for a moment, not getting out of the car. I looked at the large house. 'Philippa's mother must be pretty well off,' I said, stating the obvious.

'Very,' said Bella. She drummed her fingers on the steering-wheel. 'Look, Kit, have you got anything?'

'I don't know.'

She looked hard at me with an expression of just the mildest anxiety. She was trying to work me out. Could I have gone mad? Her jaw tightened and she opened the door.

I talked to Jeremy Burton outside in his mother-in-law's beautiful back garden, where the smooth lawn curved around well-tended beds. Bella had introduced me vaguely as an associate and left it at that. I knew that he had worked for some sort of software company. I think he owned it, or most of it. He was thirty-eight years old but looked older. His hair was greying, his face looked drawn, his eyes bloodshot. 'Is there any progress?' he said.

'I'm sorry,' I said, 'I don't know anything about that. You'll have to ask the police.'

'The only police I see are uniformed officers. There's one supposedly lurking around somewhere. They don't know anything. I feel – I feel in the dark.' He rubbed his face.

'I don't think there's been any large step forward.'

'They won't catch anybody,' he said.

'Why do you say that?'

'Isn't that what they say? If they don't find the murderer straight away, then mostly they don't find him at all?'

'It gets harder,' I conceded.

'So what can I do for you?' he asked.

'I'm extremely sorry about your wife.'

'Thank you.' He blinked, as if he couldn't see very well.

'It must have been a terrible shock. Where were you when you heard about it?'

'I've said all this before. I've said it so many times it no longer feels like the truth to me.' He paused, then managed a sad smile. 'Sorry. I'm not my normal merry self. I was at home. I usually work from home at least one day a week.'

'Was Philippa distressed? I'm sorry, is it all right if I call her Philippa? It sounds strange talking like this about someone I never met. It's just that if I call her Mrs Burton I feel like a tax inspector.'

'Thank you,' he said.

'What do you mean?'

'For asking. You know, in the papers they call her Pippa. She was never called Pippa in her life. I called her Phil, sometimes. Now it's the tragedy of Pippa – Pippa this, Pippa that. I think they use it because it fits into a headline. Philippa's got too many letters.' He sighed and ran a hand through his hair. 'And the answer is, no, she didn't seem distressed. She was happy. The same as always. Nothing was different. It was just life as normal. We were happy together – though sometimes now it seems as if I can't remember anything properly any more.'

'Mr Burton . . .'

'What I really don't understand is what Phil's mood could have to do with her death.'

'I'm interested in patterns of behaviour. Maybe I'm asking the same question you must be asking, which is, why her?'

'Everything was normal,' he said, sounding not resentful but just puzzled. 'Normal mood, normal state of mind, normal patterns of behaviour. I say that and you look at me like that, and it all sounds suspicious and strange. Anyway, what does normal mean?'

'Did she have a routine to her life?'

'I suppose so. She looked after Em, looked after the house, saw friends, saw her mother, went shopping. Ran our life together, I suppose. We were quite a traditional couple, you know.'

'Did she see friends during that last week?'

'I've already told the police, she saw her mother and she went out with Tess Jarrett.' I made a mental note of the name.

'If anything had been troubling her, she would have told you about it?'

'Dr . . .'

'Quinn. Kit Quinn.'

'Right. There was nothing troubling her. She went out and got killed by a madman. Everyone says so. Look, I don't know what you want from me. Everyone wants something. The police want me to cry on television, or to break down and confess that I did it. The press wants God knows what. Emily wants – well, she wants to know when Mummy's coming home again, I suppose. I don't know.' He sighed and looked at me out of his bloodshot eyes. 'I don't know,' he said again.

'What do you want?'

He rubbed his eyes. He looked tired and sad. 'To go home with Emily, and go back to work, and be left alone and let everything get back to normal.'

'Except of course it can't.'

'I know that,' he said wearily. 'I know. What I really want is to wake up one morning and find it's been a dream. In fact, every morning now I wake up and for a moment I don't remember, and then I do. Do you know what that feels like? To have to realize all over again?'

I was silent for a moment, and he stared down at the grass.

'Was your wife ever involved in any kind of social work? With foster-children, that sort of thing.'

'No. She worked for an auction house when we met, but she gave that up when she had Emily.'

'She had no connections with the Kersey Town area?'

'She may have caught a train from there.'

I went round in circles several more times, always coming back to the same point: what was the use of asking Jeremy Burton about his wife's character and mood when she'd been the victim of a random attack? At last I stood up. 'I'm grateful to you for talking to me,'

I said, holding out my hand. He shook it. 'Sorry, my questions must have sounded a bit strange.'

'No stranger than most of the other things I've been asked. You know, one newspaper has offered me fifty thousand pounds to talk to them about what it's like to have my wife murdered.'

'What did you say?'

'I couldn't think of anything. I put the phone down. You want to talk to Emily. She hasn't any connections with the Kersey Town area. I can tell you that straight away.'

'I'll only be a minute.'

'Pam will show you. That's my mother-in-law.'

A handsome grey-haired woman was hovering by the French windows that led into the kitchen. There was an ashen pallor to her face, the colour of a woman who had experienced intense grief. Jeremy Burton introduced us. 'I'm very sorry about your daughter,' I said.

'Thank you,' she replied, with an inclination of her head.

'Dr Quinn wants to see Emily,' Burton said.

'What for?'

'I'll only be a moment.'

Pam Vere led me along a corridor. 'Emily's got a friend here at the moment. Is that all right?'

'Of course.'

Pam opened the door and I saw two little girls crouched on the carpet arranging some stuffed animals in a circle. Two girls, one with dark brown pigtails, the other with light brown curls and just for an instant I didn't know which was which, and I felt a pang. It was like a lottery. Which of them was going to be picked out as the one whose mother had been brutally killed? Pam stepped forward to the darker girl. 'Emily,' she said, 'there's someone to talk to you.'

The tiny little girl looked up with a fearsome frown. I sat down next to her. 'Hello, Emily. My name's Kit. What's your friend called?'

'I'm Becky,' the friend said. 'Becky Jane Tomlinson.'

Becky immediately started chatting away. I sat as I was introduced to the toys one by one. Last of all were the good bears and the bad bears.

'Why are the bears bad?' I asked.

'Cos they're bad.'

'What do you do with the toys?' I asked.

'Play,' said Emily.

'Do you ever take them to the playground?' I asked. 'Do you take them on the swings and into the sandpit?'

'I dunnit,' said Emily. 'I dunnit all with Bella.'

'Did it,' said Pam.

I laughed, outsmarted.

'You're a clever girl, Emily,' I said. 'And I am sorry your mummy died.'

'Granny says she's with the angels.'

'What do you say?'

'Oh, I don't think she's gone that far. She's coming back.'

I glanced up at Pam Vere and saw on her face an expression of such fierce anguish that I had to look away again. 'Well, can I come back again one day? If I think of a new thing to ask you?'

'Don't mind,' said Emily, but she had already turned away. She lifted up a sad-eyed koala and pressed her lips to its black plastic nose, crooning gently. 'I'm so proud of you,' I heard her whisper. 'So proud.'

16

I was tired as I drove back to my flat through the fumes of the rush-hour, and glad that Julie wasn't home. She'd said something about an interview with a record company – although what she, a maths teacher and world-traveller, knew about the music industry I didn't know. I opened the windows to let in the evening freshness. Children's voices floated up from the garden at the back. I went into the bathroom, turned on the taps, and tipped some bath oil into the water. Then I took off my clothes, which felt dirty after my day, and slid into the tub. The water was slippery and pungent, and I lay back and closed my eyes. Then the telephone rang. Damn, I hadn't turned on the answering-machine. Why did phones always ring when you were in the bath? I waited, and it went on ringing. So I clambered out, wrapped a towel round myself and dripped into the living room, leaving a trail of wet footprints behind me.

'Hello?' Little soap blisters burst along my arms.

'Is that Kit Quinn?' the voice crackled; he must be calling on a mobile.

'Speaking.'

'It's Will Pavic here.'

'Oh,' I said, into the silence that followed this announcement.

'I wanted to apologize for the other night.'

'Go on, then.'

'What?'

'You said you wanted to apologize.'

There was a splutter at the other end, which might have been outrage or amusement. 'I'm sorry I was unsociable. There you are.'

'You were obviously tired, and it was a stupid invitation anyway. Forget it. It doesn't matter, really.'

'Maybe there's something I can tell you about Lianne.'

I felt a jolt of surprise. 'Yes?'

'It's not much, really. But . . . well, I'm about a mile away from your flat, and I thought I might as well call round. Just for a few minutes. If you haven't got company.'

'Fine. It's just me.' I thought about my bath of silky water. 'See you, then. By the way, how come you found my number?'

'You were right. It wasn't so hard.'

I pulled the plug on my bath and dressed in a pair of ancient jeans and a vest top. I wasn't going to make any effort for Will Pavic. While I was waiting for him, I flicked on the television news to see if there was anything more about Philippa Burton. She'd dropped from the main story to the third one: detectives still searching the area for clues; flowers and soft toys still being left at the place where her body was found. There was a new photograph of her being shown, one of her on a hilltop in baggy canvas shorts and a T-shirt, laughing, her silky hair blowing in the breeze, her arms around her little dark-eyed daughter.

I thought of Emily burying her face into her koala and whispering words to it that her mother had said to her: 'I'm so proud of you.' Maybe my mother had said things like that to me before she went and died. My father had never been very good on details like that – he'd just say, frowning, 'Well, she loved you very much, of course,' as if that was enough. I'd always wanted so much more: all the daft diminutives and terms of endearment, the games she'd played with me, the way she'd held me and carried me, the things she'd wanted for me, the hopes she'd had. All through my life I'd made them up for myself. Every time I had done well at school, I'd told myself how pleased my mother would have been. When I became a doctor, I wondered if she would have wanted that for me. Even now, when I look at myself in the mirror, with my mother's face, my mother's grey eyes, I pretend it's not my reflection that I am gazing at, but her, standing there at last, smiling at me after so many years of waiting . . .

The doorbell rang.

Will was in a dark suit this time, no tie. His eyes were red-rimmed and his skin chalky. He looked as if he needed to sleep for a hundred years.

'Do you want a drink?' I asked.

'No thanks. Coffee maybe.' He stood in the middle of the living room, ill at ease.

I made a coffee for him, and poured myself a glass of wine. 'Milk? Sugar?'

'No.'

'Biscuit?'

'No, I'm fine.'

'Why don't you sit down? Unless you want to deliver your information like that and bolt.'

He managed a brief grimace, then sat on the sofa. I took the chair opposite him and resisted the urge to make small-talk, to fill in the silence that flowered in the space between us. He stared at me, frowning.

'I told you I didn't really know Lianne.'

'Yes, you did.'

'And it's true. Dozens of teenagers come through my

doors every week. They are given shelter if they need it, information about their options if they require it. We put them in touch with various organizations if that is what they want. But no questions are asked. That's the whole point – in a way, that's why I set up Tyndale Centre in the first place. We don't try to tell them what is best for them. We don't make any judgements – everyone else does that, not us. We lay down certain rules, but outside that we make no demands on them. That's what the centre is – a place where they are free to think for themselves, even if that means making painful mistakes about their lives –' He stopped abruptly. 'All that's beside the point.'

'No, it isn't, as a matter of –'

'Lianne had been to the centre three times in the last six months or so,' he cut in. 'The first two, she was quite optimistic about her future. She said she wanted to be a cook – you'll find that about a fifth of children in care seem to want to be cooks. We gave her some leaflets about catering courses, that kind of thing. But the third time, the last time we saw her, she was depressed. Very subdued indeed. Withdrawn and listless.'

'Do you have any idea why?'

He drained his coffee and stared into the bottom of his cup. 'Her best friend had killed herself a few weeks earlier.'

'How old was she?'

'Fourteen or fifteen. Maybe sixteen. I don't really know.'

'How did they know each other?'

'No idea. They came to the centre together once, but they'd obviously known each other before. They probably hung about in the same places.'

'Why did she do it?'

He shrugged. 'Pick a reason. Why don't more of them do it, is a better question. Daisy.'

'That was her name?'

'Daisy Gill. Sounds a happy sort of name, doesn't it?' And for the first time since I'd met him he gave me a proper smile – rueful, quick to fade, but genuine while it lasted. I smiled back and he looked away, staring out of the window at my grassy plague pit.

'Do you want a glass of wine now?'

'So now you've got another fact,' he said, ignoring me. 'I mean, to add to the one you already knew. One: Lianne was troubled. Two: Lianne was killed.'

'Maybe. Wine?'

'No. No wine. That's enough. Goodbye.'

He stood up in a single movement and held out his hand. I took it. 'Thank you,' I said, and it was at that moment that Julie sailed in through the door, with her glossy and excited face; her mouth open to tell me something. She stared at us, startled.

'This is a surprise,' she managed finally.

Will nodded at her. 'I'm just leaving.'

'Glass of wine?' she gabbled. 'Beer?'

'No,' he said. 'Thank you.'

At the door, he turned. 'I wanted to say . . .' He stopped and threw a glance at me. 'I am sorry for my rude behaviour at your dinner party. The food was delicious.'

And he was gone.

'Well,' said Julie, turning on me. 'You're a sly one.'

'He came for about two minutes. He wanted to tell me something about the young woman who was murdered.'

'Yeah, yeah. Well, I've lost interest in him anyway. He's too grim for me. Do you want to hear my news?'

'Go on.'

150

'I got the job.'

'No!'

'Yup. Starting in a month's time – I told them I had other commitments before then.'

'Do you?'

'No, of course not, but you can't seem too available, can you?'

'Congratulations, Julie. I'm sure you'll be brilliant at it – whatever it is.'

'I don't really know myself.' She giggled. Then: 'So I'll start looking for a place to live.'

'No hurry,' I said, before I could stop myself. I'd have to get used to being alone again. I closed my eyes briefly.

'Why don't you try and get him back?' Julie said.

'What the hell are you talking about?'

'Don't shout so. Albie. I bet he misses you too. Anyone in their right mind would miss you.'

'I don't want him back.' To my surprise, it wasn't so much of a lie any more. He'd left of his own accord, and if he was missing me, he was sure to be missing me in the arms of another woman; missing me while holding someone else's face in his hands. So I didn't want him. I wanted someone who would just belong to me. I wanted to be the best beloved. That's what most of us want, isn't it?

17

I was tired, I had mildly swollen glands, a sore throat that felt like glass when I swallowed. I didn't feel much like going to work, so I lingered over my breakfast of toast and honey and strong tea. The kitchen table lay in a pool of sunlight. I would have liked to sit there all day, hands round a warm mug, feet in warm slippers, listening to sounds coming from the street, maybe even watching daytime television. But then the phone rang and it was Oban. He said he wanted to talk to me. 'We are talking.'

'I mean in person.'

'When?'

'Could you be here by ten?'

I looked at my watch.

'I suppose so. I'll have to cancel a meeting.'

'Good.'

'Has there been a development?'

'Not as far as I know.'

'Then what's it about?'

'We'll talk about it face to face.'

I was puzzled all the way over, constructing good scenarios and bad scenarios in my head, but mostly bad ones. I didn't come up with anything as bad as what I found when I was shown into Oban's office at exactly ten o'clock. Oban was sitting at his desk, clearly not working but looking expectant. I saw he wasn't alone. A woman was standing with her back to me, looking out of the window. She turned round. It was Bella. She caught my eye, then looked away. And sitting on the sofa against the wall was Rosa from the Welbeck.

'What's this?' I said.

Oban gave an uneasy smile. 'Would you sit down, Kit?' he said, gesturing at the chair in front of the desk.

Unable to think clearly, I did so and immediately regretted it because it made me the lowest person in the room. Oban nodded across at Rosa.

'Dr Deitch?'

Rosa bit her lower lip. It was a way of signalling that this was going to hurt her more than it hurt me. She leaned forward and put her hands together almost in an attitude of prayer. 'Kit, I want to make it clear that I blame myself for all this.'

'All what?' I asked – knowing that that was what she wanted me to ask. I should just stay quiet, I told myself. 'All what?' I asked again helplessly.

'We feel,' said Oban, looking at me kindly, which was worse than anything else, 'or, that is, I feel and I think that Rosa agrees with me, that we rather unfairly plunged you into this case without proper regard for, er, level of expertise and . . .'

'You have become rather involved, haven't you, Kit?' said Rosa gently.

'In the first place,' said Oban, 'it was a purely routine matter, a brief assessment of a suspect. We felt we owed it to you to ask you. And you performed that task admirably. We remain indebted to you. Then – and I admit this was entirely my fault – I asked you to become more involved. But recently . . . well, there have been some murmurs . . .'

'Bella?' I said, twisting round in my chair to look at her.

Bella looked at me steadily. 'I've not made any complaint, Kit. But after you left I talked to Jeremy Burton, and to the mother, and I'm afraid I had to report to DCI Renborn that I couldn't see any point to your interview with them. I'd describe it as a fishing expedition, but I couldn't even see that you were fishing for anything. This is a delicate case. It's getting a lot of attention.'

'I know,' I said. 'I only wanted to –'

'I want to echo Dr Deitch,' said Oban. 'I blame myself for pushing you into this pressured situation.'

'You don't want me to work for you any more?'

There was a pause. 'We think it was too soon for you,' said Rosa. 'And that this particular case has touched some nerve in you that may not be particularly healthy.'

'What do you mean?'

'Rosa has told me something of your early history,' said Oban.

I stared at Rosa.

'Kit, all I have said to Dan is that personal circumstances – losing your mother so young – may, in certain ways . . .' her face was going red '. . . well, have affected your judgement in some ways.'

'Oh.' I sat there for a few minutes, my cheeks burning as well. Then I swallowed hard and painfully. 'You may be right. I may be too involved. I do care, I don't know what the right level of caring is. But that doesn't mean I'm wrong. And I haven't been derailing the investigations. I haven't been telling other people what to do. I've just been following up different lines of inquiry.'

'Well, now,' Oban said, 'this isn't one of your bits of academic research. You're talking as if we can just let anybody roam around a murder inquiry, pursuing their own interests. It's not like that. And, I'm sorry to have to say this, in a way you're in danger of derailing the investigation. You put my men's backs up, you trample on other people's turf, and it seems, I'm sorry, but it seems that you're doing it without any reason. I mean, without any proper reason. I accept that you're upset by these victims. So are we all. We all want to catch these killers. You've helped us,' he added, more gently, 'but now we think it's time for us to move on.'

'Can I say something first? Before I go, I mean?'

Oban leaned back in his chair. 'Of course.'

'First of all,' I said, 'tell me, just in a sentence, how you would describe the murder of Lianne.'

'Standard murder of an accessible victim by a psychopath,' he said. 'The crime was committed by someone with a pathological hatred and fear of women. Hence the violent stabbings.'

'And the murder of Philippa Burton?'

'Completely different. I hardly know where to start. She was severely battered with a blunt object. She is a high-risk victim for the perpetrator. She was abducted in a public place while she was with a child. Different kind of person, different method, different area, different level of violence. But you disagree.'

I stood up. I had to pretend at least to be authoritative. I walked to the window and looked out. Outside was an area of virtual wasteland at the back of the police station. There were three overflowing skips and some large metal bins, piles of planks, something covered by a tarpaulin. To one side, growing out of the concrete was a vast explosion of buddleia, flaming purple. Butterflies were fluttering around it like tiny scraps of paper tossed in the wind. That was nice. I turned back to my reluctant audience. 'When I looked through the files on Philippa Burton something rang a bell.'

'What was it, Kit?' asked Rosa, at the same time as

Oban said, 'We don't employ you to listen to bells ringing. There are psychics telephoning us every day about Philippa Burton who hear bells ringing.'

I thought of my group of men at Market Hill; I thought of the things they had done and the skewed way they looked at the world. There were things I had learned from them that nobody else in this room knew. I had that at least. 'People leave signatures behind,' I said. 'Always, even when they try to cover it up, because the signature of a murderer is a bit like the meaning of a poem. There's the meaning that the poet intended, but there may also be hidden meaning that the poet wasn't conscious of. Sometimes they think their signature is one thing but it's actually another.' I hurried on, anxious to get to the end of my last stand before they lost interest entirely. 'What caught my eye about the murder of Philippa Burton was that she was lying face down. Like Lianne.'

I paused and looked at Oban. His expression remained gentle, even pitying. 'Is that it?' he said kindly. 'We've already covered this, Kit.'

'Have you ever seen a recently killed body lying face up?' I asked.

'I suppose so,' said Oban doubtfully.

'I've seen lots of pictures of them. The eyes are open, staring upwards. You know how eyes in paintings are meant to follow you around the room. The eyes of a dead person are the opposite. They are obscenely static, just staring ahead, accusing, maybe. You can imagine that if you'd killed someone, you might want to turn them face downwards, so they weren't looking at you.'

'Maybe, but for God's sake, Kit, a body is like a piece of bread. It can only fall two ways, butter side up or butter side down. It's not enough to build a case on.'

'Remember the wounds on Lianne's body? Where were they?'

'Abdomen. Stomach, chest, shoulders.'

'On her front. And yet she was laid face down. That's like painting a watercolour then hanging it so that it faces the wall.' I looked at Rosa. She was pulling a face.

'I find it difficult,' she said, 'when you talk of these women as if they were works of art.'

'I know, but they are works of art,' I said. 'They are wicked and incompetent and of no aesthetic interest, but they are works of art and we have to read them. That's what I do at the hospital. You know that. I read crimes as if they were symptoms and patterns. I search for meanings. What about the wounds themselves?'

'Brutal,' Oban said. 'Frenzied.'

'Those aren't the words I would use. Tepid, maybe. Precise. Decorous, even. In some ways, it looked like a frenzied sexual attack but it just didn't ring true.' I saw Oban wince again. 'It's not that there were no signs of sexual assault – these psychopathic murders can be a punishment of women for their sexual threat. But in those cases you see terrible aggression directed at the breasts and genitals. Not here, though. The stabbings were all above the waist and avoided the breasts entirely. Display of this kind is very rare and this form of mutilation, it's called piquerism, is even more so. And yet she was turned face down.'

'This is just not enough, Kit,' said Oban. He was gradually losing his patience. 'Where's the connection? Two bodies lying face down?'

'I've seen a number of attacks on women that were comparable to the Philippa Burton one. They were all very violent. Also, it seemed as if the presence of the child was an attraction, as an audience or a victim. But this murderer didn't want the child present. What I felt looking at Philippa Burton's body was the relative restraint. I mean, think of it: you hate women, you've just killed a woman, and you've got something like a claw hammer in your hand. Why not really go for it?'

Oban leaned forward and put a hand on my shoulder. 'Kit, you're not giving us anything. All right, you've got a feeling. True, I don't know what the fuck it means. Sorry, ladies.' The ladies looked up, but mainly because they were being called ladies. 'But I've got nothing to take to the people who think you've been wasting our time.'

I rubbed my eyes with my fingers. I had said my piece and my mind felt empty. He was right. What was there, after all I'd said? What was there to do? I didn't want to think, I wanted to crawl away, but with a last effort, I managed to retrieve something very small from the corner of my mind.

'OK,' I said in a small voice. 'I'm finished. I'll just say one last thing. We know that Lianne's dead body was brought to the canal towpath in the back of a car.'

'We don't know that at all,' said Oban, irritably.

'And Philippa Burton's body was found a mile and a half from where she was last seen. So, in all probability she was taken by car as well. Has there been any cross-reference for fibres or traces?'

'No, there hasn't, as you well know,' Oban said truculently. 'Nor have we cross-referenced them with the Jack the Ripper murders. We don't have time.'

'That's my last suggestion. Will you do it?'

'Why would we –'

'Please,' I said. I wanted to cry. 'Please.'

18

There were fireworks in my head, hissing and wheeling, in the red and purple dark. I don't know how I managed to walk out of the station, with my chin up and my legs not giving way beneath me. I even gave a friendly nod to the woman on duty at the front desk. I reached my car, but my hands were trembling so much I dropped the key on the ground and had to scrabble around for it. My eyes stung, as if there was grit in them. I had to get out of here, to where nobody could see me. I didn't want anyone looking at me with that terrible, terrible compassion in their eyes. I had looked at people like that. Once, in a different life. Everything seemed impossibly far off, as if I was looking at my past through the wrong end of a telescope.

I made it into the car. For a minute I laid my head back against the head-rest and shut my eyes. A nasty sick headache was screwing its way into my left temple. I slid the key into the ignition and drove carefully out of the car park, looking straight ahead. I imagined the three of them watching me go from their window and looking at each other with troubled expressions. How would I ever be able to face them again?

I drove as far as the little triangular churchyard between the delicatessen and the watchmaker's, not so far from my flat, where I got out of the car and went and sat on the grass, with my back against the beautiful copper beech. Albie and I used to come here sometimes, and sit under this tree. It was still damp from last night's rain, and I felt the chill seeping into my bones. I turned my face up to the sun, which was just sliding out from behind a grey cloud. A blackbird sang full throttle just above me. I breathed in deeply. In, out, in out; trying to get rid of the bubbles of panic.

I stood up wearily and walked back to the car. My legs were no longer shaky, but they felt heavy. My head throbbed. Before driving off, I pulled down the shade and stared at myself in the mirror for a few seconds. I looked at my scar, snaking white down my cheek, then I leaned forward, so that it was just my eyes gazing into my eyes.

I hoped that Julie wouldn't be there. But as I fumbled with my key in the lock, she came to the door and pulled it open for me. Her cheeks were flushed. She threw me a rather frantic glance and said in a bright voice, 'Kit! Good. You have a visitor. I said I didn't know when you'd be back but he wanted to wait. He said he was a friend of yours.'

I took off my jacket and walked forward. I could see the back of a head above the sofa. He stood up. 'You said you would come back to see me,' he said, in his soft, high voice. Michael Doll, in the same grubby orange trousers he'd been wearing last time I saw him, and an ancient grey vest with rings of sweat under the armpits.

'Michael!' I didn't know what to say. He was like my recurring nightmare, come to squat in the corner of my flat.

'I waited,' he said plaintively.

'How did you know where I lived?'

'I followed you back from the station once,' he replied, as if it was the most normal thing in the world. 'You never noticed me.'

'I'll be going now,' said Julie. 'Is that OK, Kit? Or do you want me to stay?'

'How long's he been here?' I hissed, turning my back on Michael, who had sat back down on the sofa.

'A good hour.'

'God. God, I'm sorry. You should have rung me.'

'I did. I've left three messages on your mobile.'

'God,' I said again.

'Are you all right?'

'Yes. No. I don't know. You shouldn't have let him in.'

'Kit,' said Michael, from the sofa.

'He seems harmless enough. He just kept staring at my breasts.'

'I didn't,' said Michael, as if it didn't matter much anyway. 'Why didn't you come back to see me, like you said you would?'

'I've been busy.'

'You said you would.'

'I know, but –'

'People should keep their promises.'

'Yes.'

'Otherwise it's not fair.'

'You're right.'

Say as little as possible. Don't allow him to establish any claim on me. Above all, get him out, but without making him feel resentful. He nodded as if satisfied and put his hands on his knees. There was a recent scar running down his left forearm, and a messy scab on his wrist.

'Can I have coffee now? I gave you coffee.'

'You've had three cups already,' interjected Julie.

'Four sugars, please.'

'I have to go out again now, Michael. I'm sorry, but you can't stay here.'

'And one of those biscuits I had before with your lady-friend.' He ran his tongue round his mouth.

I felt sick. 'Michael, listen –'

'And can I, you know, use your bathroom?' There were little beads of sweat on his forehead and above his upper lip.

'It's through there.'

As soon as he had shut the door, I turned to Julie. 'Listen, can you do something for me? Can you take my mobile and ring the police from outside the flat? I'll give you the number.' The horror of ringing the people who thought I was going crazy, and asking them to come and protect me from the man I had prevented them arresting, swept over me. I buried my head in my hands.

'Kit?'

'Yeah. Sorry. It's just – oh, shit. I don't know what to do. He's probably fine, but I don't want to take stupid risks.'

'Give me the phone, then.' She held out her hand. 'Come on, let's get on with it.'

'I might be about to do something terrible to him. Or to me.'

'I don't have a clue what you're going on about, but if he's dangerous, let's get him out of here. Come on.'

'No. Wait. Wait one moment.' I could hear the toilet flushing. 'I know. Ring Will Pavic. He'll know how to deal with this.'

'Him?'

'Please. I can't think of anyone else just now. Do it from outside.'

'What's his number?'

'It's in the phone's memory. Pavic.'

'OK, OK. This is crazy.'

'I know. Thanks.'

'What if he's not there, or if he –'

Doll came out of the bathroom, and Julie bolted for the front door. I noticed approvingly that she left it on the latch.

'I'll put the kettle on, shall I?' I said, too brightly.

'Do you live here alone?'

'No.'

'Are you married?'

'Why are you asking?'

'Your friend said you weren't married.'

'Then you already know.' Avoid conflict. Don't back him into a corner. Don't catch him out. 'Four sugars, you said?'

'And a biscuit.'

'Was there something you came here to tell me, Michael?'

'Why don't you have carpets?'

'Michael, is there –'

'It's funny, not having a carpet. It's like not being in a proper house somehow. Even in the home, we had carpets in every room. Mine was brown. Brown carpet and white wall, with those little bits in the paper.'

'Woodchip.'

'Yeah. I used to lie in bed and pick the bits off with my fingernails. I used to get beaten for that, when they found out in the morning. But I couldn't stop myself. Like picking off a scab. I used to do it for hours sometimes. There'd be little bits of lumpy paper all over the bed, under the sheets. Like having crumbs in your bed, and even when you can't see them you can feel them against your skin. Know what I mean?'

'Yes,' I said helplessly. I poured the boiling water over his coffee and added milk. 'Here. And help yourself to biscuits.'

'Got any fags?'

I went over to my bag and took out the packet of ten that was left over from the time I'd visited him in his bedsit. There was one left. 'Take this.'

'Match?'

I handed him a box; he struck a match, and put the box into his pocket.

'You had to pretend not to mind when you were beaten. But I always cried. Even when I was fourteen, fifteen, I cried. I couldn't help myself. Cry-baby. And then they'd jeer at you, and then I'd cry some more. So when I lay in bed, picking off the wallpaper all night, I'd cry then too, while I was doing it. Because I knew I'd get caught and beaten, and I knew I'd cry in front of everyone, and get picked on more by the other boys.'

He picked up his mug and slurped at the coffee. Bits of ash scattered from his cigarette and he brushed them off his clothes on to the sofa. 'You don't know what it's like.'

'No,' I said.

'I still cry. I cried at the police station. Did they tell you that?'

'No.'

'They laughed at me when I cried.'

'That wasn't kind.'

'I thought you liked me.'

Be firm. 'Michael, I told you. I've been busy.'

'I waited. I didn't go to the canal. I waited for you to come back to talk to me.'

'I've been working.'

'You're just like the others. I thought you were different.'

A chimney of ash fell on his knee. He dropped the glowing cigarette end into the coffee cup and I heard it hiss. He could have killed Lianne, I thought. Easily. If she had laughed at him when he tried to pick her up, say, or laughed at him when he cried.

'Can I have another fag?'

'I'm out of them. We could go to the shops together and buy some more?'

'It's all right.' He took a packet out of his pocket. It was almost full. He offered one to me but I shook my head. 'I need to go out, Michael,' I said. Will was never going to come.

He frowned. 'Not yet. I want to talk.'

'What about?'

'Just talk. You know. Like you said. You said I could say anything.'

'That was a professional interview, Michael,' I said gently. A look of incomprehension crossed his face. 'It was for work.'

'You mean, you weren't telling me the truth?'

'That's not what I mean.'

'I still think about her.'

'Lianne?'

'Yes. Nobody wants to hear me, but I was there, wasn't I? I was there.'

'Maybe.'

'No. No. Not maybe. Why do you say maybe? I was there and . . .'

The door swung open. I hadn't heard his footsteps. Doll sprang out of the sofa, tipping his cup on to the floor, where it dribbled coffee dregs and wet ash.

'Hello, Michael,' said Will. He came forward with his hand outstretched and Doll took it and held on to it.

'I wasn't doing anything wrong.'

'Of course you weren't.'

'Why are you here, then?'

'Dr Quinn is a friend of mine.' He hadn't looked in my direction yet.

'You know each other?'

'Yes.'

'So I know Kit and you know Kit, and I know you and you know me. We all know each other.' Suddenly he looked small and skinny, standing there in his horrible orange trousers. And I felt foolish and ashamed of my fears.

'You know each other?' I echoed Doll.

Will turned to me, perplexed. 'I thought you must have realized. It's not such a coincidence, if you think about it. How's the fishing, Michael?'

'Haven't been,' muttered Doll.

'Pity, now the weather's getting better. Michael's a great fisherman, you know,' he said to me.

'Yes, I know.'

'I'm driving your way, Michael. Shall I give you a lift?' He glanced at his watch. 'You could still have a good few hours by the canal before it goes dark.'

'I don't mind the dark.'

'Well, let me drive you anyway. I'm sure Dr Quinn has work to do.'

'Yes,' I murmured. 'Thank you.'

'Are you all right?'

'Yes.'

'Well, you don't look it. Maybe you should take a bit more care of yourself.' He glanced sharply at me. 'And put an inside chain on your door, perhaps.'

'I've got one. Julie just . . . oh, well, you know.'

'She's lurking outside, in her slippers. Ready, Michael?'

They left together. I watched from the window as Will put Doll into the passenger seat. Doll said something to him and Will laughed and patted his shoulder. Then he shut the door. He looked up at the window. I mouthed a thank-you through the glass but he didn't react. He just stared, as if he couldn't make out my face properly. Then he turned away.

Julie burst in through the door. 'Tell me everything.'

'I can't,' I said. 'I think I'm going to be sick.'

19

The press conference was organized at the very last minute but there was a buzz about this one and nowhere in the Stretton Green police station was remotely big enough, even though a good half of the rooms had now been stripped of all their furniture. A conference room was hastily booked at the Shackleton Hotel just around the corner and it was jammed with jostling men and women in suits shouting into mobile phones. The room was horribly hot and I saw a man in a uniform trying and failing to open a window. I stood right at the back, near the door, where there was a welcome breeze of slightly less unpleasant warm air.

Four men in grey suits swaggered through the door. Oban, Furth, Renborn and Renborn's deputy, Paul Crosby. They almost brushed against me, but didn't notice, insulated as they were by three uniformed officers as well as by their air of businesslike urgency. They made their way through the crowd and up on to the platform at the far end. They sat down at the table and were instantly blasted by television lights, which suddenly made them look more real than anything else in the room. A female officer came forward with a jug of water and four glasses. They all took sips with serious frowns. There was a microphone on the table. Oban tapped it with a finger. It sounded like someone banging on the wall with a broomstick. The noise subsided as if he had turned a dial.

'Ladies and gentlemen,' he began, 'most of you won't

know me. I'm Detective Chief Inspector Daniel Oban from Stretton Green. I won't beat about the bush. We're here to announce a significant step forward in the Philippa Burton murder inquiry.' There was a slight buzz and Oban, big ham that he was, paused, visibly savouring the moment. 'Ten days before the murder of Mrs Burton, a young woman, known to her friends as Lianne, was found murdered by the stretch of canal that passes through the Kersey Town area. We now believe that these two murders were committed by the same person.'

After saying this, he took a sip of water then clenched his jaw. I suspected that this may have been to prevent himself breaking into an inappropriate smile of pleasure at the excitement his words had provoked.

'If you'll let me finish,' he said. 'One result of this is that two separate murder inquiries will now be combined. I happen to be the senior officer and I will take nominal charge. But it goes without saying that Vic Renborn and his team have been doing an outstanding job so far and we'll be working closely together.'

He gave a sombre nod at Renborn, who gave a brief, businesslike inclination of his head in acknowledgement. There was an immediate forest of hands at the front. Oban pointed at someone I couldn't see. 'Yes, Ken?'

'What's the basis for the connection?'

'As most of you probably know, fibre analysis is gener-ally used to establish connections between a body and a suspect. But in this case we found matching fibres on the clothes of the two women.'

'What sort of fibres?'

'Originally we thought the two women had been murdered where they were found. We now suspect they were killed elsewhere and that they were then transported in a vehicle to a relatively secluded spot

169

where the body was dumped. We believe these fibres may come from the vehicle in which they were transported. What we found was a form of . . .' Oban looked down at a piece of paper on the table '. . . of synthetic polymer that is common to both bodies.'

Someone else stood up. A woman holding a microphone. 'But how did you come to make the connection?'

Now Oban allowed himself a slight smile. 'A crucial aspect of any murder inquiry is the control of information, and the pooling of it between different parts of the Metropolitan Police and beyond. I would like to say that this has so far been a model of co-operation and I'd like to pay tribute once again to Vic Renborn and his team.'

'But why did you compare these two murders? Are they very similar?'

'Not at first sight, no,' said Oban. 'But there are one or two possibly linking factors.'

'Such as?'

He looked mysterious. 'I hope you'll understand if we don't discuss these at this time.'

'Can you say anything about the sort of person you're looking for?' Oban looked across. 'Vic? You want to take this one?'

'Thanks,' said Renborn, giving a modest smile. 'What we think we're seeing here is a progression. The first victim, Lianne, was what we call a soft target. She was a runaway, living in hostels, in a world of drugs and prostitution. She was accessible and vulnerable. With Philippa Burton he was bolder. I'm not saying anything against Lianne, who was of course tragically murdered, but Mrs Burton was a respectable woman with a child. She was a more difficult target. This is a person who committed what you might call an easy murder and has now moved on to a more difficult one.'

Another hand bobbed up. 'Have you got anything more specific?'

'The murderer makes use of a car. We had also had advice from a highly experienced psychological profiler with an excellent track record.'

I knew who this was. Seb Weller.

'He has provided us with a tentative profile of which I'm authorized to give just a few details. He's white. Twenty-five to thirty-five, probably the upper end of that range. We suspect that he saw Philippa Burton, and the murder was partly committed because the killer didn't just desire her, he envied what she had, she was obviously well-off, with a child.'

'So you're saying it's a serial killer.'

'No,' said Oban hurriedly. 'Let's be sensible here. I'm just saying that we've got a dangerous man moving around, probably in a vehicle, so we ask for any possible co-operation from the public.'

'So he'll strike again,' shouted a voice from the back.

'I certainly don't want to alarm anyone,' said Oban. 'He will be caught. But in the meantime people – especially women in public places – should exercise especial caution. Let's keep 'em skinned, all right?' He looked around. 'Any further questions?'

A middle-aged woman stood up. 'You haven't explained what made you compare these two cases.'

Oban dealt with this himself. 'That's not an easy question to answer,' he said. 'As you've heard, an investigation like this depends on highly technical forensic analysis but also on old-fashioned shoe leather. We have already interviewed hundreds of potential witnesses, we've dragged the canal, we've conducted house-to-house inquiries, we've conducted intensive searches of the two areas where the bodies were found. But all the same, some of it comes down to experience and instinct.' Now he gave an avuncular smile. 'Call it the copper's instinct, for want of a better term. We had a feeling that there was a connection, even if we weren't sure exactly what it was. That was what made us check it out. Things just rang bells.'

'Why did he choose those victims?'

'We believe the choices were opportunistic. He saw his chance, acted. That's what makes psychopathic killers of that kind especially difficult to catch.'

'Do you have any suspects?'

'I don't want to make any comment about that at this time. I'll just say that we're interviewing some people.'

'Is it true that you're employing a psychic to find the killer? And is it a proper use of taxpayers' money?'

'For a start, I am not employing any psychics. On the other hand, if someone can help me find the killer, I don't care if they use tea-leaves to do it. And on that hopeful note, I think we'd better draw proceedings to a close. Rest assured, we'll keep you in touch with any developments. For the moment you'll understand that it's back to business. We've got work to do.'

Twenty minutes later we were sitting in the Lamb and Flag, a nearby pub that was decorated with a large collection of horse brasses and much frequented by policemen. Oban took a sip from his pint of bitter and held the glass reflectively up to the light.

'When I was talking about "us coppers", obviously you were included, Kit. I know that in an ideal world I should have singled you out for credit . . .'

I took a sip of my fizzy water and felt very prim. I didn't want to seem like a dour teetotaller but it was only eleven on a weekday morning. 'I'm not interested in credit . . .' I began.

'The point is,' Oban continued, 'that it's good for morale to talk about how well they've done. Deserved or not. But rest assured, if it all goes wrong, we'll single you out for public blame.'

'Yeah,' said Furth, from across the table. He had just placed a second pint next to the first, which was looking dangerously close to empty. 'We'll see you all right, Kit. As long as you don't walk out again. I can never keep track with whether you're on or off the case. You've retired more often than Frank Sinatra. Anyway, cheers.'

The final contents of pint number one disappeared. This was the boys being nice to me. It was often difficult to distinguish it from when they were being nasty. I wasn't always sure whether I was getting a slap on the back or a jab in the ribs. Perhaps you needed to be a bloke to tell. 'I wasn't sure about your profile, Vic,' I volunteered gingerly.

'Don't blame me, love. I was just quoting Seb. Are you saying he's wrong?'

'No. But what we're doing is playing the odds. We're saying the killer is white because most serial killers don't cross racial divides. I know all that. The danger of these profiles is that they cut off lines of inquiry.'

'I thought that was the point.'

'It's not much good if it cuts off the *right* line of inquiry.'

'I've heard your theory,' said Furth, a bit too loudly. 'A nice psychopathic killer. Wanna crisp, by the way?'

Offering me his crisps. I was certainly back on board. I took one and crunched it loudly.

'I wasn't saying he was nice. But there are nice killers, in a kind of way I mean.' There was a guffaw from somewhere. 'I mean it. I've come across a case where a child was murdered and buried by its mother, and the mother had wrapped it up as if she was putting it to bed. I just think that we should be careful about making assumptions,' I said. 'That's all.'

'So what do we do?' said Oban. 'That's our problem. You keep saying what it isn't. But what *is* it? Where do we look?'

'I don't know,' I said, and swallowed the last of my water. 'We need to be open to possibility, that's all.'

'Nah,' said Furth. 'You're making it too hard for yourself, darling. He started being careful, then he snatched someone in broad daylight. He's getting bolder. He needs to get the same buzz. I'll bet you anything he'll get more and more careless and we'll pick him up the next time or the time after that. And guess what? His name will be Mickey Doll.'

I ignored the mention of Doll. 'You make it sound like a game.'

'No,' said Oban. 'That's not fair.' He took a deep drink and wiped his mouth with the back of his hand. 'We may behave like a bunch of piss artists, but that doesn't mean we are.'

'Er, it does actually, guv,' said Furth, to great laughter. It was like having a meeting in the middle of a rugby club dinner.

20

I had a free afternoon after the morning at the clinic. I bought myself a warm croissant stuffed with cheese and spinach from the deli for lunch, then ate a heaped bowl of raspberries, which were large, purple, cool from the fridge and sweet with the hint of fermentation. I ate them slowly, one at a time, relishing this oasis of empty time. The fruit stained my fingers. Outside, the air was thick and bright after last night's rain. The leaves shone on the trees, glossy. I tried to think. I thought about Lianne and Philippa, letting their faces glow in my mind. I knew what Philippa had looked like alive – there had been so many photographs, with her slender, toned body and silky cap of hair, every bit of her looking buffed and polished. I only knew what Lianne had looked like dead, bitten nails and ragged hair. I didn't know the colour of her eyes or the shape of her smile. I needed to know about these two young women, because even random violence has a kind of reason. And I wanted to start with Lianne because she'd died first, but she seemed to have left no trail.

I finished the last raspberry and rinsed out the bowl. The police weren't any real help. They didn't know who Lianne was; they didn't know where she came from; they hadn't tracked down people who had known her; they could tell me nothing except what I already knew, that she had been a runaway, one of the missing thousands who drift round the streets of the big cities. The police came across people like Lianne all the time.

Runaways took drugs. Runaways stole. Runaways became prostitutes. 'They are victims and then they turn into criminals,' said Furth, and I opened my mouth to snap something at him, but then closed it. We were back to being enemies pretending to be friends.

I didn't know what else to do so I turned to Pavic again. I had to nerve myself to call him. In each of our meetings, I had been at a hopeless disadvantage, but the last had been the worst. I took a deep breath and dialled the number. A woman answered and said he wasn't there, but he was expected at any moment. I left my number, almost relieved. Then I waited, prowling round the flat, looking out of the window, picking up magazines and letting them drop again, but really just waiting.

The telephone rang fifteen minutes later. I picked it up on the third ring so he wouldn't think I was sitting by it.

'Will Pavic here.'

'I'm really sorry to bother you again,' I said. There was a pause, which he didn't fill. 'I need your help.'

'So I assumed,' he said drily.

'I need to talk to people who knew Lianne. Just a pointer in the right direction.'

'Kit . . .'

'Please.'

'All right.'

'God, that was easier than I expected.' He didn't laugh. Maybe he'd forgotten how to. 'Shall I come to your centre?'

'Let's see. Are you free at, say, six?'

'Yes.'

'Meet me at the car-wash centre on Sheffield Street. It's just up the road from here.'

'The car-wash centre?'

'That's right. Big place. You can't miss it. See you then.'

'About the other day –' I said, but he'd already gone.

I reviewed my notes, and rang through to the clinic for messages. Then I went round the corner to the hairdresser's, though it had recently started calling itself a salon and had been redecorated in silver and white, with harsh slabs of light. A young man with a shaved head, wearing loose black trousers and a sleeveless black T-shirt, tied me into a white nylon robe and sat me down in front of a huge, unforgiving mirror. He stood behind me, held my skull in his practised hands and asked me what I wanted done.

'A cut,' I said.

He lifted up strands of my brown hair and considered me for a few seconds. 'Make it a bit more choppy, perhaps? Muss it up?'

'Just a cut.'

'Highlights? A bit of copper. That's very popular at the moment.'

'Maybe next time.'

'Nice hair, though,' he mused, sliding it through his fingers before laying a towel round my shoulder and leading me over to a basin. I sat back and let a tiny young woman, with hair that looked as if it had been cut with garden shears, sluice warm water over my head, and massage shampoo that smelt of coconut into my scalp. It felt wonderful. I closed my eyes against the light. Then the young man hovered round me with long-bladed scissors and a forest of clips that he took from his belt and snapped into my hair. He cut off thick shanks of hair with a crisp sound, and they fell softly to the floor. When bits of hair prickled on my face, he leaned forward and blew softly on to my cheek.

Afterwards, I felt much better. My hair swung when I shook my head, like one of those advertisements for miracle conditioner. I ran home and had a quick shower, then dressed in my white jeans, biscuit-coloured T-shirt, pumps and ancient suede jacket. I felt clean, fresh, alert.

The car-wash centre was in a row of old and dilapidated warehouses near the canal. I got there just before six, but as I approached, I saw that Will was already waiting for me on the pavement. I drew up and he climbed into the passenger seat. Another car drew in front of us and turned into the depot.

'Where's your car?'

'Being cleaned, of course.'

'Is that why we're meeting here – because you want your car washed?'

'Lianne worked here for a few weeks earlier this year. I thought it might be a good place for you to begin. Though I'm not sure how many of the people who worked here then are still here. It's got rather a transient population.'

'Here? Washing cars?'

'No. That's strictly for the men. Collecting the money and handing out the tickets. The woman who runs it was in hospital for a bit, having a hip replacement. She's a friend of mine.' As he spoke, a woman came out of the depot towards us. She was enormous, with bristles on her chin and thin hair. Will opened his door and she bent down, with difficulty. 'Diana, this is Kit. Kit, Diana.'

I leaned across Will and shook her hand. She had a firm grip and clever eyes. 'You're interested in Lianne?'

She sounded the E at the end of the name. I wondered

where she came from. 'Yes. It's kind of you to help.'

'Do you want to come in, then? I'll be with you in a few minutes.'

'I think I'd better have a car wash first, don't you?'

She smiled at me then. 'Which one?'

I looked at the different washes chalked up on a big board outside the depot. 'I'll have the superior.'

For the first time, Will looked at me with a glimmer of approval.

'That's twelve fifty, then.'

I handed her the money, which she slipped deftly into a pocket in her skirt. Then she straightened up and beckoned me in through the giant doors. 'Wind up your windows,' she ordered.

'Are you staying in?' I asked Will.

'Looks like it.'

I edged through the doors and immediately I was in another world, dark and wet and swarming with activity. Sharp jets of water hit us from all directions, and about six men, wearing wellington boots and rubber gloves, were on the car, scrubbing it down with long brushes. I watched them through the sudsy windows. The man leaning over my bonnet had a walrus moustache and sad wrinkles on his jowly face and Slavic cheekbones. The one on Will's side looked about seventeen, very black, very tall and thin, startlingly beautiful with sloe eyes. He looked like a film star. There was an older man, Chinese maybe, who wiped my window assiduously. He caught my eyes and smiled at me through the water streaming between us.

'What is this place?'

'A car-wash centre.'

'Thanks,' I said sarcastically. 'I mean, where do all these people come from?'

Will cast a sideways glance at me. 'Refugees mostly. They work here for a while, no questions asked. Cash in hand.'

'And people like Lianne.'

'Sometimes I send kids here. It's safe work. The money's not derisory. They're off the streets, earning till they find something else maybe.'

A man in a yellow mac beckoned me forward. I moved slowly into a new set of jets: clean water to rinse off the soap. More men, this time with cloths, approached. Behind us another car moved into position.

'This is amazing!'

Will looked smug, as if he'd arranged it all for my benefit.

'About Doll,' I said at last. 'I'm sorry about that.'

'Why?'

'I mean, sorry to trouble you like that. After all, you hardly know me – but I couldn't think what else to do.'

'Why didn't you call the police?'

'I didn't want to get him into trouble – and, to be honest, I was in a bit of an awkward position myself. It's a long story. Too long.'

He nodded as if he wasn't curious. 'You were right to call me.'

'Is he dangerous, then?'

'I don't know. He's . . .' He hesitated for a few seconds. 'He's wretched.'

Once again, I was signalled forward, this time into a small bay ahead.

'We get out here,' said Will. 'Now they clean inside. He'll be back, though.'

'Doll?'

'He's fallen for you. He thinks you understand him.'

'Oh.' I didn't know what to say.

'And he thinks you're beautiful,' he said, as if that was rather funny.

I climbed out of the car and waited for Will. Instantly, four other men climbed in, two with cloths and buckets, one with a paintbrush to get at the crevices and corners, one with an industrial vacuum cleaner. Diana appeared, with two cups of coffee. 'This is Gonzalo,' she said, gesturing. 'He knew Lianne when she worked here.'

He had floppy black hair, olive skin, the shyest smile, and a soft, limp hand when I shook it.

'Hello,' I said, and he ducked his head. He was wearing a pink Bart Simpson T-shirt. 'So you knew Lianne?'

'Lianne. Yes. Lianne.'

'Were you her friend?'

'Friend?' His accent was thick. I couldn't tell if he understood a word I was saying to him.

'Were you Lianne's friend?' I repeated. He frowned at me. 'Where are you from, Gonzalo?'

His face cleared. He jabbed himself in the chest. 'Colombia. Beautiful.'

'I don't speak Spanish.' I turned to Will. 'Do you speak Spanish?'

'Nope. But I bet Lianne didn't either. Gonzalo, was Lianne happy?'

'Happy?' He shook his head. 'Not happy.'

'Sad?'

'Sad, yes, and this.' He put his hand to his mouth in a theatrical manner.

'Scared?' I asked.

'Angry?' suggested Will.

'Lost,' said Diana. She pushed a mug of coffee into my hand and I sipped it. It was bitter and tepid. 'You see it in the eyes. There are people who aren't quite with you any more. You see it a lot here.' She jerked her massive bristly chin in the direction of the men, swarming like bees over the cars.

'And you saw that in Lianne's eyes?'

She shrugged. 'I hardly met her. She was here when I wasn't. She seemed a bit withdrawn maybe. She didn't engage with people much. Did you find that?' She turned to Will.

'Maybe,' he said cautiously. I had never met a man so unwilling to commit himself.

'Well, who can blame her, eh? But she was honest, I'll say that for her. She didn't pocket any money that I could work out.'

I watched them, the fat woman and the surly man. Gonzalo shifted from one foot to the other. 'Thank you,' I said to him.

He gave me his shy smile and backed away. My car was shining, inside and out. The man with the walrus moustache was giving it a last look over.

'And thank you,' I said to Diana. 'I appreciate it.'

She shrugged. 'You're Will's friend.'

I wasn't so sure about that. I looked over at Will. 'Do you fancy a drink?'

He seemed slightly taken aback. 'OK,' he said, as if he hadn't been able to think of an excuse in time. 'Why don't you follow me? There's a place I know near here.'

I clinked some coins into the tip-box, and then we drove in convoy in our gleaming cars, down small back streets by the side of old warehouses. I'd never been here – this was a London I had never visited.

We went to a pub on the canal-side. From the front, it looked rather dreary and run down, but at the back there was a deck over the water, where we sat with our tomato juice. The sky was turning a strange brown, little sighs of wind rippled across the oily dark water, and a few large drops of rain fell.

'You like it?' said Will dreamily.

'What? My drink?'

'The canal.'

'It looks a bit dirty to me.'

He sipped his drink. 'They're going to clean it up. Have you heard about the development project?'

I looked at the black water. The warehouse on the far side was open to the sky; all the windows had been broken and inside there were piles of twisted, rusty machinery. Everywhere there was rubble and strange sorts of rubbish that I didn't want to think about too much. 'Who'd want to develop this?'

'Are you kidding? A couple of hundred acres of prime land right in the middle of London? In a couple of years this will all be wine bars, health clubs and apartment blocks with private garages.'

'Is that good?'

He drained his glass. 'It'll be respectable,' he said.

'You make that sound like a dirty word. Won't it help your young people? There'll be jobs for them.'

'I don't think most of them will fit in here. They'll be pushed somewhere else where they can be someone else's problem.' I shivered and he looked at me. 'Are you cold?'

I shook my head. 'Someone walked over my grave.'

But he took off his jacket and hung it round my shoulders. For a moment I was surprised by the thrill that ran through me when I felt his hands touch my shoulders. It had been such a long time since anyone had touched me.

21

'I still can't believe it.'

'No,' I said meaninglessly.

'I mean, that kind of thing doesn't happen, does it? Not to people you know. I can't get over it.' She shook her head from side to side, as if to clear it. 'Poor Philippa,' she said.

'Mmm.'

'And Jeremy. And poor, poor Emily. What will happen to Emily? What a thing. Who would want to do a thing like that?'

Since this wasn't a real question, I didn't answer. I sipped the coffee she had made for me and waited. Tess Jarrett looked like a small, glowing chestnut. She sat curled up in a large easy chair in the conservatory of her elegant home, small and round without being plump. She had burnished brown curls all over her head, flecked brown eyes, honey skin that glowed with health and wealth, round tanned arms, a small mouth, perfect white teeth, pearly nails on her small hands and her neat, sandalled feet. She was, she said, Philippa's best friend. Her very, very best. She shone with horror and excitement.

'We were inseparable,' she said. 'Even more since Emily and Lara were born. They're almost exactly the same age as each other, you see, and we both gave up work, so we spent lots of time together. It was nice.' It was difficult to imagine Tess as a mother. Though she was thirty-two years old, she looked so young and girlish, as if she was about to put her thumb in her mouth.

'How long had you known each other?'

'We were at sixth-form college together.' Her eyes widened. 'That means I've known her for half my life. Knew, rather. I can't get used to saying that.'

'It's hard,' I agreed.

'And then, of course, after we got married, we lived near to each other. Hampstead and Belsize Park are ten minutes' walk apart. We'd meet several times a week. We used to go shopping together.' She fingered the pastel folds of her cotton dress. 'We bought this together two weeks ago, for when Rick and the children and I go to Greece. And Rick and Jeremy get on well too. Poor Jeremy.' She sighed gustily.

'Tess,' I said into the silence that followed, 'sometimes we can find out about the killer by finding out about his victim. That's why I'm here.'

She nodded. Her face took on a tragic cast. 'Yes,' she murmured. 'I know that.'

'So I don't need to know about her last movements, or that kind of thing. That's for the police. I'm more interested in her moods, what was going on in her life. And sometimes friends know more about that than family.'

'I knew everything about Philippa,' she said emphatically. 'We had no secrets. For instance,' she lowered her voice and leaned forward, 'I told her when I was having problems with Rick, shortly after Lara was born. I think men often find it difficult when their wife has a baby, don't you? You can't give them all your attention any more. You're so tired, anyway, getting up in the night, and breast-feeding, and things like that. I think they're jealous, really. Men are like children themselves, aren't they? What was I saying? Yes, so Rick was getting very short-tempered and rather demanding, you know what I mean, and I didn't want – well, I told Philippa about that. It helped, just to talk about it. She was very good at listening, Philippa was. She wasn't a chatterbox, not like me.' She laughed girlishly, and I joined in politely for a couple of beats. 'Sometimes,' she went on, 'I think that was why we were such good friends. I was the chatty extrovert, and she was more –' She stopped and frowned at me.

'Yes?' I didn't want Tess to stop now that she'd finally worked her way round to Philippa.

'More someone who is a bit on the outside of things, if you see what I mean. Whereas I'm right at the centre.'

'Was that how she chose to be, do you think? On the outside.'

'Oh, yes, she was quite happy. I never saw her cry. Isn't that odd? I cry all the time. I cry in *Dumbo* and *Bambi* when I watch them with Lara, and any film, really, that's a bit soppy, and at the television news if they show starving children, and when Lara cries I sometimes cry as well, even if she's crying because I've told her off, and we sit there like a couple of babies howling, and I cry when she does something for the first time as well – I was in floods of tears when she said "Mummy" for the first time. I can't help it, stupid, isn't it? I cry when I'm happy and I cry when I'm sad. But Philippa wasn't like that. Even when I first met her, she wasn't.'

'Which doesn't mean she was happy,' I said neutrally.

'No.' She uncurled her legs and wiggled her toes. 'Of course not. But she always seemed a steady kind of person. Not up and down like me. I'm a pendulum. Over the moon then down in the dumps, that's me. Even when she was young and had boyfriends, she didn't fall head over heels in love. She did it – patiently, I suppose.

She was good at waiting and seeing. Anyway, she didn't have that many boyfriends. She was very calm. She never lost her temper with Emily, not like I do with Lara, little monkey. She was very firm with her, but she didn't just blow. "How on earth do you do it?" I used to ask her. Used to. Can't get used to that.' She blinked her brown eyes at me, and a single tear rolled down her cheek, then another. I handed her a tissue. 'Thanks. Sorry.'

'What was her relationship like with Jeremy?'

'Well, how should I describe it? Me and Rick, we argue sometimes, and then make up – arguments are almost worth it when you make up at the end, aren't they? But she and Jeremy didn't argue. They were very courteous with each other. He bought her flowers every Friday, without fail. Isn't that nice? I wish Rick did that. Yellow roses were her favourites, and sweet peas, though you can't usually buy sweet peas from the florist's, can you? She was good at gardening – have you seen her garden? Jeremy and Emily are back there again, I think, after staying at her mother's. I must go and see them soon. Anyway, I never saw them being lovey-dovey – but maybe that's just the way they were. I mean, you never know what goes on in other people's lives, do you? And when Emily was born, they were thrilled. Do you know? I've lied to you, I have seen Philippa cry. I went to see her just after Emily was born, the next day I think it was, in hospital. I was enormous with Lara, like one of those little round-bottomed toys you push over and then they pop up again, except if anyone had pushed me over I would just have lain on the floor for ever. I hate hospitals, don't you? They make me think I'm about to die. All those depressing green walls. Philippa was sitting up in bed, and holding this little bundle and staring down at it, and when I came in, she looked up and there were tears streaming down her face. A great sheet of tears. She said, "She's so beautiful. Look how beautiful she is. My own little daughter." Then of course I had to go and cry too, and then Emily woke up and began roaring. She loved Emily. That's why –' She stopped abruptly.

'Yes?' I said delicately.

'Oh, it's probably nothing.'

I waited. She was aching to tell me.

'I sometimes think she was having an affair.'

'Mmm?' I murmured.

'I don't know why, and maybe I shouldn't say it, but I just sensed it in her behaviour, and she wasn't at home in the day so much. I think women have an instinct for that kind of thing. I wouldn't dream of telling anyone else this, it's probably not true, but I'm sure there was something like that going on.'

'Do you know who she might have been having an affair with?'

'No. Could have been loads of people. I mean, she is lovely to look at. Was. Slim and blonde, lucky thing. Lots of men would jump at the chance. Rick, even. I don't mean that, of course, but you know how men are after the first flush of passion is over with their wives and they've settled down and their life seems a bit dull, everyone gets like that, I think, and anyway Rick always had a bit of a soft spot for Philippa. But don't get me wrong, no way am I saying it was him – God, I'm sure I'd know that, woman's instinct, and I'd kill Rick if he did anything like that, and of course Philippa was my best friend for ever . . .' She came to a halt and looked at me in a bewildered kind of way, as if she'd tied herself up in her words. 'I'm just saying there were lots of men she knew, husbands of friends, men who moved in the same circle. But I don't suspect anyone particularly, I just think in the last few weeks of her life there was something going on.'

'Something?'

'Hmm, maybe I should say someone. Her attention kept wandering. She had this excited, secret look. She let me down a couple of times when we'd arranged to meet, which she never used to do, and then made some pathetic excuse. She was fidgety, kind of. Not all there. She'd fallen for a man. I'm sure of it.'

I left Tess's house half an hour later, at midday. I felt drained. Before Tess, I had revisited Philippa's husband and her mother. Jeremy had moved back into his house which was a bit smaller and a bit newer than Pam Vere's. The long, narrow garden had an orchard at the bottom, a swing hanging from one of the apple trees. They had been rather less forthcoming about Philippa than Tess had been. I didn't think they were holding anything back, but they seemed naturally reticent. He was bewildered and helplessly sad. She seemed dazed and numb.

I had two messages on my mobile. One was from Poppy, asking me why I hadn't been in touch with her for so long. The other was from Will. 'Please ring,' was all he said.

'Yes?' he barked into the phone, when I dialled.

'It's Kit.'

'Hang on a minute.' I heard him giving some kind of instructions to whoever was with him. 'Kit? Can you be here this evening, at about six thirty?'

'Why?'

'There are some people coming to meet you.'

'Who knew Lianne?'

'Why else would they be coming to meet you?'

I opened my mouth to snap back, then closed it again. 'I should be able to get there in time.'

'See you, then.' And he was gone. He was like a man with a swarm of bees in his head.

22

I rang the bell and a young man with dreadlocks and a tattoo of a ladybird on his forearm answered. I assumed he was one of the residents, but he turned out to be a volunteer member of staff, and introduced himself as Greg. Unlike the time I had been here before, the centre was buzzing with activity. A knot of teenagers stood about in the hall, smoking cigarettes. Through an open door, I could see into a games room, where a loud game of snooker was in progress. The sound of voices drifted down from upstairs. Greg took me across the hall to Will's office and pushed open the door without knocking.

'Hi,' I said to Will. 'This is good of you. Thanks.'

'Thank them, not me. They're waiting for you in an upstairs room. Shall I show you up?'

'How many of them?'

'Five, I think, unless any have wandered off. They may have done.'

The room was hot, and thick with smoke. There was a pinball machine in the corner, and two boys were standing idly by it in a fog of cigarette smoke. One had a shaved head with a white scar running across his scalp, and the other was squat and rather hairy. They looked up when I came in but didn't acknowledge me. The other three were girls, or young women. They sat in the three easy chairs and on the floor. Among them was the startlingly pretty girl that I'd seen the first time I'd met Will Pavic. She looked up, frowning slightly. She had thick dark brows and spooky green eyes.

'Hello,' I said, walking into their midst. 'I'm Kit.'

No one said anything. I went round shaking their hands one by one, realizing almost at once that this was a mistake but unable to stop what I'd started. Most of them looked self-conscious; their hands were limp and sweaty in the baking room.

'Thank you very much for seeing me.' I sat on the floor and pulled out a packet of cigarettes I had bought, offering them round. That got their attention. Everyone took one, even if they already had one on the go. 'How about if you all tell me your names?'

'Spike,' said the boy with the shaven head by the pinball machine. There was a splutter of laughter from the others. A joke I didn't get.

'Laurie.' That was the hairy one.

'Carla,' said the black girl sitting on my right, in a whisper.

'Catrina.' She had the worst acne I'd ever seen, and a beautiful mane of red hair.

'Sylvia.' That was the green-eyed girl. She smiled knowingly. 'That's the name I've given myself, at any rate.'

'I'll try and remember. Will's probably told you why I'm here. I want to find out as much as I can about Lianne, because the more we know the more chance there'll be of finding who killed her. For instance, if we could find out where she had come from, what her real name was, her background, that might help a lot.' There was a stony silence. 'But apart from that,' I went on, 'I just want to find out, well, what she was like. The kind of person she was.'

'Will said you were all right,' said Spike. He made the sentence sound like a question.

'He means, you won't go running to the cops with things we tell you,' added Sylvia. 'Not that we'd tell you anyway. We never told the other one.'

'What other one?'

'You're not the first.'

'The police talked to you already?'

Sylvia shrugged and a shuffling kind of silence descended on the room, broken only by the flare of a match as Spike lit up again.

'Anyway,' I said at last, 'I won't tell them anything that isn't connected to Lianne. OK?' There was a general grunting of assent. 'How long had she been around here, do you know? In this area, I mean.'

'Will said about five months,' said Spike. I wished Will had told me that.

'Which of you saw her last, do you reckon?'

'That'd be me.' Carla wouldn't look up to catch my eyes. She talked to her folded hands.

'What did you do together?'

'We just walked around together, looking in shop windows. We talked about the things we'd buy if we had the money. Clothes and nice food and stuff. CDs. We didn't have any money though, did we? Unless Lianne – ' She stopped.

'Yes?'

'She was a pretty good pickpocket,' interrupted Laurie admiringly. 'She could slide her hand into anyone's bag. She and Daisy used to go round the underground stations together. They were a wicked pair. One would bump into the person and the other would lift their wallet.'

'Cool,' said Spike.

'Daisy Gill?' I asked.

'Yeah, the one who topped herself.'

'How did you two meet?' I asked Sylvia.

'Here. She was quite shy, really. Or rather . . .' she wrinkled up her little nose and pushed her blonde hair fastidiously behind her ears '. . . she didn't talk much. Not about herself, if that's what you're wanting. She never said where she came from. I bet it was somewhere in London, though. She knew London really well.'

'I bet she'd been in care for ages.' This was Catrina.

'Why do you say that?'

'You can tell. I only met her the once. I met her here, like Sylvia, a couple of months back. We had a game of table tennis, and she was crap at it and stormed off when one of the others teased her. But if you've been in care, you can tell.'

'It's like a smell.' Spike sniggered.

'That's horrible.' Sylvia turned on him. 'That's a stupid thing to say.'

He winked at her. 'Don't worry, you don't smell, Sylvia. You're lush.'

'Anyway, I know for a fact she was in care because she once told me about a home she'd been in,' said Sylvia, ignoring him. 'She tried to organize a sleepover with her friend at Christmas. They slept in next-door rooms anyway, so it was no big deal, but the staff wouldn't let them have a sleepover. That's typical of the way things are run. Red tape. They said nobody was allowed to share rooms. Against the rules. So Lianne said she barricaded herself and her friend into her room and they wouldn't come out and then the next day as a punishment they weren't allowed Christmas dinner. Or crackers or anything. But she said she was still pleased she did it, just to make a stand. She didn't say where the home was. She was dead secretive, really.'

'You don't ask?'

'You respect people's privacy.'

'I know she slept in the park sometimes. She said it was better than most of the poxy hostels round here.'

'Had she been in lots of homes?' I asked.

'Probably,' said Sylvia. 'Most of us have by the time you get to our age.' She looked almost smug as she said this, her beautiful face demure. 'If she was a runaway, then like as not she'd been round the houses.'

'Look at me.' I turned to Catrina's soft monotonous voice. 'I've been in twelve foster-families and eight homes.'

'I was with a foster-family once for nearly two years,' said Laurie. His face was plump and young behind all the hair. He didn't look more than fourteen.

'Yeah? What did you do wrong, then?' asked Catrina.

'They moved up north. They said there wasn't room in their new house. It sounded really cool there, with a garden and all. Close to the sea.' There was no self-pity in his voice. He sounded quite matter-of-fact.

'Can you tell me about Lianne's sexual relationships?' I asked cautiously. There was silence. Spike ground out his cigarette furiously. 'I'm asking because it might help. Had she been abused, for instance?'

'Probably,' said Sylvia casually.

Spike rattled the pinball handle loudly. There was a nasty kind of sneer on his face. I thought he was trying to stop himself crying.

'Why do you say that?'

'If she'd been in care for a long time, I mean.'

'You mean, you expect people in long-term care to have been sexually abused?'

'I've had enough now,' said Spike. 'I'm off.' But he didn't move.

I looked at him. His pasty face had flushed; there were red blotches on his cheeks. 'So you reckon she'd been sexually abused.'

'I wouldn't say sexually, necessarily,' said Catrina, 'but you don't get through it unharmed, if you see what I mean. You stop being a child pretty quickly.'

'You don't trust anyone,' agreed Laurie. He came and sat down among the girls at last, while Spike hovered by the door. I took out my packet of cigarettes again and he moved forward to take one, but still didn't sit.

'Did she have boyfriends?'

They looked at each other.

'I didn't see anything,' said Sylvia. 'And she never said. I mean, lots of people say, don't they? They like to brag about things. But Lianne never mentioned anything like that. Mind, none of us knew her that well, did we?' Again, she looked round the group and they shook their heads. 'She was just around.'

'She was close to Daisy,' said Carla. 'They painted each other's toenails once, I remember. I came into Lianne's room and they were giggling and painting each other's toenails. One colour for each nail. It was nice,' she said, a bit wistfully. 'Lianne didn't giggle much. They told me they were going to save up the money Lianne stole and have a restaurant together.'

A silence fell on the group as they thought of the two girls, both dead now. All of a sudden, they looked young and defenceless. Even Spike, still on his feet, with his cigarette hanging off his upper lip and his hands in his pockets, looked as if he had been caught off-guard. I sat quite still, not wanting to interrupt the moment.

'She once kissed me,' said Laurie, his face scarlet. 'I told her I'd never, you know.' He ground to a halt. Carla took his hand and put it on her lap with a gesture that was unexpectedly touching and maternal. 'Anyway, I told her, I don't know why, maybe because I had had a review that week, with my social workers, you know, and I'd heard there was still no one who wanted to foster me, and I just felt rotten that day, you know, lonely or something, like you get every now and then, and she was sitting there, downstairs where the snooker table is, just sitting and not doing anything, and no one else was around. And all of a sudden she kissed me. Held my face and kissed me.' His eyes filled with tears. Carla patted his hand.

'I heard her cry,' said Spike, suddenly and hoarsely. As he spoke, he moved closer to the door, as if he was going to bolt. No one said a word. 'I'd only met her the day before. We had a blazing argument because she nicked my radio and said it was hers. She was a right little thief. Anyway, it was in the day, and there was no one around, and I came back from doing some business.' He cast a furtive look at me and continued: 'Anyway, I heard this sound coming from upstairs. I didn't realize at first what it was. It sounded so odd. Like a cat being tortured or something. I crept up the stairs and it was coming from her room. She was kind of mewling and whimpering, just like a cat. I stood there for ages and she didn't stop. She went on and on, just crying and crying and crying like her heart was breaking.'

'Did you go in?' I asked.

He frowned. 'I didn't want to embarrass her,' he said.

I poked my head round Will's door. He was staring at his computer screen, but his hands were slack on the desk.

'Working late?' I leaned against the wall. My legs felt weak and my head buzzed with fatigue.

'What? Yes, I guess so.'

'Can I ask you something?'

'Mmm?'

'Do you have anyone to go home to?'

'No.'

'I didn't think so.' I looked at him. His face was like a stone. I leaned forward, took it in my two hands and I kissed him on his lips. Then I turned and left, and he went on sitting there.

23

People should enjoy their work. One of the great pleasures of life is activity and work is the main activity for most people. Whatever it is, it should be fun and people somehow have the capacity to turn the strangest things into fun, and it's right that they should. I would almost prescribe this capacity for taking pleasure as a medicine against depression, against the boredom and fear in most lives; I know that, and feel it as well, yet sometimes it seems difficult to bear.

When I was twelve I went to the funeral of my grandmother. We came out of the crematorium and were ushered over to the Garden of Remembrance, an area with short formal hedges and a small lawn that looked as though it should contain a miniature putting green. Grown-ups stood around awkwardly, reading the messages on the wreaths. After a few minutes I wandered away. I remember seeing two things. The first was smoke coming from the chimney and wondering if my grandmother was in that. Then, around the side, I entered the parking area for the hearses. It was a warm spring day and the undertakers were sitting on the bonnets of the cars. Several of them had taken off their jackets and rolled up their sleeves. They were smoking cigarettes and talking. A couple of them laughed at a joke I was too far away to hear.

It's stupid, I know, even for a twelve-year-old, but it was then that I realized the undertakers weren't really sad that my granny had died. In fact, they didn't care at all. When I was driving back with my father I told him angrily about what I had seen and said that they shouldn't pay them because they had been so disrespectful. My father explained patiently that the undertakers went to two or three funerals every day and they couldn't be sad for everybody. Why not? I said. It was their job to be sad.

My father failed to convince me. In fact, I decided that only unfeeling people could possibly become undertakers. If you were a good, sensitive person, all those deaths, all that grief, would send you mad. So, by definition, the people left doing the job must be psychopaths who were able to look serious while they carried the coffin, then rush home to watch TV and play with their children and say that they'd had a good day at work.

Of course, I'd grown up and learned that the surgeon you'd want to operate on your baby's defective heart valve was not someone who was as worried as you were but the person who was best at the job, even if he was a bow-tied prima donna only thinking of his reputation and about getting out to the golf course as early as possible.

So what did I expect of Oban and Furth and the rest of the men, and a very few women, in suits? They assumed the requisite sombre expressions with language to match when the cameras were around. They were gutted, absolutely gutted. This was an appalling case, everyone involved was deeply shocked. But the fact is that they were having a great time. Take DCI Oban. He wasn't being festive exactly, but there was a new bounce to his step. It was understandable. He had been stuck with an obscure, hopeless murder case that no one else wanted. No one was paying any attention, except when it went wrong. Now, Cinderella-like, it had turned into the murder case of the year and everyone wanted to be his friend.

When I called on him the morning after my visit to Kersey Town, it was like trying to see the prime minister. He gave me a friendly nod. 'Are you in a rush?' he asked.

'Not especially,' I said.

'Good,' he said. 'You can talk to me as we go.'

This wasn't an easy matter. He was always taking a call, always between meetings. He was always that few minutes late to demonstrate he was the most important person. It was like talking from the platform to someone who was on a train pulling out of a station. I started telling him about my conversation with people who knew Lianne, but he interrupted quickly, 'Do I need to know this, Kit?'

'Look, Oban . . .'

'Dan,' he insisted.

'The background to the victims is all we have.'

He stopped for a moment and gave a doubtful grunt. 'I'm not convinced, Kit. Until I see something specific, we've got to stick with what I said at the press conference. The presumption must be that what we have is an opportunist killer. Have you talked to Seb? He agrees with that.'

'No, I haven't talked to him.' In fact, I had been putting it off. That was one of the reasons I hadn't returned Poppy's phone calls in the last few days – I didn't want to get Seb instead.

'We'll see him in a minute. You can talk it over.'

'That won't be necessary.'

'And I don't want any rivalry between you.'

'There isn't any rivalry.'

'By the way, Kit, have you been talking to anybody about our Mr Doll?'

'No,' I said. 'Who would I talk to about him?' A thought struck me. 'He came round to my flat.'

Oban shrugged. 'I'd watch yourself.'

'So obviously Julie knows about him.'

'Obviously,' said Oban, with a twinkle in his eye.

'Oh, and I've talked to Will Pavic about him. Will knows him anyway.'

'Pavic again?' Oban gave another grunt. 'You're getting into some strange company. He's treading a fine line, that one.'

'So people keep saying.'

Oban's expression became sombre. 'No, I mean it, Kit. Pavic has rubbed a lot of people up the wrong way in this area. The social-service people hate him. I think a few journos are out to get him.'

'What on earth for?' I said. 'I know he's not exactly easy to get on with but he's only trying to help.'

'Really?' said Oban dubiously. 'Not everyone would agree about that. There are rumours, more than rumours, about drug-dealing in that hostel of his. Some people say that he's just turning a blind eye to it, but others are saying he rakes a percentage off the top. I can tell you that if he makes one false move he's going down. Anyway, that wasn't what I was saying. I've been phoned up by a couple of journalists about Mickey Doll.'

'What for?'

'Just questions. Is it true that he's been questioned for the murders? Is there a prospect of his being charged? Why did we let him go?'

'How did they hear about him?'

'This station's like a bloody news agency. If someone farts in here, someone else will be on the blower to the *Mail* about it.'

'What did you say?'

'Just bare bones. If anybody rings you about it, refer them to me. Ah, here he is now.'

I half expected to see Michael Doll but he was referring to Seb, the media's favourite psychiatrist. Poppy's husband, my kind-of friend. Today, he looked as if he was ready to go on the one o'clock news. He was wearing crisply pressed black trousers, boots and a rather spectacular black-leather jacket over a shiny white shirt. His hair was deftly tousled and he had the appropriate day or so's growth of stubble. He stepped forward, kissed me on both cheeks then gave me a hug. 'Kit,' he said. 'Isn't this great? Working on the same case, I mean.'

'Wonderful,' I said, wrapped in his arms and deeply uncomfortable there. 'How's Poppy?'

'What? Oh fine, hunky-dory. You know Poppy.' He gave a light laugh and winked at Oban. 'Kit and I go way back.'

'Obviously.'

'She and my wife are thick as thieves. So this is like a family affair.'

'So you know Julie?' asked Oban.

'Julie?' Seb frowned. 'Do I know Julie, Kit?'

'I hope I'm not putting my foot in it,' Oban said roguishly.

'No,' I said frantically, feeling my cheeks burn. 'Look, I keep wanting to say –'

'Never mind. There are things we need to discuss. Hang on.' His mobile was ringing again.

'Oban was telling me about your views on the case,' I said to Seb as we waited. 'I knew some of them already, though. I think I heard you talking about the case on the radio, but I'm not sure if I heard your conclusion. I think they had to play a record.'

'Oh, that,' he said absently.

Oban put his phone in his pocket and joined us again. 'We need to talk integration here,' he said.

'Well, of course I'm completely delighted that Kit's on board.' Seb gave his wide smile once more and touched my shoulder. 'I've always wanted to see her being a bit more ambitious about her work. But I suppose we should just formalize the pecking order. Two separate inquiries have been merged into one, and I was the consultant for the primary murder.'

'But the murder of Lianne happened first, Seb. Do you mean that the murder of Philippa Burton is more important?'

'I mean it was a larger-scale inquiry. What I'm saying is that we have two psychological consultants and I want matters made clear. Just to formalize things.'

'I don't quite understand,' I said.

'Well, for instance – just a random example – there should be a consistency in the public presentation of the psychological expertise.'

'You mean, you want to appear on television and at press conferences,' said Oban drily.

'That's fine by me,' I said hastily.

'So that's agreed,' said Oban.

'It was only a hypothetical example,' Seb said, 'but very well, if that's what you want, then I accept the responsibility.'

'However, Kit remains centrally involved,' said Oban firmly. 'After all, she is the person responsible for the two inquiries being merged.'

'Yes, I heard about that,' said Seb. 'What a piece of luck.'

I took a deep breath. I wasn't going to be goaded. 'How is the fibre analysis going?' I asked. 'Have they managed to get any closer to the car type?'

Oban shook his head. 'You can see the technical stuff if you want. It's a very specific kind of coloured synthetic fibre. It definitely comes from the same source but that doesn't mean it's actually the carpet from the car itself. It could be from a blanket or a piece of cloth or a hundred other things. The result's no bloody help at all.' He put his hands in his trouser pockets and looked blank. 'I've got to be going. There's a meeting with someone from the Home Office. Then I've got to see a collection of people who're going to dowse for the murderer. Or at least I think that's what it was. Idiots with forked sticks.'

He went and Seb and I were left awkwardly together with nowhere to go. 'How's Poppy?' I said, then remembered I'd asked that already.

'Oh, you know,' he said, looking over my shoulder. 'By the way, I've been meaning to call you. Did Poppy tell you? Megan and Amy hardly slept for days after your goodnight story. Woke screaming in the night.'

'I'm sorry,' I said. 'I didn't mean . . .'

'No, I was only joking. Interesting idea, though. I've been thinking about it. Did you get it from somewhere?'

'I think I told you that it was a dream I've been having since my accident.'

'Red room. Interesting idea. A bloody chamber. Do you think it's a sort of womb? Your mother died, didn't she? Do you think you're expressing a wish to return to her dead womb?'

I had a strong impulse to beat Seb around the head with a heavy object. 'No, I don't,' I said. 'It's a story about being very afraid because being slashed across the face made me very afraid.'

'Possibly,' Seb said reflectively. 'Have you written about it? Are you planning a paper on it?'

'No,' I said. 'My subject is usually other people's dreams.'

'Good,' he said. 'Good.'

The next morning, very early, the phone rang. It was Oban. 'Get a paper.'

'What do you mean? What paper?'

'One of the tabloids. Any of them. Fuck it.' And he put the phone down.

Five minutes later after a breathless run down to the man outside the tube station, a selection of the day's tabloid newspapers was spread out on my table. The familiar, slightly eager, slightly dazed expression of Michael Doll was staring up at Julie and me out of a mess of huge, raucous headlines: 'ARREST IN PIPPA MURDER. "I'M INNOCENT" SAYS PIPPA SUS-PECT. PIPPA SUSPECT'S "WEIRD" PAST.'

Pippa. That name again. The right length for a head-line. And where was Lianne? Who cared about her? I scanned the papers. It was all there. The questioning, a suspiciously detailed account of what had been obtained by Colette's wire, the release on what were described as 'technical grounds'. There was a sketchy account of his life and times: children's home, Borstal, minor sexual offences. A young woman from the *Daily News* had managed to get an 'exclusive' interview, as if there was any problem in getting this pathetically lonely man to talk to a young woman. Here, at least, Lianne was mentioned. Doll boasted that he had been close by. To make things worse, he tried to deny that he had been a suspect. No, not at all, he said, he was an important witness, he was the only person who had actually seen anything. There was a photograph of him in his room looking proud of himself.

That room. There was a description of the room by the journalist – a rich, clever young woman coming face to face with a desperate, poor, fucked-up man – that was a form of accusation in itself. The article ended on a note of caution that looked as if it had been composed with a lawyer looking over the writer's shoulder: 'We do not suggest that Mickey Doll has any involvement in the crime. He is not a suspect. No evidence has been found linking him to the tragic murders of Lianne and young mum Philippa Burton. Yet men like Mickey Doll, with his porn-fuelled fantasies and his criminal record, are an obvious threat to the community, to our families, to our children. In identifying a man like Doll, in printing his photograph, in revealing where he lives, we are not, of course, recommending any actions against him by members of the public. That would be illegal, however understandable, however legitimate the concerns of ordinary people. It is time for the politicians to act.'

Julie took away the interview and read it with her coffee and a bowl of the fruit she ate for her breakfast. 'Hmm,' she said, when she had finished. 'It doesn't really capture his full charm.'

But the following day Oban told me, rather casually, I thought, that Doll was in hospital. A concerned citizen had walked up to him in a pub and smashed him in the face with a broken bottle. 'So he's scarred too,' he added cheerfully. 'He's apparently been asking for you, but I wouldn't visit, if I was you.'

'No, it's probably not a good idea,' I agreed, with a pang of guilt, and put Doll out of my mind.

24

Two days after Doll had been attacked, I went back to the Burtons' house, not because I thought it was a particularly fruitful idea but because Oban pressed me into it. 'Something odd about the bloke,' he'd said.

'Something odd about most people,' I replied.

'He's not upset enough.'

I wondered what that meant. Jeremy Burton had seemed upset enough to me, with his hopeless, tired face, his little grimaces of bafflement and misery. Was there a right amount of grief, then? How did you measure it? I thought about the thousands of people who'd laid flowers on the site where Philippa's body had been found, and wept copiously for a pretty young mother and for the little girl she had left behind. Was that grief ? I didn't say any of this to Oban, of course – he'd just have raised his eyebrows ironically and sent Seb instead.

I arrived at the house on a Sunday morning, as Jeremy Burton had requested. Philippa's mother opened the door, and ushered me through the hall and into the gleaming kitchen. There were flowers everywhere – faded velvet irises, shrivelled ox-eyed daisies, and numerous vases of white lilies, whose thick, oppressive fragrance filled the house. As I passed the living room, I saw banks of condolence cards on the mantelpiece and the table.

I looked out of the kitchen window. The father and daughter were in the garden together, sitting on a wrought-iron bench with their backs to the window. He was doing a crossword, and she was kicking her legs back and forth. Something made him look round, and I raised a hand and made my way out into the garden and across the lawn. He gave a nod of recognition. I had worried about blundering back in but he didn't seem displeased to see me.

We shook hands and he folded up the paper self-consciously, although not before I'd noticed he hadn't filled in a single clue. He was wearing an open-necked T-shirt and khaki shorts, but nevertheless looked rather neat and smart. Some people always look respectable, I thought, and some people never do. Give Doll a bath, a haircut, a shave, a manicure, dress him in a thousand-pound suit, and he'd still look unwashed and somehow unsavoury. You couldn't clean off his past.

'Look,' said Emily.

I crouched down. She had laid her treasures on the bench beside her. There was a round grey stone and a sharp white one, a forked stick, a feather, a clump of moss, a small pink bouncing ball smeared with mud, an old cat's collar, a wooden ice-cream stick, a plastic tube.

'Look,' she said again, and uncurled her plump fist. There was a small shell on the palm of her hand.

'Where did you find that?' I asked.

She pointed to the gravelled area near the kitchen door.

'It's lovely,' I said, and she closed her fist over it again. She was wearing a spotted sundress, and her hair was clipped back behind her ears, making her face seem thinner than I'd remembered.

'I'm going to give them to Mummy,' she said, in a self-important voice. I glanced at her father.

'She means, put them on Phil's grave after she's

buried,' he explained, wincing. 'It was my mother-in-law's idea, that Emily should collect things for her. I'm not so sure. She seems to be taking the idea a bit too literally.' He frowned so that a small furrow appeared over the bridge of his nose.

'What else have you found?' I asked Emily.

She climbed carefully down from the bench, shell in one hand, and started to gather up the treasures with the other. 'Come and see,' she said.

'Can I come in a minute? First I need to talk to your father.'

She nodded. The stones and moss and plastic tube fell on the grass. She knelt down and started to pick them up. Her father made no move to help her. His hands were thrust into the pockets of his shorts, his newspaper tucked under one arm. I glanced across at him. His face looked bruised with tiredness. 'I tell you what, Emily, why don't I bring those to you when I come and see what else you've found for your mother?'

'Promise?'

'Yes.'

'Don't forget that.' She pointed to the plastic tube, lying at my feet.

'I won't.'

We watched her as she plodded away from us.

'She thinks Philippa's coming back.'

'Does she?' I looked at her straight back and spindly legs as she disappeared through the kitchen door.

'Won't you sit down?' He pointed to the bench.

'Thanks.'

'Coffee?'

'No, thanks, I'm fine.'

He sat down too, at the other end of the bench.

'I heard about your contribution,' he said.

'Oh, well . . .'

'I underestimated you, I think.'

'How are you doing?' I asked.

'All right.'

'Sleeping OK?'

'Yes. Well, no, not really. You know. I wake and . . .' He trailed off.

'Eating?'

He nodded.

'I talked to Tess Jarrett a few days ago. She said that Philippa seemed distracted during the last few weeks before her death. Do you think that's true?'

'No, I don't.' I waited. 'I'm sorry. That's all I can say.'

'She didn't seem to have anything on her mind?'

He stared down at the ground, as if he was trying to pretend I wasn't there. 'She seemed the same as usual.'

'Tell me about the night before she died. Describe your evening together.'

He sighed and started intoning in a monotonous voice: 'I came back from work at seven. Emily was in bed and Philippa was reading her a story. We both said good-night to Emily.'

'What did Philippa say, when she said good-night?'

'What did she say?' He blinked at me. 'Do you know, I can't remember. We went downstairs and I poured us both a glass of wine and we walked round the garden together. It was a nice evening.' His voice was getting a bit less clipped. 'We had supper outside, there.' He pointed at the table on the patio.

'What did you eat?'

'Moussaka. Green salad.'

'What did you talk about?'

'I can't remember.' He looked distressed. 'I can't

remember anything, except at some point she asked me if I thought she was looking older.'

'What did you say?'

He flicked something I couldn't see off his shorts. 'I must have said something about how she always looked beautiful to me, but I can't remember the exact words.'

'So, there was nothing different about her, or your relationship with her?'

He spoke now as if he were waking from a deep sleep. 'Different? I don't know what you're digging for. Do you think this was something to do with me? Or her? She wasn't depressed. She didn't drink. She didn't take drugs. She didn't wander round Kersey Town like that girl . . .'

'Lianne.'

'Yes. She got up in the morning and made me breakfast. She looked after the house. She looked after Emily. She met friends. She was happy. She talked about when she should return to work. She talked about having more children one day. Soon.' His voice cracked slightly, but he went on, 'Then, one morning, after she had made breakfast and tidied up the house, she went out with her child and she was suddenly murdered. End of story. That's what the police think anyway, and so does that other doctor who's been round here asking questions. If you've got reasons for thinking differently, please tell me what they are. I want to know.'

I stood up. 'I'm sorry to distress you.' I stooped down and picked up the clump of moss, the two stones, the plastic tube. 'Is it OK if I take these to Emily?'

'She'll probably be in her bedroom. Top of the first flight of stairs.'

'Thanks.'

★

She was arranging small plastic animals on a shelf. I squatted beside her with my hands cupped. 'Here are your things.'

'Do elephants go with lions or horses?'

'If it were up to me, I'd put them with the lions. Do you want to show me what you've collected for your mother?'

She stood up and crossed over to her bed where she pulled out a large cardboard box. One by one, she placed things on the floor: a small jam-jar, a thistle head, several cards from cereal packets, three buttons, a string of plastic beads, a marble, a small shred of orange silken material, some spangled wrapping-paper, a chipped china dog, an apple. I watched her face. She was perfectly intent on her task.

'Which is your favourite?'

She pointed at the marble.

'Which would your mother have liked?'

She hesitated, then pointed at the orange rag.

The door opened and Philippa's mother put her head round the door. 'Excuse me,' she said, in her firm, pleasant voice, 'but a friend is due to arrive for Emily any minute.' She made me feel as if I had sneaked in under false pretences.

'Of course.' I put the objects I was holding carefully into the cardboard box. ' 'Bye, Emily.'

'And the shell,' she said, not looking up. 'The shell's pretty. She liked pretty things.'

Albie phoned up. He just wanted to say hello, he said. He just wanted to see how I was getting on. I held the phone carefully, as if it could hurt me, and waited. We waited for the other person to say something. Then we both said goodbye politely.

I phoned my father but he wasn't there. I wanted someone to say to me, 'Life can be hard, but don't worry, my darling, everything is going to be all right.' I wanted someone to hug me tight and stroke my hair. I wanted my mother. Ridiculous, but true. Would it never go away, that feeling? Would I miss my mother for my whole life, not a day going by without missing her? I picked up the phone to ring Will. It was so quiet in my flat that I could hear my watch ticking on my wrist and my heart beating, and the occasional rattle of dry leaves in the trees outside. But I didn't ring him. What would I say? 'I'm on my own, come round and hold me, please'?

I poured myself a glass of wine and lit two candles. Then I turned off the light and sat on the sofa. Somewhere, a mosquito whined in the half-darkness. Outside it began to rain again and the wind sighed in the trees. What did I know about him? Nothing, except he'd given up a top job in the City to run a hostel for homeless young people who'd fallen through all the safety-nets; that the police distrusted him and suspected him of allowing drugs to be sold on his premises; that he was sour and ill-humoured and dark. I wanted him now because he was so unlike ebullient Albie, and because he looked like a crow, a solitary bird. I wanted to wrap myself up in his ragged misery and make us both better.

In the end I didn't have to seek out Will because he came to me. The following night, when I had already gone to bed after a busy day, the doorbell rang. I pulled on my dressing-gown and looked at my watch. It was past midnight: probably Julie had forgotten her key again. I stumbled to the door, still tangled up in strange dreams. He was standing there and when he saw me he gave a kind of shrug. 'I couldn't sleep,' he said.

I stood back and he went up the stairs in front of me. He sat on the sofa, and I poured out a tumbler of whisky for him, and a smaller one for me. I was very conscious of my tousled hair and tatty dressing-gown. I couldn't think of a single thing to say to him. He seemed so big and alien in my flat. How had I ever dared to kiss him, or to dream of him? We sat and sipped our drinks. He hadn't even taken off his coat, and he stared into the glass as if it held some answer.

In the end, I made a move, because I couldn't bear to go on sitting there in the gloom and heavy silence. I crossed over to the sofa, and I leaned down towards him. I didn't kiss him: that would have seemed too intimate. I undid the buttons on his coat, and then on his shirt and he lay back with his pale torso gleaming and his eyes closed, while I touched him with tentative hands, and watched him. He put up his hands and held my face blindly and I sat astride him, pulled open my dressing-gown and pressed his head against my breast, listening to the hammering of my heart. 'You should be careful,' he muttered.

I didn't know what he was talking about; I didn't care. We were just strangers, in need of comfort. Outside, the rain was blown in waves against the window.

25

As soon as the phone rang, it felt like the wrong time. It was dark outside. My eyelids felt glued together. How long had I been asleep? I was in my own bed but it felt strange. I was in an unusual part of the bed, to one side; Albie's side. As I reached across I realized with an ache in my stomach that I was alone. Will had gone.

'Yes?' was all I could manage.

'Is that Kit?'

'Who's this?'

'Furth. You all right?'

'What?' I said stupidly. 'Sorry, you just woke me up.'

'There's a car on the way to fetch you. Can you manage that?'

'What for?'

'The boss says he'll see you at the hospital.'

'What hospital?'

There was a pause.

'What's it matter what hospital?'

'Don't know. What's happened?'

'Haven't time. We'll fill you in when you get here. Can you manage that? Or shall I say you can't come?'

My brain was coming to life now, though slowly, like a lizard sitting on a stone in the morning sun. I was able to think. For example, I could now see that Furth was hoping I would say grumpily that I was too tired and slam down the phone.

'No problem,' I said. 'Where do we meet?'

'The driver knows,' Furth said, and the line went dead.

The car was on its way. I had only a couple of minutes. I ran into the shower, switched the water on very cold and allowed myself to think about Will, the way we'd held each other like two drowning swimmers. Which one was dragging the other down? What the fuck had it all been about? Why had he gone like that, like a thief? I turned the shower to very hot so it stung my skin. I thought of his expression as he'd come inside me, almost a sob, the closeness I'd been without for so long. Then I'd come as well, just from the look of him, I'd felt. He had held me so close that I had been scared and now he was gone. Was that it? Well, I thought. Well what?

I dried myself quickly and began to get dressed. I was doing up the buttons on my shirt when Julie came in, naked. She didn't seem to have seen the films in which the actress gets out of bed then immediately wraps a towel around herself. I had wondered if she did it to demonstrate that she had irritatingly large breasts for such a slim figure but really I knew she wasn't like that. She just didn't think about it, which I found even more alarming. 'What's going on?' she said. 'House on fire?'

'Work,' I said. 'Something seems to have come up. Don't know what.'

'God,' she said. 'Sounds important.'

'Don't know. Someone just phoned.' I still didn't feel awake enough to formulate complex sentences.

'You want some coffee?'

'I don't think there's time. A car's on its way to pick me up.'

Julie gave a smile. 'I heard you had company.'

'Who from?'

'No, I mean I *heard*. Through the wall.'

'Oh, for God's sake, Julie . . .'

'No, no,' she said. 'There was nothing I could do about it. It's the walls. They're like paper.'

I felt myself go very red. 'Well, that's very embarrassing. I'm sorry if I kept you awake. I thought you were out.'

'Well, I came in again. But don't be sorry, I was glad. You deserve some fun.'

'It wasn't exactly fun,' I said, feeling in some deranged way like Julie's prudish elderly relative.

'Really?' she said, her expression changing to one of concern. 'Well, it sounded fun. Who was the guy?'

I gave a huffy sort of deep breath. 'As it happens it was Will. You know, Will Pavic.'

'Christ,' she said. 'That's weird. I mean great. Pavic. God. Is he awake?'

'No. Actually he's gone, as a matter of fact.'

'Gone? Right. Will Pavic. That's incredible. When you get back, I want to hear every single detail.'

'Julie! One, I'm not going to tell you every detail. And two, you seem to know everything already.' There was a ring at the door. In the quiet of two thirty a.m. it sounded like a fire alarm. 'And three, I've got to go.'

As I walked out, Julie was saying, 'Will Pavic. That's great. It's fantastic. But isn't he a bit strange?'

I just shook my head and left. The car outside looked like a minicab. A man in a suit was holding the front passenger door open.

'Dr Quinn?' he said.

'You're taking me to see DCI Oban?'

'I don't know about that. I'm just dropping you at St Edmund's.'

'Fine.'

As we set off I asked him if he knew what this was

about. When he said he didn't, I stayed silent and just looked out of the window. It was the dead time of night, but London never really went quiet. There were newspaper vans, the occasional car, people walking purposefully, the leftovers from yesterday mixing with the people preparing for tomorrow. I felt that my pulse was starting to race. I worked through alternatives in my mind. Another murder. An arrest. What else could be important enough for this?

'You a real doctor?' the driver asked.

'Sort of.'

'Know people at this hospital, do you?'

'Not at this time of night.'

The car pulled up outside the entrance to the casualty department of St Edmund's. A uniformed officer was standing outside like a doorman. As I got out of the car he muttered something into the radio on his lapel. It crackled something unintelligible back.

'I'm Kit Quinn,' I said.

'Yeah,' he said. 'I'll take you up.'

I seem to have spent a lot of my life in the sort of places that never entirely close – airports, police stations, hospitals – and I rather like them for their slightly forlorn bustle that continues even when it is dark outside and good citizens are asleep. There were ambulances outside, a doctor and nurse ran past, there were cries from various directions. A pale young woman in a white coat was sitting in a corner drinking coffee and eating a mangy-looking sandwich while somehow attempting to fill in a form. Work was being done. The officer led me past all that, up some stairs and along a corridor. From a good fifty yards away I could see Oban sitting on a bench. He caught sight of me too early so we had that embarrassing hiatus where we were too far away to speak, so he nodded at me, then pretended to inspect his nails as if there was something urgent and fascinating about them, and then he looked back up at me.

I was intensely curious about his expression. Sad? Triumphant? But I couldn't read it. He looked like a troubled relative waiting for news, an expectant but worried father. And he looked awful. Rumpled, unshaven, grey with fatigue. 'Thanks for coming, Kit,' he muttered.

'So?' I said. 'What is it? Another murder?'

'No,' he said, and with obvious effort he made an attempt at a smile. 'I think I've won my bet with you. If it was a bet. I wish I felt better about it.'

'What bet?'

'I think I said something to the effect that our murderer was cruising around in his car and he would strike again when he had the chance. You were dubious. Now he has struck again. Or tried to.'

'What do you mean? Who have you got in here?'

'Ms or Mrs, or whatever you call it, Bryony Teale. Aged thirty-four.'

'Is she badly injured?'

'Not physically. I've asked for a doctor to come and talk to you.'

'What happened?'

'Bryony Teale was walking along the canal this evening, silly girl. These people behave as if it were some country riverbank. She was approached and attacked by a man. But in the middle of it, two people stumbled on them on the towpath. The man fled. A car was heard driving away at speed.'

I was silent, thinking furiously. 'Are you sure there's a connection?'

'We're working on it. But it was at the same spot,

almost to the yard, where Lianne's body was found. It seems compelling to me.'

'Bloody hell. And there were witnesses?'

'Two of them.'

'Did they get a description of the car?'

Oban shook his head gloomily. 'That would be too easy, wouldn't it? They were helping Bryony. Terrible state she was in.'

'Has she said anything?'

'Not yet. She's terribly shocked. She can hardly speak.'

'So what am I doing here?'

'I want you to talk to her. Now, later, whenever she can talk. I want to see what you can get out of her. Hypnotize her, shine a light in her eyes, hold an object in front of her, anything, just find out what she knows.'

'Of course. But what about Seb?'

'It's not his sort of job. Don't worry. I'll deal with Seb. And it would be better if it was a woman.'

'Dr Quinn?'

I looked round. A doctor was standing next to me, a balding, very pale man of about my own age with a slightly resentful expression. Here we were, taking up space, time. He had the air of someone who had to be in two other places.

'Yes.'

'I'm Dr Steen. Apparently you want to know about Bryony Teale here.' He looked at his clipboard. 'She's not my patient but I've checked her card. No injuries except some superficial bruising. She's been suffering from shock, which is understandable. Dr Lander just did the usual – rehydration, warming her up, keeping her under observation. She should be fine in the morning.'

'Has she got family? Has anybody been notified?'

Steen gave a shrug. 'She's not my patient,' he said. 'I'm sorry.'

'Can I talk to her?'

He looked down at his clipboard helplessly, as if he expected it to tell him something. It didn't. 'I don't know,' he said. 'It may not be a good idea.'

'It's all right,' I said. 'I'm used to patients like this. I won't be intrusive.'

'OK,' he said. 'There's a nurse in there, I think. I've got to run.'

And he did.

'So,' I said, 'shall I go in and see her?'

'For what it's worth,' Oban said.

My hand had been on the door handle, but I stopped. 'I don't understand,' I said. 'At least this is some kind of positive development in the case. We've got witnesses. Nobody has been killed. Why so gloomy?'

'I'm not exactly gloomy,' Oban said. 'Just confused. And I don't like it.'

'What do you mean?'

'There was one thing I didn't mention.'

'What's that?'

'Those two witnesses, the ones who saved Bryony.'

'Yes?'

'One of them was Mickey Doll.'

26

I would have liked to see my face.

'Doll?' I said stupidly. 'Doll?' Oban stared glumly at me and nodded. 'He was a witness *again*?'

'That's right.'

'But that's . . .' I stopped. I didn't know what to say or what to think.

'Yeah.'

'But why?'

'I'm working on it.'

There was a very long pause. I was incapable of movement or speech or thought. 'So,' I finally managed, 'I'd better talk to this woman.'

The first thing that struck me was her hair, which was long and the colour of ripe apricots. The second was her hands, clenched into fierce fists on the sheet that was pulled up over her. I went across to the bed, the duty nurse beside me – a huge woman who walked with a roll like a pitching ship, her shoes creaking loudly on the scuffed linoleum. 'Don't go distressing her now,' she said, and picked up one of the woman's slim wrists in her enormous fingers and held it for a minute, head cocked on one side as if she was listening. Then she squeaked away again, and the door shut with a click behind her.

'Hello, Bryony,' I said, and she stared up at me as if I was indistinct to her. Her pupils were dilated. I pulled up a metal chair and sat down, noticing as I did so that I was wearing odd socks. 'My name's Kit.'

'Hello,' she murmured, struggling into a sitting position so that her pale orange hair fell forward. She had a striking, slightly flat face, with high cheekbones and a firm jaw. Her eyes were pale brown, almost golden.

'You've had a shock,' I continued, 'but you're quite safe now. There is no need for you to be frightened. All right?'

She nodded and half smiled. 'Sorry,' she said, in a low voice. 'Sorry to be so feeble.'

I smiled back. 'Don't apologize. Is there anything you need? Tea? Something to eat?'

'No.'

'Look, it's beginning to get light outside.' I gestured to the small window. Outside, the dark had become grey. 'Night's nearly over.'

'I want to go home.'

'I'm sure you'll be able to very soon. Where is home?'

'Home,' she repeated vaguely, and lifted a hand to her head. 'Why do I feel so strange?'

'You've had a shocking experience. It's normal to feel strange.'

'Like people after the football-disaster thing?'

'That's right.'

'But I'm not that kind of person.' She trailed her fingers over her face, as if she were tracing her features to remind herself of who she was. 'What happened?'

'You don't remember?' Oban was going to be even more glum when he heard that.

'I remember bits, like in a fog. Tell me what happened. Please.' She leaned forward and touched the back of my hand softly.

I thought of those confused misty few seconds in Stretton Green police station, the warm feeling of the blood on my face. 'You were attacked by the canal late last night. But you were lucky. Two men came to your aid. Your attacker ran off. Obviously anything you can remember will be a help but don't force anything. Just let it come back of its own accord, don't block it out.'

She nodded and sat up straighter, pulling the sheet around her. 'My head aches,' she said, 'and I'm thirsty. Can I have a glass of water?'

I poured water from the jug on the locker beside her into a plastic beaker, and held it out. When she took it, her hand was trembling violently, so that drops spilt on to the sheet and she had to wrap the other hand round the beaker as well.

'Thank you,' she said. 'God, I'm tired. I'm so tired now. Is Gabriel coming soon?'

'Gabriel?'

'My husband.'

'I'm sure the police will have contacted him.'

'Good.' She lay back and her hair spread on the pillow.

'Before you rest, Bryony, could you tell me what you remember?'

'I remember . . . I remember a shape in the darkness. Coming out of the darkness.' She closed her eyes. 'And someone shouting.' Her eyes snapped open. 'I can't,' she said. 'Please. Not yet. It's a jumble. When I try and grab hold of something it slides away from me, like trying to remember a dream. A horrible, horrible dream.'

'It's OK. Take your time. Did you recognize the person who attacked you?'

'No! No, I'm sure I would remember that, wouldn't I? Or would I?'

'And what,' I asked her as neutrally as I could, 'about the men who helped you?'

'What?' She blinked and rubbed her face again.

'Had you seen them before, those two men?'

'Seen them? No. I don't know. I don't know. Who were they? Wait a minute, wait a minute.'

I stood up and crossed to the little window, where morning was breaking. It looked straight into another room. I could see an empty bed, a locker, a phone on wheels, just like the ones in Bryony's room. My brain was seething. What the fuck had Doll been doing there? I would have to speak to him too. Later, though. My mouth was parched from the whisky I'd downed last night, my eyes ached in their sockets. I needed caffeine.

'I don't know,' she said at last. 'I'm sorry.'

'Bryony.' I turned back to her. She was staring at me, waiting for me to speak. 'It's very important that if you remember anything, anything at all, any detail, no matter how irrelevant it seems to you, you tell someone. The police. Me. But someone. All right?'

She nodded. At that moment, the door swung open and Oban pushed his head into the room. 'Mrs Teale,' he said, 'you have a visitor to see you. Your husband is on his way up now.'

'I'll leave you now, Bryony, but I'll come and see you later, if that's all right,' I said, moving towards the door where Oban was waiting, his great weary brow puckered with anxiety. She nodded at me and half closed her eyes.

'Well?' hissed Oban, as soon as we were in the corridor.

'She doesn't remember much.'

'Fuck,' he said. Then: 'Fuck, fuck, fuck.'

'She will, though,' I said. 'She's just had a shock. Give her time.'

'Time, you say. Time is the one thing I don't want to give. What if he strikes again?'

A tall man strode past us, the husband, I guessed. He had a straight nose, dark hair and thick dark eyebrows, and he reminded me of a picture of a Roman emperor in one of the books I'd had as a child.

'Do you want me to speak to her later?' I asked Oban.

'Would you?'

'Sure. And, as you said yourself, I think it's best for a woman to talk to her, given what's just happened.'

'Yes,' he said.

'What about Doll? Should I see him?'

'Fuck,' he said again. 'I don't know. He's at the police station now, making a statement.'

'So he definitely wasn't the attacker?' I asked cautiously.

'Oh, God, Kit, ask me in a few hours' time. The other witness is there as well. Sensible type, for once.'

'A man in a suit with a mobile phone, you mean.'

'Yeah, all that. Anyway, I'm on my way back there now, so I'll find out more, maybe.' He gave a disgusted grunt. 'Just maybe.'

'OK, well, give me a call. On my mobile – I may well be out.'

'Sure. Thanks.' His tone was preoccupied. I could almost hear his brain churning round and round, like a wheel in mud. Then he said, 'Do you know what really pisses me off?'

'What?'

'We've got three witnesses, if you count bloody Mickey Doll. One's a bereaved little child. One's in shock. One's a fucking pervert and weirdo who can't string three thoughts together, and who's a suspect anyway – or would be if it was possible. I need a break here.'

'Give it time. Maybe you've just got a break.'

'Maybe.'

'Speak to you later, then.'

★

I was driven back in a police car through the early morning. The roads were already full of traffic. The wet pavements gleamed in the low sunlight. The metal shutters outside newsagents were being scrolled up. Asian grocers were arranging oranges and baskets of plums in pyramids outside their shops. A refuse van moved slowly along, picking up sacks that had been left by the side of the road. I lay back and watched London move past me. I thought about Will, his frowning face in the candlelight, and about Bryony Teale with her apricot hair and her smile and trembling hands. I pictured Bryony alongside Lianne, and Philippa. I touched my scar. Welcome to the club, I thought to myself. Then I tried not to think at all.

27

Julie was still in bed. I could hear her turning over on her divan in the room that a long time ago had been my study. I boiled the kettle and heaped several tablespoons of coffee beans into the grinder. I covered it with a tea-towel before turning it on, but still I heard Julie groan through the walls. I put my nose close to the coffee and inhaled deeply. In the fridge I found a nectarine, which I quartered and put on a plate, and a small pot of Greek yoghurt. I drank the strong, rich coffee slowly, between small bites of sweet juicy nectarine and creamy spoonfuls of yoghurt. It was seven o'clock.

I had to arrange to see Doll and maybe the other witness. I had to visit Bryony Teale. And I wanted to see Will. I lifted my hand and put it against my neck, my cheek. My skin felt soft and tender. I closed my eyes and let his face come into my mind. Maybe he didn't want to see me again, though – maybe that was it, a few hours in the middle of one sleepless night.

Julie staggered in, wearing a man's shirt that looked suspiciously like one of Albie's. Where had she found that? 'Hi,' she said vaguely, and padded over to the fridge. She poured herself a mug of milk and drank it in one go. Then she turned to me, with a white moustache on her upper lip. 'Everything OK?'

'Yes. I guess.'

'Emergency over?'

'For the time being.'

'Good. Want a slice of toast?'

'No thanks.'

I went and stood by the window, looking out on to the street, as if he'd be walking there.

'I wish . . .' I stopped.

'Yes? Tell me?'

I had his home number. Why not? I rang him. There were several rings before he answered. The receiver was picked up and there was a muffled greeting. It sounded something like: 'Unngh.'

'It's me,' I said. 'Kit.'

There was another unintelligible sound followed by a pause. Gathering his faculties perhaps. 'Did you just wake up?' he said.

'I've just got in,' I said.

'What do you mean?'

'I was called out.'

'Oh.' There was a pause. 'Do you want to have breakfast?'

'Now?'

'What's the time?' I heard some fumbling and a groan. 'At about eight?'

'At your place?'

'I don't really eat much at my place.'

I was disappointed. I wanted to see his home. People say that you're strongest on your own territory. It's not true. Your own territory is where you're vulnerable. You can play at being a tourist everywhere else, but the place where you sleep will give things away about you. Somehow I found it hard to imagine Will Pavic living anywhere. He gave me directions to what he described as a pretty basic café that he went to on his way to work. I put the phone down. How many hours' sleep had I had? One. Maybe two. I felt as if there was somebody small inside my head jabbing the back of my eyeballs

with slightly warmed needle points. I went to the bathroom, filled the basin with cold water, dipped my face
in it and held it under for as long as I could manage. I
looked at it in the mirror, water running off it. Had last
night really happened? It felt confused in my mind now,
different bits running together, like in a dream. That
face, my face, was the best evidence that something had
occurred. Pale, hollow-eyed – what a sight.

Andy's Café was full of smoke and people in donkey-
jackets and steel-capped boots. Will waved me over from
the far corner. I sat opposite him and we didn't touch.
    'I'm having a basic fry-up,' he said. 'What about you?'
    'I'll just have coffee.'
    'I wouldn't recommend their coffee.'
    'Tea, then.'
    'What about food?'
    'I ate something when I got in.'
    Will's food arrived, stacked on a large oval plate, with
two uncompromisingly dark brown cups of tea. He
loaded some fried egg, bacon and tomato on to his fork.
    'I'm sorry,' he said, before filling his mouth.
    'What about?'
    He had to chew and swallow for a long time before
he was able to speak. He took a gulp of tea. I took a gulp
of tea. 'Leaving like that,' he said. 'I don't sleep. I get
restless. It's better to go.'
    I didn't speak and Will carried on eating. He wasn't
looking at me.
    'You don't need to make excuses,' I said. 'I suppose
I'd like you to be honest with me. I'm tired of playing
games with people. Or maybe just tired.'
    Will was mopping up egg yolk from his plate with a
piece of fried bread. It was almost more than I could

bear at this time of the morning. He put it into his mouth and chewed it vigorously. He wiped his mouth with a paper napkin. He raised his eyes and looked at me. As he did so I realized how rare that was. He was always looking to one side, over my shoulder. I had seen him naked, I had been to bed with him, yet I had hardly looked in his eyes. He was some years older than me, about forty, but looked older with greying hair and a face that wasn't so much wrinkled as creased over his ferocious high cheekbones. But his eyes were grey and very clear, like a child's eyes.

'It wasn't just that,' he said, his face colouring slightly. 'I looked at you when you'd fallen asleep. I brushed the hair off your face. You're a heavy sleeper.' He smiled slightly. 'You looked lovely.'

'Look, you don't have to . . . I know I'm not . . .'

'Shut up and listen. What I was trying to say is that you looked different. It was the first time I had ever seen you when you didn't look sad or anxious or . . .' He hesitated and then said, 'Or too hopeful.'

'Oh, well, hopeful,' I said. It made me sound pathetic, like a spaniel that was going to be kicked.

'You'd even looked a bit sad when you'd walked across your room and kissed me. But then, when you were asleep and didn't know anyone was there, you looked young and peaceful.'

I took a sip of the last of my tea. It was even browner and more bitter than the rest had been.

'And,' continued Will, 'I just had the sudden feeling that the best favour I could do you was not to be around.'

'I don't need to be protected,' I said. 'I can make up my own mind about what's best for me. And, anyway, I think you're maybe quite a happy person, in your own grim sort of way. Especially considering the number of people who hate you. It's amazing, I would have thought that a part of your job was to get on with the police and the social services.'

'I don't have a job,' Will said, frowning. 'A lot of these kids I'm trying to keep clear of the police and social services.'

'You talk as if they're out to get you.'

'They are out to get me.'

'I've heard people talk about drug-dealing on your premises. They said they'll charge you with conspiracy. You could go down for ten years.'

'Fuck them,' he said dismissively.

'Well, *do* you allow it?'

He gave a noncommittal grunt.

'I'm not wired, you know.'

He shrugged. 'You've seen the place. Obviously we keep dealers out, or try to. But it's the culture. We're trying to help these people. It's complicated and messy. It's not like reading out a paper at a seminar.'

'Do you know what I think?'

Now he did allow his features to relax into a sort of good humour. 'No, Kit. I don't know what you think.'

'I think there's a bit of you that would like to be arrested and sent to prison, just to confirm your view of what the world is like.'

'I'm not interested in gestures.'

'That depends if you count martyrdom as a gesture.'

I looked at him, unsure whether he would flare up or give his sarcastic laugh. He seemed unsure himself. 'Maybe it's flattering to be hated,' he said finally.

'I think that might be one of the definitions of paranoia,' I responded. 'Maybe the idea that everybody's out to get you is preferable to the fear of just being ignored.'

'But you just said that everybody *was* out to get me.'

'Yeah, I forgot. Are you ever going to ask me back to your place?'

'What do you mean?'

'You talked about not being able to sleep in unfamiliar surroundings. I'm curious to see how you manage it in your own bed.'

He looked at his watch. 'I'd invite you back now but it's about twenty to nine. I've got people to meet.'

'I didn't mean that.'

He looked the closest to embarrassed that I'd ever seen. 'Sure,' he said. 'Any time.'

'What about tonight?'

'That's a possibility,' he said. 'I'd just have to warn you, among various warnings, that it's quite austere. I mean, it lacks a woman's touch.'

'I'm glad to hear that.'

Suddenly he looked more sombre. 'Don't expect too much from me, Kit,' he said, in a return to his usual starker tone.

I gave a sigh. 'I don't think I expect very much at all,' I said, and I gave a huge yawn.

'Tired?'

'I think today's going to be a bit of a struggle.'

'What happened last night?'

I sat back in my chair and looked at him. 'Do you really want to know?' I said. 'It's nothing interesting.'

'Yes, I want to know.'

So I ordered two more teas for us and I gave him a précis of my night at the hospital.

'So what are you going to do now?' he said, when I'd finished.

'She was deeply shocked when I saw her. I'll talk to her over the next few days and see if I can find out anything.'

'Walking along the canal after midnight,' Will said scornfully. 'Honestly!'

'You mean she was asking for it?'

'I mean she was a fucking idiot.' He took a sip of tea. 'What was her husband called?'

I thought for a moment, trying to get the pea-soup fog in my brain to disperse. 'Gabriel,' I said. That sarcastic smile again. 'Do you know him?

'I know who he is.'

'Who is he?'

'Haven't you heard of that theatre building that's opened in one of the warehouses by the railway? The Sugarhouse or something. You know, Hungarian mime artists on stilts, that sort of thing. That's him.'

'I think I've heard of it.'

'Lottery grants. Revitalizing the community. He should just fuck off back over the hill to Islington and then his wife wouldn't get attacked.'

'Revitalizing the community is your job, is it?'

Will didn't reply but ran his finger around the rim of his cup. Then he looked at me. 'What are you doing?' he asked.

'What do you mean?'

'I mean, what are you doing? Are you trying to make them better or do you think you'll catch the murderer all on your own?'

'I'm an adviser, that's all,' I said uncomfortably.

'You don't need to convince *me*,' he said. 'What do I know? As far as I can see, there's someone driving around attacking women. They are dangerous, they need to be caught. All that's clear. I don't understand what you're doing. Or why. Why you're so involved. I don't understand what you're after.' With his finger he gently traced the scar on my face. It made me shiver.

'You've already been attacked once. Isn't that enough?'

I took his hand in mine. 'Stop that,' I said. 'I should introduce you to some detectives. You all seem to feel the same about what I'm up to. Meanwhile I've got to do some of this useless work.'

'I didn't say it was useless. I said I didn't understand it.'

I leaned down and kissed him. 'The problem,' I said, 'with everything, really, is that you only know at the end, when it's too late, if it was worthwhile. I'll see you.'

'Tonight?'

'You want me to?'

'You want me to get down on one knee?'

I looked around the café. 'Not here,' I said. 'Look, here I am, all hopeful, as you put it. I'm saying I want to see you again, tonight, at your place. Now, what about you?'

'Yes,' he said, in a voice so low it was almost a whisper. 'Yes.' We stared at each other.

When I left he was still sitting there, with his greasy plate and cold tea and stern face. In twelve hours, I would hold him again.

28

At last, I thought, a witness who was straightforward, a man who spoke his mind, dealt in facts and nothing else, saw what there was to be seen, never let fancies cloud his judgement. He shook my hand firmly and cleared his throat as a preliminary to speaking. My eyes felt scorched in their sockets. All the coffee and the dark brown tea I had drunk this morning was toxic in my system.

'Dr Quinn,' I said.

'I'm Terence Mack. But people call me Terry.'

'Do you make a habit of walking along the canal after midnight?' I asked.

He gave a sniff. 'I don't think someone like me needs to worry.'

I couldn't help but agree. He was compact and gingery, with hairy knuckles and wrists, and long ear-lobes. His dark grey suit was rather too tight round his waist, and he wore, over his white shirt, a striped red and black tie that made my head ache even more. He, too, must have been up half the night, but he didn't look weary at all. He sat upright and alert.

But he was a dead loss, for all that. Like most witnesses, he had only realized after the event that something was happening. I had his statement in front of me. It was short and precise; he had even noted the exact time of the attack immediately afterwards, 1.19 a.m., according to his watch, which was set at the correct time, to be sure. He had, he said, been walking along the canal because he had been at a meeting with clients from

Singapore at the Pelham Hotel, just up the road, and afterwards had been unable to find a taxi. The path was the shortest route to the busy intersection of roads near Kersey Town station, where he knew there was a cab rank.

'I was coming out of the tunnel,' he said to me now. 'There's a light there. So I stepped out into the darkness and for a moment I couldn't see anything at all. You know how it is.' I nodded. 'I just heard a noise. I could make out some shapes, scuffling, by the water's edge. Then the next thing I knew there was this woman in my arms, screaming.'

'And she said . . .' I looked back at the statement '. . . "Help! Help, please help."'

'Maybe she said help more times than that, I can't be exact. She screamed from an inch away. Her hair was in my eyes, so I couldn't see much at all, but her voice was clear enough.'

'And you saw nothing after that.'

'Just this other fellow standing there.'

'The other witness?'

He raised his bushy eyebrows. 'Weird-looking guy.'

'What did he do?'

'Who?'

'The weird-looking guy.'

'He helped.'

'And there was definitely another man?'

'What do you mean? What do you think this is all about?'

I looked at the statement once more. 'There isn't much of a description here.'

He looked a little shamefaced. 'It was over so quickly. Just shapes in the darkness and the woman flying at me. I didn't really know what was going on. At least I noticed the time.'

'That was good,' I said. 'How was Bryony, I mean, the woman?'

'A bit shocked,' said Terence. 'A bit hysterical. She was saying it was all right, there was no need to do anything, even though she was in a terrible state. Poor girl. Is she all right?'

'She's traumatized. But she will be, I think. What was Doll – the other guy – doing while you were phoning?'

'Doing? Not very much. Holding on to her, seeing if she was all right. Not the kind you need around in an emergency. She was crying by then, but softly. Holding on to my arm and whimpering and saying would I stay with her. She was in shock, I could see that. Her hands were trembling. She was breathing in these short gasps. I hope they gave her tea with lots of sugar, that's always best for shock. Can I ask you something?'

'Yes.'

'The fellow I gave my statement to, name of Gil I think, he said the attacker was probably the same man who murdered Philippa Burton.'

'He did?' I said drily.

'Is he?'

'I don't know.'

'I should have got him. I could've. I didn't know what was going on.'

'You're sure there was nothing about the fourth shape you remember – height, hair, clothing?'

He shook his head regretfully. 'It was over so quickly.'

'Did you see where he went?'

'No. I presumed up the steps to the road, but I didn't see him. I should have followed, shouldn't I?'

'You phoned for help. That was the main thing. It's for the police to run after people.'

'She was shivering. I put my jacket over her shoulders until the police and ambulance arrived.'

'Good. That was good.'

'But Philippa Burton's murderer. That would have been something . . .'

'A pretty lady,' he said, and his voice trembled. 'Such a pretty little lady.'

'Michael,' I said, trying to hold his eyes, which wandered all over the room, not resting on anything for long, except the view out of the window, which overlooked the car park.

'Twice,' he said, in a strange, high tone. 'Two times it's happened now to me. I've been there twice, Kit.'

He looked dreadful. There was an ugly, suppurating gash running from his left nostril, over the corner of his mouth and down his chin, which gave his face a distorted appearance, and set his mouth into a vague twitchy smile. The wound was swollen and purple, and it looked to me as if he'd been tugging at the stitches: ends of nylon thread stuck out of his skin. Even as we spoke, he couldn't keep his hands off it, but touched and picked at it. His lip was swollen, and he kept dabbing it with the tip of his tongue. There was a large graze on his forehead. One wandering eye was bloodshot. His hair was greasy. His clothes hung off him, as if in a couple of days he'd lost several pounds in weight. He smelt bad, too – a thick, sour odour that filled the poky room.

'Why me, Kit?' he asked, in his fretful voice. 'Why am I always the one?'

'I don't know,' I answered, truthfully enough. 'You're all right, though, aren't you? Hero of the hour.'

'Pretty lady,' he said again. His eyes flickered round to rest on me for a moment. 'Not as pretty as you. You're always the prettiest, don't worry about that. Soft hair, though.' He made a faint mewing sound, that made me shudder.

His statement was a jumble of contradictory assertions – that he'd seen a huge man, a giant of a man, trying to strangle Bryony, that she'd run from her attacker and straight into his outstretched arms, that he'd rescued her himself, that he'd seen the man drive off in a blue estate car, maybe it wasn't blue, maybe it was red, maybe it wasn't an estate car, that maybe, come to think of it, he'd seen him run off down the canal, that Bryony had fainted.

'Just tell me the things that you know for sure, Michael. Why were you by the canal so late?'

'Fishing. Good time for it. Full moon. Nobody around, no bloody noise.'

'Where were you? Right on the edge?'

'My patch. In the shadows, just near the tunnel, where no one can see me, but I can see them.'

'What did you see?'

'You know,' he said. 'The lady. The man after her. And the other man. Terry. Have you met Terry? We both rescued her. Chased him off, saved her.'

'Can you describe him?'

'A man. A big man.'

'Anything more?'

'Not exactly. I just saw shapes and then I got up, I think I got up, I don't know exactly, I was confused, anybody'd have been confused, Kit, and I held on to her so he couldn't get her.'

'Are you sure? You are quite sure it happened like that? You pulled her away?'

'Oh, yes.' He smiled with his misshapen mouth. 'I saved her. I'm sure I saved her. Does she realize that?

The papers say terrible things about me, but I saved her from him. Tell them that, will you? Tell everyone what I did, Kit, so then they'll know. They'll be sorry for the things they did. Everyone'll be sorry then.' Once again he touched his face, licked his cut lip.

'What happened after that?'

'After?'

'After you pulled her.'

'Then this other man came out of the tunnel, and she ran to him and the other one ran off. And she screamed and screamed and screamed. I didn't know anyone could scream that loudly.'

'Michael, listen. You must think. Is there anything you can remember, anything at all, anything you saw, or you heard, no matter what, that you haven't told the police or me?'

'I stroked her hair to comfort her.'

'Yes.'

'And the other man, the one who came out of the tunnel, he said – excuse me, Kit – he said very loudly: "Fucking hell." Sorry.' Doll looked prim.

'Where are you going now, Michael?'

'Where?' His eyes wavered on me. 'I don't suppose I could come to . . .'

'You should go home, Michael. Get yourself a solid meal. Clean clothes. Rest up.'

'Rest up,' he repeated. 'Yes. Things have got a bit out of hand, really. They gave me pills but I don't know where I put them.'

'Go home, Michael.'

'Am I safe?'

'Are the police protecting you?'

'They said they'd keep an eye out.'

'Good,' I said. I smiled at him. In the middle of my

confusion about what had happened, my deep weariness, my distaste for Doll, I felt a jolt of surprising and unwelcome tenderness for him, with his slashed face and reddened eyes and his general squalid hopelessness and helplessness. 'I think you're quite safe, really. It won't happen again. Just take care.'

'Kit. Kit.'

'Yes.'

But he didn't have anything to say to me. He just stared at me for a few seconds. His eyes filled up with tears. They ran down his cheeks, over his cut face, into his dirty neck.

It was eleven o'clock. I had two hours before my meeting with Oban and Furth, three before I was due at Bryony Teale's house. I thought about going home and taking a shower, maybe lying down. But suddenly I didn't feel tired any more. I felt sharp and clear with lack of sleep, as if I was standing on a high mountain, breathing in thin air. I thought about getting myself something to eat, but the idea of food made me feel slightly nauseous. All I wanted was a glass of cold water to wash through my body, dilute some of the bitter coffee I'd gulped down.

I walked out of the station, and on the high street I bought a large bottle of carbonated water and took it to a patch of green nearby, where there were seats and drooping rose bushes. There, I sat on a bench in the sun, drinking my water and watching the people who walked past. The warmth felt lovely on my skin, gentle and soothing. I sighed and closed my eyes and felt sunlight trickle down my neck. My head buzzed lightly with fragments of the last twenty-four hours: I heard Will's groan of last night, felt his hand on my breast. I saw him as he had been this morning, so careful not to promise me anything. I pictured Bryony's face on the hospital pillow; her pale orange hair and caramel eyes, her trembling hands. I let Doll into my mind, with his plaintive incoherence and his blotchy oozing face. The other witness – Terence Mack with the square, hairy hands – had been momentarily blinded by the light of the tunnel. Nobody had seen anything that mattered. Everyone was always looking in the wrong direction. Drama happened in the dark shadows.

I sat there for a long while, thinking and not thinking, letting the images drift across my brain like wisps of fog, insubstantial but suggestive. The sun moved in and out of clouds. People came out of their offices and sat on the patch of grass to eat their sandwiches. I thought about Albie, but he seemed a long way off now – a man laughing in the distance, head thrown back, white teeth gleaming; a stranger. It was hard to believe that for months on end I had gone to sleep wishing he was beside me, and woken each morning remembering all over again that he had hurt me and that he wasn't coming back to take me in his arms and say that he was sorry. Never again. He'd never again hold me and touch me. Such a hard, sharp word: never. Definite, like a knife, like a line drawn under something.

And tonight I'd see Will. I'd go to his house and I'd make him look at me and see me, and I'd feel happy for a while. I stood up, and wrenched my mind back to Bryony Teale.

29

'Nice,' I said, looking out of the window.

'Bad area, though,' said Oban, sniffily.

Oban had told me that Bryony Teale was willing to talk to me. Especially to me. A sympathetic female ear, Oban had said on the phone. Not as a compliment. I had walked over, and as I approached the house, the window of a car outside had slid down and a hand emerged, beckoning me over. Oban peered out. He opened the door and invited me to sit next to him on the back seat. He said he wanted to talk first. It would have been nicer outside, even on this grey day, but Oban was obviously more comfortable in the car. Maybe it seemed like a mobile office.

The house was part of a terrace that curved in a gentle crescent, not so much a bold letter C, more a parenthesis. The houses were tall and narrow, late Victorian. Some were shabby, one was boarded up, but a few bore the tell-tale signs of gentrification: shiny-painted front doors with brass knobs and knockers, freshly pointed brickwork, metal shutters on the lower windows. Oban pointed down the street. 'Ten years ago a stack of flowers was piled up there.'

'Why?'

'A couple of boys were walking along down towards Euston Road when they ran into a gang of other kids. They chased them and they caught one by those railings. They beat him up and then when they were done someone pushed a knife into him.' He looked back at the house. 'I don't know why people like that want to move here.'

'From what I hear they're trying to do some good to the area, show some faith in the local people.'

Oban pulled a face. 'Right,' he said. 'And this is the thanks they get. They're so bloody naïve. I've seen it all before. That woman walking down the canal as if it's a country lane. I mean, I'm not a particular fan of country lanes, but this is stupid. Did you hear of the woman a few years ago who was staying in one of the local hotels?'

'I don't know,' I said. 'I hear stories about lots of women.'

'This one stayed on the road, but some boys dragged her down on to the towpath. She was raped. They asked her if she could swim. She said no, clever thing. So they threw her in. She swam across to the other side. Got away.'

'What's your advice?' I asked. 'To stay indoors with the door locked and the TV on?'

'It would be safer.'

'The best idea would be if *everybody* went walking by the canal.'

'Who wants to walk by a smelly canal?'

Enough was enough. 'Do you think we should go in and talk to Bryony Teale?' I asked.

Oban looked thoughtful. 'It might be better if you talked to her on your own,' he said. 'At first anyway.'

'I'm not sure if we'll get anything from her at all yet,' I said. 'She seemed in a bad way last night.'

'Just do what you can. Give us something, anything.' Then Oban's voice dropped into a mutter that I couldn't make out at all.

'What was that?'

Oban started to speak but nothing except a sort of

twitching splutter emerged. 'It's that bloody Doll,' he finally managed. 'He's in it somewhere. I don't know how but he is.'

'You said he was just a witness.'

'Witness my arse,' said Oban, his face a fiery red now. The police driver sitting in the front of the car turned round and gave me a look. 'I want to bury that bastard. Ask her about Doll. Ask her what he was doing there.'

'Sorry,' I said. 'As I understand it, the point of the connection was the place, this same area of canal, and the same method of abduction. That's where Doll spends his life, sitting there with his rod and his maggots. And there was the girl and the witness. He helped her.'

Oban gave a sarcastic laugh that was part grunt, part cough. 'I haven't got a bloody clue what's going on,' he said. 'But Doll has been in this from the beginning like a bad smell. He's bound up with it somewhere. I just know. So do you. You've seen him, you've seen where he lives.'

I gave a shudder. 'I know. All right, I'll ask. Do I just knock at the door?'

'That's right. We've had an officer there all day, just to make cups of tea probably. She'll answer.'

'What are *you* going to do?'

'I'm off. If she's able to make a statement, I'll send one of my DCs over.' As I opened the car door, Oban put his hand on my wrist. 'Get me something, Kit. I'm desperate.'

The young female officer opened the door. 'Dr Quinn?'

'That's right. How is she?'

'Dunno. She hasn't said much.'

I looked around. The floor and the stairs were stripped and polished but there was a casual, slightly raffish feel to the interior. A bike hung from a heavy-duty hook on one wall. There were shelves with rows of battered paperbacks in the hall and I could see more shelves with more books on the landing at the top of the stairs. The hall led through to the kitchen and I could see a garden beyond that. The door opened next to me and a man came out, the man I'd seen at the hospital. He was unshaven now, and his dark curly hair was rumpled. He was dressed in a navy blue sweatshirt, jeans and worn tennis shoes with no socks. He looked the way I felt. I guessed he'd slept even less than I had. He was tall, six foot or so. He shook my hand. 'I'm Gabe,' he said.

'I saw you,' I said. He looked puzzled. 'At the hospital. Last night. This morning. Whatever.'

'Oh, yes, sorry, I wasn't at my best. Can I get you something?'

'I'll make some tea,' said WPC Devlin, officiously, and padded off towards the kitchen like an Edwardian maid.

'How's your wife?'

Gabe's expression changed to one of concern. 'I don't know. Better than last night.'

'That's good. Can I have a word with her?'

Gabe looked uncomfortable. He put his hands in his trouser pockets, then took them out again. 'Can I ask you something first?'

'Of course.'

'Bry was attacked by this person who did these other awful murders?'

'It seems possible, at least. It was in exactly the same place as one of the bodies was found.'

'But it seems so far-fetched,' he said. 'Why on earth would someone come back to the spot where he'd already committed a murder? It sounds so risky.'

'Yes, but murderers do that. It's not a theory, it happens. Murderers go back.'

'Right, right,' said Gabe, as if he were talking to himself. I had an impulse to put my hand on him, to offer him comfort, but it was better to let him talk. 'What I wanted to ask, I mean it probably sounds stupid or paranoid, but I just wanted to know if Bry could be in any danger. Could he want to get at her again?'

I thought for a moment. I wanted to be precise about this.

'The opinion of the investigating officers is that the perpetrator of these crimes is an opportunist. Late at night, on the canal, your wife was an obviously vulnerable target.'

Gabe's eyes narrowed and he looked at me. 'But what do *you* think?'

'I should say that I'm hired by the police to suggest possible ideas. I consider different directions. I have always suspected that something links the first two victims.'

'What? Why?' Gabe Teale sounded as if he was in the middle of a bad dream.

'I don't know. It's just a feeling. It may be wrong. It's probably wrong. The police don't agree with me, that's for sure. I just wanted to be frank with you.'

'But if you're not wrong . . .' he was speaking slowly, in a fog of tiredness and stress '. . . that would mean Bry was still in danger.'

'Don't worry about that,' I said. 'There is no question whatever that the police will provide basic protection. All right?'

'That's good,' he said, not looking very reassured. 'Thank you.'

'Can I see your wife now?' I said, as gently as I could.

'I'll take you through. Would you rather talk to her alone?'

'That's up to you,' I said. 'I'm sure she'd rather you were there.'

'She's in here,' he said, leaning against the door, pushing it open. He looked through. 'Bry? The doctor's here.'

I followed him in. Two rooms had been knocked into one, making a large space that ran the depth of the house. I could see the street through the large window at one end and the garden through the french windows at the other. Towards the garden end Bryony Teale was sitting on a large rust-coloured sofa. She was wearing a bright orange sweater and blue three-quarter-length trousers. Her bare feet were tucked up under her. I walked over and her husband pulled up an armchair for me. Then he sat down on the sofa, lifting her up so that she could lean against him. They exchanged glances and Gabe gave her a reassuring smile.

Above her on the wall was a large, poster-sized photograph showing a little girl standing in a deserted city street. The child was ornately dressed, she almost looked like a gypsy fortune-teller, but what struck me most were her dark, fiery eyes, which gazed directly into the lens. It was as if the girl had that moment looked round, and focused her extraordinarily intense glare on the photographer. You knew that at the next she must have looked away again, but it was enough. It made you want to know about the girl, what had happened to her, where she was now.

'That's amazing,' I said.

Bryony looked round then forced the beginning of a smile. 'Thanks,' she said. 'I took it.'

'You're a photographer,' I said.

'I don't know if I can still call myself that,' she said

ruefully. 'I have difficulty finding people who want to publish the sort of pictures I want to take.'

'I can't believe that,' I said.

'I took that one last year about a quarter of a mile from here,' said Bryony. 'I was walking and I met her with her family. They were refugees from Romania. Isn't she beautiful?'

I looked again. 'She's fierce,' I said.

'Maybe I scared her,' said Bryony.

'How are you feeling?' I said.

'Sorry to be so collapsed.'

'Don't be ridiculous,' I said. 'You don't have to prove anything. You don't even have to talk to me if you don't feel like it.'

'No, no, I want to. This isn't like me.'

I looked closely at her. She was obviously better than when I'd seen her at the hospital, but she was still pale with dark rings under her eyes. 'Anyone would have been shocked by what you went through,' I said. 'So I suppose your work means you do a lot of walking around in strange places.'

'A bit,' she said.

'But you should be careful. I was just talking to the head of the murder inquiry. He doesn't think that walking by the canal at night is such a good idea.'

'I keep telling her that,' said Gabe. 'But she's fearless. And stubborn. She's always loved to walk.'

'I feel a bit differently now,' she said.

'Well, maybe not alone at night,' I said cheerily, noticing the first stirrings of an argument. 'Do you feel all right to talk about it?'

'I want to help.'

'If it feels bad, just tell me and I'll stop.'

'I'm all right.'

'Can you tell me what happened?'

'I've spent today going over and over it in my mind, but I don't think I'll be of much use. It happened so quickly. I was walking along the canal towpath. I felt an arm on me, pulling at me. Pulling and pulling, and I gave a scream. Then immediately there were these other people grabbing at me. It sounds so stupid but at first I didn't realize that they were trying to help. Before I knew what was going on, the man had run away.'

'That was all?'

'All?'

'Look, Bryony, after the attack you were in a state of shock. Trauma. You don't need to downplay what happened to you.'

'Oh.' She gave a shaky laugh. 'Well, to be honest, I was scared shitless. It's true that the kind of work I do means that I wander around in the strangest places, and if you let yourself be frightened by things then you'd never get anything worthwhile done. I'd just take self-portraits of myself in my garden.' She gave another small laugh. 'But, to be honest, I think I almost walked along the canal as a kind of dare to myself – does that sound completely mad to you?'

'No. It sounds reckless, not mad.'

'Well, so I was a bit spooked anyway, walking along in the shadows' – she glanced up at Gabe who gave her an encouraging little nod – 'and then this shape loomed up at me and his hands were all over me. I thought I was going to die, or be drowned. Or raped.' She gave a shudder. 'When I look back on it, I try to tell myself it was nothing, but I thought I was going to be killed, just because I was stupid enough to be by the canal in the middle of the night. I dreamed about it last night and I woke up crying.'

'Did you notice anything about the man?'

She shook her head hopelessly. 'It was dark. This is going to be so pathetic. I think he was fairly short. He may have had closely cropped hair. I've got an image of that in my mind. That's all.'

'White?'

'Yes. Or I think so.'

'Do you remember what he was wearing?'

'No.'

'Or what he wasn't wearing? A suit? A long coat? Jogging shorts?'

She gave a thin smile. 'No, none of that,' she said.

'One last thing,' I said. 'I wonder if you could say anything about the two witnesses.'

'What do you mean?'

'What did they do?'

Bryony looked puzzled. 'I don't understand. You know what they did, they scared the man off.'

I couldn't quite think of what to say. I had another try. 'From what you say, it was all terribly confusing. It might have felt like you were being attacked by three people. Or attacked by two people who were scared off by the third person.'

'Why?'

'I was just wondering.'

Bryony looked thoughtful. 'I'm trying to go over it in my mind. All I can say is what I've said all along. I was attacked by a man and he ran away. That's it.'

'Just the one attacker and two witnesses who scared him off?'

'Yes.' She looked more confused than ever.

'Sure?'

'Yes. No. Well, as sure as I can be of anything, that is.'

'If you give a statement to the police, they'll ask you a lot more questions along those sort of lines. It's amazing what you can remember if you approach it in the right way.'

'I'll do my best, Dr Quinn, I really will.'

'Please call me Kit. When people call me Dr Quinn I look around the room for someone else.'

'All right, Kit. Can I say something else?'

'Anything.'

She swallowed. 'I'm so grateful for everything that's being done for me but . . . but . . .'

'What?'

'I wonder whether it was just an attempt at a mugging. Maybe he was going for my purse.'

'Yes,' I said. 'One of the witnesses mentioned that. He said that you said it was nothing, that you didn't even want to phone the police. He insisted on doing it with his mobile.'

She pulled up her legs even further so that her knees were under her chin. She looked into my tired eyes with her tired eyes. 'Does that seem strange to you?'

I gave my best doctor's smile of reassurance. 'Not at all. Have you ever been walking along the street when you've seen someone trip and fall over? Sometimes they'll give themselves a nasty knock but as often as not they won't wait to get over it. They'll try to walk on as if nothing has happened. It's a strong human impulse to try to insist that things are carrying on as normal. You see it even in quite serious accidents. People with severe bleeding try to continue on their way to work. It's completely natural to try to persuade yourself that nothing serious has happened. Maybe it's the brain trying to protect itself from stress.'

'But it might be true.' There was a tone of appeal in

her voice. 'It might be, mightn't it, just a mugging? A horrible coincidence.'

'You may be right. We'll definitely consider it. But I've already been talking to your husband about this. We won't take any chances.'

'That's good,' she said bleakly.

I leaned forward. 'You've probably already been told this, but I want to tell you again. It's very common for people who've been through experiences like yours to suffer depression. You feel confused about it, you may even blame yourself, or be blamed.'

I looked at Gabe. 'I know what you mean,' he said. 'I know we're sometimes a bit ratty with each other. But I couldn't possibly blame Bry for anything.'

'I didn't mean that,' I said. 'I was just trying to say that these things are difficult for you in ways you don't expect. And it's difficult for partners as well.'

Bryony sat back on the sofa and closed her eyes. 'I just want it all to go away,' she said.

'I think it has, for you,' I said. 'I believe that. What we really want is to make it go away for everybody.'

She leaned back against Gabe, who stroked her hair. Suddenly I felt a bit envious and entirely unnecessary and made an awkward exit.

30

When I turned left, off the busy arterial road and into the cul-de-sac where Will lived, I was slightly taken aback. His house, as he'd said on the phone, was a smallish Victorian semi, the one with a bottle-green door and a black iron gate, not the one with the straggly privet hedge and the boarded-up window on the first floor. What he hadn't said was that these two were the only old houses in a large new estate, with high-rise blocks of flats, a network of walkways and car parks, and a small playground whose roundabout had been chained up. Two teenagers swung on the swings meant for toddlers, smoking and dragging their heels on the rubberized Tarmac. Will's house, with its front garden and neat fencing, looked quite surreal, as if it had been plucked out of some middle-class residential street and been placed here by mistake.

I think I'd been imagining that he would open the door and draw me inside and we'd gaze at each other then fall into each other's arms. Of course, it didn't happen like that. Will opened the door with a cordless phone tucked under his chin, and beckoned me in without saying anything. Then he disappeared into the kitchen with his phone, leaving me standing alone in the living room with the smile dying on my lips.

But at least it gave me the chance to look around a bit. The room was almost empty. If I called out, my voice would probably echo. There were, I saw, precisely four objects in it: a splendidly large and deep mustard-yellow sofa; a sleek hi-fi system in the corner; a revolving CD stack full of discs; and one of those beautiful apothecary chests with dozens of tiny drawers that you buy for several thousand pounds in overpriced antiques shops in north London. And that was all. No table. No other chairs. No TV or video player. No bookshelves. No hooks where coats and jackets hung. No pictures or photographs on the white walls. No random objects scattered round the place. I thought of my flat: however neat and bare it is, it's full of odd things – pens and notepads, books, newspapers and magazines, decorative bowls with dice or keys or a pair of earrings in them, candlesticks, mirrors, glasses, flowers. But here, there was absolutely none of the clutter of daily life.

I slipped off my suede jacket, slung it on the sofa arm, and peered at the CDs. I couldn't find a single name I recognized there. I walked over to the chest and cautiously opened one of the drawers. It was empty. So were the next three. I found a stash of paper-clips in the fifth and a broken chesspiece several drawers later. Nothing more.

'Sorry about that.'

I was startled. He'd padded in silently, like a cat, and caught me snooping among his things, except that he didn't seem to possess any things.

'Do you really live here?'

'How do you mean?'

'Well, this.' I gestured round the room. 'What do you do when you're here? There's nothing in it. There's no sign of you being here. It's spooky, really. It's not so much minimalist as utterly minimal.'

'That's the general idea.'

'How long have you lived here?'

'A couple of years.'

'Two years! You've collected nothing in two years? Where were you before?'

'In a very full house.'

'With a wife?'

'That was one of the things it was full of, yes.'

'So you walked out on everything?'

'You don't go in for small-talk, do you? Do you want a drink?'

'Yes. What have you got?'

I followed him into the kitchen, which bore only a faint resemblance to any kitchen I'd been in before. There was a sink near the back window, a large stainless-steel rubbish bin, a fridge in the corner. But there were none of the usual kitchen units and surfaces, and I couldn't see a cooker. Instead, there was an old pine table against one wall, on which stood a kettle, a toaster, a coffee grinder and two sharp knives.

'Christ, Will, this is a bit weird.'

'Whisky, gin, brandy, vodka, Campari, some strange Icelandic schnapps that I've never opened.' He was rummaging in a tall cupboard. 'Or there's beer and wine in the fridge. Or tomato juice.'

I didn't fancy beer or wine, certainly not tomato juice. I wanted something that I could feel burning my throat and coursing through my veins. 'I'll try the Icelandic stuff.'

'Brave of you. I'd better join you.'

I went to the back door and looked out into the garden. It was dusk, but I could see in the gloom that it consisted of a small lawn and a large bay tree set bang in the middle. Will put several chunks of ice into two tumblers, then glugged in several fingers of a clear liquid.

'Thanks.' I raised my glass to him formally, then tossed

half the drink down my open throat. 'Fuck!' It hit me in the back of my throat and my eyes watered.

'All right?'

'You haven't drunk any.'

He drank without flinching, then set down his tumbler on the table. Yards of floor separated us. He seemed miles away and unreachable.

'I don't really know why you wanted to come,' he said, over the great space that divided us.

I didn't bother to answer. I drank the rest of my liquor in one. The room tipped then righted itself again. Who cared what happened? At least I was here, and something was going to happen. 'Do you want me to go away, then?'

'No.'

'Good. I'm over the limit anyway. So what next?'

'Something to eat?'

'No thanks.'

'Have you slept?'

'No.'

'No sleep, no food.'

'I'm not going to make the first move, Will.' Drink made me brave.

'All right.'

'Because it's your turn.'

'To answer your question, I left because one day I woke up with a hangover and I felt unutterably sick of it all.'

'Of your job?'

'My job, my slickness at it, my amazing ability to obey the letter of the law and never the spirit, my petty triumphs and successes, my drinking, my increasing cocaine habit, my house with its fine period furniture, my bank balance, my briefcase and laptop and mobile phone, which I carried to work early every morning on the underground, pressed up against all the other men just like me. Sick to death of all my things. The more you have the more you find you need. The latest, smallest mobile, fancy gadgets, a watch that's a computer. Sick of the fucking trouser press, the suits and ties, the drinks parties, the meetings with lots of other men in suits just like mine who owned trouser presses and period furniture, the holidays in Cape Cod that people talked about, the conversations about golf and school fees and fine wines. I just woke up and knew I couldn't do it. I couldn't go there for one single day more. It was a bit like alcohol poisoning. I felt sick of myself, allergic to the world I lived in. Disgusted by how oblivious I was to everything around me. Do you know? Every morning, and every evening, I walked past these groups of homeless kids, like the ones I spend my days with now, and past winos and prostitutes, and I literally didn't see them, unless they were in my way. I was blind to them.'

'Then you suddenly saw them?'

'It wasn't exactly the road to Damascus.'

'But it was your conscience that made you leave and start the centre?' I wanted him to say something good about himself.

'I don't use that word unless I'm trying to squeeze a donation for the centre out of a businessman who wants to feel virtuous. Politicians have degraded it. Conscience. Integrity. Honour. Truth. Sincerity. Love.' His voice was scornful. 'It was more like compulsion. Don't make me out to be a crusader. I did it for me, to rescue myself. I'm the only person I'm trying to save. Do you want more drink?'

'OK. Why not? What about your wife?'

'She stayed.'

'In the full house.'
'Yes.'
'Children?'
'No.'
'Do you ever see her?'
'No.'
'Do you miss her?'
'No.'
'Do you get lonely?'
'No. Or not until now.'
'Why now?'
'Why do you think, Kit?'
'Do you do this often?'
'What?'
'What we are about to do.'
'No. Do you?'
'No. Can't you tell?'
'People seem one thing and are actually something quite different.'
'How do I seem?'
'Like someone who's scared and making herself do it anyway.'
'What am I scared of?'
'I don't know. Me?'
'Why should I be scared of you?' I was, though – dread and excitement filled me.
'The world, then. Scared of getting hurt?'
'I'm the one who's supposed to say trite therapeutic things like that.'
'Drink up.'
'Finished. Now what?'
'If I asked you to come upstairs, what would you say?'
'Ask me, and you'll find out.'
'Will you come upstairs?'

'Yes.'

He picked up the bottle by its neck and I followed him out of the kitchen and up the narrow, uncarpeted stairs into his bedroom: one futon, one wardrobe, a tall standard lamp, and unexpectedly cheery yellow curtains, half open, that twitched in the breeze from the open window.

'Undo the buttons on your blouse.'

'Give me the bottle first. I need Dutch courage. There. Like that?'

'Yes. You're really very lovely.'

'Then why do you look as if you're in pain?'

'Because you're lovely.'

'It's all right.'

'You don't want to trust me, Kit.'

'I don't. I don't trust you at all. That's the point.'

'I'll be no good for you.'

'That doesn't really matter at all.'

Afterwards, I lay on his futon and stared out of the window at the gibbous moon in the inky sky. Will lay beside me, silent, looking up at the ceiling through half-closed eyes. Then he said, 'I'm hungry.'

'I'm thirsty.'

'Do you want something to eat?'

'It didn't look as if you kept much food here.'

'I don't. I could get us a takeaway. Italian, Indian, Chinese, Thai, Greek. Or there's even a Japanese not so far off.'

'I don't mind. Anything.'

'I won't be long.' He pulled on his old jeans and a grey sweatshirt. 'Don't go away.'

I lay on the bed and listened to his footsteps clattering down the wooden stairs; heard the front door open and close. I was all alone, in Will's house. After a few minutes, I went into the bathroom. Very clean and functional. I washed myself and put on the thick blue towelling robe that was hanging on the back of the door, then I wandered into the second upstairs room, a square room overlooking the back garden. All there was in here was a grand piano and a piano stool. I touched one of the ivory keys and a single note hung in the air. It sounded a bit out of tune. I opened the lid of the stool and found a few dog-eared pieces of music with pencilled instructions scribbled across the top and a can of beer.

I went downstairs to find something to drink, for my mouth felt dry after all the alcohol. In the hallway, the phone rang and an answering-machine clicked on. 'Will,' said a man's voice, in a stage-whisper. 'Will, it's me, mate. I need to talk to you. Will, are you there? Please? It's urgent.' There was a silence, during which I could hear him breathing heavily. Madly, I held my own breath, as if the caller could somehow hear me too. Then the machine clicked off.

I took a bottle of fizzy water out of the fridge and drank two glasses of it. It was nearly eleven. In the past forty hours, I'd had about two hours' sleep, if that. But I didn't feel tired, not exactly; I felt strangely over-focused. My skin tingled; my heart pounded; my brain raced; all the objects in the room seemed unnaturally clear to me, as if they were back-lit. I went into the living room and sat on the soft, deep sofa with my feet curled up under me. That was how Will found me, when he returned fifteen minutes later. He came into the room carrying a large bag and his face looked preoccupied and wearily bleak – the face he wore when alone. Then he saw me. He didn't smile, but it was as if a shadow moved away from him. I did that, I thought, as I moved up to make room. He didn't say anything, but put his arm around me and pulled me against me. His cheek was cold from the night air. Then he sighed and leaned forward to pull two black trays from his bag.

'That looks beautiful, like a work of art. It's a pity to wreck it.'

'We should be drinking sake with this.'

'I don't want anything more to drink.'

'Here, eat this.'

He fed me a chunk of raw tuna smeared with a hot green paste and dipped into soy sauce, and I chewed it obediently. It didn't taste of fish or brine. It just tasted of freshness. 'Nice.'

'And another.'

'Mmm.'

'Don't close your eyes.'

'No, of course not.'

'Eat this. Kit, Kit.'

I tried to keep my eyes open, but it was all too lovely for me to bear any longer – the warm room, the deep sofa, his dressing-gown with his smell on it wrapped around my naked body, the unfamiliar food, the vague prickle of fear somewhere in my belly, the feel of his hand stroking my hair, the sound of his voice in my ear, calling my name. His breath on my cheek. I felt myself sliding into a blissful darkness.

31

I looked at Michael Doll for a minute before I approached
him. There was a line of men along the edge of the canal.
It was a Wednesday morning. Didn't these people have
jobs to go to? A couple of radios were tuned to different
stations and turned up loud. The fishermen's telescopic
rods were enormously long, sometimes extending back
across the towpath and forward across to the far side of
the canal. As I stood there a young cyclist came along
the path forcing much grumbling and moving of rods
out of the way.

There were one or two clusters of fishermen, huddled
together over a cup of something warm poured from a
Thermos flask, but mainly they sat alone. Somehow
Michael Doll was even more alone, further along the
bank, away from the others. Had they heard about him?
His dog sat beside him, motionless except for the saliva
that dribbled from between his yellow teeth. I walked
towards him, stepping over rods and between plastic
boxes of hooks, reels, maggots. Although it wasn't a cold
day, Doll was wearing a red and black checked coat like
a Canadian lumberjack and a rather jaunty navy blue
cap. He was looking directly ahead, and as I got closer I
could hear that he was singing under his breath. Then it
was as if he had felt my gaze on his face, like a breath of
wind, and he turned. He smiled, but not with surprise.
He had an air of expectancy that chilled me. 'Hello, Kit,'
he said. 'How are you?'

'Fine,' I said, pushing my hands into my pockets

and looking around. 'I've never actually seen you fish before.'

He gave a little throaty chuckle. 'It's a good life down here,' he said. 'Good people.' He lifted the rod up. There was nothing on the hook. 'They nibble the worms off, canny blighters.' Another chuckle. He moved the rod so that the hook swung towards him and he caught it deftly. He was sitting on a fold-up camp stool. Down by his left boot there was a tobacco tin full of earthworms. He sorted among them with his fingers until he had apparently found one with which he was satisfied.

'The others seem to be using maggots,' I said.

'Maggots is a waste of money,' he said. 'You can dig up the worms round the back. Many as you want. Besides, worms is more meaty.' He almost closed one eye and narrowed the other as he lined up the unfortunate worm so that it could be impaled on his hook. 'You know, it's a funny thing, people worry about foxes and baby seals but they don't worry about fishes or worms. I mean, like, look at this worm. People say a worm don't feel pain but look at this worm.' He pushed the point of his hook through the worm. Some grey liquid came out. Did worms have blood? I thought I'd done it in biology when I was about thirteen but I couldn't remember. 'Look,' he said unnecessarily, 'it's wriggling more. You'd think for all the world that it was in pain and trying to escape, wouldn't you? Steady now.' This last was addressed to the worm. Far from escaping, the worm was now impaled a second time on the barbed hook. 'Who's to say that a worm don't feel pain like you or me do?'

'So why do you do it?'

Doll swung the rod again and the worm disappeared into the dark waters of the canal. The little float tipped and bobbed and finally settled in an upright position. 'I don't think about it,' he said.

'Yes, you do. You were just talking about it.'

He frowned with concentration. 'Well it goes into my brain, if that's what you mean. But it don't bother me. It's just a worm, isn't it?'

'I suppose so. Do you catch many fish?'

'Sometimes I get ten. Sometimes I sit the whole day in the rain and get nothing.'

'What do you do with them?'

'I just throw them back. Except sometimes the hook's in too deep. You pull the hook out and it rips their mouth or pulls their guts out with it. Then I snap their neck and give them to a cat that lives round where my flat is. Loves them, he does.'

I pushed my hands deeper into my pockets and tried to maintain an expression of polite interest. I could hear Doll muttering to himself, but then I listened more closely and realized he was talking to the fish, the invisible fish down in the oily dark water, trying to coax them on to his hook. 'There you are,' he whispered. 'Come on, my beauties. Come on.' He lifted the hook out of the water. There was no fish but half of the worm was gone. He gave a wheezing laugh. 'Crafty buggers.'

'Michael, I'm really here to talk about what happened on the canal.' He murmured something unintelligible. 'Didn't you think it was strange that you should be here when this happened?'

He looked round. 'Not strange,' he said. 'I'm always here. It's my patch. If he wants to kill girls on my patch then I'm here.'

'All right,' I said. 'This is your patch. You know it. Did you recognize the man? Was there anything familiar about him?'

'Nah,' said Doll. 'It was all on top of me so quick. Dark. Saw nothing.'

'Are you all right, Michael? You haven't been attacked again?'

'Nah,' he said, smiling at me. 'It's all forgotten. Forgotten and forgiven.'

I looked warily at his float. The worm would have been chewed about three-quarters of the way down by now. I didn't feel I could face the torment of a second worm at this time of the morning. 'Try to think, Michael,' I said. 'If you remember anything, anything at all, just get in touch with me. You can get in touch with me via the police.'

'Nah, I got your number.'

'All right,' I said doubtfully.

'I know where you live.'

'Or you can tell the police.'

'Look, a fish, a bloody fish.'

There it was flashing silver dangling from Doll's line. I left at speed before there was any chance of watching its intestines pulled through its mouth.

Walking home I passed a coffee shop with a temptingly empty table outside in the sunshine. I sat down, ordered a double espresso and tried to make some sense of the clutter in my brain.

When the second cup arrived, I phoned Oban. Yes, Bryony *had* given them a statement and he was in low spirits. 'As you know we got fuck all out of Mickey Doll that made any sense, pardon my French, and as far as our description goes we've got Terence Mack's fairly tall man and Bryony's fairly short man. Maybe we can get the two of them together and they can get their stories straight.'

'It was a scramble in the middle of the night,' I said. 'What did you expect?'

'I can't believe that this bastard broke cover, people saw him, and we've still got bloody nothing. What are *you* up to?'

'I'm sitting in a café drinking coffee.'

'I wish I was bloody with you. By the way, are you going to give us some kind of report on the incident? What do you reckon about it?'

'Bryony told me that she thought it might have been a straightforward mugging gone wrong, nothing to do with the case at all.'

'Yeah, she said the same to us. What's the matter with her? Doesn't she want to be famous?'

'We should consider it.'

'Do you want to put her in charge of the inquiry? I'd be glad to be shot of it.' I couldn't help laughing. 'Are you still there, Kit?'

'We don't want to be sidetracked,' I said. 'It's not just Bryony. It doesn't quite fit the pattern.'

'What do you mean it doesn't fit the pattern? It fits too many bloody patterns. There's the spot on the canal, there's Doll. That should be enough, even for you.'

'I was thinking of the attack itself. The other two were done quite skilfully, in a way. But this was so clumsy.'

'Come off it, Kit. These killers escalate, they get more reckless. They need to take more risks to get the same thrill. If the witnesses hadn't been a wimp and a headcase we'd have had him. And as for that bloody headcase . . .'

'I don't know, Dan, I just went and talked to Doll down by the canal.'

'Don't tell me. You think he's too nice to have done it.'

'The opposite. If Doll were a murderer, he would be

269

much worse than this. I should know. I've just watched him putting a worm on a hook.'

'Is that the basis for your judgement?'

'One of them.'

'Well, I'll keep you away from my thirteen-year-old, then. You should see what he does with beetles and a magnifying glass.'

My coffee cup was empty. I couldn't manage any more. My head was already buzzing. The sun had gone behind a cloud. It was surprisingly cold.

'So what are your plans?' I asked.

There was a silence on the line for a few seconds so that I began to think we had been cut off.

'I've got a horrible feeling that what we're really doing is sitting and waiting for him to do something even more stupid and get caught. In the meantime we're going to try some more publicity. I've briefed some journalists on the new attack. I was trying to persuade Mrs Teale to go on television but she didn't seem keen. Maybe you could work on her.'

'All right.'

'Any other ideas? What are *you* up to?'

Now *I* was silent for a few seconds. What *was* I up to? 'I suppose I'm trying to look at everything again. I have this feeling we're missing something.'

'Are you looking for some connection between them all?'

'I don't know.'

'But, Kit,' said Oban, with only the smallest hint of exasperation, 'we've already got connections. You established one of the main ones. Why are you looking for others?'

'I don't know,' I said, suddenly lacking in all energy. 'Maybe I'm just blundering around in the dark.'

'You said it, not me,' said Oban. 'Let me know if you find the light switch.'

And now he really was gone.

I went into the clinic and spent a busy day taking calls, answering mail, chairing a case meeting on a boy who had set fire to his foster-home, sitting in on interviews of two hopeless applicants for a job. I made concerned comments, I discussed and argued, and all the time my mind was somewhere else. I didn't get home until eight and there was a note on the table: 'Out. Back very late. The weirdo called. Love J.' Had he remembered something?

I had a long bath during which I briefly fell asleep. I knew that you could fall asleep while driving, then crash and die. Could you fall asleep and drown in the bath? I didn't take the risk. I got out and put on a dressing-gown. I phoned Will. No answer. I looked in the fridge and found a bowl of rice there, so I ate it standing up. It would have been better heated, with olive oil and Parmesan on it. Then I ate two gherkins and a tomato. There was an open bottle of wine in the fridge and I poured myself a glass.

I turned on the radio and, with no surprise, realized that the voice I heard belonged to Seb Weller and he was talking about Lianne and Philippa. God, he was a pro. Words flowed smoothly from him, no hesitations, occasionally a small pause to establish his spontaneity.

'Obviously this case touches on a central nerve for many women living in the area,' he said. 'I often think that men do not understand it properly.'

'Except you, of course,' I muttered, then felt ashamed of myself.

'Men don't know what it is like for women to walk

down a dark street, stand in a lonely subway hearing footsteps coming towards them, lie in bed at night and listen to the strange sounds outside. All women, bold or cautious, always have this hidden basement of fear. I like to call it . . .' he paused once more '. . . like to call it their red room . . .'

'Oh, Christ!' I exclaimed loudly.

'A red room where all the things they fear the most . . .'

The phone rang and I banged the off-knob on the radio angrily.

'It's me.'

'Who?'

'Mike.'

It took me a second to connect this name with Michael Doll. So it was Mike now.

'Hello.'

'What are you doing?'

I felt a slight wave of nausea. Was he going to ask me next what I was wearing? I pulled my dressing-gown more firmly around me. 'Why are you calling, Michael? Have you remembered something?'

'I was just calling,' he said. 'You just called on me, down at the canal. I'm just calling you.' There was a pause. 'It was good to see you.'

'I've got to go now,' I said.

'That's all right,' he said.

'Good-night.'

'Sleep well.'

I didn't. Not after that. Not for hours. I woke up feeling as if I hadn't slept at all. My tongue felt as if it had been glued to the roof of my mouth. I hadn't drunk that much, had I? It was half past eight when I got up. Julie was sitting at the table with a pot of coffee, looking through a newspaper. Others were scattered on the table. It felt like Sunday morning, but it was Thursday. She'd gone to sleep about four hours after me and she looked like someone in an advertisement for being young and fresh-faced.

'What's up?' I said.

'I went to get a paper and there was stuff about your crime in the papers, so I bought some of them.'

'It's not really *my* crime.'

'It's amazing. There's a woman who says she can find the murderer using crystals. There's someone else who thinks it's to do with the moon. There's another psychologist. There's a photofit picture.' She held up the newspaper. 'He definitely reminds me of someone. It's been driving me mad.'

'Buster Keaton,' I said.

'That's right. But he's dead, isn't he?'

'I think so. Also, it's the way he looked in about 1925.'

So that was what they had got out of Terence and Bryony. God, they must be desperate.

'It doesn't mention you, though,' said Julie, in a slightly disappointed tone. Maybe she suspected that I'd been making it all up, that I wasn't really involved, or just at some very, very low level. Tea-girl or something. 'Do you want to read it?'

'I don't think so.'

I drank some coffee and dressed quickly. There were things I wanted to do. If I drew a blank, then I would call a halt, make an attempt to become normal again, stop seeing patterns everywhere, shapes in the clouds.

'We need to talk,' said Julie, as I rushed past on my way out.

'Later,' I said, racing down the stairs.

273

As I came out of the door, I sensed someone close by. I could smell it. I turned.

'Morning, Kit.'

It was Doll, his dog beside him. He was wearing the same jacket as the day before and the same hat. He had added a scarf, which was tied around his neck with two ferociously tight knots. How could he ever untie them? And how long had he been waiting for me?

'Michael,' I said. 'What's up?'

'I need to talk to you.'

'You've got some evidence?'

'I just need to talk to you.'

'I'm in a hurry.'

'I'm not.'

The oddness of the reply stopped me in my tracks. 'I've got to go,' I said.

I began to walk but he walked along with me. 'I wanted to call round,' he said. 'I wanted to see you.'

'What about?'

'You understand. I need to talk about things.'

I stopped. 'You mean the murders?'

He shook his head too vigorously. It looked as if it must hurt. 'Things. You understand.'

I tried to think clearly. What I really wanted was to get away and never see him again. But did he have something important to tell me? 'Michael, I'm working on these murders. You know that. If you've anything to say about that, I'll listen. I haven't time for anything else.'

'Why?'

'Because I'm busy.'

'That's all you care about, isn't it? You only care about me because you think I might tell you something. You're like all the others.'

274

'Which others?'

'I'll talk to you later,' he said, his face a fiery red now. 'I'll talk to you later when I feel like it. I've got my eye on you now, Kit. But I'm going. I'm busy as well, you know. It's not just bloody you.'

And he was away, muttering and twitching. A young man walking towards him crossed the road.

32

'I don't know how I can help you,' said Pam Vere. She had placed herself in the armchair opposite me, but upright, with her hands tense on the armrests, as if she was about to stand up again and show me the door.

I sat in the room where Philippa used to sit, where the light flooded in through the french windows. The bouquets of flowers that had been standing on every surface last time I'd been here had all gone now; people lose interest pretty quickly. Only a vase of massed pink and dark purple sweet peas stood on the table between us – I remembered that her talkative friend, Tess, had said they were Philippa's favourite flowers. There was a large black-and-white photograph of the dead woman on the mantelpiece behind Mrs Vere, so that in looking at the mother I was also looking at her murdered daughter, whose grave smile and dark eyes seemed to be staring intently into the room she'd left.

Pam Vere seemed to have aged ten years since I last saw her. She was probably still in her fifties, or early sixties, but her face was pale and weary, and the wrinkles on it were so deep that they were like grooves carved in stone. Her mouth was a thin line. There were dark smudges under her eyes. When I had been here before, I had been touched by Emily, and had imagined what it must be like for her to lose her mother so young, but I hadn't really imagined what it must be like for Pam to lose her daughter, her beloved only child – not until now, when I looked into her bleak face and saw how her hands, when they released the arms of the chair, trembled on her lap.

'I don't know how I can help you,' she repeated.

'I'm so sorry to disturb you again. I just wondered if it was possible to look through some of Philippa's things.'

'Why?'

'Have the police already been through her possessions?'

'No. Of course not. Why on earth would they? She was killed by a mad person, out there . . .' Her hands gestured towards the windows.

'I'd like to take a look.'

'You don't want to talk to Emily again, do you?'

'Not at the moment. Is she here?'

'She's upstairs, in her room. I look after her at the moment, most of the time at least. I come in the mornings and I stay until her father gets back. Until things get on an even keel. She spends half her time in her room. She'll be going to nursery school, anyway.'

'How's she doing?'

'There's a cardigan Philippa used to wear a lot, which she uses as a blanket. She curls up on it and just lies there sucking her thumb. The doctor said I should let her. He said she was coming to terms with Philippa's death in her own way.'

'That sounds right,' I said, looking at her intently. Was I making her angry? Was I blundering in?

'Jeremy does his interminable crosswords and cries when he thinks no one can hear him. Emily lies on her carpet . . .' She rubbed her eyes. 'I don't know. I don't know what's best.'

'What do you do?' I asked.

'Me?' She gave a faint shrug. 'I get through the day.' She stood up abruptly. 'What are you looking for?'

'Did she have somewhere she kept her things – letters, diaries, things like that?'

She took a deep breath, flinching as if there were a pain deep in her chest. I knew that she must be toying with the idea of telling me to go away and never come back.

'There's the desk in the bedroom upstairs,' she said finally. 'I'm not sure there's much in there, except bills and letters. We haven't been through all her things yet.' She glanced up at her daughter's photograph for an instant, then looked away. 'Jeremy's packed up most of her clothes now. He gave most of them to Oxfam. It makes me feel odd to think of strangers walking around wearing her nice dresses. She had some lovely clothes, you know. The police took away her diary.'

'Yes, I know.'

'There's nothing to find. She just went to the park one day, and she didn't come home.'

'Can I see her desk anyway?'

'All right. What does it matter?'

It felt illicit to be in the large bedroom, which had clearly been decorated by a woman, and still looked as if it was shared by a couple, with a cluttered dressing-table against one wall, and two plumped-up pillows on the bed. But one side of the open wardrobe was empty, except for dozens of bare hangers on the rail, and only men's clothes were slung on the chair near the door.

The bureau-style desk was near the window that overlooked their back garden. There was a little jug of dried flowers, a cordless telephone and several photographs on its top. I sat down at it, looking once more into the face of Philippa Burton, this time holding a younger Emily, legs wrapped around her mother's waist, round flushed cheek pressed against Philippa's smooth pale one.

I pulled down the lid. Inside, it was unpromisingly neat and empty. I started with the little compartments, lined with green baize. There were pens, sharpened pencils, paper glue, Sellotape, two books of stamps, one first and one second-class. Also a stack of headed stationery, white envelopes, brown envelopes, ink cartridges in a small plastic bag, blank postcards, a collection of bills with 'Paid' written across them. I examined them, but there was nothing odd there: £80 to unblock the drain; £109 for a case of wine; £750 for a set of eight ladder-backed chairs, including two carvers; that kind of thing. There was a bundle of drawings by Emily – people with heads and legs and no bodies, blotchy rainbows, wonky flowers, crooked patterns. Phillippa had written the dates when they were drawn on the back; clearly she had been a methodical woman.

I found a stiff glossy card showing National Trust paints that were called things like sepia and old linen, saffron yellow and drawing-room red. There were circulars from charities appealing for donations; three invitations, inviting Philippa and Jeremy to parties that she would never attend now; quite a few summer postcards – scrawled, barely legible messages sent by Pam and Luke, Bill and Carrie, Rachel and John, Donald and Pascal, sent from Greece, Dorset, Sardinia, Scotland. And there were also a couple of handwritten letters. One was from a woman called Laura, thanking Philippa and Jeremy for the lovely dinner. The other was from someone called Roberta Bishop, introducing herself as a near-neighbour and proposing that Philippa should come to the next residents' meeting to discuss parking on the road and the plan for traffic calmers. She used lots of exclamation marks.

I shut the lid and opened the first drawer. A stash of A4

paper, a pile of holiday brochures, old bank statements chronologically arranged and neatly clipped together. I leafed through them, looking for anything that might snag my attention. Nothing did. Philippa hadn't been extravagant. She spent about the same amount each month; withdrew the same amount each week from the cash machine. I was about to close the drawer when I felt something right at the back, pushed up behind the pile of paper: a slim paperback book with a pink cover called *Lucy's Dream*. It was, it announced on the cover, 'an erotic novel for women'. There was a soft-focus image of a woman with blurred bare breasts, the dark shadow of one nipple, head thrown back, hair falling over her shoulders like water. I toyed with the idea of taking the book away before Jeremy started to clear out his wife's desk, but decided against it. Philippa wouldn't mind now what he found out.

In the bottom drawer there was a large doll in an unopened box. Her name, apparently, was Sally; she had brown ringlets, long brown lashes, and wide blue eyes that stared up through the Cellophane. She gave me the shivers. There was a dummy and a bottle tied into the cardboard. The writing on the box announced that if you gave Sally water, she cried and wet herself. Probably, I thought, Philippa had bought the doll for Emily; maybe for a birthday that was coming up. There was also a small notepad, which I opened. On the first page was a shopping list with items ticked off. The second page was a list of things to do: ring plumber, buy shoelaces, defrost fridge, take car to garage for service.

The next page was covered in rather superior doodles of various kinds of fruit. The fourth page was empty, apart from several London phone numbers jotted in the margin. The fifth page had a few words scrawled across it, which I glanced at casually as I licked one finger, ready to turn over the leaf. I stopped dead, finger in mid-air.

'Lianne' was written in a scrawl. I stared at the letters, hardly daring to move in case they should disappear, blur into something else. Suddenly my mouth felt dry. The word didn't change, however long I stared at it. It still said 'Lianne'.

I looked down the page, gazed as if I was in a dream. For there, near the bottom and ringed in question marks and in smaller writing, still unmistakably Philippa's: 'Bryony Teal'. Lianne and Bryony Teale, misspelt. Philippa had written down the names of the two other victims. There was another name, as well, with a little flower doodled next to it, symbol of the word. 'Daisy'.

Very carefully, as if it was a bomb that would go off in my hand, I lifted the notepad and dropped it into my bag. I closed the drawer.

For a minute, I sat at the desk and stared out of the window, allowing the knowledge of what I had just seen to sink through my brain and take root there. A small dark cloud moved across the sun, so that the garden lay in shadows. As I looked, Emily, dressed in denim shorts and a striped top, ran on to the lawn and stood there, calling something to her grandmother who was still in the house. Suddenly she looked up and saw me, sitting at her mother's window and for one terrible moment her whole face lit up into unbearable joy and she stretched out her arms to me; her mouth opened to call out a name, a word. Then her body sagged and her arms dropped limply to her side. I felt tears prick my eyes.

I stood up and left the room, the bag with its precious cargo slung over my shoulder. All that I could think about were those names in the notebook. And that I had told Bryony she was not in danger.

33

I phoned in my apologies to the management meeting at the Welbeck. I cancelled my lunch with Poppy. I sat in the car next to Oban, while he swore and sweated and told me for the hundredth time that it made no fucking sense. His voice was just a drone, like the traffic. I pressed my fingers against my temples. There had to be an explanation. We were just looking at this in the wrong way, somehow. If we approached it from a different angle, we would see it differently. All the things that made no sense at all would shine with meaning. I closed my eyes and tried to relax my mind, so that the knot of incomprehension would unsnarl. I waited for clarity to float down. Nothing happened. I groaned to myself and rubbed my eyes. Beside me, Oban's face was glum. He wasn't looking forward to this visit either.

His mobile rang and he picked it up. 'Yes,' he barked. 'Yes. Go on.' His expression changed, and he leaned forward slightly in his seat, gripping the steering-wheel with his free hand. 'Say that again. OK, OK, we'll be on our way back in, say, half an hour. No more. Stay put.'

He put the phone down. 'Fuck,' he said once more.
'What?'
'Fuck.'
'Yeah, but what else, Daniel?'
He pulled up outside the Teales' house with a shriek of brakes. 'You'll never believe what I just heard.'
'Tell me! What?'

'No time now, I'll save it,' he said, and sprang from the car.

'No,' she said, in a whisper. Her face drained of colour as she stared at us. Her eyes looked huge and dark. 'No!' She spoke louder this time, fiercely, and lifted both hands to her mouth as if she was praying. 'I don't understand. It can't be true. What does it mean?'

'We don't know,' I said. I glanced briefly at Oban to see if he wanted to add anything to my bald statement, but he was sitting perfectly still, staring down at his hands, which were resting on the kitchen table, as if he was trying to remember a fragment of a dream.

She opened her mouth to say something, but then dropped her head into her hands. Her glorious hair hung over her face like a curtain. 'Can't be happening,' I heard her mutter. And then again. 'It can't be happening.'

Behind us on the cooker something hissed then boiled over. A smell of burning sugar filled the kitchen but Bryony didn't move. Oban lumbered to his feet and lifted a pan off the hob, then came back to where Bryony was crouched over the table.

'One of the victims wrote down your name,' I said. 'Yet you say that you never met her?'

'I didn't,' she said slowly. 'I really didn't.'

Oban lowered his big, tired face into his hands.

'You're sure, Bryony? We meet so many people, maybe you didn't know her name. Maybe she knew *you*.'

'I've never met her. Don't you think I'd have remembered, with all the stuff in the papers? I've never set eyes on her. I'd never heard her name before she was killed.'

'Nor Lianne?'

'For God's sake, I didn't meet her. What more can I say?' Her voice was a wail.

'What about the name Daisy? Daisy Gill?' This from Oban, who had suddenly lifted his head.

'No! No! Who's she? Another victim?'

Oban silently handed her a photograph I had never seen before. The police can work fast when they have to. It was one of those strips of four, taken in a photo booth, of a girl with a peaky triangular face and spiky black hair. In the first she was serious, her lips slightly open to show a chipped tooth. In the second she was beginning to grin, and was glancing sideways, presumably at some invisible friend. In the third, Daisy was giggling, and had shifted sideways, so that the left slice of her face was cut off. In the fourth, she was gone and only a hand waved in the air.

Bryony stared at the photo for a minute then pushed it away, shaking her head violently. 'No,' she spluttered, then burst into tears. I leaned across the table and took her hand. She held on to it as if she was drowning and only I could save her.

'Yet Philippa Burton wrote down your name before she died,' said Oban quietly, almost as if he was talking to himself.

'I know she fucking did!' snapped Bryony, through her tears. 'I heard you loud and clear. Sorry. Sorry. Shooting the messenger and all that. This is a shock, to say the least.' She wiped away her tears with the heel of her hand, and made a visible effort to compose herself, sitting up straighter in the chair and pushing her hair behind her ears. 'I need to get a grip on this. Shall I get us all some coffee?'

'I never say no to coffee,' I replied, at the same moment as Oban said, 'Not for me, thanks.'

She stood up in one graceful movement. She was wearing a long black cotton skirt with a black T-shirt over it and her feet were bare. There was a silver chain around her ankle.

'Give me a few seconds to let this sink in,' she said, as she padded over to the kettle. 'Please.'

Oban smiled tiredly at me and undid the top button of his shirt. His blue eyes seemed even smaller and paler than usual, and he kept blinking them, as if he could somehow clear his vision. His straggly hair was greasy and his face unshaven. On the way over here, between frantic calls on his mobile, he had turned to me and said, 'I want you with me on this from now on.' It hadn't sounded peremptory, but humble, as if he had turned from boss to supplicant in an instant. There was no doubt that I was the hero of the hour: the woman who had seen what was invisible to everyone else. I didn't feel particularly good about it. I had discovered a pattern, sure, but one that made no sense. Rather, it actually destroyed whatever sense there had been remaining to us. In the meantime, there was a killer out there.

I picked up the picture of Daisy Gill and stared at it. There was a stud in her eyebrow and, I saw, one in her tongue. There was a locket round her neck. In the third photo, the one where she was sliding out of the frame, I could see it more clearly. It was a little heart, like the one that Lianne had been wearing when she was killed, bearing the word 'Best . . .' I wondered if Daisy's locket said '. . . Friend'.

I watched Bryony as she spooned coffee into two mugs. She was biting her lower lip and frowning slightly, but when she felt my gaze on her she turned her head and gave me a rueful grimace.

'Is your husband here?' I asked.

'Gabe? No, he's just gone down the road to the post office. He'll be here any minute. He doesn't usually work until mid-afternoon. Here, you don't take milk, do you?'

'No milk, no sugar. Thanks.'

She sat down at the kitchen table again, wrapping her fingers around her mug as if for comfort. Suddenly she looked terribly young and vulnerable.

'All right,' she said to us. 'What happens now?'

Oban cleared his throat, and said, with portentous meaninglessness, 'We'll be making extensive inquiries.'

Bryony stared at him, looking baffled.

'Look,' I said, 'it makes no obvious sense that a victim should know the identities of two other victims or potential victims. We don't know when she wrote down the names, of course, so we don't know if Lianne was already dead, or not.' I hesitated for a beat, but she was an intelligent woman: she already knew what I was about to say. 'One thing it seems to suggest is that it wasn't just a mugger by the canalside.'

She nodded. Her lips were white.

'And that the killer isn't just acting randomly,' I added gently.

'No,' she murmured. 'I see.'

'So the police will be spending some time with you now, trying to find out . . .'

As I spoke, I heard the sound of a key turning in the front door, then someone whistling tunelessly in the hall.

'Gabe!' called Bryony. 'Gabe, I'm in the kitchen. With the police.'

The whistling stopped abruptly. When he came in, he was shrugging off a battered leather jacket. His face was tense. 'What's happened?' he asked. 'Bry? Are you OK?'

'Please don't be alarmed, Mr Teale,' said Oban, but

Bryony cut in, 'Philippa Burton wrote my name down before she was killed.'

Gabriel opened his mouth but didn't seem able to say anything: he just stared at her, at us. He looked absolutely stricken.

'Mine and the girl Lianne's, and someone called Daisy,' continued Bryony slowly, as if to make sure he was taking it in. His horror seemed to give her new calm and resolve. 'Daisy Gill, did you say?'

'That's right, Mrs Teale.'

'So it looks like it wasn't just a mugging. And it looks as if he wanted to get *me*, not just anyone.'

Gabriel came over and knelt beside her chair. He gathered both her hands in his and kissed them, and then he buried his head in her lap. She stroked his dark, tousled hair softly, then took his head and lifted it so that he was looking at her. 'It's all right, you know,' she said. I thought she was probably reassuring herself as well as him. 'It's all going to be all right, I promise. Nothing will happen. Do you hear, my darling?'

'Can we ask you a few more questions before we leave you in the capable hands of my detectives?' said Oban.

Gabriel got up, and stood behind Bryony, both hands on her shoulders.

'Do you know a man called Will Pavic?' asked Oban.

I stared at him – why was he asking that?

'I don't think so. Do we, Gabe?'

'Well, of course I know who he is,' said Gabriel. 'I mean, most people know him in this area.'

'Why?' Oban asked. 'I mean, I don't even know the woman who lives next door, let alone the couple across the road.'

Gabriel raised his palms. 'I meant, we're all in the

same kind of world. I run a community theatre and one of the things we do is to try and get some of the people who feel most isolated and abandoned by their community involved again. He runs a hostel for young people. And he's kind of famous, isn't he? He's always, er, how shall I put it? Making waves. We come across each other, sure. That's all, though. Why? Why do you ask about him?'

'That's all for now,' Oban said. 'Detective Inspector Furth will be wanting to talk to you, though.'

We left them in the kitchen, Gabriel with his hands still on his wife's shoulders; she with her head twisted round to look up at him. She looked terrified, and I was flooded by a sense of dread.

'What do you make of this, Kit?' Oban said, as we drove back towards the station. 'Guess what I heard on the way over: three calls were made between the Burton household and Pavic's centre during the month leading up to Mrs Burton's death.'

'Oh,' I said. I felt cold to the bones, though the day was sticky.

'Oh? Is that all? Jesus, Kit, did you hear? The first two calls were just a minute or so long. The final one lasted eighty-seven minutes. What do you make of that, eh?'

'I don't know.'

'Pavic, eh? This is going to be interesting.'

'Very interesting,' I said slowly. Then: 'I think,' I said painfully, 'that I ought to mention something.'

'Hang on.' He punched some numbers into his phone. 'Tell me later.'

'All right.'

I leaned my forehead against the window and briefly closed my eyes. What a colossal mess.

34

We pulled in at the police station and Oban leaped out and set off at speed so that I had to run to keep up with him.

'What are we doing?' I said breathlessly, to the back of his head.

'Talking to some people.'

A uniformed officer joined from a corridor to one side and moved into step with Oban. 'Is he here yet?' Oban asked.

'He's in Two,' the man replied. 'You want me to talk to him?'

'We'll do it straight away. Won't take a minute.'

I followed Oban as he turned left and then right down the corridor. We came to a door and Oban knocked briskly. It opened and a policewoman stepped out. She nodded respectfully.

'Is he all right?'

'Don't know, sir,' said the woman. 'He hasn't really opened his mouth. Except to yawn.'

'Stay here,' he said, to her, not to me. 'We won't be more than five minutes.'

He held the door open for me and I stepped inside. I don't know what I was expecting. I hadn't really had time to think. So when I saw Will Pavic I felt as if, quite unexpectedly, I had been punched in the face. He was leaning on the far side of the table, his hands in his pockets. He looked round and caught my eye. Even my legs felt unsteady. He displayed almost no reaction except for the smallest trace of a sardonic smile. He was wearing a grey suit and a white shirt with no tie. I wondered if he had actually been arrested. Did they still take ties away from men to stop them hanging themselves? I turned towards Oban. 'I didn't . . .' was all I managed at first. 'I didn't realize . . .'

'Mr Pavic has kindly come in for a quick word. Obviously we need to clear one or two things up. Please sit down.'

Oban gestured at one of the chairs by the table. Will sat down. He still didn't speak. I leaned on the wall just inside the door, as far away from him as I could get. I looked at him but his bored gaze was on the table. It was an expression I already recognized, unyielding, opaque. I was gibbering by the door but Oban was affable and relaxed, sitting down opposite Will as if they were having a drink together.

'There've been developments in the murder case involving Lianne and Philippa Burton.' No response from Will. Oban gave a cough. 'Maybe you know there was a further attack by the canal on a woman named Bryony Teale. I think you may know her husband, Gabriel.'

'I've heard of him,' Will said tonelessly. 'I don't know him.'

'He'd heard of you. But then, you're pretty well known, aren't you, Mr Pavic? And you'd had contact with Lianne, of course. Until this morning, I must admit that I doubted there was anything that connected the women in this case.'

Will's eyes narrowed and the sour smile became more apparent, but he didn't speak.

'You've never come across Bryony Teale?' Oban continued. 'She's a photographer. Apparently she spends a lot of time walking around this area, in the streets and by the canal.'

'No,' Will said.

'What about Philippa Burton? Do you know her? Have you met her? Heard of her?'

Behind my back I clenched my fists, my fingernails digging into the palms of my hands.

Will shook his head. 'No,' he said.

'Why should you?' said Oban. 'She lives over in Hampstead. Married to a businessman. But I suppose you meet all sorts of people.'

No reply. This time he looked over at me. I didn't look away. I tried to make a face at him conveying that, although I was a part of the investigation, I was still aware of the awkwardness of the situation and also how completely unnecessary it was to interrogate him in this way. It was a lot for one expression to convey, and it probably came out as a form of panic. It didn't seem to matter, though. Will was looking at me as if I was a coat Oban had hung up on the way in.

'As I was saying,' said Oban, 'I wasn't convinced of any sort of link. I just assumed women were being attacked at random. Dr Quinn, though, she nagged away at the idea of a link. Now she's found a note kept by Philippa Burton. It was all there: Lianne's name, Bryony Teale's. Amazing, don't you reckon? Two of the victims' names written down by the other victim.'

Will gave a tired shrug. 'What's this about?'

'That's what I was getting on to. We checked her phone calls for the last month or so. It was mostly what you'd expect, her mum, husband at work, couple of friends, a travel agent, that sort of stuff, but there was a funny thing. On July the ninth, a call was made from the house to your hostel. Now, I know what you're going to say, but it wasn't to the payphone you've got in the hallway, the one that people use to do their drug deals.'

'They don't use that phone to make drug deals,' Will said. 'I think you'll find that dealers prefer their own mobile phones.'

'The point I was making is that the call was made to the phone in your office. We were interested in any comment you might like to make on that.'

If this had been an exam testing impassivity, Will would have got ten out of ten. But it wasn't an exam, and I knew that any normal person in Will's situation would have been startled by the connection between the women, then thoroughly taken aback by the call made to his own phone. A normal innocent person would have started behaving like a guilty person. Will just looked bored. 'I have no comment,' he said.

'Do you mean you're refusing to answer? That is your right.'

'No, I don't mean that. I don't know what sort of comment you're expecting. Ask me questions and I'll answer them.'

'Did you talk on the phone to Philippa Burton?'
'No.'
'Do other people have access to the phone?'
Another shrug. 'Probably.'
'I don't want "probably". Yes or no.'
Will clenched his jaw. 'Yes,' he said.
'Supervised access?'
'I'm out a lot. My assistant, Fran, is there most of the time. We have lots of casual helpers and volunteers. But I'm sure the phone is left unattended at times.'

'Was Lianne staying at the hostel at that time?'

'She never stayed at the hostel. She might have been around.'

'It's an important point because this call was made before either of the murders occurred.'

'Obviously,' said Will.

'I'm sorry,' said Oban. 'Am I missing something? What's so obvious?'

Will drummed his fingers lightly on the table. 'It's not important,' he said.

'But what did you mean?'

Will sighed. 'If these people were talking to each other, then it was before they were murdered. That's all I meant.'

'Who said they were talking to each other?'

'You did.'

'No. I said a call had been made from Philippa's phone to yours. She could have talked to you. For example. Except, of course, now you've assured us that she didn't. But it might have been someone else. Or else somebody else rang from that phone. There are endless possibilities. So it would now be more useful than ever to know when Lianne was at the hostel. Do you have records?'

'They're not very precise.'

'That's a pity,' Oban said, his benign tone cracking at the edges. 'Some detailed records might have been extremely helpful.'

Will pushed back his chair, the way people used to do after finishing large Victorian meals. Its metal legs squeaked horribly on the linoleum floor. He looked engaged for the first time, which with Will Pavic was the same as saying he was angry. 'You know,' he said, 'after years of experience, I've discovered that the only way to stop people like you getting at my records is not to keep them.'

For a moment Oban concentrated very hard on removing invisible dirt from his fingernails. 'Mr Pavic,

I'm not much interested in whatever political point it is you're trying to make. A young woman who spent time at your hostel has been murdered. Another victim called the hostel. I'm sorry if you find that boring.'

Then there was a silence. When Will spoke his voice was very quiet, but also clear and icy, so I could hear it from across the room. 'I work with these people all the time,' he said. 'They're invisible. Something happens and people like you get terribly interested. Then you go away. So you'll forgive me for not being grateful for the attention.' He stood up. 'You don't seem to understand how my house works. People don't punch a clock. They don't write in a little book when they use the phone.' Now, for the first time, he looked at me with clear recognition. 'It's not Cheltenham Ladies' College. It's more like a little rock in the middle of the sea. People get washed up on it. They cling to it for a bit. Then they get washed away again. If they are a little stronger than they were when they arrived, that's about the best I can hope for.'

'Was Lianne stronger when she left?'

Now, despite everything, Will couldn't hide the sadness in his eyes. 'I don't know,' he said.

When he left, he didn't look at me and I didn't hold out my hand or say anything. But when he was gone, I bit my lip and told Oban in faltering, half-formed sentences that in the last week or so I had been seeing Will Pavic. Sort of. Oban looked punch-drunk and flabbergasted, as if I had woken him from a very deep sleep only to tell him something incomprehensible.

'Pavic?' he said dully. 'But I thought . . . But what about . . . You and him? Oh, well.' He gave a puzzled frown. 'Pavic? You're sure? You and him, a couple?'

'We're not exactly a couple.'

'Like my wife and me. I know what you mean.'

35

'I want you to stick with me now,' Oban had said. So here I was beside him, standing once more on Jeremy Burton's waterlogged lawn and conscious all the while of Emily – watching us out of her bedroom window with her thumb stuck in her mouth. Jeremy had insisted we go outside to talk, as if he felt oppressed in the house. He was wearing only a short-sleeved shirt, no jacket, but he didn't seem to feel the chilly wind that was rippling round the garden. I was wearing a cardigan but I still felt cold. Water seeped through my shoes.

'I don't understand,' he repeated. That was almost all that he'd said since we arrived. He had looked at the photographs of Daisy, Lianne and Bryony, picking each one up and holding them away from his face as if he was long-sighted, before handing it back to Oban. 'No,' he had said to each one. 'No. I've never seen this face. I've never heard this name. No, no, no. I don't understand why you're showing them to me.'

'Your wife wrote down the names of the other victims before she died,' Oban said patiently. 'Lianne. And the name of the woman who was recently attacked by the canal, Mrs Teale – Bryony Teale. And Daisy Gill was a girl who killed herself a few months ago, and was apparently a friend of Lianne's. Your wife also wrote down her name.'

'Why?' He shook his head vigorously, and frowned at us as if he couldn't quite make out our shapes. 'Why?' His face sagged. He looked tired. His skin had a grey pallor to it and his eyes were red-rimmed and looked sore.

'We don't know why, Mr Burton,' said Oban. 'We have only just found this new evidence, and obviously it changes the way we're looking at everything.'

'Philippa never knew them,' he insisted. 'She didn't.'

'She wrote down their names.'

'It's all a mistake,' he said frantically. 'I can't explain it but it's all a mistake. She never knew them.'

'What makes you so sure?' I asked, as gently as possible.

'She would have told me.'

'What would she have told you?'

'Anything. Everything. All the things in her life.' For a moment he looked as if he was going to burst into tears, but then he glared at us and started striding down the garden.

'Mr Burton,' interjected Oban firmly, 'I know this is a shock but –'

'It's not a shock, it's – it's like a bad dream.'

'Could she have been threatened or . . . ?'

'I don't know why she wrote them down. Why would anyone threaten her?' He suddenly stopped walking and turned on us, so that we were standing in a tight knot. 'I know what you're thinking.'

'What are we thinking?'

'That she was up to something. Having an affair, or some such rubbish. Or maybe that I was. Maybe I was having an affair with all those women and she found out. Is that what you want me to deny? All right, I deny it.'

He walked away again.

'Jeremy.' I caught up with him and put my hand on his arm to slow him down. 'Please listen carefully. We are not suggesting anything or assuming anything. Please listen. I know –'

'What do you know? Nothing. I'm not much good at showing my emotions. I never have been. That doesn't mean I don't feel them. Phil knew that. She could see when I was down or worried about something, or if work had got to me. I would walk in through the door, and she would look at my face and she'd know if I was all right or not. I didn't have to say anything with her. We weren't all over each other, nobody would call us a passionate couple. But there are ways and ways of loving someone. And I loved her and she loved me, and now she's dead and you stand there insinuating things about us and our life together. We had a good life. The life we both wanted. Not glamorous or anything like that. But we had each other and then we had Emily. And we were trying for another child. Then we would be a family, complete. That's what she said. Now she's dead and we're never going to be complete, are we?'

'Mr Burton . . .'

And then we both saw that he was crying. He stood under the apple tree, bowed down by its half-ripe fruit, and howled like a little boy until his face was blotchy, and shiny with tears.

'No,' said Pam Vere, sitting upright in a chair. Her amber earrings swung as she shook her head firmly. She didn't recognize any of the faces. Yes, she was sure. Perfectly sure.

'How long was Daisy here, Mrs Winston?'

Mrs Winston was plump and curly-haired, and would have looked cosy except that she wore too much make-up and her eyes were shrewd and appraising behind her thick glasses. We sat in her warm kitchen, three cats winding themselves round my legs, and ate chocolate digestive biscuits. Oban was back at the police station and dismissive of my desire to find out about Daisy. 'We've got to concentrate on the main players, Kit,' he'd said. 'And, anyway, my men have been there, done that.'

'How long?' Mrs Winston frowned and took a noisy slurp of her tea. 'Now, let me think. What exactly did I tell those nice officers who were here? Well, it wasn't that long, as a matter of fact. Usually, we like our children to stay a long time, build up a proper relationship, you know, give them a family life. One girl we had for nearly two years. Didn't we, Ken?'

Ken, who was half her size, nodded. 'That's right.'

'Georgina, that was, lovely girl.'

'Lovely,' echoed Ken.

'But Daisy, now, she didn't stay long at all. Three months, maybe a bit longer.'

'Why such a short stay?'

'She never settled. We tried, you know. We gave her her own room, with new curtains that I made for her, and nice furniture. And we made her welcome, didn't we, Ken?'

'We did.'

'I said to her, the day she came, I said, "Daisy, treat this house as your home. And if you have any problems, however big or small, then come to me."'

'And did she? Come to you with problems, I mean?'

'Oh, no. Never. She was tight as a clam, that one. I knew, that first week, I knew it wasn't going to work, didn't I, Ken?'

'You did.'

'She kept herself to herself. Ate in her room. Crumbs

everywhere. Didn't join in or make an effort. And she said dreadful things about my boy Bernie.' I'd met Bernie – a great hulking boy of about seventeen in a T-shirt with a skull on the front who'd opened the door to me. 'When he was only trying to be companionable.'

'So, Daisy never told you much about what was going on in her life?'

'No. Hardly anything at all. Secretive little thing.'

'Did you meet any of her friends?'

'No. She went out, but never brought anyone back here. Sometimes she stayed out all night. I told her, "Daisy, I don't mind you going out, and here's a key, but you have to tell me what time you're coming back." Not that she ever did, mind.'

I spread out the photographs in front of her.

'No,' she said, flicking through them. 'I already said. Of course, I recognize this one, but only from the telly.'

'Philippa Burton.'

'What's someone like her got to do with Daisy?'

'So you're quite sure you never met any of them?'

'I told the officers already, no.'

'Thank you,' I said wearily. 'Just double-checking.'

'It's not easy being a foster-parent, you know. You probably think I didn't care about Daisy, but I did my best. I was very sorry when I heard about what had happened to her. "Poor little thing," I said, didn't I, Ken? But I wasn't surprised.'

'Why not?'

She shrugged. 'She was an angry, wretched girl, really. Prickly and rude, flaring up over nothing, crying in her room, throwing things. She kicked the cats sometimes. I caught her at it. It was like a final straw. She thought the world was against her, that one. It was all too late.'

'What was too late?'

'Us. Everything, I suppose.'

'Thank you,' I said, getting up to go, wanting to leave the overheated kitchen and the winding cats.

'We did our best.'

'I'm sure you did.'

'But some people, you can't help them.'

'I'll let myself out.'

'She was her own worst enemy.'

'In a way, I blame myself,' said Carol Harman.

'Who found her?'

'I did. My staff called me because her door was locked and she wasn't answering their knocks. So I opened it with my master key from the outside and found her there. She'd hanged herself – but you knew that, didn't you?'

'Yes, I did.'

'We knew she was at risk, cutting herself and starving herself. She was on special measures at the home – one-to-ones with the staff, things like that. It shouldn't have happened.'

'She must have been determined,' I said. I liked this woman, who was making no attempt to justify herself to me. 'It wasn't a cry for help.'

'If she hadn't succeeded, she might well never have tried again. You don't know. She was a difficult girl, very stubborn, very needy. Terrible life. She once said to me, "No one's ever said they loved me."'

'What did you say back?'

'That I loved her, of course – but it doesn't really ring true, does it, coming from a woman who's only known you for a few weeks, and is paid to look after you?'

'At least you said it.'

'Hmmm. Anyway, you want to know if I ever saw

any of these women. I met her once.' She put the tip of one finger on Lianne's face. 'She came to call for Daisy. They went up to Daisy's room together. That's all.'

'None of the others?'

'No.'

'Why do you think she did it?'

'Killed herself? I don't know. She had a sad life, didn't she? I don't know of any particular circumstances, but that doesn't mean there weren't any. Probably because in the end it was easier than being alive.'

36

The next day I drove to the clinic, sat through a meeting about staff structures and pretended to do some paper-work. My brain was teeming with the events of the last twenty-four hours. I thought about the list of names; about Bryony's white, shattered face when she heard; Jeremy's howls under the apple tree.

And I didn't know what to do about Will. Would he be so angry with me he wouldn't talk to me? Did I want to see him again? At a quarter past six I phoned him. At about ten to nine I looked at my watch as Will removed it from my wrist and put it on the floor by his bed. When I put it back on my wrist I had come out of the shower. It was just after ten. He was lying in bed. I lay down beside him. I was still damp from the shower and he was still damp from sweat and sex and me. I smelt of his soap and I could smell me all over him.

'That was wonderful,' I said, and then started to apologize. 'I always feel stupid saying that. I feel as if I'm saying thank you for something.' I sat up with my back against the wall, propped up with a pillow, and looked at the room. There were the remains of a Chinese takeaway. An empty wine bottle lying down and another a third full. Our clothes were scattered.

'I'm sorry about yesterday afternoon,' I said. 'I didn't know what to do.'

'It doesn't matter,' he said. He was trailing his fingers over my body, but not looking at me.

'That was what surprised me,' I said. 'It really didn't

seem to matter to you. I get scared by police and I'm working with them. You didn't seem bothered.'

'Is that a problem?'

'Maybe I get more scared than you do.'

'That's understandable.'

'Oh, you mean this?' I raised my hand and touched my cheek, my scar.

'What did you want?' he asked. 'Should I have got on my knees and started pleading my innocence?'

'What do you mean, your "innocence"?'

'That's what you want as well, isn't it? You want me to look you in the eye and say, "Kit, I'm innocent. So help me God."'

'No,' I protested. 'But . . .'

'Aha, so there is a but after all.' He stood up. 'I'm going to have a shower.'

I lay in bed, half covered by the thin sheet, thinking. As soon as he came back into the room, wrapped in a large white towel, I said, 'You know what the problem is?'

'Whose problem? Mine or yours?'

'You didn't lose your cool for a second in there. You were perfectly in control.'

'And the question is, would an innocent man behave like that?'

'Don't you care, though?'

'What?' He raised his eyebrows. 'About what people think of me? Why should I?'

'No. No, I don't mean about what people think of you. I mean about – well, all of it. Lianne and Philippa and Daisy and now Bryony, and you're involved in it somehow. Even if you have absolutely nothing to do with it in a technical term, you're *involved*. And you knew some of them, Will. You knew Lianne, and she was young and lonely and in need of help, and now she's dead, they're dead, and yet you just sat there with your ironic smile, scoring points. I mean, I know you must care somewhere, deep down, because otherwise why are you doing this job and everything, so I know you care, of course . . .'

'No, you don't. It doesn't follow.'

'Well, all right, maybe you don't care one bit and I find that chilling.'

Will gave a nasty smile. 'More chilling than the possibility that I might be capable of murder? Maybe,' he let his towel drop to the floor in a white puddle, then pulled on a robe, 'maybe the possibility even excites you? Do you like to think I'd be capable of killing someone? I know you – you like to face your fears, don't you? Feel the fear and do it anyway?' The tone was mocking and cruel.

I sat up in the bed. 'Listen, Will, let's not play games like this. Please. For what it's worth, I've met a few dozen killers, I suppose. Maybe more. For all of them there are big fat reports explaining why they did it. I don't know of a single example where somebody spotted them in advance as potential murderers. In fact, several of them were let out by people like me and killed somebody else. So I'm not going to stand here and say that you couldn't kill a woman.'

'Sit.'

'What?'

'You're not standing, you're sitting.'

'Oh, for God's sake. You're proving what I'm saying. Look, what I'm trying to say is that I was looking at you this afternoon. And I suddenly thought you'd quite like people to think you'd done it. It would be great in every way. You would be a victim yet again. The great misunderstood Will Pavic. And it would show how stupid the police were. It would be pretty much your ideal situation – you being right and everybody else being wrong. Which is your basic world view.'

Pavic's slow smile didn't waver. 'So I didn't manage to fool you?' he said.

I reached over and took his hand and pulled him down beside me on the bed. I stroked his bristly short hair. I kissed his forehead. I laid the palm of my hand against his cheek and for the briefest moment he leaned into it. 'I've had rather a bad year,' I said. 'I have bad dreams.'

'Kit . . .'

'My sex life had been non-existent for a bit and just now it's been the best, and that's been so nice. Nice is the wrong word. You know what I mean, anyway. And sometimes I wonder whether I'm falling in love with you.'

'Kit . . .' he said again. He wasn't joking or sneering any longer. That was something. Even if everything was about to come to an end, that was better than his contempt.

'Maybe you're right,' I continued. 'And I'm drawn to you because you're bad-tempered and intimidating, and you scare me in some way. Or maybe I want you because you seem unhappy and I'm kidding myself that I can make you happy again – you know, that mad female fantasy you've probably read about. Whatever. I've been happy, anyway, just feeling wanted again like this. I've been happy when I've been working and suddenly I let myself think of you. I have felt myself coming back to life again. But I don't want to be with someone who doesn't care about anything, and who won't yield to anyone. I'm not much good at passion with no tenderness. I'm not tough enough. And I'm really very bad at playing games – well, here I am putting all my cards on the table. No aces, as you can see.' I gave a small laugh and he still didn't say anything. 'So, maybe I need someone with softer edges.'

Will put up a hand and tucked a strand of wet hair behind my ear.

'I think it will be harder for me than for you if we stop seeing each other,' I said. 'I'm a rotten leaver. I've never been any good at it. You're probably better at it, though – I bet you don't spend much time looking back.'

'I still want to see you, Kit.'

'You want to see me on your terms.'

'What are your terms, then?'

'I don't know.' I gave a small sob. 'But the point is, there are some.'

He smiled. 'That's completely incomprehensible, you know.'

'I know.' He handed me a tissue and I blew my nose. 'Anyway, for tonight at least, I'm going. And maybe that's what I should be doing altogether.' I put a finger on his lip. 'Ssh, don't say anything else. Not now.'

I stood up and pulled on my trousers and shirt.

'I don't like the idea of you walking around here at this time of night,' Will said.

'I think I'll be all right,' I said. 'My name wasn't on the list.'

I stepped out of the house and walked away without looking back. There was a full moon so bright that it lit wavelike rims on the clouds across the sky. My body was quivering with tension. I felt tears running down my cheek, hot, stinging, but I took some deep breaths. I wiped my face. That was better. I'd done the right thing, there was nothing to get in a flap about. It was probably all over now, anyway, but I went over and over it in my mind. Move on, I told myself. Move on. I had other things to think about.

I've never been worried about walking in cities late at night. I have a theory that if you walk briskly, and look as if you know where you're going, you'll be safe. I've spent quite a lot of my career talking to dangerous men, and I've frequently asked them how they select their victims. I think the answer is that they pick on people, women mainly, who, through weakness or lack of judgement or insecurity, seem to be inviting their attentions. I've tried to make myself believe that if you don't look like a victim, you won't become one. Maybe I'm just kidding myself. The randomness of suffering is unbearable. Better to believe that people are responsible for the things they bring on themselves.

I walked through empty dark streets until I reached the brightness and noise of the main road and Kersey Town station. The taxis were squealing, the stall was there selling tomorrow's newspapers, as if there wasn't time enough for that tomorrow. Usually I would have been fascinated with the sights of the late-night city. I love looking at people who seem to be in the wrong place at the wrong time. I try to imagine what strange errands and wrong turnings have brought them here, I tell myself stories about them. But now there were other stories in my head, interrupting each other, shouting to be heard. I crossed the busy road and cut across the square, leaving the bustle behind me. I thought of Bryony, walking late at night along the canal. It was stupid, as Oban had said, but I understood the impulse. The darkness, the quiet, the barely shifting black water, a strange secret world right in the middle of the city.

I thought of Philippa, on Hampstead Heath in broad daylight, in a crowded children's playground.

My mind was working so furiously that my walk home had become almost unconscious, even though I was following a complicated route through back streets and small alleyways. I was barely a hundred yards from my front door when something jerked me out of my reverie and I looked around feeling startled. Had I heard something? I was in a quiet street with a row of houses on one side and a churchyard on the other. I saw nobody but then, in the corner of my eye, I caught a movement. When I looked more carefully in the direction I'd come from, there was nothing. Had someone moved back into a shadow? I'd be at my front door in a minute. I started walking briskly, my hand closed around the key in my jacket pocket. A minute, less, thirty seconds. I broke into a run and reached my door. At the moment I pushed the key into the lock, I felt a hand on my shoulder and gave a stupid little cry of shock. There was a tightness across my chest as I looked round. It was Michael Doll. His sour-sweet breath was on my face.

'I just caught up with you,' he said, with a smile.

I tried to think. Be calm. Defuse it. Make him go away. But I had to seem surprised. I mustn't seem to take his presence for granted. 'What on earth are you doing here?'

'I missed you,' he said. 'You didn't come and see me.'

'Why should I come and see you?'

'I've been thinking about you.'

'Were you following me?' I asked.

'No, why should I?' he said, taking a step back, looking away.

He had been following me. For how long? Had he been outside Will Pavic's house?

'You been with someone else?'

Someone *else*? What was going on?

'I've got to go now, Michael,' I said.

'Can I come in?' he said.

'No, you can't.'

'Just for a few minutes.'

'It's too late. My friend's up there.'

He looked up at the flat.

'There's no light on.'

'She's in bed.'

'I want to talk.'

I couldn't believe that I was standing on my doorstep at half past midnight negotiating with Michael Doll about whether he could come in. 'I've got to go.'

'You'd let other people.'

'Michael, it's late. You've got to go home.'

'I hate my home.'

'Good-night, Michael.' I said it with a slight, but not a welcoming, smile and a touch on his arm, which signalled sympathy but not real warmth.

'I want to see you,' he said, but more feebly.

'It's late,' I said. 'I'm going.'

Not too quickly, I eased myself back into the doorway and pushed the door shut but it jammed. He had his foot against it. He leaned forward so that his face was in the gap. 'You hate me?' he said. It was hardly a question. 'You want me to go. Never see me.'

Oh, how I wanted him to go. To scuttle out of my life, and if he was going to fasten himself to somebody, then let it be to somebody else. 'I don't mean that at all,' I said. 'I'm tired. I've had a difficult day. Please.'

His face was quite close to mine now. He was breathing with a wheezing whistling sound. His arm reached through the gap and I felt his hand on my cheek.

'Night, Kit,' he said.

I didn't reply. The hand withdrew. I felt the pressure against the door relent and I was able to push it shut. I leaned against it and felt a sudden rush of nausea. I could still feel the traces of Michael Doll on my face. I could still feel Will Pavic inside me. It seemed to me that I was smelling of these men. I ran upstairs and, although I'd already had a shower at Will's, I had another long one, until the water ran cold. Then I rummaged in a cupboard and found a bottle of whisky. I took a glass to bed with me and sat in the dark sipping at it in mouthfuls that burned me inside and dulled my brain.

37

The next morning I phoned Oban and told him about Michael Doll. He seemed to find it mildly amusing.

'So you've got an admirer,' he said. 'Another admirer, I should say.'

'It's not funny,' I said. 'I think he may have been following me.'

'Why?'

I hesitated. I didn't want to talk about Doll following me back from Will's place. 'It's getting more serious,' I said. 'He's hanging around the house, watching me. I don't feel safe.'

There was a cough that might have been a laugh.

'I don't believe this,' he said. 'We've spent the last few weeks trying to convince you that Doll is dangerous and you've been trying to convince us that he's a sweet, misunderstood boy.'

'That's not what I was saying.'

'I know, love, can't you take a joke? But what do you want me to do about it?'

'I'm not sure. But I'm starting to feel threatened by him.'

'Dear me,' said Oban. 'And I was just starting to get more interested in your other friend.'

'What?'

'It's hard to avoid. I've been thinking about it and all roads seem to lead to Will Pavic and his bloody drug-dealing centre.'

'That's ridiculous.'

'Maybe. But we need to think about it. If you like I can send someone round to whisper in Mickey Doll's ear.'

I gave a sigh of relief. 'That might be a good idea,' I said. 'The problem is, everything I say to him, whether I'm friendly or angry, just seems to encourage him. I don't want to bully him but it's getting out of hand.'

'Don't worry. We'll lean on him. In a nice way, of course. Are you coming in today?'

'Maybe later,' I said. 'I'll be at the clinic for most of the day.'

In the morning, I was sitting in one of the seminar rooms at the clinic with a fifteen-year-old girl called Anita, her whey-faced, stunned mother, a social worker and a solicitor. I was looking through a file. It was the usual disaster. Worse than the usual disaster. Supervisory visits had been omitted, medication not administered, papers lost. That was all standard. But a school building had been set on fire. That had certainly done the trick. Anita had attempted suicide twice, repeatedly mutilated herself and her case had got stuck in the in-tray. But if you set fire to public buildings, you get attention.

There was a knock and the door was pushed open. It was the clinic's receptionist. 'Phone for you,' she said to me.

I looked round in disbelief.

'I'll call back later.'

'It's the police. He said he tried your mobile.'

'It's switched off. Tell him I'll ring back in a minute.'

'He said to get you out of wherever you were. And he'd hang on.'

I made profuse apologies, ran down the corridor and picked up the phone. 'This had better be –'

'Doll's dead.'

'What?'

'In his flat. Get there now.'

When I'd visited Michael Doll in his flat before, I'd thought it a squalid, desolate home for a strange and lonely man. He had seemed the sort of person who would have been obscure while he was alive and whose death would have been ignored. No longer. He had become notorious. There were three police cars, an ambulance and other unmarked cars double-parked along the road. The area around the street entrance was taped off. Two policemen stood outside, and there was a small crowd of people with nothing better to do on a weekday afternoon in Hackney.

I pushed my way through with murmured apologies, and as I approached the policemen I saw the old women with wheeled shopping baskets looking at me with new interest. What could I be? A detective? An undertaker? One of the police went inside and I heard a muffled shout. After a few moments Oban emerged. He seemed deeply shocked, his face a startling grey-green colour. I found myself asking how he was.

'Jesus,' he said in a low voice. 'Un-fucking-believable. Pardon me.' He looked around guiltily at the old women.

'What's happened?' I asked.

'The scene-of-crime guys are just starting,' he said. 'I wanted you to have a quick look. Just so you've seen it before they take him away. Are you up to it?'

'I think so,' I said, gulping slightly.

'It's not pretty,' he said.

I had to put things like miniature hairnets over my shoes. Oban told me not to touch anything. Mounting the stairs required some care because they were covered with a sheet. At the top Oban turned to me and told me to take a deep breath. He pushed the door open and stood back, leaving me to go in first.

The body was sprawled on the floor, face downwards, except there was no face. It looked like an effigy but the head wasn't finished. I recognized the clothes from the previous night. The soles of his shoes were pointing up at me. The lace on the right shoe was undone. Brown corduroy trousers. Anorak. Above that just dark wetness. I started to speak but my mouth was too dry. I had to swallow several times. I felt a hand on my back. 'Steady, love,' said Oban.

'Where's his head?' I asked, in a voice that didn't sound like my own.

'All over the place,' said Oban. 'Repeated massive blows with a very heavy, very blunt object, much of it after death. It was a fucking frenzy. Hence all this.'

I looked around. It was the red room. It was the red room of my nightmares. I had thought of it as an idea, a symbol, but I was standing in it. It looked as if the room had been sprayed with blood from a hose. The walls, even the ceiling, thick globs on the ceiling that looked as if they were about to drop on us but they had coagulated.

'You know, head wounds,' said Oban, looking round. 'They always bleed a lot, don't they?'

I looked around. I tried to be dispassionate, but I kept thinking about that irritating disgusting presence on my doorstep last night, that repellent urgency, all reduced to that wretched bundle on the floor. I had put some sort of curse on him. I had wanted him out of my life for ever. Had I wanted him dead?

'Take a look at this,' said Oban.

He held a transparent folder, which contained a piece

of paper. Written on it in crude capital letters was:
MURDRUS BASTAD.

'That was lying on the body. Do you see?' he said.
'They can't even bloody spell.'

'So they caught up with him,' I said.

Oban nodded. 'What a shithouse,' he said. 'You've
been here before?'

'Yes,' I said.

'I thought it might be useful for you to have a look at
it. Take as long as you want. Or as short.'

My legs shook and I moved to sit down on the arm
of a chair but a man stepped forward and prevented me.
I apologized.

'What a fucking mess,' Oban said, again. 'It looks like
a slaughterhouse in a museum.'

'Michael Doll was a collector,' I said. I mustn't be sick.
I swallowed hard and breathed shallowly through my
mouth.

Oban pulled a face. 'Really? What did he collect?'

'Just anything he found. Stuff by the canal. Anything
he could carry. It was a kind of illness.'

'I don't envy the people who have to clear this out . . .'
Oban carried on talking but I couldn't hear him. I
couldn't hear anything. Because suddenly I had seen it.
I walked across the room, I had to manoeuvre carefully
around the body. I walked across and reached for something on a shelf. It was between a jam-jar and a coil of
rusting wire. Somebody shouted something and I felt a
hand tugging at me.

'Don't touch,' a voice said.

'That,' I said, pointing. 'That.'

The man was wearing gloves and he leaned forward
and picked it up, very carefully.

'What's that?' Oban asked.

'You tell me,' I said.

'It's a feeding cup, the kind you give to toddlers. What's that written on it?'

'Emily,' I said.

He looked puzzled. 'You're not going to tell me that Mickey Doll had a daughter called Emily, are you?'

'No,' I said. 'But Philippa Burton did.'

38

'All right?' asked Oban, as we drew away from the pavement where the group of people had become a small crowd.

'Fine.' I kept my voice firm and smiled at him. I wasn't shaking. My voice was steady. My breathing was even. I wound down the window and let the warm wind blow into my face.

'It was unbelievable, wasn't it?' His face had returned to normal, and his tone was jovial, even gleeful. He looked more alert yet more relaxed than I'd seen him in weeks. I half expected him to start whistling through his teeth.

'Yes.'

'Tough job for the scene-of-crime lads. Nightmare. But there will be a lot of sympathy for the people who did it, even so. Rough justice and all of that. We have to tread carefully at the press conference.'

I closed my eyes for a minute and thought of Doll's pulped remains, the sea of blood. Red blood everywhere; a room dark red with blood.

'So we come full circle, Kit.'

'What?'

'It was Doll all along. After everything.'

I made a noncommittal noise and gazed out of the open window. The sky was blue and cloudless, the sun golden; people on the street were dressed in bright colours. It was a day of heat and light, like the last gift of summer.

'Come on, Kit. You can put it behind you now. It's over, admit it.'

'Well . . .'

'Let me guess. You're still not convinced. We find Emily's drinking cup in Doll's room, for Christ's sake, with her name written across it – of course we'll have to confirm it with Mr Burton, but I think that's just crossing the Ts, don't you? But you're not convinced. What would it take?' He turned his head and grinned across at me as he said it. He sounded fond, rather than exasperated.

'It's just that I don't understand.'

'So? Who does? We don't need you to understand any more. You're not required to conduct a seminar about it to your colleagues, or whatever it is you do. We just needed to find the person who killed the women, and we have, thank God.'

'No. I meant it doesn't make sense.'

'Lots of things don't make sense.' He swerved to avoid a cyclist in neon Lycra, leaned briefly on his horn. 'But Doll was the murderer, Kit.'

I didn't reply.

'Kit? Come on, say it. Just once. It won't hurt.'

'I'm not saying that I think you're wrong . . .'

'But you won't say I'm right either.'

'No.'

He laughed. Then he put a warm hand over mine. 'You did well, Kit. Even though, in the end, your instincts were mistaken, you did excellently. Don't think I haven't realized how hard it must have been for you, after everything. But we'd have been all over the place without you. You kept us on the straight and narrow.'

'No,' I said, and was surprised by how firm my voice was. 'No. I stopped you from charging Doll weeks ago.

If you'd charged him then, guilty or not, he'd be alive now. In a year's time, maybe he would have landed up in my hospital. I told him he was safe.'

'It does no good to think like that. We've all made our mistakes on this one, but you saw connections we didn't see. You stopped us from making mistakes we were poised to make. You prevented a Godawful mess.'

'But . . .'

'Christ, Kit, give it a rest. No more buts. You're the most bloody-minded woman it's ever been my pleasure and privilege to work with.'

'I'll put it on my CV,' I said drily.

'And the most honourable,' he added. I looked at him, but he was staring straight at the road ahead.

I put a hand on his arm, lightly. 'Thank you, Daniel.'

My flat looked neglected, as if no one was living there any longer. All the windows were shut, the curtains ambiguously half closed as if I had gone on holiday, the surfaces dusty. There were no fresh flowers, as there usually are, except some dead ones in a vase on the kitchen window-sill; no fruit in the bowl on the kitchen table; no books lying open on the arm of the sofa; no notes from Julie stuck on the fridge door. I opened the fridge. It was clean and almost empty: one carton of semi-skimmed milk, a tub of butter, a little jar of pesto, half full, a bag of coffee beans.

And when had I last properly seen Julie? With a little jolt of shame, I realized that I couldn't remember. Over the last few frantic days, she had been like a hazy outline on the edge of my vision, hovering there but ignored, blinked away. I had a vague recollection of her saying we needed to talk as I rushed past her, on my way somewhere else. When had that been?

The door to what I had grown used to thinking of as her bedroom was open, so I put my head round it. It looked too tidy. Julie always left clothes on the floor, the bed unmade, lipstick and pots of face-cream open on the filing cabinet that she had turned into her dressing-table. For a moment, I wondered if she had gone altogether, but her suitcase was still on the floor, and the cupboard was full of clothes.

I went back into the main room and opened some windows. I wiped the surfaces. Then I ran out of the flat, down to the deli on the corner, where I bought goat's cheese and a rough slab of Parmesan, fresh pasta, single cream, Italian salami and ham, olives stuffed with anchovies, little almond biscuits, basil growing in a small pot, artichoke hearts, four plump figs. It wasn't that I wanted to eat any of these things; I just wanted to have them in my house, like a welcome for whoever came through the door.

After the deli, I visited the greengrocer's further up the road: red peppers, yellow peppers, green apples, one pale-striped melon, nectarines, purple plums and a bunch of black grapes. At the florist's, I bought a huge, brash bunch of yellow and orange dahlias. I staggered home with the plastic bags digging into my fingers and the flowers tickling my nose. I put the kettle on, ground coffee beans, stuck the flowers in a glass vase, put the cheese in the fridge, piled the fruit and vegetables into a large bowl. There. If Julie came in now, she'd know I was back home again.

I was just thinking about a bath when the phone rang.
'Yes?'

'Kit, I'm going to pick you up in about five minutes, OK? I'm nearly with you now.'

'I thought you said it was over, Daniel.'

'It is, it is. This is just a coda. You'll appreciate it, I promise you.'

'I don't like surprises –' I began, but the phone had gone dead.

'You've been in on this from the beginning. I thought you should be here at the end as well.'

'I still want to know where we're going.'

Oban grinned. 'Don't grumble so much.'

A few minutes later, we were standing at the Teales' front door.

'Are you sure she's here?'

'I rang in advance.'

When Bryony opened the door, I was taken aback by her appearance. She had tied back her orange hair and her face looked pale. There were smudges under her eyes, as if she hadn't slept for days. She looked thinner under the old blue jeans and an oversized white shirt that she was wearing, and the smile she gave us didn't reach her eyes.

'Come in.'

'This won't take long, Mrs Teale,' said Oban, as soon as we were in the living room. 'I just wanted to ask you if you'd ever seen this.' Then he pulled a thin glove on to his right hand, leaned down into the bag he was carrying and, like a conjuror, he flamboyantly produced a small leather pouch.

Bryony took one look at it, and her hands flew up to her mouth. 'Yes,' she whispered.

'It was found in Michael Doll's house.' He darted a look of pure triumph at me.

'Oh!' She gasped, as if someone had punched her in the stomach and all her breath was being expelled. Abruptly, she started to cry, bending her face into her hands and whimpering. Tears dribbled between her fingers.

I glared at Oban, who got up and crossed over to her, putting a hand clumsily on her shoulder. 'There, now. It's all right. It's all over, Mrs Teale, Bryony. He's dead, you see. You are safe now.'

'Safe?' She lifted her drenched face, looking bewildered. 'Safe?'

'Yes. I can't tell you the details, but I can say that we are confident that Doll – the man who passed himself off as a witness to your attack – was the murderer. He has always been a suspect, and he was found dead in his flat this morning. He had in his possession items belonging to both you and to Philippa Burton. We knew this was yours' – and he held up the pouch, jingling it – 'because it contains, among other things, your labelled house keys. Maybe he'd collected something belonging to Lianne, too, but we'll probably never know that.' He nodded at her genially. 'Trophies, you see.'

'But how . . . what . . . ?'

'He had been the target of a vigilante attack before, so we're working on the supposition that they killed him. Early days yet.'

'My pouch,' she said slowly. 'He had my pouch.'

'Do you remember losing it?'

'No. I don't know. I mean, I must have lost it on the night of the attack. But I didn't think . . . I knew it had gone, but I didn't remember where I'd last had it. I was too confused. When I fell, he must have . . . I thought he was helping me . . . How did I think that?' She shuddered violently and wrapped her arms tightly round herself.

'Are you all right?' I asked.

She turned to me. 'I suppose I must be,' she said. 'I

feel a bit sick, all of a sudden. I mean, it's all going to be all right now, isn't it? I suppose it hasn't quite sunk in.' She made an effort, and smiled. 'It's been an interesting few days.'

He held out his hand. 'Goodbye, Mrs Teale, we'll be in touch again soon. Tying up the many loose ends, as it were. Though it won't ever be quite tidy enough for you, Kit.' He looked smugly at me.

'Goodbye, Bryony.' I was going to shake her hand as well, but she put her arms round me and kissed me on both cheeks. She smelt clean and felt soft and fragile. 'You've been lovely,' she whispered in my ear. 'Thanks.'

'Satisfied?' said Oban, as we left.

'Don't crow, Dan, it doesn't suit you. Where are you off to now?'

'Press conference. I hope you're coming.'

'You don't hang around, do you?'

'Not when we've got a result. Jump in.' He held open the passenger door.

'I don't know why I let you bully me.'

He snorted with laughter. 'That's a joke.'

I don't know why, but I put my fingers up and touched my scar lightly. 'It's funny,' I said, 'but I can no longer remember a time when I didn't look like this.'

'Like what?'

'Scarred.'

'You're all right,' he said, self-consciously. Then: 'Come on, climb in, we can't stand outside Mrs Teale's front door discussing your looks all afternoon.'

It was getting dark by the time I returned home. The windows were dark, which meant that Julie hadn't come back yet. I let myself in and immediately ran myself a bath. Less than twelve hours ago I'd been staring down at Doll. His face rose unbidden in my mind, not just the mess I had seen on the carpet but the face he'd turned towards me when he'd sat fishing by the canal. That expectant smile. He had killed two women, Lianne and Philippa. He had tried to kill a third, Bryony. Yet despite that, I couldn't stop myself feeling a spasm of pity for the man. He'd never had a chance. He had been vicious, repellent, perverse, murderous, but he'd never had a chance. I'd met too many people like Doll.

'Hi. You've got foam in your hair.'

I sat up. 'I didn't hear you come in.'

'That's probably because you were under the water. The flat looks nice.'

'Good. I'd been neglecting it.'

'Yes.'

'It's finished.'

'What?'

'The case. It's over. It looks like it was Michael Doll all along.'

'Doll? The man who was in the flat?'

'Yes.'

'Christ. That'll make me more careful about whom I open the door to.'

'Julie, why don't we go out this evening? Unless you've got something else on.'

'I'd love that. But I'm rather out of money at the –'

'On me. I've got plenty of money and nothing to spend it on.'

'Oh, I'm brilliant at spending.'

I ordered clear soup, Thai fishcakes, pork and chicken satay, noodles and rice, steamed spicy dumplings, king prawns in chilli, squid with lemongrass and coriander, spare ribs, a bottle of South American wine. Julie looked impressed and alarmed.

'And two glasses of champagne,' I added.

'What's all this about?'

'What?'

'You're ordering enough for six of us. You're not pregnant, are you?'

The champagne arrived and I chinked my glass against Julie's. 'This is my New Year's Eve.'

'It's August, Kit.'

'The New Year can begin anywhere.'

'I can't work out if you're celebrating or drowning your sorrows.'

'Bit of both. I'm glad it's over. I'm glad Doll isn't going to do any more harm. But I don't understand how it all happened, it's completely baffling, it doesn't add up. And that makes me feel . . .'

'Frustrated?' supplied Julie.

'More than that. As if I've failed them. Philippa and Lianne. Does that sound mad?'

'Yes. It does. You've been worrying me with your –'

'At the press conference today, Oban went out of his way to praise me. He was effusive, even. I felt a complete fraud.'

'Because?'

'Because I feel as if I haven't laid them to rest yet. It sounds stupid, doesn't it?'

'They're dead so they're already at rest. And surely what most matters is that he's been caught.'

'He's dead.'

'Oh.' She looked taken aback.

'Killed by vigilantes who'll feel completely justified when they find out what he'd done. Here we are, our meal.'

I drank the whole bowl of soup. It was so spicy it was like swallowing pins and needles. My body glowed with the after-effect. Then I ate three of the spicy dumplings. I chewed them lots of times and had to make an effort to swallow them. But I managed it.

'I'm sorry I've been so obsessed.'

'That's OK. I just want to know what happened with Will Pavic.'

'That's over too. Or it might be, at least.'

'Really? That was quick. But maybe that's not such a bad thing. He was rather grim, wasn't he?'

'I think his grimness is the point,' I said. I bit into my spare rib and took a large gulp of wine to swill it down. Doll's pulped face floated in front of my eyes. The room was in my head, sprayed with his blood, with mine.

'So why end it?'

'What? Oh, because I don't want to go down that road. I think, well, I think I should try to be happy.'

'That sounds like a good idea.'

I picked up a ring of squid. It looked like rubber. Or guts. I laid it back on the plate and stared at the beige rice. I drank some more wine. I felt extremely odd.

'I've got something to tell you,' Julie was saying, through the mist in front of my eyes.

I blinked. 'What's that?'

'I'm leaving.'

'I know, you're going to find a flat of your own.'

'No. I'm leaving the country again. I can't stand it. I feel trapped. I don't want to be a teacher, or work in a record company, turn up at an office every day in my boring suit, with tights and leather shoes. So I'm going away again. Do I sound like someone who's having trouble coming to terms with real life?'

'I've always thought that there's nothing wrong with

escapism,' I said, and my voice seemed to come from a long way off.

'I just want to be happy too. Like you.'

I raised my glass. 'To your happiness.'

'Don't cry, Kit. We can both be happy. At the same time.' We giggled tearfully at each other. 'And while you're drunk and emotional,' she added, 'I think I ought to tell you that I borrowed your black velvet dress without asking you, then I washed it in hot water and it's gone all funny. The hem looks like a wave. Sorry.'

39

I woke the next morning to the sound of wind rattling at the panes and clattering in the trees outside. A few yellow leaves scratched at the windows as they fell. For a horrible moment I couldn't remember anything: not what day it was, where I was, who I was. All I knew was that I couldn't remember anything, that I was a blank. I lay waiting for the vacuum in me to be filled up with memories. And sure enough, the memories came flooding in. Doll without a face, first of all, lying in his blood and all around him blood dripping from the walls, from the ceiling. A torture chamber. Then Doll with a face, his arm raised, the jagged porcelain in his fist, the blood spraying everywhere, and it was my blood. I lay pressed back against my pillow with my eyes open but seeing what was inside my head. I felt as if I had been running and running for all these months, thinking I was leaving the red room behind. And all the time I had been coming full circle, back to where I had begun.

I drove straight from Market Hill to Kersey Town, where I parked. On an impulse, I ran to buy some flowers. I didn't have a clue what kind of flowers she had liked, if she liked any, but I bought a fat bunch of anemones, purple and red and pink, still dewy and like a cluster of soft jewels. I ran along the pavement, for I didn't want to be late. It seemed to me that to turn up on time was the least I could do. I wanted to pay tribute. I wanted to say sorry.

I don't know why Lianne had touched me so deeply. I had never known her, but she was motherless, like me. I had only seen her face when she was dead, a round face with freckles on the bridge of her nose. I knew nothing about her, and perhaps if I'd met her when she was alive, I wouldn't have liked her or felt any kind of tenderness towards her. I knew nothing about her life. I didn't even know her real name. No one did. She might have been a Lizzie or a Susan or a Charlotte or an Alex. Anyone. She was an unknown girl, being buried in a council plot, and maybe a woman who had never met her would be her chief and only mourner.

As I arrived people were coming out of the previous ceremony – the taped organ music ushered them out and then, after a few minutes of silence, the music ushered me in. The room was quite long, painted cream, and was lined with new wooden pews. In front of them stood Lianne's coffin. I was the only one here. I didn't know what to do with my flowers. Should I put them on the coffin? Was that what people did? I glanced round, then laid the bright anemones on top of the pale shiny coffin with its gilt handles. Then I sat down in the front pew and waited while the taped music played. After a minute or so, there was a rustle behind me, and a woman came and sat down beside me. She had her hair tied back in a headscarf and wore a dark-grey jacket over her flowery dress, as if she'd pulled it on in a hurry.

We smiled warily at each other, then she leaned across to me and said in a whisper, 'Hello, I'm Paula Mann, from the council.' She waited a beat, then went on, 'I didn't know her, but I'm the one who organized this. She died in our district, see, and with no one else . . . poor mite, whoever she was. It falls to us. We like to come and pay our respects if we get the time. Sometimes

329

we can't manage it. But it's not right they should be sent off with no one.'

'Kit Quinn,' I said, and we shook hands, and I thought, Not just one but two mourners who only ever saw you when you were dead.

'I don't suppose you knew her either?'

'No.'

'Thought not. Usually we manage to find someone if there's someone to be found,' she said. 'It's amazing how many people die all alone, and you don't even know where they came from. Says something about the way we live, I reckon. So much loneliness.' Her nice face creased.

'Did you try and find out who she was, then?'

'That's my job, see. I'm like a detective, really, except usually there hasn't been a crime. I get the corpses that haven't been claimed and I've got to see if there's a next of kin, or a friend, even, who'll take responsibility – and if there isn't I arrange the funeral and sort out all the possessions. Throw them away in most cases. Sometimes I feel terrible, when I come across photographs, or letters, or things that must've meant an awful lot to someone once. And we just bundle them all up, and keep them in a big cabinet for a few months, then chuck them. Burn them.'

'What did you do with Lianne's stuff ?'

'She was different – we don't even know if she had any stuff. All we got was a dead body found by the canal.'

'And that doesn't happen often?'

'Not so much – though it happens more often than you'd care to think.'

The organ music changed and the chaplain came in, so the two of us hushed. He looked at us solemnly and laid his hand on Lianne's plain coffin, just above my bunch of flowers. But before he could say anything there was a noise behind us. I turned and saw four young people hovering awkwardly on the threshold. I recognized them at once, though they were dressed very differently, in strange assorted black garments that they'd probably cobbled together from friends. There was Sylvia with the green eyes, who looked like a sprite, the shy black girl, Carla, who'd been the last of the group to see Lianne alive, Spike with the shaved head, hairy Laurie. Each of them held a small bunch of flowers, though Sylvia's looked as if it had been grabbed from a front garden as she had passed. Carla had bought huge, waxy lilies that must have cost a lot; I could smell them from where I sat. I smiled at them but they didn't smile back. Perhaps they didn't remember me. They looked embarrassed, self-conscious, and Spike was giggling and nudging Laurie as they shuffled up to the coffin and laid their flowers next to mine, then trailed back to the pew across from us.

The service began at last. At least the chaplain didn't pretend he knew Lianne or could say anything about her. He just made his way quickly through the required ritual. Half-way through, I felt as though someone was staring at me and turned round. A small pain jabbed me in the chest. He was there. Will. Dressed in an austere black suit and looking more like a crow than ever. He sat at the back with his arms crossed and stared at me. No, that wasn't it. He was staring through me, as if I wasn't there at all. His eyes looked like holes in his gaunt, stubbly face. His hair was cropped to his skull, and I could see a small white scar on his scalp. I turned back, but it was as if his gaze was burning a hole in my neck.

When the coffin slid away I imagined Lianne's body inside it, burning up. From a fridge to a fire. I imagined her sweet little face, her bitten nails, that heart locket: 'Best . . .' Tears pricked at my eyes but I blinked them back. Across the aisle, there was the sound of weeping. When I glanced over, it was not one of the girls but Laurie. Laurie who had once been kissed by Lianne, who'd let her take his clumsy face in her hands and kiss him full on his hopeless mouth. Timid Carla was holding his hand. Spike was looking down at his big black boots and I couldn't see his face. Only Sylvia gazed ahead, with her calm, sea-green eyes.

The piped music played, and we stood up to leave. Will was still sitting at the back. His gaze was fixed on the space where the coffin had been. He looked impassive until I saw that his face was a sheet of tears. He didn't bother to wipe them away or conceal them. I walked to his pew and held out a hand. 'Come on,' I said. He looked at me then, but I might have been a stranger. I took his hand and pulled. 'Come on, it's the next funeral in a minute. You don't want to sit through another one, do you?'

I steered him out, blinking, into the sunlight. His hand was cold and he moved stiffly.

'Are you all right, Will?'

He didn't answer but he looked at me at last, blindly. I pulled a tissue out of my bag and wiped his face. He stood still and let me. I put a hand on his shoulder, but it was like touching a board. 'Will? Will, can I drive you home?'

'No.' He jerked away from me.

'Where's your car?'

'I walked,' he managed. His face was stunned, as if someone had brought a brick down on his head.

'Let me help you.'

'I don't need help.'

I looked at his closed face, his stony despair, and all the old tenderness welled up in me. He needed help more than anyone I'd ever met.

'Come on,' I said, and put my arm through his. 'Let's walk a bit.'

We walked in silence away from the crematorium. He went whichever way I steered him, as if he were stumbling along in a pitch-dark cave. I could have led him to the canal and pushed him over into the brown water and he wouldn't have noticed. But bit by bit I felt him relax against me. I wanted to take him home with me and take care of him. I wanted to rub the back of his neck, run him a bath, cook him a meal, make him smile, watch him sleep in the darkness, hold him tight, kiss the side of his unhappy mouth – not for sex but for intimacy. Human contact: the feel of someone else alongside you in this crappy cold world. But he was never going to let me in. Not like that.

'Here's my car. I'll run you home.'

He didn't argue. I opened the passenger door and pushed him inside. He looked up at me and seemed to be about to say something, but he changed his mind. I drove in silence, and left him at his front door. The last I saw of him, he was still standing there like a stranger who had no idea where he was. He looked so lonely.

I rang Poppy. Her greeting sounded a bit brittle.

'What's up?' I asked.

'Nothing,' she said huffily. But then she added, 'I've just been calling and leaving messages with that Julie and you never bothered to call back.'

'I'm so very sorry,' I said. 'I've been busy.'

'Fine. But you can't put people on hold.'

'Oh, Poppy, look, I really am sorry. Shall I come round now?'

'No. Seb and I are going out for a talk – not that it'll do any good.' She gave a bitter laugh.

'What's wrong? Is something up?'

'Oh, you know, the usual. Successful man and stay-at-home wife.'

'You mean . . .'

'I don't know, Kit. Let's talk later. OK? I've got to go and put some make-up on. I look like a frumpy old matron at the moment.'

'Don't say things like that.'

'Why not? It's true.'

'No, it's not. You're lovely.'

'Don't be stupid. I can't fit into any of my dresses any more.'

'No, I mean it. You're lovely and wonderful and he doesn't know how lucky he is.'

She sniffed. 'Sorry to have been curt.'

'No. I'm sorry.'

I put the kettle on to boil water for some pasta. What I really wanted was to sit on my sofa and have someone serve me tea and crumpets, cosset me, look after me. For the briefest second, I let myself dream of my mother stroking my hair and telling me I could rest now. I felt shaky with fatigue and emotion as I thought of Lianne's coffin sliding into the flames. I imagined Poppy desperately trying on clothes in front of the tall mirror in her room, and saw her disappointed face as she stared at her reflection. And then I imagined Will, all alone in his echoing house.

Suddenly, I could bear it no longer. I pulled on my suede jacket and ran to the car. I drove very fast, impatient with every traffic light. When he opened the door, he was still wearing his black suit. He stood back and let me in, and I pushed the door shut behind me. I led him to the sofa and pushed him into it and sat beside him. I took his two cold hands between my warm ones and blew on them. I undid the top buttons of his shirt. I eased off his stiff black shoes.

'I'll make you a cup of tea,' I said, and he didn't protest.

In his kitchen, I toasted two slices of bread and spread them with the marmalade that I found in the fridge.

'You're mothering me,' he said, but he took a large bite of the toast anyway.

I didn't ask him why he'd been so sad. I just watched him eating his toast and drinking his tea. Then I led him upstairs and took off all his clothes as if he was a child, and he lay in bed and I sat beside him and stroked his bristly head. At last he closed his eyes and I took away my hand. 'I'm not asleep,' he said softly.

'I only came to make sure you were all right.'

'Yeah, yeah. You shouldn't worry so much about other people, Kit.'

'I can't help it.'

'Ah.' He was slipping away from me. 'You should worry more about yourself, you know.'

'Why?'

'The good doctor.'

'Will?'

'Mmm.'

'About what I said . . .'

But he was asleep at last. His weary face softened, his lips parted slightly, his fingers relaxed and curled gently against the sheet. I watched him for a while, then I got up, closed the curtains, and left.

40

My date hadn't arrived so I bought myself a beer and stood outside on the steps watching the theatre-goers arrive. Gabe Teale's theatre, the Sugarhouse, was an abandoned warehouse that stood on railway land between the huge gas works and the canal. There had been what looked like a hasty conversion with scaffolding and Portakabins but the people in nice suits or high heels were still picking their way from the road between piles of rubble. The West End was only a quarter of an hour's walk away but it seemed like a different continent. I loved that about London. However safe and familiar you were, you were never more than five minutes' walk away from something strange.

The respectable people shuffled across to the improvised main entrance and then, almost without exception, they looked around at their surroundings and smiled with that childlike pleasure of doing something familiar in an improbable, almost secret place. Or maybe it was self-congratulation at having ventured into such a dangerous, out-of-the-way spot.

The crowd was starting to thin as people drifted to their seats. I looked at my watch. Twenty-two minutes past. I wasn't going to be stood up, was I? But there he was, puffing a little as he caught sight of me and did that rather pathetic attempt at a slow-motion jog to show that he was in a hurry.

'I'm not late, am I?' Oban said, looking around sheepishly.

'We've got a few minutes. Can I get you a drink?'

He perked up. 'Is there a bar here?' he asked. I held up my beer in response. 'Double Scotch.'

I fought my way through the crowd. By the time I'd got it for him a bell had rung. 'We'll need to be fairly quick,' I said, giving him the drink. He swallowed it in a single gulp.

'I needed that,' he said hoarsely. 'I'm not used to this sort of thing.'

'Nor am I,' I protested. 'I haven't been to the theatre for months, years. I thought it would be a good thing to come to this. A sort of celebration.'

Oban looked dubious. 'The last time I went was in about 1985. It was some sort of musical. On roller skates. I never felt the need to go again. What's this one about?'

I looked at my programme. 'I don't know,' I said. 'It's something to do with the history of this area.'

Oban looked wistfully into his empty glass. 'I didn't know there was any history, apart from criminality.'

A voice came over the Tannoy telling us that the performance was about to begin. We went in to take our seats, except that it turned out that there weren't any seats.

Market Day wasn't a normal play, any more than the Sugarhouse was a normal theatre. It was more like wandering around an indoor carnival. There were jugglers, clowns, performers on stilts, people on soapboxes giving speeches. There were children playing games, singing and shouting. There were stylized sketches performed by people of different ages in costumes they got out of a chest in the middle of the arena. The action happened all over the place, sometimes at the same time, and you had to wander around trying to catch what you could. At first I was irritated, tantalized by the feeling that I was missing something important on the other side of the hall, but after a bit I relaxed and treated it like a walk through an exotic foreign city. Oban grumbled at first about there not being a proper story but he was suddenly pulled out of the crowd by a rather beautiful young female magician. She asked him his name and what he did, and there was a big laugh when he confessed to being a policeman. He went very red and then was wonderfully startled when she found an egg in his inside jacket pocket.

I loved it, and I loved it partly because in a strange way it freed me to think. I gazed with immense pleasure at the man walking across the wire above us but at the same time my head was buzzing as I remembered all I'd been through in the last month. I went over it and tried to assemble it in some kind of order and of course it wouldn't go. But for the first time, in the middle of a happy crowd, it didn't seem to matter so very much.

In the interval the performers didn't disappear into their changing rooms but wandered through the crowd introducing themselves and chatting. Oban and I talked to one of the jugglers, an accordion player and a group of children who went to the local primary school. Oban suggested in a hopeful tone that we go and talk to the young woman behind the bar so we walked out into the 'foyer', which was really just another section of the old warehouse. Oban bought me a gin and tonic and another double Scotch for himself. The girl who served him must have been a teenager. Her hair was cut quite short and bleached. She had rings all round her ears, in her nose and through her lower lip. I asked her how long she'd been working there.

'A few weeks,' she said.

'Are you from around here?' I asked.

'I s'pose,' she said.

'It must be good to have a place like this in the area.'

'I s'pose,' she said, and then someone behind me ordered a bottle of Mexican beer from her rather crossly and we moved away.

'Cheers,' I said to Oban, and we clinked glasses. 'Clearly Gabe is doing his bit for local people. It seems as if this theatre is a bit like Will Pavic's hostel.'

Oban sipped his drink with a murmur of pleasure. 'I think he's doing a bit better than Will Pavic,' he said. 'This isn't exactly my sort of show. I prefer a good story. I couldn't follow most of it. But I can see that it's a clever bit of work. Hello, look who's here.'

He nodded at something and I looked round and saw Gabe Teale in conversation with a seriously trendy-looking couple. 'Let's go over,' I said.

'He looks busy.'

'Then we'll interrupt him.'

We pushed our way through the crowd and I nudged Gabriel's arm. He looked round and gave a start, as well he might. 'Surprise, surprise,' I said.

'Indeed,' he said.

He introduced us to the two people he was talking to. I didn't catch their names but it didn't matter because, with a slightly curious look at us, they drifted away towards another group of people who looked as if they, too, were in the know.

'You didn't think we were the cultural types,' I said.

He looked at us with genuine confusion. Did he think we were a couple? What was it about me? Was there anybody in the world so weird that if they were standing next to me people wouldn't assume I was going out with them?

'Well . . .' he began.

'It's fantastic,' I said. 'I hadn't realized this was such a huge set-up. And this amazing show. And employing these local people.' I was babbling. Stop babbling, Kit.

'It's not just me,' he said. 'I'm just the artistic director. There's a board of directors and various other people.'

'Don't be modest,' I said. 'Is Bryony here?'

'She doesn't work here,' he said. 'She's at home. She's still not very well.'

There was a moment of silence.

'So,' I said, 'you've probably got things to see to.'

'Yes,' he said. 'There are a couple of things.'

We shook hands formally in one of those curious goodbyes that aren't very momentous. It wasn't exactly as if Gabriel and Bryony were emigrating. He would be working in the area, I would be living in the area, and yet, London being London, we would probably never meet again.

When he was gone, Oban gave me a smile.

'You look very cheerful,' I said.

'I am. I've spent about an hour and a half with you and you haven't told me that I've been all wrong about everything.'

I couldn't suppress a smile. 'I was working my way to that,' I said. The bell rang for the second half. I took a sip. 'You know, I'm feeling quite cheerful as well. It's been a nice evening. I've got out of the house. Trouble is, when I'm feeling cheerful, that's when I start worrying. I'm a Puritan, you see. I believe that people are only happy when there's something somewhere that they don't know about.'

'You're never going to be happy with that attitude,' Oban said.

'People keep telling me that. I just want to say one thing and then I'll shut up. I know we should be pleased with ourselves, job well done and all that, but things keep nagging away at me – you know, like when you buy a shirt and, however careful you are, there's always a pin left over that sticks into you.'

Oban looked baffled. 'Is that the one thing you wanted to say? About shirts?'

'No, listen. Michael Doll was found dead with these trophies.'

'There's no problem with that, is there? You're the one who knows about these men. Murderers keep trophies, don't they?'

'They do,' I agreed. 'It's absolutely standard. They do it to maintain power over their victims, to relive the experience. Obviously these aren't normal trophies. The feeding cup belonged to the little girl, who wasn't his victim.'

'Yes, but it's still a trophy, isn't it? It was the reminder that he killed her mother. And for all that we know there could be something else that belonged to Philippa Burton in that rubbish dump he lived in.'

'You're right,' I said. 'And in the same way, the leather pouch he got from Bryony wasn't a normal trophy. For a start she wasn't dead.'

'He grabbed it during the struggle and kept it. Handy as well. It had the key to Bryony Teale's house. He could have made use of it.'

'Yes,' I said. 'So I'm just going to mention two loose ends and then we'll go and look at the play and that will be the end of it. We're now assuming that it was Michael Doll who was attacking Bryony Teale on the towpath. That would certainly deal with the coincidence of him being on the scene. But what about the other man?'

'I've thought about that,' said Oban, taking another sip of his drink. 'We were looking at it from the wrong angle. Instead of Terence Mack and Mickey Doll rescuing Bryony from unknown man, we have Terence Mack and unknown man rescuing Bryony from Mickey Doll. We knew that the different accounts were totally hopeless anyway, so it's not surprising that Mack and Bryony didn't realize what was going on.'

'And this unknown hero ran away because he was too modest to take all the credit?'

'There are plenty of people who don't want to meet the police, even as a witness. Maybe he was carrying drugs, something like that.'

'All right,' I said. 'Last question. What about Philippa Burton's list? What about the phone calls to the hostel?'

Oban drained his glass and placed it on the bar. 'The first thing is that we don't need to know. When a murderer dies before being tried, there are always details you never recover. It could be anything. Maybe . . . maybe . . .' he cast around '. . . maybe Bryony took a photograph of Lianne, and . . . and Philippa saw it in an exhibition and wanted to get a copy of it and . . .'

'Bryony said she didn't know either of them and why would she want to phone the hostel? And why would that make Michael Doll kill them all?'

'That was just off the top of my head,' Oban said, a little irritably. 'Given time I could come up with something better.'

'Doesn't it worry you?'

'What worries me is the half-dozen or so murders I've worked on where we never found anybody at all. I think of those every evening before I go to sleep. About once a year I dig out the old files and I wonder if we missed anything or if something new has been developed that we can try on it. This case is closed. That's what makes me happy. I don't mind a few gaps. Remember, reality is cleverer than we are. You can't expect to understand it all.'

I wanted to say more but I'd promised and, besides, a brass band was striking up inside.

41

Lottie and Megan were playing an intricate, unintelligible game on the grass. An hour earlier I had given a bright purple floppy dinosaur to Lottie and a red and white floppy snail to Megan, and both featured prominently in their game. I had given a green and blue floppy crab to Amy and she was rolling down the hill and trying to encourage the crab to roll with her. Behind them was London, looking pleasantly hazy in this hot afternoon from high on Primrose Hill.

I was lying on a rug, propped up on an elbow. I took another sip of cold white wine.

'I want to hear all about it,' Poppy said. 'Of course, Seb has told me some . . .' She glanced over at Megan and then at Amy. 'Megan, stop that! Stop it now or I'll take it away from you. But Seb's version is probably rather different from yours.' Her tone was dry.

I lay back on the rug.

'I don't know if I can tell it coherently,' I said. 'Especially on an afternoon like this, with two glasses of white wine already coursing round my blood.'

It was an all-female picnic. Three girls playing on the grass, while two mothers and one non-mother sat on the rug. The other mother was Ginny, an old friend of Poppy. The fathers were elsewhere. Ginny's husband was playing cricket – somewhere in the Home Counties, she said – and Seb was in a television studio somewhere in front of us in central London.

'What's he talking about now?' I asked. 'Still the Philippa Burton case?'

'I think so. He's plugging this book he's nearly finished.'

'About the case? That's amazingly quick.'

'He was writing it as it went.'

'Is everything all right between you now?'

'Not really.' She glanced over at the girls again. 'But I can't talk about it now.'

'Of course. Later.'

'About the book – actually, you'll be really flattered. Guess why?'

I took a sip of wine. 'I don't know,' I said. 'Why?'

'He partly got the idea from that bedtime story you told the girls when you came round for dinner a few months ago. Kept them awake for about a month. Something about a castle, wasn't it?'

'What's the book called?'

'*The Red Room*, I think. Could that be it?'

'Yes, it could be. It was a nightmare I was having. That's what it was about.'

'Oh, I see. Seb must have talked to you about it.'

I didn't reply because for the moment I was drenched, smothered, plunged in self-pity. I had been slashed in the face and had a nightmare that had haunted me. And now I felt as if I had been mugged and my nightmare, my own personal private nightmare, had been stolen from me. I drained my glass and then I thought, So fucking what? Who cares?

Scattered around the blanket were sandwiches, fruit, fizzy drinks and some things I'd grabbed during a swoop on a supermarket: plastic tubs of hummus and taramasalata, pitta bread, olives, breadsticks, miniature pork pies, baby carrots, chopped cauliflower. I prodded the tip of a baby carrot into some pink-coloured dip and nibbled it experimentally.

I felt numb – almost pleasantly so – as I lay and nibbled, sipped, chatted, but I could see that the attention of the other two women was always incomplete. Whether they were telling me something urgent, or crunching on a floret of cauliflower, they would always be glancing around or looking over my shoulder in search of the little girls. At one point I murmured something intended to be reassuring about how they were only a few yards away, and Ginny immediately responded with a story of a friend of a friend who had left a three-year-old unattended for just two or three minutes in a garden with a little pond that was hardly more than an inch deep. Well, you can imagine the rest. Ginny was a comfy-looking dark-haired woman with a lovely laugh. She was such a motherly mother, I wondered who she was before having Lottie. Someone like me, probably, thinking she was all right as she was.

I lay back and closed my eyes. Close to my ear, Poppy shouted for the girls to come and have their lunch right now and I mean right now. There was a scramble of small bodies and screams because someone had arrived at the blanket without waiting for someone else and I suddenly felt a shock of cold on my jeans. I sat up with a yell and saw the wine bottle had been tipped over on to me by Megan as she clambered across towards the chicken drumsticks. When she saw what she had done, her howls drowned even those of her little sister. Poppy took her in her arms.

'That's absolutely all right, Megan, my darling. Don't cry. It doesn't matter at all, does it? Kit, could you tell Megan that it doesn't matter?'

'It doesn't matter, Megan,' I said obediently.

'I'm sorry, Kit,' Poppy said, 'but Megan gets ridiculously upset by these things.'

By this time Megan seemed already to have recovered her spirits and was gnawing at a piece of chicken.

'Anyway,' said Ginny cheerfully, 'white wine doesn't stain. In fact, it's what you use for getting red wine stains *out*, isn't it?'

'It's just a bit wet,' I said dabbing at it with a sheet of kitchen roll. I felt that it was me who should be saying it didn't matter, rather than them.

'God,' laughed Poppy, 'you should be grateful it's just wine. You couldn't begin to imagine the stains I've had on my clothes.'

I smiled, with only a small hint of strain, and filled my glass again.

'You know,' said Ginny, 'I think lots of mothers have been particularly affected by your murders.'

'Hardly mine,' I objected.

'That poor little girl whose mother was snatched away while she was playing in the playground. I've hardly let Lottie out of my sight ever since it happened. I know it's irrational.'

I murmured assent.

'Didn't it get you down terribly, Kit? Didn't you find it unbearable?'

I placed my wineglass on the rug, then thought better of it and picked it up again. 'I don't know if that's the right word,' I said. 'It made me feel sad.'

'Speaking for myself, I feel safer, anyway, now that the person who did it isn't around any more. I saw the detective on telly. He was being so nice about you.'

I looked at the little girls. Amy had reached the pudding course. She was supposedly eating a chocolate

347

muffin but this involved so much mashing up of the muffin, so much smearing of it over her face and such a vast spillage of crumbs on to the blanket that it was difficult to believe any of it had ended up in her mouth.

'It wasn't as satisfying as you might think,' I said. 'This man – he was called Michael Doll – he was just found dead –'

'Killed by vigilantes,' Poppy interrupted.

'Obviously I wouldn't defend something like that,' said Ginny. 'But I must admit when I read about it, my first thought was, great.' She pulled Lottie close to her and hugged her. 'It may be rough justice, but there's a man who won't do harm again.'

'Or good,' I added.

'But you must know all about him.' Poppy said in an encouraging tone, sensing my distress.

'I'd met him.'

'Ugh,' said Ginny. 'Creepy. What was he like?'

'He *was* creepy,' I said. 'He was very disturbed, he was repulsive in many ways, a bit pathetic.'

'But what's it like having known somebody who's done these terrible things?' Poppy asked.

'I'm not sure,' I said. 'You should ask Seb. But I didn't think he had done the murders. And he died before things were properly sorted out.'

'But there was solid evidence. The police said so.'

'That's right. There was solid evidence. Lots of evidence. Unfortunately it doesn't really fit together very well. But you don't want to hear about that.'

I looked at them. They really didn't want to hear about it. The girls, who had wandered away, had come back now and were demanding attention. The two mothers were tied to their children as if by steel wires, their faces jerking round ceaselessly. Had they fallen over? Had they run away? Were they being too noisy? Were they being too quiet? Had they been murdered? I thought of little Emily in the playground, digging in the sandpit while her mother was seized and taken away and beaten to death. I created the scenario in my mind as I had so many hundreds of times before and played through it with Michael Doll in the role of the psychopathic killer. That was it. I jumped to my feet.

'Where are you going?' asked Poppy. 'You look as if you've seen a ghost.'

'Maybe I have. Sorry. Got to rush. Something . . .'

'Can I look at the sun?' said Megan.

'No,' cried Poppy. 'You must never ever *ever* look at the sun.'

'Why not?' said Megan.

'It'll burn your eyes.'

'If I close my eyes.' She closed her eyes. 'Is it all right if I close my eyes?'

'I suppose so. But you can't see anything.'

'It's not dark,' said Megan. 'It's red. Where's the red from?'

'I don't know,' said Poppy. 'I suppose it's the blood in your eyelids.'

'Blood?' said Megan. 'Yippee. I'm looking at my blood. Let's all look at our blood.'

And the little girls staggered blindly around on the sunny green hillside looking at their blood while I ran from them as if I was being pursued.

42

I was breathless when I arrived back at my flat, and my head buzzed with the white wine and the sun, but I immediately picked up the phone and called Oban. He was out somewhere. I could hear traffic, people talking. 'Are you busy?' I asked.

'It's the weekend, Kit,' he said. 'What is it? Want to take me to the opera?'

'I wanted to alert you that I'm going to see the little girl, Emily Burton.'

'What?'

'You know, Philippa Burton's daughter.'

'I know who she fucking is. That . . . that . . .' He seemed to be gasping for breath. 'That is *such* a bad idea.'

'There's just one question I've got to ask.'

'Kit, Kit,' he said soothingly, as if he were trying to talk me off a window-ledge, 'there's always one more question. Think of what you're doing. You'll stir up that poor family all over again. You'll drive yourself crazy. You'll drive me crazy. Just leave it.'

'I wanted to ask if you thought a police officer should come along with me.'

'No, definitely not. The case is closed. This is a free country. You can call on anybody you like but it's nothing to do with us. Honestly, Kit, I like you but you need something, I don't know what it is –'

And the line went dead. I don't know whether Oban had walked into a tunnel or just given up in despair. A tape-recorder. That's what I needed. I had one somewhere. A few minutes' rummaging produced a tatty little cassette player from the bottom of a cupboard and then, in a drawer of old plugs, rubber bands, pens without caps and a huge daisy chain of paperclips, I found a dusty cassette tape, a party tape from when I was at college. That would do. I phoned the house. A woman answered.

'Hello. Is that Pam Vere?'

'Yes.'

'This is Kit Quinn. Do you remember? I'm the –'

'Yes. I remember.'

'I wondered if I could come and spend a few minutes with Emily.'

'She's not here at the moment.'

'Could I come later?'

'But I thought it was over.'

'I just want to dot some Is, cross some Ts. And I wanted to see how Emily is.'

'She seems to be all right. She's happy with friends. And an au pair has started.'

'Can I come? I'll be five minutes.'

'I don't want to be difficult, but is it really necessary?'

'I'd be very grateful,' I said firmly, unrelentingly.

There was a pause. 'She'll be back at just past four. Maybe you could talk to her before she has tea.'

'I'll be there.'

It was more formal than before. I had arrived before Emily and I found a spot in the kitchen where I could plug in my tape-recorder. Neurotically I tested it a couple of times, saying one-two, one-two into it and playing it back. The second time I suddenly wasn't sure whether it was the first one-two or the second, so I did it again saying A-B-C-D, for want of anything better.

Emily burst into the room like a little chattering

gremlin in paint-spattered red dungarees, a blonde au pair running to keep up with her. She looked so happy. Suddenly I pictured her in five years' time, with no surviving memory of her mother, nothing that could be disentangled from snapshots and half made-up stories told to her about Philippa by others. She ran forward and hugged her grandmother's knees. When she saw me, she fell silent. I walked over and knelt down beside her.

'Remember me?' I said. She shook her head solemnly and looked away. 'I've got something to show you.'

She had just been getting ready to be shy but in her interest she forgot. She gave me her hand and we walked over to the kitchen table and my tape-recorder. Pam sat opposite us, watchful.

'Look at this,' I said.

'What?' she said.

I pressed the record button.

'Say something.'

'Don't want to say something.'

'What do you do at play-school?'

'I do *anything*,' she said firmly.

I switched it off, rewound and played the tape back. Her mouth fell open in amazement.

'Do it again,' she said.

'All right.' I pressed the record button. I sat very close to her. I could smell soap and paint.

'Well,' I said, 'so what shall we talk about?'

Emily crinkled her nose and giggled. 'Dunno,' she said. 'That's your mark,' she said pointing at my face.

'That's right,' I said. 'See? You remember.'

'Does it hurt?'

'Not so much,' I said. 'It's got better.'

'Can I feel it?'

'All right.'

I leaned forward and Emily stretched out a stubby forefinger. She traced a stinging, itching progress from near my ear, down my cheek to the edge of my jaw. No pain now.

'When we talked before,' I said, 'you were playing with your friend and we talked about the playground. You were playing in the playground when your mummy went away. Do you remember that?'

'Yeah,' she said.

'Lots of people talked to you about that, didn't they?' I said.

'Pleecemen,' she said.

'That's right,' I said. 'And those policemen and -women, they asked you if you had seen your mummy go away with somebody and you said you hadn't.'

Emily was scratching on the table. I could feel I was losing her. The tiny attention span of a nearly-four-year-old was almost at an end. I looked at the tape-recorder. The spools were rotating. I had come here with just one shot in my gun. I would fire it, and if nothing came of it, that really would be it. I would say goodbye politely, go home and return to those bits of my life I had neglected for too long. I put my hand out and enfolded Emily's own tiny, warm, sticky hand. I gave a little squeeze to attract her attention. She looked at me.

'I don't want to ask you about that, Emily. I want to ask you about something different. Could you tell me about the nice woman?'

'What?' Emily said.

'What are you . . . ?' Pam said.

'Sssh,' I said abruptly, holding up my hand. 'Emily, what did she give you?'

'Nuffing.'

'Nothing?'

'A lolly.'

'That's nice,' I said. I could feel the thump of my heart all over my body, even in my head. 'What did she do? Did she push you on the swing?'

'A bit. She took me to the sand.'

I tried to picture the playground. Yes, of course. The sandpit was the furthest point from the railings where Philippa had been standing, watching her daughter.

'That's fun,' I said. 'And then she went away. She left you there?'

'Dunno.'

'What did the lady look like?'

'I'm bo-ored,' Emily said loudly.

'Was she big?'

'Bo-or-or-ored.'

'That's lovely, Emily,' I said. 'Thank you very much.' I gave her a hug. She wrestled herself free and ran to the door and out into the garden. I switched off the tape-machine. I looked over at Pam. She seemed lost in distressing thought.

'But . . .' she said. 'It was that man. What was she . . . ?'

I had been intending just to get up and leave but I owed her something.

'I should have thought of it ages ago,' I said. 'You can abduct a woman on a dark night, in a lonely place, without too much fuss. You can do it in a crowded place as well, though it takes a bit more care. But you can't trick a mother into leaving her child alone, not even in a playground, not even for a single minute. There'd have to be somebody to look after the child. That's what I suddenly thought. And I guessed it would have to be a woman. And Emily always said her mother was coming

354

back, didn't she?' Pam nodded, staring at me. 'Because that's probably the last thing Philippa said to her. She would have said something like, "Don't worry, I'll be back soon," and Emily's still waiting.'

I unplugged the tape-recorder then stood up, clutching it to my chest as if someone was going to try to steal it from me. 'I've got to go,' I said.

'So he had an accomplice,' Pam said.

I shook my head. 'I knew Michael Doll,' I said. 'I don't think he was on genuine speaking terms with a single woman.' Except me, I thought to myself. And with a pang I left her sitting at the kitchen table, with her hands folded as if she was praying.

43

I rang the Tyndale Centre for Young People on my mobile when I was just a few minutes down the road. When the woman who answered the phone said that Will wasn't there, I drove the rest of the way, parked right outside and rang the doorbell.

'Is Sylvia here, by any chance?' I asked the young woman on duty, who had cropped hair, a spider-web tattoo on her cheek and who didn't look much older than the residents.

'Nope.' The spider-web moved and stretched when she spoke.

'Are you expecting her?'

'Couldn't say.'

'Do you have any idea where I might find her?'

'Couldn't say.' She took a cigarette from behind her ear and stuck it between her lips. 'Confidential,' she said. She lit the cigarette.

'Oh. Of course. If you do see her, could you tell her that Kit Quinn wanted to ask her something? I'll write down my phone numbers.' The young woman didn't answer, just looked at me suspiciously. 'She knows me,' I added. I pulled my notepad out of my bag, jotted down the numbers on a page and handed it over. She put it on the front desk without looking at it. I had little hope she would do anything about it. 'Thanks anyway, and sorry to bother you.'

But as I turned to leave, with no idea of where to try next, a voice piped up, 'You could try the fair.'

I turned to see a boy squatting by the front door. He looked about ten, except he had a cigarette in the corner of his mouth and was playing with a flick-knife.

'The fair? The one on Bibury Common?' I'd passed it on my way, feeling a tremor of nostalgia for the days when I'd loved the swoop and sickening fall of high rides, the tacky fluffy toys and giant plastic hammers you won when you shot all the targets down with a misaligned air rifle.

'Yup.' He hesitated. 'Could you lend me a couple of fags, miss?'

'Sorry, I don't smoke.'

'Money, then.' He put his hands together in a self-mocking gesture of pleading. I slid a glance at the girl on duty then passed over some coins. 'Cool! Thanks.'

Evening was drawing in, and the fair was just getting going. Men in leather jackets, with oiled-back hair and manky teeth, were tightening things with spanners. The big dipper was circling slowly round through the dusk, though its chairs were all unoccupied. There was a helter-skelter, a merry-go-round of teacups, one of animals, the dodgem cars watched over by lean young men in tight jeans who were chewing gum, a haunted castle, a rickety-looking hall of mirrors whose last segment was being wheeled into place, stalls where you had to toss hoops over bottles and win dolphins, stalls where you could win bags of liquorice allsorts and nasty vases if you threw a dart into the bullseye, vans selling greasy burgers and fat orange sausages. And there was mud, squelchy brown mud, liquid streams of mud where the caravans had churned ruts; mud everywhere.

I looked around for Sylvia. People were just beginning

to arrive. Tinny music was starting to play. A helium balloon, let loose from the grasp of a howling toddler, floated up into the sky. The smell of frying and of cigarette smoke filled the air. Perhaps she wasn't here. I picked my way through the mud, staring at the knots of people, and was thinking of giving up when I saw her. She was climbing into a dodgem car with a boy of about sixteen. As they sat down, he put his arm around her shoulders but she pushed it away contemptuously. Her hair was tied into ridiculous bunches, and she looked much younger than I'd remembered her, and happy, as if she hadn't a care in the world. I watched her as she bumped her way round the circuit, screeching in pretend fear when she was smashed into, whooping when she wrenched her car round to hit someone else.

When she climbed out, I went to meet her. 'Hello, Sylvia.'

'Hi.' She didn't seem in the least surprised to see me there.

'I was looking for you.'

'Yeah?'

'I wanted to ask you something. But I don't want to interrupt your evening, so if you'd prefer, we could meet after.'

'It's OK. I haven't any money anyway. I'll see you around, Robbie,' she said, dismissively, to the boy by her side, who slouched off, his long flappy trousers dragging in the mud.

'Do you want something to eat? Or drink?'

'I don't mind.'

'What about . . . ?'

'OK. A burger with fried onions and ketchup, some chips, and a Coke.'

We walked over to one of the vans, where I got the

food. 'There's a bench over there, where we can talk,' I said.

'Sure,' she said, amiably. She didn't seem curious, but she was certainly hungry. She had eaten most of her food by the time we sat down. There was grease running down her chin and ketchup on her lips. She dragged her sleeve across her face and sighed.

'There was just something I thought you might be able to help me with,' I began.

'About Lianne?'

'Kind of. Well, about Daisy as well. Lianne's friend.'

'Sure. The one who topped herself.'

'Yes. Did you know her well?'

'Saw her around. Hung around with her sometimes. You know. Same crowd.'

'Do you know if Will Pavic knew her?'

'Probably. I mean, he would, wouldn't he?' Her gaze wandered off. 'Could I get some candyfloss too?'

'Definitely. In a minute. This is a difficult question, Sylvia, but do you know – do you have any idea if Will Pavic ever, well, got involved with any of the young people in his care?'

'Involved?' she repeated, as if it was a foreign word.

'Yes. If he had sexual relationships with any of them.'

'Oh, *fucked* them, you mean?' She giggled and patted me kindly on the shoulder. '"Sexual relationships",' she said, mimicking my voice.

'Did he?'

'Got a fag?'

'No.'

'Oh, well.' She pulled her own cigarettes out of her jeans pocket and lit one. 'Don't think so.'

'Are you sure?'

'Sure? Course not. You can never be sure about things

like that, can you? Just, not that I know of.' She wrinkled her little nose and puffed away. 'He's not a toucher, though.'

'A toucher?'

'Some of them put their hand on your shoulder, on your knee, pat you when they're talking to you. Ugh!' She shuddered. 'Creeps, as if we don't know what they're doing. Will doesn't do that. He keeps his distance.'

'OK. What about Gabriel Teale? Did Daisy ever mention his name?'

'Gabriel? What kind of stupid name is that for a man? Never heard of him.'

'He runs the Sugarhouse.'

'Oh, *that*. I know that, of course.'

'Did Daisy ever go there?' I asked, trying to keep the urgency out of my voice.

'Sure. Loads of us have been there. Not me. Not my thing. Daisy did, definite. She had to learn how to do cartwheels.' She smiled. 'She was brilliant at them by the end. She could do it completely straight, lots in a row. She used to cartwheel into rooms.'

Excitement prickled up and down my spine. I pulled the theatre programme out of my bag and turned to the back of it. 'You know when we first met, you said that someone was asking questions about Lianne? Is that the man?' I put my finger on the photograph of Gabe.

She glanced at it. 'No way!' She giggled. 'The person who was after Lianne was a woman.'

I stopped dead in my tracks. 'You never said that,' I managed.

'You never asked.'

I pulled Bryony's picture from my bag. 'Was it her, then?'

Sylvia squinted in the half-light. 'Nope,' she said.

'You're sure?'

'Sure. They're nothing like. The woman I saw was blonde, for a start.'

In a daze, I pulled out another photograph. 'Like this?'

'Yeah. Yeah, that's the one. I'm certain. She was snooping around, asking things in her hoity-toity accent. Who is she?'

I looked down at the face, touched it softly with a finger. 'A woman called Philippa Burton.'

'Philippa Burton.' Sylvia looked at the photograph and a shadow passed across her face, a kind of hardness. 'Did she kill Lianne, then?'

'No,' I said. Then: 'I don't know.'

'You look funny, are you ill?'

'No. I'm just confused, Sylvia. Do you want your candyfloss now?'

'Are you having one too?'

'No.'

'Why not? Let yourself go, why don't you?' She turned her shrewd, delicate face to me and looked at me assessingly. 'You want to relax.'

A curious feeling of lightheadedness took over. 'OK. I'll have a giant pink candyfloss.'

'Cool. And then we'll go on that.' She pointed towards the Waltzers, which were spinning round so fast that I could only just make out the faces of the yelling passengers.

'I'll think about it.'

'Don't think. Come on.'

I ate the candyfloss. It fizzed against my teeth, stuck in my hair and melted on my cheek. Then Sylvia and I climbed into one of the Waltzers.

'I don't want to do this.'

Sylvia giggled. The car started to move, slowly at first, but then faster, faster, and each car was whirling round in its own dizzying circle as well. I tried to say something, but my cheek muscles seemed to have gone slack. The world was a hurtling blur. The centrifugal force pinned me back against the seat; my stomach was somewhere else, my sticky hair whipped against my face.

'Fuck,' I managed to gasp.

'Scream,' said Sylvia, in my ear. 'Scream your heart out.'

I tipped my head back and I opened my mouth. I screamed, until I could hear my scream ripping above everyone else's. I screamed my heart out.

44

There was more fumbling with my tape-recorder, which became worse under the sceptical, snorting, frankly disapproving gaze of Detective Inspector Guy Furth, and the disappointed and embarrassed one of Detective Chief Inspector Oban. They were two men with their minds on other things, new cases, who were confronted with an obsessed woman who wouldn't let go. Worse than that, it was a woman who was crouched under a table in Oban's office trying and failing to fit a simple plug into a socket. I cursed silently and then loudly. A plug was a fucking plug, wasn't it?

I finally managed it and positioned the machine on Oban's desk.

'You'll have to listen carefully,' I said. 'The recording isn't brilliant quality. I did it on an old tape I found at the back of a drawer and I think it's a bit past its best.'

The two detectives exchanged glances as I pressed the 'play' button. It was a little embarrassing, because I hadn't rewound it properly and the tape began with me saying one-two, one-two, and then the alphabet. I looked at Oban. He was biting his lip as if he was trying to stop himself laughing. It didn't get much better. There was the seemingly endless prattling between me and Emily about her play-school and my injury. Oban was shifting impatiently in his seat.

'Was it hailing when you did the interview?' Furth asked, with a curl of his lip.

'There's a sort of crackle on the tape, I know,' I

admitted. 'Sorry about all this but I wanted you to hear the whole thing so that you got the context.'

He muttered something under his breath.

'What was that?' I asked.

'Nothing,' he said.

I switched off the tape and rewound it a bit.

'For God's sake,' he cried, 'we're not going to listen to it again, are we?'

'I want to make sure you don't miss anything.'

He groaned. As the conversation moved on to the events in the playground he gave a frown of concentration. Suddenly Emily was saying she was bored, there was a click and a crackle and there we were in the middle of 'Hotel California' – it had been a party tape in the mid-eighties. The two men grinned.

'I like this bit,' said Furth. 'Better sound quality as well.'

'So what do you think?' I said impatiently.

'Play it again,' said Oban. 'Just the last bit,' he added hastily.

With a bit of trial and error I rewound the tape and played Emily's responses about the woman. Before the end, he leaned over and switched it off himself. He sat back with a look of discomfort.

'Well?' I said.

He was looking out of the window as if he had just noticed something fascinating that required his full attention. He glanced round as if he was surprised I was still here.

'Sorry,' he said. 'I was just thinking of a few weeks ago when we were playing *you* a tape. Funny how things work out.'

'Not really,' I said.

'What do you want me to say?' he said.

I already had that queasy feeling that things weren't going my way. 'I'm not sure I wanted you to say anything,' I said. 'I thought you might jump up in the air and get excited.'

'What should I get excited about?'

I looked at both of them. Furth's expression was oddly kind, which made me feel worse. 'Are you not hearing what I'm hearing? We should have thought of this ages ago. People don't grab mothers while they're supervising their children with lots of other people around. There was a woman involved, a woman who spent a few minutes with Emily while Philippa Burton was lured away to the car where she was killed.'

'I don't hear that,' said Oban.

'What do you hear?'

He gave a dismissive sniff. 'I hear leading questions being put to a three-year-old girl who's giving vague answers. I mean "the nice woman", what's that? That could be any woman in the past year who bought her a lolly.'

'So you don't believe Emily.'

'For a start, as you know, that tape would be totally inadmissible as evidence. I also think it's bullshit. I'm sorry, Kit, but I think you've got carried away and you're starting to waste my time.'

'So you're not going to consider the possibility that a woman was involved?'

'Do you have one in mind?'

'Yes.'

'Who?'

'Bryony Teale.'

'You what?'

'You can kick me out in five minutes but listen to me.'

★

'And did he listen?' said Julie, sipping at her drink.

We were sitting in a new bar in Soho called Bar Nothing. Apparently hard edges and straight lines were out. This was all pastel sofas and large cushions on the floor. We were sitting at the bar. It wasn't actually soft. It couldn't be soft. Your drinks would fall over. But even that had a gently swirling curve.

I had met Julie in the early evening and I had shouted and raged and metaphorically headbutted the wall, so she insisted that the only solution was for us to dress up and go out on the town together. She put on and looked wonderful in yet another of my dresses, a black one with chiffon sleeves. I was wearing my special figure-hugging pink dress that was part of a fantasy of being the subject of one of those blues songs in which the singer complains about having been lured away from home by a devil woman. I sort of hoped someone would come up to the two of us and tell us we were violating city ordinances.

I think I immediately embarrassed Julie by ordering two margaritas, which is probably a bit nineties, if not eighties, but I needed something quick.

'You know, pink is your colour,' said Julie, as we took our first sips. 'It goes with your grey eyes, somehow.'

'Goes with my scar.'

'Don't say that,' she said.

'I think I'm getting better,' I said. 'I used to talk about the Phantom of the Opera, didn't I? I don't worry about people feeling that any more. Now I think they probably just assume I had some cosmetic surgery that went wrong.'

Julie didn't reply. Instead she touched my face, tipping it so she could see the side fully in the light. She scrutinized it as if she were assessing an ornament in my flat. I thought of little Emily running her finger down the

366

scar. Her inspection finished, Julie smiled. 'It looks like something that tells a story.'

'The only story that scar tells is how little time he had.'

Julie flinched and I apologized. We ordered another drink each and I steered the conversation on to her. She talked about travels, about terrible men and a couple of nice men, and about her plans and suddenly she asked me if I wanted to go along and I horrified myself by thinking, Well, why not? Why not just drop everything and go? Towards the end of my second drink I thought, Why not drop everything and go that very evening?

We found a table and ordered a couple of salads and a bottle of wine, but suddenly this didn't seem enough. I felt a craving for red meat. I thought I even saw Julie blanch when it arrived, thin slices of raw beef with shavings of Parmesan, drizzled with olive oil and lemon juice. 'I know I'm a carnivore,' she said. 'But I think I prefer it when the meat goes a nice brown colour.'

I tried to keep the conversation to Julie and her life and times, I really did, but it was no good. I was like an unstable smoking volcano and while we were still picking at our salads the volcano erupted and started giving her an animated account of the last couple of days.

'Yes, Oban did listen,' I said, our glasses full once more. 'I mean, he heard what I was saying. That's the expression, isn't it? He heard me out. Then it was just, the case is closed, don't waste our time, don't make us think that life is more complicated than we thought, don't make us do our job properly.'

I stopped and laughed. I had caught myself actually jabbing my finger fiercely at Julie. She had moved away slightly to avoid being stabbed by it.

'It's not me,' she said, laughing as well. 'You don't

have to convince me. Well, you do. I must admit I don't understand what you're on about. Are you saying that that nice photographer woman was helping that weirdo Doll murder people?'

'No, no, Doll had nothing to do with it. She was helping her husband, Gabriel.'

Julie took another sip of red wine. 'I dunno,' she said. 'I should have been asking you about this three drinks ago at least. I mean, these are nice people. He works for a theatre. Why would they kill those women?'

'And Doll as well.'

'What do you mean? That was done by those vigilantes, wasn't it?'

'No, it wasn't.'

'But you told me that they even left a message.'

'Yeah, I know. "Murderous Bastard" with those ridiculous misspellings. That was so pathetic, but I was shocked by the scene and I didn't think about it. Is someone who can't even spell "bastard" going to use a word like "murderous"? Remember what I thought about the bodies of Lianne and Philippa? The wounds were like someone pretending to be a psychopath but without the real conviction. You should see what a real sexual psychopath does to a woman's body.'

'I don't think so,' Julie said. 'So these are nice murderers, right?'

'They weren't doing it for fun. It was because they felt they had to.'

'What the fuck for?'

'I haven't a clue. But it doesn't matter. That's the good bit. Before, none of it fitted together. Now it all does. This poor girl, Daisy, it turns out that she had a connection to Gabe Teale. I saw a friend of hers yesterday who told me she'd been working at the Sugarhouse.

Lianne was concerned about Daisy, and she gets killed. I've discovered that Philippa Burton was after Lianne.'

'Why?'

'No idea. The note I found in her room showed that she had made the connection between Lianne and Bryony. Anyway, she gets killed. I've now shown that Bryony was involved in abducting Philippa.'

'Have you?' said Julie doubtfully.

'Absolutely. So, now where was I?'

'Not sure.'

'Michael Doll. That so-called attack on Bryony never made any sense. All that coverage of Michael Doll made almost everybody think he had murdered Lianne. But for Gabriel and Bryony, it placed Doll at the scene. Maybe he had seen something. Maybe he even got in touch with them and threatened Gabriel. They made a half-arsed attempt to attack him, knock him on the head, dump him in the canal, whatever, make it look like vigilantes, but then that Terence Mack man pops up, Bryony is grabbed, Gabe legs it, Doll hasn't got a fucking clue what's going on, and it looks to everybody like an attack on Bryony. No wonder she was in such a traumatized state.'

'Well . . .'

'And so they – or probably just Gabe, since by now Bryony is assumed to be in danger and is under police protection – go to Michael Doll's flat to do the job properly. Bryony had got Emily's cup from when they tricked Philippa into going off with Gabe for a chat in their car. Gabe murders Doll, leaves the cup. Doll is dead, well and truly framed, the case is closed.'

Julie tipped the last drops of wine into our two glasses. 'More?' she said.

'No,' I said. 'I'm sobering up.'

'Doesn't sound like it. Now, wait a minute,' she said, 'it wasn't just the drinking cup, was it? There was also that leather pouch. Do you really think he would leave that deliberately? That was a bit of a risk.'

'I thought about that,' I said. 'I don't think it was deliberate. You should have been there. The room was just blood. Gabe must have been covered.'

'If he was there,' Julie added.

'He was there. He's covered in blood, strips down to wash in the bathroom, leaves the pouch. It's found, but it turns out not to matter because it's seen as another of Doll's trophies.'

Julie didn't speak for a moment. She looked as if she was doing long division in her head. 'You said all that to Oban in five minutes?' she said finally.

'I gave him the shortened version.'

'No wonder he kicked you out.'

'You're not convinced?'

'I don't know. I'll have to let it settle in my brain for a bit. I don't care what you say, I'm going to have another drink.'

She ordered two brandies, took a gulp of hers and winced. 'So what're you going to do? Are you going to have another go at Oban?'

I flicked my finger against my glass, making it ring.

'No,' I said reflectively. 'I think I've used up my store of goodwill with him. I don't know. I've been going over and over it in my mind. You know when Paul McCartney thought of "Yesterday", he spent days trying to work out where he had heard it before. He couldn't believe he'd really thought it up. I've been wondering whether I'm imagining patterns that aren't really there.' I picked up the glass and drank a burning gulp. 'Maybe I should go and talk to them,' I said.

'Who?'

'Bryony and Gabe.'

'You mean, tell them you think they're mass murderers?'

'Give them a little prod, make them worried. Maybe they'll do something.'

Julie drained her glass. 'Like nothing, if they're innocent,' she said. 'And kill you, if they're guilty.'

'I can't think of what else to do.'

Now it was Julie's turn to point her finger at me. It was a little unsteady. 'How much have you had to drink?' she said.

'Two margaritas. About a bottle of wine. And this brandy.' I finished it off.

'Exactly,' said Julie. 'What I hope is that it's the drink talking. It's probably all been the drink talking. But the last bit. I'm absolutely sure that tomorrow morning neither of us is going to remember anything about this evening. Especially me. But I want you to promise me that you won't do anything really, really stupid. Do you promise that?'

'Of course I promise,' I said, with a smile.

'I don't know if I believe you.' She put a hand on my shoulder and shook me, as if she wanted to wake me up. 'Look, Kit, don't you see that what you're doing here is completely crazy? And I mean *completely*.'

'No, I –'

'It's one thing to put yourself at risk for a reason – I still wouldn't advise it.' She paused to hiccup violently, then continued, 'But you're talking about putting yourself at risk for no reason at all. As if the lives of two dead women were somehow more important than your own living life, if you see what I mean.'

'Yes. But that's not the way I'm looking at it.'

'Sure, you're looking at it from back-to-front and inside out. You're trying to save dead people. You can't.'

'I know that.'

She brought her face closer to mine and repeated, louder, 'You can't save dead people, Kit. You can't bring anyone dead back to life. Let it go.'

45

When I was a teenager, my father used to make me drink a big glass of milk before going out to a party. He said it lined the stomach. I should have drunk a glass of milk last night, I thought, when I woke the next morning. The light shining in through my half-open curtains hurt my eyes even before I opened them, and my mouth felt dry. I squinted at my clock. It was half past six. I'd give myself five more minutes. Just five, no more. Never had my pillow felt so soft or my limbs so heavy or my eyelids so glued together.

I peered groggily at the clock again, and the digits clicked round to six thirty-five. Just a few more minutes. I remembered a time as a child when I'd been ill, and my aunt had come to stay with us so my father could still go to work. For those few days, I pretended to myself that my aunt was my mother – that this was what it would have been like if she hadn't gone and died. I'd lain in bed with my comics and a drink of lemon barley water on the table beside me, and the curtains half open just as they were now, dust drifting in the sunbeams. And each time I surfaced from my feverish dreams, I could hear her downstairs: cupboards being opened and closed, a vacuum-cleaner purring, the washing-machine humming, glasses chinking, shoes clicking across the hallway, murmuring voices at the front door. I'd felt so safe, under my covers, knowing she was just a few yards away. I wished I could give myself a day like that now. I could lie here until tomorrow morning, slipping in and out of sleep, drifting between insubstantial dreams and dozy wakefulness; occasionally padding out to the kitchen in my dressing-gown to make a cup of tea. Waiting for a cool hand on my brow.

A violent snore reached me from Julie's room. I opened one eye. Six forty. Up, I told myself, and my legs slid round to the floor. My head pounded as I brought it upright, then steadied to a mild, manageable throb. Not too bad after all. I went to the bathroom and splashed cold water over my face. Then I dressed as quickly and quietly as I could. Before leaving, I drank three glasses of water. I longed for a strong black coffee but I didn't dare in case I woke Julie. She'd probably lock the door and throw the key out the window if she knew where I was going. But I had it all worked out.

It was a misty morning. The shapes of the houses at the end of the street were vague, and cars had their lights on. Later it would probably be bright and warm, but now it was chilly. I should have brought a jacket with me, put on a sweater instead of my thin cotton shirt. There was already a fair amount of traffic. London is never dark, never quiet. But I still got there by half past seven. That was fine; surely theatre directors never got up earlier than eight.

The curtains of the Teales' house were all closed. No light seemed to be on. Good. I tried to make myself comfortable in the car seat. I had no idea how long I would have to sit here: I should have bought a cup of coffee on my way, at least. I should have bought something to read. All I had was the car manual and a ten-day-old newspaper. I read the paper, all the already-forgotten stories about a fashion model here, and a war there, a dead boy here and an Internet millionaire there. I felt cold, stiff, sore. I brushed my hair and twisted it back. I peered at my face in the car mirror and winced at my morning-after pallor. I fidgeted. The Teales' curtains remained closed. I could have slept longer after all.

At a quarter to nine, a light went on upstairs. My mouth was dry. Questions pulsed behind my eyes: why am I here? What on earth am I doing?

At five to nine, the curtain was opened and for a brief moment I saw Gabriel's shape in the window. I slid lower in my seat and peered at the house through my gritty eyes. I needed a pee.

A few minutes later, the curtains were opened downstairs. There were two shapes; they were both up. I imagined them in their nice kitchen, making coffee, toasting bread, talking to each other about their day, kissing each other goodbye. The front door remained shut. I could go home, I thought. Drive home and climb back into bed. Julie was probably still asleep, lying wrapped in her covers with her arm over her eyes.

At last the door opened and Gabriel appeared. He stood on the step for a few seconds, patting his pockets to make sure he had keys, calling something over his shoulder. He was dressed in black jeans and a grey woollen jacket, and he looked like the kind of person I know; like one of my friends.

I had to wait a bit. I stared at the car clock. I counted ten minutes, then got out of the car. It still wasn't too late to change my mind, even now. It wasn't too late right up to the moment that I rapped louder than necessary on the front door and heard footsteps.

'Yes?'

Bryony was in her dressing-gown, holding it shut at the top in a gesture I recognized from myself. She was staring at me with dazed eyes, as if I had got her out of bed. I saw her swallow hard. 'Bryony,' I said warmly. 'I hope this is OK. I was passing by on my way to see a client. I literally saw your road ahead of me and since I was running ridiculously early, I popped in on the off-chance.'

'Kit?' she murmured.

'And to be honest, I could do with a lavatory and a cup of coffee before my meeting. I didn't wake you, did I?'

'No, no, sorry.' She made a visible effort. 'I just wasn't expecting – but come in, of course. I'll put the kettle on. The loo's down the hall.' She gestured with a hand. Newly bitten nails, I noticed. Bitten like Lianne's nails had been bitten.

'Thanks.'

When I came out she was spooning coffee beans into a grinder. 'You look tired,' I said. She looked more than tired. Weight seemed to have dropped off her, so that her body was slack where it had been strong. Her collarbones were sharp. Her face was puffy; her glorious hair was greasy; she had a faint red rash on her left cheek. As she lifted the kettle to the cafetière, I saw she had a bracelet of eczema round one wrist. 'Are you all right?'

'I've been a bit under the weather,' she said.

'Yes, Gabriel said. Did he tell you I went to the Sugarhouse the other evening?'

'No, he didn't.'

'Is it the worry that made you ill?' I asked.

'Perhaps,' she said slowly. She poured two cups of coffee and set them down on the table. 'Do you want something to eat – or maybe you're in a bit of a hurry for your meeting?'

'I've plenty of time,' I replied cheerfully. 'But I don't want anything to eat. This is what I need.' I sipped the scalding coffee. 'Have you seen the doctor?'

'What about?'

'About how you feel.'

'I'll be fine. After all, everything's all right now, isn't it?'

'Is it?'

'I mean, it's over. The worry.' I looked at her, and she fumbled with her cup. 'That's what the police said.'

'I know. The police love things being over, you see. They love closing a case. Solved. Big tick. Celebration down the pub. Move on.'

'I don't know anything about that.'

'But it's different for you and me, isn't it?'

'Maybe it's time I got dressed.' She stood up, clutching her dressing-gown once more. 'It's getting on. Things to do.'

'You're left with what you've suffered, what's inside your head.' She looked at me with heavy-lidded eyes, as if just keeping awake was a supreme effort. 'And for me there are questions that I can't stop myself asking. I know it's stupid, but I can't stop myself. Why would one victim write down the name of another before she died? How could a killer snatch a woman from a park, in broad daylight, in front of her child? Why did a reliable witness think that Michael Doll was just an innocent bystander?'

'I can't help . . .' Bryony's lips were bloodless. 'I don't know.'

'Why would a woman let herself be snatched from the playground without screaming and shouting, and why didn't the child make a fuss when her mother disappeared?' I made myself smile. 'The police weren't really interested in any of this. Especially once Michael Doll had died. I have a problem with cutting off from things. That's what people always say about me. Anyway, with this, I've got all these bits of a story and I've been trying to fit them together. Do you mind if I tell it to you?' She didn't react. 'There was a girl called Daisy. Daisy Gill. Fourteen years old, though she may have looked older. I never met her. I just saw her photograph and talked to her friends. She was an unhappy child, I know that. Parents who abandoned her, carers who deserted her, or worse. She badly needed friends. She needed adults she could trust, who would make the world a little bit safer for her. It's hard for people like you and me to imagine what her life must have been like. Often angry and always lonely and always scared.'

There was a scraping noise as Bryony pulled out her chair and sat down again. She cupped her chin in her hands and for the first time looked steadily at me out of her caramel eyes. The colour stood out against her pale skin.

'Daisy had one friend. Lianne. I don't know Lianne's real name, I don't know where she came from. But I do know that she, too, was a broken child. Desperate, even. But at least Lianne and Daisy had each other. They had precious little else, but they had that. Perhaps it was their lifeline. When they were both old enough, they wanted to live together and run a restaurant, cooking macaroni cheese. That's what their friends said.'

'Why are you telling me this?'

'Daisy killed herself. Hanged herself in her drab little room in the place she was supposed to call home. Then a few months later, Lianne was killed, down by the canal. And then, shortly after, Philippa Burton was killed by the same person. Philippa knew Lianne – we have no idea how or why. Lianne knew Daisy. And the funny thing is that Daisy worked at the Sugarhouse. So everything is connected.'

'It's not really connected,' Bryony said. 'This is a small area. Anyway, I was a victim as well.'

'Michael Doll.' For a brief instant, I remembered my last sights of him. Michael Doll alive. Michael Doll dead. 'He just blundered into the story. That was all there was to it. He was just there, by the canal where no one could bother him, catching his wretched fish then throwing them back into the water.'

'He killed those women.' She put her hands in front of her on the table and sat up straighter.

'He was a terrible sight,' I said. 'I saw his body, you know.'

'I always wanted to take photographs,' Bryony said softly. 'Ever since I was nine years old and my uncle gave me a cheap little Instamatic for my birthday. It's a curious thing, how you know suddenly – but I always felt I could see the world more clearly when I saw it through a camera lens, like it made sense. Even ugly things can look beautiful through a lens. Meaningless things make sense.' She glanced up at the photograph of her little gypsy girl. 'And I'm good at it, you know. Not just at taking the actual picture, but knowing what I'm looking for. I can go weeks and nothing happens, then one day I'll see something. A face. Something happening. The way the light falls. Like a click in my mind. And it made me feel I was doing my bit, being a witness.' She licked her pale lips. 'For society, or something, as well as for me. Like Gabe and his theatre. He's good at what he does too, you know.'

'I know,' I said. 'I saw it.' It felt very quiet in the kitchen, as if the world outside had stopped.

'We got dragged into the story as well,' she said, with a long sigh. 'It doesn't matter anyway, does it? It's over. The police said it's over, that I'm safe. That's what you said as well. I'd feel better eventually. But I'm so tired. I'm so tired I could sleep for a hundred years.'

There was a soft click behind us and a hush fell on the room. Every object seemed clear and sharp: the pot plant on the window-sill, the cups hanging from hooks, the tiny web on the light bulb, the sun glinting off the copper pans, making geometric patterns on the wall, my hands, folded peacefully on my lap. All that I could hear was myself, breathing calmly, and the faint tick of my watch. It was twenty-two minutes past ten. Bryony sat very still.

At last I turned around. Gabriel stood framed in the doorway. He closed the door with a second soft click and looked at us; from Bryony to me, and back again. Nobody said anything. The sun shone through the window.

I opened my mouth to speak then closed it again. What was the use? I had nothing more to say. I put up a finger and traced my scar, from hairline to jaw. It comforted me, somehow. It reminded me of who I was.

'I forgot my bag,' said Gabriel.

'I'd better go,' I said. But I didn't get up.

'She was just passing,' said Bryony at last, in her new flat voice.

Gabriel nodded.

'I want to go to bed,' she muttered, and stood up unsteadily. 'I'm ill.'

'It was just a social call,' I said. 'We were talking about things. You know.'

'What things?' He looked across at his wife.

'She was talking about it all,' Bryony said. 'She mentioned a girl. What was her name?'

'Daisy,' I said. 'Daisy Gill.'

'She killed herself. And she was a friend of Lianne's. And she worked at the Sugarhouse.'

'This is so stupid,' Gabriel said wearily. 'This was all meant to be over. What do the police say about this?'

'It's just her,' said Bryony, almost inaudibly. 'She's alone.'

He came over to me. 'What did you want?' he asked. He bent down and touched my shoulder, softly at first, then he gripped my shirt and pulled me to my feet.

'Gabe!' Bryony exclaimed.

I looked into his exhausted face, his bloodshot eyes. Behind him I saw Bryony's wan face. Beyond her, a closed door. There was no escape.

'Are you going to kill everybody in the world?' I said.

His hands were warm when he put them around my neck. I let myself remember my mother's face in the photograph I carried with me wherever I went, as if she could protect me. The way she smiled and the sunlight stroked her pale skin. My mother, sitting on the grass. Gabriel's face was very close to me now, like a lover's, and I heard him whispering, 'We didn't want this.' His face was set in a grimace of horror. His eyes were half closed, as if he couldn't bear to see what he was doing. I lashed out at him, but his body was solid and unyielding, like a grim tower. So I made myself go slack, and he began to squeeze. Against every instinct in me, I let my knees buckle slightly. The world was red and black and pain, and the sound of someone crying. And then, with my body as limp as I could make it, as if I was about to go under, I brought my right hand up as fast and as hard as I could and I opened my fingers into a V and jabbed into the direction of his eyes. I felt a soft wetness, and I heard a yelp. His fingers loosened for an instant then tightened once more. I tore my hand down his cheek, feeling the rip of skin under my nails, then hooked them into his screaming mouth and yanked back as hard as I could. His roar filled my ears; pain was pumping round my head and all that I could see was red. Blood filled my vision. I jabbed again and again, hitting something soft, feeling the stickiness of his blood, the wet of his saliva, the jelly of his eyes.

'Bryony. Finish it now, for fuck's sake! Bryony.'

Something black arced through the red fog in front of me. I closed my eyes at last, but there was a loud crack, like a gun going off a few inches from me, and his fingers fell from my throat. I toppled on to the floor, feeling the wood of the boards splintering into my cheek. Another noise and I could just make out a black tripod, coming down once more. Then Gabriel fell on top of me. His body covered mine and his blood ran down my face and his gasps were in my ears, and her screams. I pushed him off, and stood up although the world was still howling around me, and the floor tipped dangerously beneath my feet. Gabriel was lying in his own blood with his eyes closed. There was a violent gash in his head, his face was ripped and one eye was entirely red. But his chest moved up and down with his breathing. I took the tripod off Bryony and, half leaning on her for support, led her to a chair, pushing her down into it.

'I'm not a bad person,' she sobbed at me. 'I'm not a bad person. I'm good. Good. I'm a good person. This was all just a mistake. A horrible mistake.'

46

The visitors' room at Salton Hill remand centre was like a squalid cafeteria in a very bad area. There was even a hatchway to one side where a woman who looked as if she might be an inmate filled paper cups with tea from a large metal urn or poured industrial-looking orange squash. There were plastic plates of biscuits with circles of jam in the middle. Children were running around, there was shouting, the squeak of chair legs on the floor, cigarette smoke, and the reek of poverty everywhere.

In men's prisons there are all sorts: thugs, psychos, rapists, tricksters, professional crooks, minor drug-dealers. But in a women's prison the inmates mostly look mad, sad, bereft. There aren't any female bank robbers. There aren't any rapists. There aren't any vil-lains who regard a year inside as a form of sabbatical. There are desperate, confused people who were caught shoplifting because they had no money, or women who heard voices and put a pillow over their baby's face. They were scattered around the tables, smoking, always smoking, and talking to their baffled, shy mums and dads, boyfriends, fidgeting children.

I was told by the woman who checked my pass at the door that Bryony was on her way, so I bought two teas and a miniature packet of biscuits, and took two small paper packets of sugar with one of those little plastic spatulas, as if a plastic spoon would have been too much of a luxury. I placed them all on a cardboard tray.

Nothing that could be used as a weapon or, since this was a women's prison, for self-mutilation.

I sat at my designated table, number twenty-four, and took a sip of my tea, which was so hot that it burned my upper lip. And before I had time to sit back and gather my thoughts, there she was. She was in her own clothes, of course, a brown round-necked sweater, navy blue trousers, tennis shoes on bare feet. I saw her silver ankle chain, still there; her wedding ring had been pulled off, though. There was just a faint white mark where it had been. Her blazing hair was pulled back tightly and tied behind. But it was no good. She wore no make-up, which made me realize how carefully made up she had been before, even when lying on the sofa, the morning after the attack. There were new lines around her eyes and a pallor that made her look as if she had emerged from a cave. She sat down without a word.

'I got you tea,' I said, lifting a cup across to her side of the table.

'Thanks,' she said.

She leaned across for the two packets of sugar. She tore the corner off each in turn and poured the sugar into the tea, watching it. Then she stirred the tea jerkily. As she did so I saw the bandages around her wrists. 'I heard about that,' I said.

She looked down. 'I did it wrong,' she said. 'Someone told me. People cut across because they've seen it done that way on TV. But it heals too quickly. I should have cut along the arm. Lengthways. Lengthwise. Whatever. You've come here to thank me, I guess.'

I was startled by the abrupt change of subject. 'I came because Oban said you wanted to see me. But I suppose I do want to thank you. I was going to die. You saved my life.'

'That'll count for something, don't you think? That I saved your life.'

'I think they'll take it into consideration,' I said.

'I've co-operated,' she said. 'I've told them everything. Did you bring the cigarettes?'

I reached into my jacket pocket and took out four packets. I slid them across the table, looking around. 'Is this all right?' I asked.

'So long as they've still got the wrapping on it's all right. They worry about things being smuggled.' She took a cigarette from a packet of her own and lit it. 'I'd got down to about one cigarette a week. Then suddenly, in here, I thought, Why not? There's not much else to do.'

'I can imagine.'

She looked around and smiled. 'Bit of a change,' she said. 'You wouldn't think of me in a place like this, would you?'

I looked at this woman, who had killed Lianne and Philippa and Michael Doll, and then, like her, I looked at those other pathetic women who had had break-downs, or failed to pay their bills and panicked and cracked up.

'I met Gabe at college. Everybody loved him. I'd only had two boyfriends before him. I fell for him completely. I thought I was the luckiest girl in the world. Ironic, isn't it? If I hadn't been the girl who nabbed Gabe Teale, I wouldn't be sitting here.'

'I suppose you could say that about anything,' I said. 'That's what life is, isn't it? One thing leading on to another.'

'I find that rather hard to live with. I feel I found myself in this situation. I feel I'm a good person. And I loved Gabe and I was in his power and then I made one decision, I mean I was put in a situation, and then I was put in another situation, and then I couldn't take it any more. I finally fought back. That was with you. And now I'm here.'

She paused, waiting for some kind of an answer, but disgust clogged my throat and I couldn't speak, so she continued. 'You know the funniest thing? When I met you, well, not in the hospital but when you came to the house, I thought you were the sort of person I'd like for a friend. We'd go for lunch and talk about things.'

I was finding it difficult to breathe. I had to say something. It took an effort to maintain an even tone. 'You didn't feel that with Lianne?' I said. 'Or with Philippa? That they could have been your friends, that they were humans, like you, with hopes and fears, just like you? With futures?'

She stubbed out her cigarette in a little tin-foil ashtray on the table. Nothing you could pick up and hit someone with. 'I wanted to see you because you were the only person I could think of to talk to. Who wouldn't judge me. I thought you would understand. How's Gabe, by the way? Have you seen him?'

'I'm sorry,' I said. 'I'm under strict instructions not to talk about Gabe with you. There are legal reasons, apparently. He's better, though. Physically, I mean.'

'Good,' she said. 'Where was I? Yes, about you. You know about these things, don't you? I've been working it all out. I saved your life. That was a mitigating circumstance, don't you think?'

'It might be,' I said, 'but maybe I'm biased.'

'I think it's unfair that we're both being treated as murderers, as if we are both equally to blame for what happened. You're a woman, you're an expert, I had hoped you could understand that these were his murders.

In a way, I was under his control. I thought people might understand that. If you look at it one way, I'm one of his victims as well. I finally rebelled against that when I saved you. I returned to myself, if you like. It's as if it wasn't me until I saved you.'

With that, she looked me full in the eyes for the first time. Was she saying that I owed her something? Her life for mine?

'What happened?' I said. 'With Daisy.'

'Nothing,' she said. 'She killed herself. You know that.'

'She was involved with your husband.'

'I don't know that much. The fact is, young girls have always been throwing themselves at Gabe. It's not something I'm going to defend. I'm not going to pretend I like it. From the sound of it she was pretty unstable. She didn't report it to the police, did she?'

'No.'

'Well, then. It's all nonsense.'

'She was fourteen years old, Bryony. *Fourteen.*'

'As I say, I don't know anything about that. But the fact is that this other girl, this Lianne, came round and she was hysterical. She had completely the wrong idea about Daisy. She was probably on something.'

'I saw her autopsy report,' I said. 'No traces of drugs were found in her bloodstream.'

'I was just saying that she was out of control. She started flailing around. I came in in the middle, I hardly knew what was going on. One moment she was shouting and lashing out at Gabe and me, and the next moment she had fallen over and she must have banged her head. It was like this nightmare. I didn't know what was going on. All I know is that she was dead and I panicked. We tried to revive her, you know.'

'You panicked,' I said. 'So you and Gabe stabbed

her dead body lots of times. Around the breasts and abdomen. And then you dumped the body by the canal. That might have been your idea. You knew it after your long walks around the area.'

'No,' she said dreamily. 'No, it was Gabe's idea. All Gabe. He was hysterical. He said we had to make it another sort of murder, as if it was done by different sorts of people from us. "Us", that's what he said. He said we were in it together. He said that it could have ruined everything and that now we would be safe. He said that he wouldn't let me go.'

'But you weren't safe, were you?'

'No, we weren't. This woman . . .'

'Philippa Burton. She had a name, you know.'

'Yes, she'd got our address from the other girl, from Lianne. She came to see us looking for Lianne. She knew she'd been there.'

'Why?'

'Lianne had told her about Gabe. That's what she said.'

'No, I mean why was she looking for Lianne?'

'What does that matter? Gabe was frantic. He couldn't think what to do. I'm trying to explain why it all looks so bad as a whole, but when you break it down into bits, there's an . . . an explanation for it.'

'Were you going to say an *innocent* explanation?'

Bryony paused. She was on her third cigarette now. 'I was going to, but it sounded callous. I don't want you to think that about me, Kit. I don't mind what most people think, but I want you to understand me.'

'So what happened with Philippa?'

'Gabe said he had an idea. He was going to talk to her, talk sense into her. We arranged to meet her.'

'On Hampstead Heath.'

'That's right. I didn't know what was going to happen. He told her that he wanted to talk to her, make up a story that would satisfy her. I stayed and looked after the little girl. I had no idea what he was going to do. I'm not sure if he did. He said later that he panicked and attacked her.'

'And battered her body with a hammer and dumped it on the other side of the Heath. So he presumably had the hammer with him.'

'Presumably,' said Bryony. 'That's damning against Gabe, isn't it?'

'Yes, it is. And you were with Emily, waiting for her mother to come back?'

'After a while I got scared. Nobody came. So I ran away. There were lots of people around, she was going to be all right. But that's what I feel most guilty about, leaving a little girl alone like that.'

'I can see that,' I said. 'And it came as a terrible shock when you came back and Gabe told you what had happened.'

'He wasn't there. He didn't come back for a whole day. He told me he was thinking of killing himself.'

'And he had to clean the car as well.'

'I never even thought about that. All I could do was shut it out. I was in purgatory. I wanted to shout it out. I wanted to tell everything. It feels better just telling you. I've so wanted to tell the whole truth.'

'Then there was Michael Doll. He had bad luck as well, didn't he? As well as you, I mean. The place you chose to dump Lianne's body was the place where Mickey Doll sat all day fishing. You saw that in the papers.'

'That's right.'

'What did he have on you? Did he see you?'

'I don't think so. I don't know. Gabe did it. He didn't see anything.'

'Did Gabe drop something that Doll found?'

'No.'

'So what was it?'

'Nothing.'

'What do you mean?'

'I don't think he knew anything. But Gabe became obsessed with the idea that this man had been there, that he might know something. He said that he was the only way we could possibly be caught.'

'So you went down to see him at the canal. You can't deny being present that time.'

'No, I was there. I admit it. By then I would have done anything to help Gabe, to make it all go away.'

'What was the plan? To knock him on the head and push him into the water?'

She started to cry. I was prepared for this. I passed a couple of tissues across the table. She wiped her eyes and blew her nose.

'I don't know,' she said.

'But you were caught,' I said. 'You were brilliant. Your description once you had recovered from your trauma was a particularly nice touch. That mysterious criminal who was just different enough from the other descriptions to make them all seem unreliable. What a performance.'

'It wasn't a performance. I thought I was going to go mad.'

'And then you got Doll after all.'

'That was Gabriel. He said that with Doll gone, and blamed for it, that would be the end.'

'What did you say?'

'I had no will left. I just wanted it all to end.'

'When you ran away from Emily, when you were so worried, you took her cup with you. That came in useful. You, or maybe I should say Gabriel, left the cup there. Of course, he also left a leather pouch. But it didn't matter. It was another miracle. It just incriminated poor Mickey Doll even more. After all, what murderer would deliberately leave behind something that identified them? A bit tough on Doll, though.'

She blew her nose again. 'I know,' she said. 'It torments me. But I can't think of what else I could have done.'

'And then there was me,' I said.

'I was on the verge of telling you,' she said. 'You knew that. I was going to confess when he came back. You're not sure. I can see that in your eyes. You're not sure whether to believe me. But I didn't let him kill you. You're sure of that.'

'Yes, I'm sure of that. You suddenly resisted him. Why was that?'

She lit another cigarette while she thought, her pretty face screwed up. 'I thought it was going to go on for ever and we would never be safe, not safe enough for Gabe. Maybe I was just tired.'

I took a sip of my tea. It was very cold now, with a metallic taste, though it might just have been my dry mouth.

Bryony leaned forward with an urgent expression. 'I've been reading,' she said. 'I think I was mentally ill. I've read about it. It's an emotional-dependence syndrome. It's a well-known pattern. Women get into the power of men and become helpless. I had years of abuse with Gabe. He's a difficult man. A violent man. And it wasn't a black-and-white situation. The first death was a suicide, a tragedy. Then there was the accident. By the time we were in the middle of it, I had lost any sense of self.' She took another drag of her cigarette and looked at me with narrowed eyes. 'Do you think people will believe that?'

'Very possibly,' I said. 'People believe the strangest things, I've found. And you're young and pretty and middle-class, which always helps.'

'You're an expert,' she said. 'You were the crucial person in this case. The police trust you. Will you help me?'

I took a deep breath and put my hands in my pockets, perhaps to conceal that they were trembling. 'I think I may be too involved in the case to appear as an expert witness,' I said.

Her expression hardened. 'Kit,' she said, 'I could have let you die. I saved you. We could have been sitting at home now and you would be dead. I saved you.'

I stood up. 'I'm glad to have been spared,' I said. 'I'm sorry not to be more effusive. I keep thinking of Emily and the dead bodies. I can't get them out of my mind. They were alive and you killed them. Well, you seem to have forgiven yourself for that without too much difficulty. It never ceases to amaze me, the ability of people to justify themselves and never feel guilty.'

'But haven't you heard what I've been saying?' Bryony said. 'I'm as devastated as anybody.'

'I've heard you say that none of it was your fault,' I said. 'I've heard you say that it was all Gabe and not you. It seems that I should be feeling sorry for you as well as Daisy and Lianne and Philippa and Michael.'

'Help is what I need.' Her voice was a wail. 'Help is what I've always needed.'

Oban was waiting outside in the car park. There was a fierce cold autumn wind and I closed my eyes and took it full in the face. I wanted it to blow the last hour out of me. He smiled at me.

'Was it like you said it was going to be?' he asked. 'Was she presenting herself as one of Gabriel Teale's victims as well?'

'Something like that.'

'You think she'll get away with it?'

'Not if I have anything to do with it,' I said, and shivered. My eyes filled with tears.

The light was failing by the time Oban dropped me off at the top of my street, but even from a distance I knew who it was standing at my door. He was wearing a long coat; his hands were thrust into his pockets; his shoulders were hunched. He looked as if he was standing on a crag and cold winds were blowing round him.

I stopped dead, and for a moment I considered running away. Or running towards him and putting my arms around his grim figure. Of course, I did neither. I walked as casually as I could up the pavement, and when he finally heard me and turned round, I managed a smile.

'I've just come from Salton Hill,' I said.

'Oh,' he said, pulling a face. 'Her.'

'Yes.'

He gave a grunt and pushed his hands deep in his pocket. 'At least there won't be any more of his crappy plays,' he said, shoving his hands even deeper in his pockets.

'I didn't know you'd seen any of them.'

'I didn't need to.' There was a silence. Will looked as if he had been assigned to some sort of compulsory sentry duty outside my flat. He gave a sniff. 'I suppose you're expecting me to congratulate you.'

'Well . . .'

'I suppose you want me to go on about how you were right and everybody else in the world including me was wrong. Is that it? Give you a fucking medal or something.'

I giggled then. 'You're welcome,' I said.

I pushed open the door and kicked aside a bundle of mail lying on the mat. 'Do you want to come in?' He hesitated. 'Glass of wine? Beer? Come on.'

He followed me up the stairs. In the kitchen, I handed him a bottle of beer from the fridge and poured myself a glass of red wine. I closed the curtains, then lit a candle and put it on the table between us. He took a sip. 'How's your neck?' he asked. 'Or whatever other bit of you he . . .'

'Fine,' I said. I looked at his face in the shadowy, shifting light. I knew he wouldn't change. And I knew what it would be like: me hoping all the time for something more, always asking for something he couldn't give.

'Will . . .' I began.

'Please,' he said then. He shut his eyes for a moment. 'Please.' I wondered whom he was pleading with. It no longer felt as if he was talking to me, but to someone inside his head.

I leaned across the table and put a hand on his arm. It was like touching a steel girder. I wanted to take his face in my hands and kiss him till he kissed me back. I wanted him to hold me, tight. If he did that, I didn't stand a chance. But he didn't move, although his eyes were open again.

'It's not fair of you,' I said at last.

'No, I guess not.' He tipped back the last of his beer and stood up, the chair scraping on the floor. He looked around. 'Are you moving out of the area?'

'Why should I?'

'I don't know,' he said. 'Bad associations. Trauma.'

I shook my head. 'What bad associations?' I said. 'I'm staying.'

'That's good,' he said, then caught himself. 'I mean, it's an interesting area. In some ways.'

'That's what I think.'

'Good.' He lowered his head and kissed me on my cheek. I felt his breath; his stubble. For a moment we stood like that, close to each other in the candlelight. Then he drew back.

'You did well,' he said. 'I told you that, didn't I?'

'Not in those words.'

'I can't believe you going in like that, on your own,' he said. 'You should look after yourself more.'

And then he was going, his coat flapping behind him, and I stood where I was and watched him leave.

47

I was helping Julie to pack. It was a friendly but melancholy kind of business, made more so by the soft autumnal weather outside my windows. The beech and chestnut trees were yellow and gold and russet-red now, and a warm wind gusted through their branches, scattering leaves in radiant showers. Drifts of brown leaves piled up in the courtyard and occasionally children crunched into them, wearing boots and shouting with glee. The sun shone through a thin gauze of clouds. Summer, which had never really arrived, was leaving. Julie was leaving. I was staying behind.

'Here, this is yours.' She chucked over a lavender-coloured top, which I'd hardly ever worn. 'And this.' A flimsy cardigan winged across the room, the arms flapping. 'God, I didn't realize how much of your stuff I'd borrowed over the months. I'm like a magpie.' She giggled. Her eyes were bright and she glowed with energy and excitement.

We had been at it all morning, in an aimless kind of way, stopping every half-hour or so for tea. We were separating her possessions into piles: one pile for the things she was going to take with her; one for the stuff she wanted to store for when she returned; one for the rubbish bin or the charity shop or me. This third pile was by far the biggest – she was on a binge of freeing herself of possessions, throwing away all her baggage.

She slung a pair of strappy black shoes on top of a violently yellow mac that she'd bought only a few weeks ago, when she was fed up with the rain. She added some beige cotton trousers that she said made her bottom look a funny shape, a jacket that she'd never really liked, three or four sweatshirts, tights with ladders, a beaded bag, a black skirt, bought for her supposed office job, which she picked up between finger and thumb as if it smelt bad, a lime-green T-shirt, a purple roll-neck jersey. 'Here. Your red dress,' she said, unhooking it from the hanger and passing it across.

'Keep it.'

'What? Don't be stupid. It's yours and you look beautiful in it.'

'I'd like you to have it.'

'It's not exactly practical.' She looked tempted, though, and stroked it as if it were alive.

'Stuff it in the bottom of your rucksack. It hardly weighs anything.'

'What if it gets ruined, or I lose it?'

'It's yours to lose or ruin. Go on, you're throwing things away as if there was no tomorrow. Let me have a turn.'

'OK.' She leaned across and kissed my cheek. 'Every time I wear it I'll think of you.'

'Do that.' I was alarmed to find there were tears in my eyes, and busied myself with uselessly refolding items of clothing.

'You've been lovely.'

'Hardly. I've been anti-social and grumpy half the time, and neurotic the other half.'

'Talking about grumpy, what's happening with Will?'

'Nothing.'

'You mean it's over?'

'I don't know. "Over" is a big word, though. I've hardly ever ended anything in my life, even when I wanted to. So perhaps I'm letting him do the ending, by not contacting me. Or perhaps he will contact me and then – I don't know. I don't know what I will do. But he's not good for me. He's too harsh, like a rock I was always going to cut myself on.'

'You're probably right. You'll meet someone else soon, you'll see.'

'What about these shorts?'

'Chuck them. Your bruise has faded, you know. It's gone yellow and brown, not that extraordinary purple any longer. Does it still hurt?'

'Not much – a bit sore.' I touched it lightly.

'Strange summer.'

'You can say that again. It all feels unreal now, like a story that happened to someone else.'

'Do you ever feel you're playing at being grown-up?'

I sat back on my haunches and picked up an electric-blue vest-top. 'You should take this.'

'I mean, I don't feel grown-up at all – I feel as if I was just a step away from when I was a child. But, then, I don't live in a very grown-up way, do I? Drifting around, not settling, not having a career or long-term prospects, wearing clothes for teenagers – like that top,' she added, picking up the blue vest and adding it to her to-take pile. 'But you've got this amazing proper job, and a flat that looks light years away from your student days – you even give papers at conferences, for God's sake. But is that how you feel inside, as well?'

'No.' I hurled a pair of silk knickers at her and she stuffed them into her backpack. 'I feel as if it's all a charade that I'm hiding behind. But we all feel like that. That everyone else is different, and sorted out in a way we'll never be. If we live to a hundred we'll probably feel like that. When we're on our deathbed we'll still be waiting to feel grown-up.'

'Maybe.' She grinned across at me. 'But I really *am* like that. That's why I'm running away again. I don't like real life.'

'Who said I did?'

She looked across at me, a mermaid in a bright sea of clothes. 'You should come with me, then.'

'It's too late.'

'It's never too late.'

'I don't believe that.'

The phone rang.

'I'll get it,' said Julie, clambering to her feet. 'You put the kettle on.'

But it was for me. 'The police,' she mouthed, handing over the receiver with a shrug.

'Kit Quinn?'

'Speaking.'

'DCI Oban told me to call you. Apparently a Mrs Dear wants to get in touch with you.'

'Mrs Dear? I've never heard of her.'

'Something about her daughter, Philippa Burton.'

'Pam *Vere*?'

'Anyway, she wants to talk to you.'

'OK, give me her number, then.'

'She probably wants me to tell her about the Teales,' I said, after I'd put the phone down. 'Though Oban went and visited Jeremy Burton straight away. There's nothing left to say.'

'Poor woman.'

'It's the funeral the day after tomorrow – finally. Philippa was her only child. She's just got Emily now.'

'Are you going?'

'Probably. Though it'll be crowded out.'

'I'll be in the air. Far away.'

'I just wish I knew why she had to die. I feel it's all

unfinished still. It haunts me and it must haunt them a hundred, a thousand times more – not knowing anything at all.'

Pam Vere was clipped and strained on the phone. She wanted to meet before the funeral, she said. Today, if possible. She was free any time. I grimaced across at Julie, and said that I could be at her house in half an hour.

'I'd rather meet outside.'

'All right.' I glanced at the uncertain skies. 'How about the Heath – that's near you, isn't it?'

'I thought we could meet by the canal.'

'The canal?'

'Where the girl was killed.'

'Lianne.' I hated the way that nobody called her by her chosen name. Even in the papers, she was always 'the homeless girl', 'the drifter'. And I hated the way adjectives were applied by an unimaginative press: Philippa was tragic, Lianne was merely sad.

'Yes. Can we meet there?'

I tried not to show my surprise. 'If that's what you want.'

It was trying to rain by the time I reached the steps leading down to the canal. Occasional large drops splashed into the water, spreading ripples. It seemed ominous, except, of course, what I dreaded had already happened and was in the past.

Pam Vere was waiting, standing quite still in her scarf and camel-hair coat. She didn't smile, but she held out her hand as I came towards her. Her grip was firm and steady. Her eyes were steady too, in her chalky face. I noticed that for once she'd applied her make-up carelessly – there was a pale smudge of powder on the side of her nose and a faint fleck of mascara on one of her wrinkled and hooded eyelids. 'Thank you for coming,' she said formally.

'I wanted to,' I said.

'You're coming to the funeral.'

'Of course.'

'There was something else I wanted to say to you. I couldn't say it there.'

She looked around us, at the rash of nettles, the mucky path dotted with crisp packets, the slimy water spotted with rain. 'Was it here?'

'By the bridge,' I said, pointing.

'Did she suffer?'

That wasn't what I had been expecting and it took me a moment to gather my thoughts. 'I don't think so. They weren't serial killers, Mrs Vere, they weren't like the Wests. They didn't enjoy killing. They would have got it over as quickly as possible. Maybe the worst thing for your daughter would have been knowing that she had left Emily at risk.'

She cleared her throat. 'I meant the other girl.'

I gazed at her. 'Who? Lianne?'

'Yes.' She held my eyes. 'Would it have been painful?'

'No,' I said. 'I think it was very sudden.'

Mrs Vere nodded and then said, in a voice that had become husky, 'I heard they stabbed her all over.'

'That was after she died.'

'Poor girl.' A raindrop splashed on to her cheek and ran down it, towards her mouth. She didn't wipe it away.

'Yes,' I said, wondering why Pam Vere wanted to stand in the rain with me by a canal.

She turned her back on me and stood looking out on to the water. 'Philippa was a good girl,' she said. 'Maybe we put too much pressure on her – she was our only child, you know. Sometimes now when I look at photographs of the three of us, I think how little and single she seemed between us. Two adults and one little child. But then when she was eleven her father died, of course, and it was just her and me. And she was still a good girl, always neat, always thinking of other people, always helpful. Too helpful, perhaps. She wasn't unpopular, but she didn't have many friends when she was little. She liked playing by herself, with her blessed doll. Or being with me, making cakes and shopping and tidying the house. She never gave me any trouble.

'And she was the same at school. A hard worker – that's what school reports always said. Nothing brilliant, but a hard worker, a pleasure to teach. Always did her homework as soon as she got back from school. Good as gold. She would sit at the kitchen table and eat hot buttered toast and Marmite and then she would do her homework, in blue ink, with her neat handwriting, her looping Y. I can see her now, in her navy blue uniform, with her heels tucked up on the bar of the chair and her brow furrowed, blotting her work after each line. Or colouring in her maps for geography. She liked doing that, shading the coastline blue and the forests green, drawing lines of contour.

'I got her schoolwork out of the chest a few days ago and looked through it all, all the exercise books with the subjects written across the top right-hand corner, with a ruled line under her name and class. It seems like yesterday. There were things I could remember her doing, like the drawings of herself she did when she was tiny, with scribbled yellow hair and a pink semi-circle mouth. Children always draw themselves smiling, don't they, although Philippa wasn't a great smiler, you know. Then, later, the pencil diagrams of flowers, with their pistils and stamens. Planets. The six wives of Henry VIII. Algebra. *Je m'appelle* Philippa Vere *et j'ai onze ans.*' Pam Vere's French accent was impeccable. 'And there were her school diaries. They used to write diaries on a Monday morning – what I did at the weekend, that type of thing, you know?' I nodded. I didn't want to say anything that might stop her. 'And I read through them. And do you know what? I was in all of them. She always wrote about what she did with Mummy. Mummy and me went to the shops, Mummy and me went to the playground, Mummy got me a kitten and its name is Blackie, Mummy took me to the museum. I suddenly realized that there was almost nobody else in her diaries except me and her. I didn't know how solitary she was until I read those entries. She never complained.'

She turned fully to face me. 'You're asking yourself why on earth I am telling you all of this, aren't you?'

'You need to say it to someone.'

'I'm an old woman now. Oh, I'm not really old, I know. I'm only in my sixties and I could live for another thirty years. But I feel old now. I feel twice as old as I did a year ago. You don't have children, do you?'

'No.'

'Do you have a mother still?'

'No. My mother died when I was very young.'

'That's why, then.'

'Why what?'

'Why it was you I wanted to talk to. She was even a good girl when she was a teenager. She made a few more friends, sometimes she went out on a Saturday night. She would have a few drinks, not many. She didn't smoke. She didn't take drugs. She was very pretty but she didn't realize it, and I think that meant that other people didn't really notice how pretty she was. She wasn't showy or pushy or flirtatious. I always thought she was the loveliest girl I knew, but then I was her mother, so I would think that, wouldn't I? And fourteen- and fifteen- and sixteen-year-old boys don't look properly, do they? I was thankful for that – I always told her not to worry about what her friends were up to, she had plenty of time. Time,' she smiled grimly, 'she didn't have plenty of it, after all, did she?' She came to an abrupt halt.

'Then what?' I asked, quietly.

'Then she met someone. A boy. Well, a man, really, older than her. She was only fourteen when she met him. He looked at her properly. Suddenly she no longer seemed like a young girl, she was on the verge of womanhood. I just thought she was growing up. I find it hard to believe now, but I really didn't have any idea what was going on. I only found out about it afterwards. She was so innocent, my quiet little daughter. She thought that she was in love with him. And that he was in love with her, more to the point. If I had realized at the time, I could have warned her.'

She smiled at me. 'You see now, I'm not just talking to you like this because I need to talk to someone about Philippa. A secret is a terrible thing. The only way to stop it being terrible is to tell it, but you mustn't. He left her, of course, it only lasted a few weeks. And she was heartbroken, though I still knew nothing.'

She turned back to the canal once more, then said: 'And pregnant.'

I walked over to where she was and stood beside her, looking into the depths where Doll's fish lurked. 'She had the baby?'

'I found out that she was pregnant when she was

twenty-seven weeks and five days gone. So she had the baby. It was all done very secretly. I made sure of that. Nobody knew, just Philippa and me.'

'A girl?'

'Yes. A girl who would have been eighteen a few months ago.'

'Lianne?' She had been older than I'd thought, then.

'I told the school Philippa had glandular fever. We went away to France together while she waited. She was very quiet, as if she was in shock, but she did what I said. There wasn't really any choice. They took the baby away almost at once. Philippa wanted to hold it – her – first. She cried and sobbed and begged. She went almost mad. But I wouldn't let her. I didn't want her to get attached. She couldn't have a child, for God's sake, she was only a child herself. I wanted her to have a life, a husband, all the things I'd been planning for her. So I wouldn't let her hold the baby. She cried solidly for two days, you've never seen so many tears, it was like a dam bursting, all the tears she'd been too eager and helpful to cry all her life. And then she seemed to pull herself together. Her milk dried up, her tummy gradually got flat again. She went back to school and did her exams and went on to sixth-form college. She never talked about it again.'

'Mrs Vere . . .'

'I held the baby, though. Tiny, shrivelled, red thing with baggy skin and gummy blue eyes. She put her fist round my finger and wouldn't let it go, as though she knew.'

'Knew?'

'That I was her grandmother. Her family. Her home. Her last chance. I unpinned her strong little fingers one by one and handed her over.'

'And then she was taken away for adoption?'

'Adoption, yes, I suppose so. I didn't want Philippa to know. I thought it was best if the door was shut firmly on the whole episode. Of course, she would have been able to find out where she really came from five months ago, when she turned eighteen.'

'Those phone calls.'

'I didn't know at first, of course, not until then, when I heard about the calls, the calls between Philippa and . . . and her. I wasn't withholding evidence. I suppose you'd say that I didn't want to know. But for eighteen years not a week's gone by when I haven't thought about that little baby gripping my finger and staring at me. And I wonder if an hour went by without Philippa remembering, too. We never spoke. Not even after Emily, we never told each other what we felt.'

She looked at me at last. 'That's why I wanted to see you, to know if my granddaughter suffered.'

So this whole sad tale had been about a daughter looking for her mother, a mother searching for her daughter.

'I wonder if they ever found each other, before they were killed,' I said at last.

'Sometimes I comfort myself by imagining that they did. That Philippa was allowed to hug and hold her baby at last. But we'll never know, will we?'

'No. We'll never know.'

We were just about to part when Pam Vere put her hand on my sleeve. 'I was going to ask,' she said, 'whether it might be possible for my granddaughter to be buried in the same grave as my daughter. Do you think it might be?'

'Lianne was cremated,' I said. 'And her ashes were scattered.'

'Oh, I see,' said Pam. 'Well, that's that, then.'

★

I walked back home. Up the steps away from the canal, along the shabby streets. Through the windows I could see people leading their own particular lives: a man holding a violin, bow poised; a woman on the phone, animated, hand lifted in the air; a naked little boy sitting in an upstairs room, looking out over the street with a doleful expression. I looked at people's faces as I passed them. No faces are ordinary. All faces are beautiful if you look at them in a certain way.

Julie was waiting. There was the smell of garlic coming from the kitchen, and a vase of fresh yellow roses stood on the table. Her rucksack was by the door, bulging, fastened up, an airline label attached to its strap. I sat at the table and I took out the photograph of my mother and laid it before me. She smiled up at me, gleaming through all the years of missing her. Her clear grey eyes shone with promise. The sun touched her young and happy face. I felt very peaceful and very sad. I've never been good at partings.

Read on for a taste of

Land of the Living

By Nicci French

(Penguin, £6.99)

Abbie Devereaux wakes in the dark – hooded and bound with no idea where she is or how she got there. All she knows is that a man she never sees is keeping her alive – and eventually will kill her. She dreams of returning to everyday life – to the land of the living. But in fact that may prove just as terrifying . . .

Darkness. Darkness for a long time. Open my eyes and close, open and close. The same. Darkness inside, darkness outside.

I'd been dreaming. Tossed around in a black dark sea. Staked out on a mountain in the night. An animal I couldn't see sniffed and snuffled around me. I felt a wet nose on my skin. When you know you're dreaming you wake up. Sometimes you wake into another dream. But when you wake and nothing changes, that must be reality.

Darkness and things out there in the darkness. Pain. It was far away from her and then closer to her and then part of her. Part of *me*. I was filled to the brim with hot, liquid pain. Although the darkness remained, I could see the pain. Flashes of yellow and red and blue, fireworks exploding silently behind my eyes.

I started to search for something without really knowing what it was. I didn't know where it was. I didn't know what it was. Nightingale. Farthingale. It took an effort, like hauling a package out of the water of a deep dark lake. That was it. Abigail. I recognized that. My name was Abigail. Abbie. Tabbie. Abbie the Tabbie. The other name was harder. There were bits missing from my head and it seemed to have got lost among the missing bits. I remembered a class register. Auster, Bishop, Brown, Byrne, Cassini, Cole, Daley, Devereaux, Eve, Finch, Fry. No, stop. Go back. Finch. No. Devereaux. Yes, that was it. A rhyme came to me.

A rhyme from long, long ago. Not Deverox like box. Nor Deveroo like shoe. But Devereaux like show. Abbie Devereaux. I clung to the name as if it was a life-ring that had been thrown to me in a stormy sea. The stormy sea was in my head mostly. Wave after wave of pain rolling in and dashing itself against the inside of my skull.

I closed my eyes again. I let my name go.

Everything was part of everything else. Everything existed at the same time as everything else. How long was it like that? Minutes. Hours. And then, like figures emerging from a fog, things resolved and separated. There was a taste of metal in my mouth and a smell of metal stinging my nostrils but the smell became a mustiness that made me think of garden sheds, tunnels, basements, cellars, damp dirty forgotten places.

I listened. Just the sound of my own breathing, unnaturally loud. I held my breath. No sound. Just the beating of my heart. Was that a noise or just the blood pumping inside my body, pushing against my ears?

I was uncomfortable. There was an ache down my back, my pelvis, my legs. I turned over. No. I didn't turn over. I didn't move. I couldn't move. I pulled up my arms as if to fend something off. No. The arms didn't move. I couldn't turn. Was I paralysed? I couldn't feel my legs. My toes. I concentrated everything on my toes. Left big toe rubbing against the toe beside. Right big toe rubbing against the toe beside. No problem. I could do it. Inside a sock. No shoe. I wasn't wearing shoes.

My fingers. I drummed them. The tips touched something rough. Cement or brick. Was this a hospital? Injured. An accident. Lying somewhere, waiting to be found. A railway accident. The wreckage of a train.

Machinery on top of me. Wreckage. In a tunnel. Help coming. Heat-seeking equipment. I tried to remember the train. Couldn't remember. Or a plane. Or a car. Car more likely. Driving late at night, headlights on the windscreen, falling asleep. I knew the feeling, pinching myself to stay awake, slapping my cheeks, shouting, opening the window so the cold air hit my eyeballs. Maybe this time I failed. Veered off the road, down an embankment, rolled over, the car lost in undergrowth. When would I be reported missing? How do you look for a lost car?

I mustn't wait to be rescued. I might die of dehydration or blood loss just yards from people driving to work. I would have to move. If only I could see the way. No moon. No stars. It might only be twenty yards to safety. Up an embankment. If I could feel my toes, then I could move. Turn over first. Ignore the pain. I turned but this time I felt something hold me back. I flexed my legs and arms, tightened and loosened the muscles. There were restraints. Over my forearms and just above my elbows. My ankles and thighs. My chest. I could lift my head, as if in the feeble beginning of an attempt at a sit-up. Something else. Not just dark. It was dark but not just that. My head was covered.

Think clearly. There must be a reason for this. Think. People in prison were restrained. Not relevant. What else? Patients in hospitals can have restraints placed on them in order to prevent them harming themselves. Lying on a trolley. Restrained on a trolley prior to being wheeled in for an operation. I've been in an accident. Say, a car accident, which is most likely. Statistically. Severe but not life-threatening. Any sudden movement could cause, and the phrase came to me out of nowhere, severe internal bleeding. The patient could fall off the trolley. It's just a matter of waiting for the nurse or the anaesthetist. Perhaps I had been given the anaesthetic already. Or a pre-anaesthetic. Hence the vacancies in my brain. Strange quiet, but you do hear of people in hospitals lying around on trolleys for hours waiting for a free operating theatre.

Problems with the theory. I didn't seem to be lying on a trolley. The smell was of darkness, mildew, things that were old and decaying. All I could feel with my fingers was concrete, or stone. My body was lying on something hard. I tried to think of other possibilities. After famous disasters bodies were stored in improvised morgues. School gymnasiums. Church halls. I could have been in a disaster. The injured could have been placed wherever there was room. Restrained to prevent them injuring themselves. Would they be hooded as well? Surgeons were hooded. But not their eyes. Perhaps to prevent infection.

I raised my head again. With my chin I felt a shirt. I was wearing clothes. Yes. I could feel them on my skin. A shirt, trousers, socks. No shoes.

There were other things at the edge, clamouring to be admitted to my brain. Bad things. Restrained. In the dark. Hooded. Ridiculous. Could it be a joke? I remembered stories of students. They get you paralytically drunk, put you on a train at Aberdeen. You wake up in London dressed only in your underwear with a fifty-pence piece in your hand. Everyone will jump out in a minute, pull off the blindfold and shout, 'April fool.' We'll all laugh. But was it April? I remembered cold. Had summer been? Was summer still to come? But of course a summer had always been and there was always another summer to come.

★

All the alleys were blind. I had gone up them all and found nothing. Something had happened. I knew that. One possibility was that it was something funny. It didn't feel funny. Another possibility, possibility number two, was that something had happened and it was in the process of being officially dealt with. The hood – or bandage, yes, very possibly a bandage. That was a thought. I might have received a head wound, eye or ear damage and my entire head was bandaged and hooded for my own protection. They would be removed. There would be some stinging. The cheery face of a nurse. A doctor frowning at me. Don't worry, nothing to worry about. That's what they'd say. Call me 'dear'.

There were other possibilities. Bad ones. I thought of the stone under my fingers. The damp air, like a cave. Until now, there had been only the pain and also the mess of my thoughts, but now there was something else. Fear in my chest like sludge. I made a sound. A low groan. I was able to speak. I didn't know who to call or what to say. I shouted more loudly. I thought the echoing or harshness of the sound might tell me something about where I was but it was muffled by my hood. I shouted again so that my throat hurt.

Now there was a movement nearby. Smells. Sweat and scent. A sound of breathing, somebody scrambling. Now my mouth was full of cloth. I couldn't breathe. Only through my nose. Something tied hard around my face. Breath on me, hot on my cheek, and then, out of the darkness, a voice, little more than a whisper, hoarse, strained, thick so I could barely make it out.

'No,' it said. 'Make another sound and I'll block your nose as well.'

★

I was gagging on the cloth. It filled my mouth, bulged in my cheeks, rubbed against my gums. The taste of grease and rancid cabbage filled my throat. A spasm jerked my body, nausea rising through me like damp. I mustn't be sick. I tried to take a breath, tried to gasp through the cloth but I couldn't. I couldn't. I was all stopped up. I tugged with my arms and my ankles against the restraints and tried to take a breath and it was as if my whole body was twitching and shuddering on the rough stone floor and no air inside me, just violent space and red behind my bulging eyes and a heart that was jolting up through my throat and a strange dry sound coming from me, like a cough that wouldn't form. I was a dying fish. A fish thrashing on the hard floor. I was hooked and tied down, but inside me I was coming loose, all my innards tearing apart. Is this what it's like? To die? To be buried alive.

I had to breathe. How do you breathe? Through your nose. He'd said so. The voice had said he'd block my nose next. Breathe through my nose. Breathe now. I couldn't take enough air in that way. I couldn't stop myself trying to gasp, trying to fill myself up with air. My tongue was too big to fit in the tiny space left in my mouth. It kept pushing against the cloth. I felt my body buck again. Breathe slowly. Calmly. In and out, in and out. Breathe like that until there's nothing except the sense of it. This is how to keep alive. Breathe. Thick, musty air in my nostrils, oily rottenness running down my throat. I tried not to swallow but then I had to and again biliousness flowed through me, filled my mouth. I couldn't bear it. I could bear it, I could, I could, I could.

Breathe in and out, Abbie. Abbie. I am Abbie. Abigail Devereaux. In and out. Don't think. Breathe. You are alive.

★

The pain inside my skull rolled back. I lifted my head a bit and the pain surged towards my eyes. I blinked my eyes and it was the same deep darkness when they were open and when they were closed. My eyelashes scraped against the hood. I was cold. I could feel that now. My feet were chilly inside the socks. Were they my socks? They felt too big and rough; unfamiliar. My left calf ached. I tried to flex my leg muscles to get rid of the crampy feeling. There was an itch on my cheek, under the hood. I lay there for a few seconds, concentrating only on the itch, then I turned my head and tried to rub the itch against a hunched shoulder. No good. So I squirmed until I could scrape my face along the floor.

And I was damp. Between my legs and under my thighs, stinging my skin beneath my trousers. Were they my trousers? I was lying in my own piss, in the dark, in a hood, tied down, gagged. Breathe in and out, I told myself. Breathe in and out all the time. Try to let thoughts out slowly, bit by bit, so you don't drown in them. I felt the pressure of the fears dammed up inside me, and my body was a fragile, cracking shell full of pounding waters. I made myself think only of breathing, in and out of my nostrils. In and out.

Someone – a man, the man who had pushed this cloth into my mouth – had put me in this place. He had taken me, strapped me down. I was his prisoner. Why? I couldn't think about that yet. I listened for a sound, any sound except the sound of my breath and the sound of my heart and, when I moved, the rasp of my hands or feet against the rough floor. Perhaps he was here with me, in the room, crouching somewhere. But there was no other sound. For the moment I was alone. I lay there. I listened to my heart. Silence pressed down on me.

Nicci French

read more

author photo © Mark Read

read more

Nicci Gerrard was born in June 1958 in Worcestershire. After graduating with a first class honours degree in English Literature from Oxford University, she began her first job, working with emotionally disturbed children in Sheffield.

In the early eighties she taught English Literature in Sheffield, London and Los Angeles, but moved into publishing in 1985 with the launch of *Women's Review*, a magazine for women on art, literature and female issues. In 1987 Nicci had a son, Edgar, followed by a daughter, Anna, but by the time she became acting literary editor at the *New Statesman* her marriage had ended. She moved to the *Observer* in 1990, where she was deputy literary editor for five years, and then a feature writer and executive editor. It was while she was at the *New Statesman* that she met Sean French.

Sean French was born in May 1959 in Bristol, to a British father and Swedish mother. He too studied English Literature at Oxford University at the same time as Nicci, also graduating with a first class degree, but their paths didn't cross until 1990. In 1981 he won *Vogue* magazine's Writing Talent Contest, and from 1981 to 1986 he was their theatre critic. During that time he also worked at the *Sunday Times* as their deputy literary editor and television critic, and was the film critic for *Marie Claire* and deputy editor of *New Society*.

Sean and Nicci were married in Hackney in October 1990. Their daughters, Hadley and Molly, were born in 1991 and 1993.

By the mid nineties Sean had had two novels published, *The Imaginary Monkey* and *The Dreamer of Dreams*, as well as numerous non-fiction books, including biographies of Jane Fonda and Brigitte Bardot.

In 1995 Nicci and Sean began work on their first joint novel and adopted the pseudonym of Nicci French. The novel, *The Memory Game*, was published to great acclaim in 1997. *The Safe House*, *Killing Me Softly*, *Beneath the Skin*, *The Red Room*, *Land of the Living*, *Secret Smile* and *Catch Me When I Fall* have since been added to the Nicci French CV. *The Safe House*, *Beneath the Skin* and *Secret Smile* have all been adapted for TV, and *Killing Me Softly* for the big screen.

But Nicci and Sean also continue to write separately. Nicci still works as a journalist for the *Observer*, covering high-profile trials including those of Fred and Rose West, and Ian Huntley and Maxine Carr. Her novel *Things We Knew Were True* was published in 2003, and her second, *Solace*, in spring 2005. Sean's latest novel *Start From Here* came out in spring 2004.

The Red Room has more police procedural material than any book you've done before, or indeed, any you've done since.

Sean: There are various reasons for that. One is that when we started the book, we thought we'd experiment with a recurring character. This was the psychiatrist, Grace Schilling, who had played quite a prominent, if largely ineffectual, role in our previous book, *Beneath the Skin*. The idea was that she would still be suffering the traumatic effects of that at the beginning of this story. There was a vague idea that we might write a series of 'Grace Schilling' novels. The interesting part of this would be to see a character develop over a series of books. The less noble part of the conception would be to save us the trouble of having to keep thinking of new leading characters. But we quickly dropped the idea.

Nicci: No – we quite slowly dropped the idea, and then had to start again. But it just didn't work for us. One of the main reasons for this is that whereas many thrillers have at their centre the 'expert' – the detective, pathologist, psychologist – who examines the crime and solves it, we have always been more interested in the people who are affected and damaged by crime. We want to think about ordinary people to whom extraordinary things happen. And it's hard to keep psychological realism with an ordinary central character who serially stumbles into solving crimes. The days of Miss Marple are over.

Sean: Most authors seem to end up trying to kill off their recurring characters, like Arthur Conan Doyle pushing Sherlock Holmes off the Reichenbach Falls and Ian Fleming having Bond poisoned at the end of *From Russia with Love*. We just did it earlier than anyone else.

So is Kit Quinn just Grace Schilling with a different name?

Sean: Not at all. Once we started writing, we realized we needed a different sort of character for this story and Kit quickly moved in a completely new direction.

Nicci: We needed to make Kit someone who wasn't assuredly professional like Grace, but young, uncertain of herself and who could be drawn into a story that at the start she was on the outside of. We gave her a certain kind of bravery or pluck: she is someone who forces herself to confront the things she most fears.

Sean: However, we have used a character twice – although we don't know if anyone's actually noticed her. The eccentric consultant psychiatrist, Thelma Scott, who comes in at the end of *The Memory Game* then appears at the beginning of *The Safe House*.

Have you noticed a canal theme in your work?

Sean: We weren't aware of it but a reader pointed out that canals occur in all the books up to that time – except for *The Safe House*, which is mainly set outside London. And it's true. Our characters walk along them and cycle them, they have significant meetings beside them. In fact, they do everything except go along them in boats. This is partly because Nicci and I just love canals. There's something so strange about them, these hidden, quiet lanes right in the heart of the noisy, crowded city. They've been done up recently, and the abandoned wharves and warehouses have been turned into offices and luxury flats but years ago they were almost forgotten about and we used to go there a lot, walking and cycling. It's a location that's always haunted us.

Nicci: Haunted us because they seem a bit like the city's unconscious. They feel full of secrets. Strange things go on beside canals. People get murdered there, take drugs there, make love there, walk alone there and you can feel far from the roar of the city even when it's just the other side of the wall. Also, you get a completely different view of London when you see it from the canal's edge. And even now, when everything's been so developed, there are still these sudden areas that remain run-down, over-grown – it's like stumbling into a different world. There are vast dilapidated buildings along the water with boarded-up windows. You walk past them and wonder who's inside, what's inside. They're scary and mysterious. And if canals were important in other books, they were central to *The Red Room*, because of the characters we were trying to describe – the loners and misfits of London, the drifters and the runaways, the people we chose not to see (see below) who seemed to us to belong to the hidden landscape of canals.

read more

the people we chose not to see

Nicci: When I left university, over twenty years ago, I took a job as a child-care officer in a home for young people with emotional and mental health problems in Sheffield. I was young, idealistic, rather naive, sentimental – and I was very touched and disturbed by the children I tried to look after. In fact, they've haunted me ever since. Sometimes I even still dream about them, particularly a chubby, mute, black-eyed escapologist called Matthew who I would fantasize about adopting. A few of them were young teenagers; others only just out of nappies.

There were about fifteen of them in the home. Some of them had severe physical and learning difficulties and others were simply marked by years of neglect and abuse. Some had parents who came to see them regularly; others had been abandoned long ago and were never visited by anyone. (One little boy had been delivered to the social services naked, in a bucket – he was so malnourished that he would never grow to a proper size.) The home wasn't a bad place, but it was cheerless and institutional, not homely at all. The food wasn't bad either, but it was like school food: catered, rather than cooked; certainly never prepared by the children themselves. The bedrooms were comfortable, but identical to each other, and most of the children didn't own possessions that would personalize them. They didn't have old teddy bears, or books or bedspreads or posters. Hardly any of them had family photographs – it had never occurred to me before how important photographs are to make us feel that we belong somewhere. Almost all of them were so hungry for affection and recognition that it could drive them to extremes of behaviour.

When we took them out in groups, sometimes they were stared at, but more frequently they were ignored. People looked away, walked in wary circles around them, made sure there was no contact. There was enormous casual and unconscious cruelty in the way the public treated them: they were so in need of acceptance and they so rarely received it. They were outsiders. They didn't belong. Really, people didn't care.

I left after a year. I wasn't very good at the job, and anyway it seemed to me that most of my work was about containment. I kissed them all goodbye and gave them presents and took them out for a treat, and then I went back to my fortunate, privileged, happy life. Many years later, when I was working on the *Observer* and covered the trial of Rosemary West, the feelings I had had about the children in care were amplified. I found it profoundly upsetting that almost all of the girls and young women who had been snatched, tortured, killed and buried underneath the terraced house in Gloucester had never been missed. Nobody had noticed their absence, worried about them, waited for them to come home. They hadn't really had a home. They'd been drifters and children in care; they'd slipped through society's nets. They weren't much mourned. They reminded me of the children I had looked after in Sheffield.

Partly because of these missing, unmissed young women, I then spent several months on the *Observer* researching and writing two stories that in my mind connected with them: stories about the people in society who are invisible to us. The first article was on children in care; the second on prostitutes. As always with the things that I write alone, Sean was my advisor, editor and first reader, and in part *The Red Room* emerged out of the many conversations we had about the invisible people in our society – all the stories that never make the news, all the people whose lives and deaths go unnoticed.

With the feature about children in care, I visited several children's homes and spent time with the residents there – partly hearing about their lives, and partly just accompanying them through their days. I also made contact with a core group of young people who lived in homes or with foster families (many children actually prefer to be in a home – they say they already have a family, albeit one who can't look after them, and they don't want a substitute). Most of them had had terrible starts to their lives: they'd been beaten and sexually abused and abandoned. Some of them had already lived with more than ten foster families. Several of them, even ones not yet in their teens, were already using drugs. Several had committed criminal offences. Some could not read or write. Most were very protective of the families who had failed them, or been simply unable to cope – the word 'Mum' can bring tears to the eyes of the most hardened teenager. These young people could be quite scary prospects, yet at the same time they were touching and sometimes had an unexpected innocence about them for all their swagger and assumed indifference. I remember taking them out for a meal: most of them had never set foot in a restaurant before. They couldn't believe they could order whatever they wanted (some of them ordered double meals), and they were nervously excited. They were also rather heartbreakingly hopeful about their futures. I found them extraordinarily touching; I don't know what has happened to them, although we corresponded for a while.

I met up with the prostitutes by ringing numbers on the call-cards that are posted up in phone booths round London. I spent days sitting in over-heated, dingy rooms that were thick with perfume and smoke, talking to them and sometimes waiting while they disappeared into the bedroom with a punter. Some of them were still very young, girls rather than women. While a couple of them were strong, purposeful and ambitious, saying that they were earning money in order to finance their future life, most of them had been in care, had been abused, and had drifted into prostitution – they got through the day on crack, cigarettes and alcohol. They dreamed of a different life – one woman said she'd always wanted to be a social worker, so that she could save children from the life she had now; another wanted to be a barrister – without having any notion of how to change the life they were in. They were very distressing.

In the UK, there's a population as big as that of Bath made up of runaways and vagrants. We see them and don't: the tramp, the beggar, the busker, the truant. In *The Red Room*, Kit finds herself in the world of these unnoticed outsiders. She is made aware of the people and the stories she simply hadn't noticed before, and she asks why some lives are deemed more precious than others. This blindness is made part of the actual plot: clues go unnoticed because people are looking the wrong way.

read more

There are of course hundreds of serial characters in fiction, especially detectives in thrillers. One of the pleasures of the form is the relationship readers build up with figures from Sherlock Holmes and Father Brown up to Morse and Rebus. There's also a pleasure in recurring villains, from Professor Moriarty to Hannibal Lecter. One of us (and it's not Nicci Gerrard) even has memories of Biggles' recurring antagonist, Erich von Stalhein.

But there are also characters that recur in odder, more interesting ways. Here are ten of them:

1) Jack Falstaff. William Shakespeare not only invented the sequel, but also the rubbish sequel. If *Henry IV Part Two* is the *Godfather Part Two* or *Aliens*, then *The Merry Wives of Windsor* is *Speed Two* or *Predator Two*. And poor Falstaff is a shadow of his former self; he doesn't even seem to remember some of his old comrades.

2 and **3) Don Quixote** and **Huckleberry Finn** both appear in a very peculiar kind of sequel, in which the previous book has not only been published, but the character has read it. In Volume Two of *Don Quixote*, the knight keeps meeting people who have read Volume One. Huckleberry Finn begins: 'You don't know about me, without you have read a book by the name of "The Adventures of Tom Sawyer"....' The famous Escher drawing of a hand sketching itself comes to mind.

4) Henry Bech. John Updike is so prolific that one career isn't enough for him, and he invented a writer who was different from him in almost every way. He was Jewish and, almost unimaginably for Updike, he suffered from writer's block. He portrayed him in a series of stories that allowed him to parody the literary life (and also use up material from his own life as a writer, attending conferences, signing special editions etc.).

5) Nathan Zuckerman. Philip Roth's alter ego is much odder than Updike's. He has led a life suspiciously like Roth's, achieved huge success and notoriety with a book very like *Portnoy's Complaint*, married an Englishwoman very like Claire Bloom and so on. Many readers will scarcely notice, but the great later novels, *American Pastoral*, *The Human Stain*, are actually narrated by Zuckerman.

6) *Before Sunset* is possibly the most remarkable sequel in film history. In *Before Sunrise*, **Ethan Hawke** and **Julie Delpy**, played two young people meeting for a romantic night in Vienna. Ten years later, they meet again in Paris. And it really was ten years later: their two extraordinary faces were marked by the passage of the years, a special effect that no make up or CGI or acting skill could have faked.

7) Seymour Glass. When Seymour Glass shot himself in J. D. Salinger's great story, 'A Perfect Day for Bananafish', readers might have thought this was the last of him. Far from it. He became a character that haunted almost all of the rest of Salinger's fiction. In fact, Salinger's last published story, 'Hapworth 16, 1924', consists in its entirety of a fifty-page letter written by Seymour from summer camp. It is, quite frankly, bonkers.

8) The Moomintroll books. Tove Jansson, a manic depressive Finn who lived half her life on a remote and tiny island and who died a few years ago, was one of the greatest writers of children's books. Her Moomintroll adventures are mysteriously funny and sad. Although at their centre is the charmingly odd Moomintroll family, Jansson also peoples her stories with strange characters who come and go and sometimes seem to be forgotten about altogether, giving her later works a dreamlike quality: a squeaky creature called Sniff who suddenly disappears and is never mentioned again, a romantic loner called Snufkin who wanders off the pages and is heard of only occasionally. Indeed, Jansson's final book, *Moominland in November*, caps all this by banishing the Momintroll family themselves, and filling the pages instead with characters who are waiting for them to return.

9) Mrs Rochester. One type of recurring character is the one who is written by more than one author. An obvious example of this is Charlotte Bronte's Mrs Rochester, who in *Jane Eyre* is the barely glimpsed mad wife in the attic, whose terrible laughter and screams haunt the novel. Jean Rhys turns her into the subject of her great *Wide Sargasso Sea* in which she becomes a mistreated victim of imperialism and misogyny.

read more

10) Henry James. In 2004 two major writers, entirely ignorant of the other's work, turned Henry James into their subject and central consciousness. Yet they produce very different versions of Henry James, reflective of their own individual voice and sensibility. In Colm Toibin's magnificent *The Master*, the writer (who in life was actually very sociable and funny) is melancholy and introverted; in David Lodge's *Author, Author* he is much more interested in the literary world that he inhabits.

read more

THE SAFE HOUSE

You let a traumatized young woman into your home.
And into your heart.
You want to protect her like a member of your own family.
To save her from the darkness that's pursuing her . . .

Samantha Laschen is a doctor specializing in post-traumatic stress disorder. She's moved to the coast to escape her problems and to be alone with her young daughter. But now the police want her to take in Fiona Mackenzie, a girl whose parents have been savagely murdered. Yet by allowing Fiona in, Sam is exposing herself – and her daughter – to risks she couldn't possibly have imagined.

'A superior psychological thriller' *The Times*

'Emotionally acute' *Mail on Sunday*

THE MEMORY GAME

You remember an ordinary, idyllic childhood.
Then one day you discover that your memory is deceitful.
And possibly deadly ...

When a skeleton is unearthed, Jane Martello is shocked to learn it's that of her childhood friend, Natalie, who went missing twenty-five years ago. Encouraged by a therapist to recover lost memories, Jane hopes to find out what really took place when she was a child – and what happened to Natalie. But in learning the truth about her and Natalie's past, is Jane putting her own future at terrible risk?

'Electrifying' *Harpers & Queen*

KILLING ME SOFTLY

You have it all: the boyfriend, the friends, the career.
Then you meet a stranger and on impulse, you sacrifice everything.
You're in passionate love.
And grave danger ...

Alice Loudon couldn't resist abandoning her old, safe life for a wild affair. And in Adam Tallis, a rugged mountaineer with a murky past, she finds a man who can teach her things about herself that she never even suspected. But sexual obsession has its dark side – and so does Adam. Soon both are threatening all that Alice has left. First her sanity. Then her life.

'Compulsive, sexy, scary' *Elle*

'Cancel all appointments and unplug the phone. Once started you will do nothing until you finish this thriller' *Harpers & Queen*

'A real frightener' *Guardian*

BENEATH THE SKIN

Someone's watching you.
You don't know who and you don't know why.
But *he* knows you ...

Zoë, Jennifer and Nadia are three women with nothing in common except the letters they receive, each one full of intimate details about every aspect of their lives – from the clothes they wear to the way they act when they think they're alone. And if that isn't terrifying enough, the letters also contain a shocking promise: that soon each life will come to a sudden, violent end. Can Zoë, Jennifer and Nadia discover who their tormentor is? And if so, will any of them live long enough to do anything about it?

'A nail-biting, can't-put-it-down read' *Marie Claire*

'Chilling, startling' *Daily Mail*

'Brilliant' *Evening Standard*

SECRET SMILE

You have an affair.
You finish it.
You think it's over.
You're dead wrong . . .

Miranda Cotton thinks she's put boyfriend Brendan out of her life for good. But two weeks later, he's intimately involved with her sister. Soon what began as an embarrassment becomes threatening – then even more terrifying than a girl's worst nightmare. Because this time Brendan will stop at nothing to be part of Miranda's life – even if it means taking it from her . . .

'Creepy, genuinely gripping' *Heat*

'A must read' *Cosmopolitan*

'Nicci French at the top of her game' *Woman & Home*

LAND OF THE LIVING

You wake in the dark, gagged and bound.
He says he will kill you – just like all the rest.

Abbie Devereaux is being held against her will. She doesn't know where she is or how she got there. She's so terrified she can barely remember her own name – and she's sure of just one thing: that she will survive this nightmare. But even if she does make it back to the land of the living, Abbie knows that he'll still be out there, looking for her.

And next time, there may be no escape.

'Shocking, uncomfortable, exhilarating' *Independent on Sunday*

'Dark, gripping' *Heat*

CATCH ME WHEN I FALL

The stunning new masterpiece of psychological suspense by Nicci French

You're a whirlwind.
You're a success.
You're living your life on the edge.
But who'll catch you when you fall?

Holly Krauss lives life in the fast lane. A successful young businesswoman with a stable home life, she is loved and admired by all who meet her.

But that's only one side of Holly. The other sees her take regular walks on the wild side – where she makes ever more reckless mistakes.

And when those mistakes start mounting up, the two sides of Holly blur together and her life quickly spirals out of control. She thinks she's being stalked, someone is demanding money from her – threats lurk around every corner and those closest to Holly are running out of patience.

But is she alone responsible for what's happening? Are her fears just the paranoia of an illness – or intimations of very real danger?

And if she can no longer rely on her own judgement, who can she trust to catch her when she falls?

TO FIND OUT MORE ABOUT NICCI FRENCH, VISIT
www.niccifrench.co.uk

Get the inside story behind all the novels.

Read fascinating interviews with Nicci Gerrard and Sean French.
Learn more about the authors individually and how they write their novels together.

Extras include a piece from Nicci French's UK editor on the publishing process, and an article from Professor Sue Black on what life is really like for a forensic anthropologist.

Take Nicci and Sean's (not too serious) test and find out if you are a sociopath!

---

r e a d   m o r e

NICCI FRENCH

If you enjoyed this book, there are several ways you can read more by the same author and make sure you get the inside track on all Penguin books.

Order any of the following titles direct:

0140271295 THE MEMORY GAME   £6.99
'A beautifully crafted psychological thriller' *Harpers & Queen*

0140270361 THE SAFE HOUSE   £6.99
'A potent, emotionally acute psychological thriller' *Mail on Sunday*

0140275290 KILLING ME SOFTLY   £6.99
'A chilling study of monstrous obsession' *Sunday Telegraph*

0140281061 BENEATH THE SKIN   £6.99
'Truly chilling . . . does not miss a beat as it courses towards its startling denouement' *Daily Mail*

014028107X THE RED ROOM   £6.99
'Very, very frightening . . . definitely one to read with the lights on' *Cosmopolitan*

0141006501 LAND OF THE LIVING   £6.99
'Steel yourself for a gripping tale of obsession…and fear' *Sunday Mirror*

Simply call Penguin c/o Bookpost on **01624 677237** and have your credit/debit card ready. Alternatively e-mail your order to **bookshop@enterprise.net**. Postage and package is free in mainland UK. Overseas customers must add £2 per book. Prices and availability subject to change without notice.

Visit www.penguin.com and find out first about forthcoming titles, read exclusive material and author interviews, and enter exciting competitions. You can also browse through thousands of Penguin books and buy online.

IT'S NEVER BEEN EASIER TO READ MORE WITH PENGUIN

Frustrated by the quality of books available at Exeter station for his journey back to London one day in 1935, Allen Lane decided to do something about it. The Penguin paperback was born that day, and with it first-class writing became available to a mass audience for the very first time. This book is a direct descendant of those original Penguins and Lane's momentous vision. What will you read next?